I0589366

"A brisk, suspenseful adventure nestled in real, historical drama"

"Irving's (*Courier*, 2015) historical thriller, the second in his Freelancer series, offers a provocative reinterpretation of the infamous Wounded Knee incident.

Irving reprises the picaresque role of Rick Putnam, a motorcycle-riding courier and war-hardened Vietnam veteran. Set in 1973, the story centers on the Wounded Knee debacle in South Dakota, in which members of the American Indian Movement seized and occupied a small town within the Pine Ridge Indian Reservation. In this fictional version, the activists, surrounded and beleaguered by U.S. law enforcement, are increasingly threatened with the possibility of a final, deadly raid that ends the standoff once and for all. Rick joins his Native American friend, Eve [Buffalo Calf], in an attempt to sneak badly needed supplies past the blockade surrounding the town. The area is crackling with violence, riddled with various tribal factions all deeply territorial, suspicious of outsiders, and accustomed to spontaneous bouts of violence. Rick, troubled by the political intrigue he encountered (and barely survived) in the previous novel, uncovers yet more subterfuge regarding the collusion of the federal government with corrupt officials within the Bureau of Indian Affairs. What follows is an action-packed adventure that includes nefarious government forces, intramural tribal conflict, and motorcycle gangs. Rick remains the constant through the two volumes: he's still a chain-smoking, wisecracking tough guy haunted by memories of service in Vietnam. His character can be a bit overdrawn, flirting with caricature as the wounded but incorruptible warrior with "eidetic memory." However, his developing romance with Eve humanizes him, adding a layer of complexity and vulnerability. Once again, the story's pace is torrid, moving from one taut scene to another while the historical drama of Wounded Knee facilitates Irving's principal strength: rendering the wildly implausible believable. Rick's irrepressible wit will help readers through the sometimes-dark material. In response to a Native American introducing himself as Pete Talltrees, Pawnee out of Oklahoma, Rick responds, "Rick Putnam, BMW out of Washington DC."

A brisk, suspenseful adventure nestled in real, historical drama."

—Kirkus Reviews

"*Warrior* takes off like a crotch rocket. Wounded Knee with more action than Custer's Last Stand and the intrigue of spy master David Ignatius novels. It's Philip Marlowe on the mean streets inside the Beltway and the dusty dirt roads of Indian country..."

—John Herrick
ABC NEWS Special Events Producer

"*Warrior* is a novel of danger and heartache, a tense military story that digs into the American Indian past and present, a narrative with lyrical passages of natural description from which the smell of cordite rises…"

—Richard Godwin
Author of *Apostle Rising,*
Mr. Glamour, One Lost Summer

"After years of watching them you've probably realized broadcast news guys are more than a little nuts. The good ones are. Overcoming deadline pressures and technology challenges isn't possible without doing crazy things. Novelist Terry Irving is a broadcast news guy. So is Rick Putnam, the protagonist of his new novel, *Warrior,* who learned to do crazy things to live through the Viet Nam war and brought that craziness home to a Nixon administration America uncertain how to treat the warriors who made it back alive. Putnam had to kill to survive Viet Nam firefights, but, on most nights, survivor's guilt brings to his nightmares the faces of those who died and any chance of sleep ends with his screams.

"In *Courier,* the first novel in this series, Putnam finds solace and some escape from the guilt when he takes a master's command of motorcycles which respond to his every whim. But the craziness isn't gone during the hours Putnam is awake. He employs it to take insane chances while racing through traffic just to deliver on time the exposed film his network needs for nightly newscasts. In *Warrior,* he puts it to better use in harrowing chase scenes as he tries to stop a madman from both defiling children and ruining Indian land for energy exploitation. Too often, action and suspense novels don't deliver on the suspense. Readers know that, whatever the odds, heroes like Clancy's Jack Ryan or Child's Jack Reacher will beat them and prevail. It's fun, but the reader knows the good guy will always win. Not so with Rick Putnam. On the surface, Putnam shares the tough guy qualities we've come to expect in the genre. He constantly works out to keep his body in fighting form and, in well written action sequences, certainly knows how to fight.

"Putnam's guilt is key. He skilled at killing but doesn't want to add more faces to those nightmares. Even in life and death struggles, Putnam risks himself and others by trying to stop the bad guys in some way other than death. His aversion is so strong, the reader is left to wonder whether the always present guilt has created a subconscious death wish that guides both his fighting and the motorcycle exploits Irving has written so well you know they'll translate easily to the big screen. Putnam is a survivor but, in Irving's hands, you just don't know whether Putnam's ghosts will keep him from surviving anymore. That's the tension, and it keeps you turning the page."

—Gary Nuremberg
Veteran Washington DC Journalist

Ronin Robot Press
A Division of
Rock Creek Consulting, LLC
9715 Holmhurst Road
Bethesda MD 20817
www.terryirving.com
www.roninrobotpress.com

First Edition – 7/1/2015
ISBN-10: 0986087386
ISBN-13: 978-0986087387
Printed and Distributed in the United States by IngramSpark

Terry Irving

WARRIOR

(The Second Book in the Freelancer Series)

RONIN ROBOT PRESS

CHAPTER 1

April 26, 1973, Wounded Knee, South Dakota

A .50 caliber machine gun bullet tore through the sky. Rick Putnam felt the hair on the top of his head suddenly rise up from the pressure suction, and in the split-second before he heard the *thwup* of the bullet, he'd already begun his dive to the ground. Fighting the pressure of the harness across his shoulders, he reached forward and grabbed the backpack of the woman in front of him and took her down with him.

Both of them slammed hard into the dirt, driving the air from their lungs. Rick could feel her intake of breath–the prelude to a sharp complaint. He scrambled up the length of her body and slid a hand over her mouth before she could speak.

"Stay quiet," he whispered urgently in her ear. "A round just went over. There could be more."

After an instant, there was a soft kiss on his palm

and Eve Buffalo Calf remained silent.

Rick Putnam raised his head slowly and scanned the South Dakota prairie that surrounded them. It was a quarter moon and its wan light didn't even compete with the broad stripe of the Milky Way as it illuminated the low hills and ravines. Someone standing still in the darkness or lying flat, as they were, was effectively invisible, but he knew that he would easily spot any headlights, flashlight beams, or, most likely, the red glow of lit cigarettes.

He relaxed his grip on Eve. "I think we're OK," he said, his voice just above a whisper.

Eve rolled onto her side as far as her backpack would allow and looked up at Rick. "What happened?" she asked softly.

"Machine gun round," he said. "Big one. It had to have been less than a foot over my head. I could feel the bow shockwave in my hair. I reacted because where there is one, there are usually more."

"Well, yeah, it would make sense that machine gun bullets would tend to travel in herds."

In her voice was a gentle humor, but her eyes held a sense of urgency. Rick knew that she felt helpless–pinned by the massive aluminum carrier frame that curved at least eight inches over her head–but there was no evidence of fear in her voice. It had been her decision to walk essential supplies in to feed the American Indian Movement activists now blockaded in the tiny crossroads town of Wounded Knee. Now, with fifty pounds of flour, corn meal, and dried milk pressing her into the dry dirt, she was as determined to continue as she'd been hours before when they'd started walking.

Rick quietly popped the release buckle at his waist and slipped out of his own, much heavier, pack. Once he'd struggled free, he lifted the massive rig of aluminum tubes and bungee cords off Eve so she could wriggle out, stand up, and stretch her sore muscles.

As he stretched, he took another long look around, seeing nothing but dim outlines of dirt, rocks, and sparse prairie grasses until he looked east, the direction they were heading. There were faint streaks of red and slowly falling pinpoints of white on the horizon. Rick thought they might even have been beautiful if he hadn't known they were the tracer rounds and parachute flares of the U.S. Marshalls and other government forces as they continued to keep pressure on the radicals who had stood them off for months now.

It didn't look much like a standoff tonight–more like a pitched battle.

In the cold silence of the prairie, Rick could make out a low mutter, the distant sound of hundreds, if not thousands, of rounds being fired.

For a moment, he wondered why the sight of combat wasn't bringing back his own bitter memories of bullets zipping and buzzing through elephant grass under a blazing jungle sun. He loosened his rigid self-control for a moment and dared to hope that his constant visions of Vietnam were beginning to fade. Then he shook his head; he knew full well he wasn't that lucky. Most likely, it was simply that distance had reduced the intensity of combat into insignificant lights on the horizon.

The nightmares would be back.

"They're getting pounded in Wounded Knee tonight," he said. "If they were getting hit by air cover, this could be a night attack on a Cong strongpoint."

At that moment, he saw the lights of two fighter jets coming in low and fast over the tiny village, and he thought, "The universe definitely has a sense of humor." They were outrunning the sound of their own engines and so were heading straight for Rick and Eve in an eerie silence.

"Jesus," muttered Eve. "Can they see us?"

"Not at that speed," he said. "Anyway, I don't think they're looking for us." The jets then went into a vertical climb, rolled over, and leveled out high over the small town. Now, the scream of the Phantom engines rolled across the flat plain.

"They're just showing off."

"That reminds me, why was someone shooting at us a minute ago?" she asked.

"I don't think they were," he answered. "The bullet wasn't going that fast when it went over me–it would have been a lot louder. That would mean it was just a stray round from a long way away."

He pulled the oversized aluminum frame with its load of desperately needed supplies back upright, crouched, and carefully began to arrange it across his broad shoulders. "It's funny. You think you're hidden out here in the dark, but a stray round can still find you. Bullets go a hell of a long way before they hit the ground."

With a grunt, he stood and re-buckled the waist belt. Then he lifted the smaller pack that Eve carried. She stood patiently while he placed it on her shoulders as gently as he could. For a few moments, he worked to adjust and settle the big pack into a position that was, if not comfortable, at least bearable.

When he had finished, he kept patting and tweaking the aluminum frame with one hand while he reached down and slid the other along the soft curve of her jeans. He could see the flash of her teeth in the darkness as she turned toward him, smiling. "None of that, trooper," she said. "We've still got a few miles to walk."

"More than a few," he said. "We won't be anywhere near Wounded Knee until right before dawn."

"Let's hope it's just a bit earlier." She turned and resumed a slow but steady walk toward the firefight. "It's really hard to make anything out in the false dawn. Things can just disappear."

Rick knew she was referring to Larissa Iron Crow, the young Lakota woman–just a teenager, really– who had prepared their packs of supplies and then walked with them under a beautiful sunset before sending them off on their nightlong journey. She'd been softly singing the entire time.

She said it was a song to give them the power to walk unseen. They would be like mist as they passed the state police, marshals, and Tribal Council goons who were trying to choke off Wounded Knee's fragile supply line.

There was no doubt that they were walking into danger. Both the radicals of the American Indian Movement and the supporters of the elected reservation leaders were capable of violence, but there were a lot more of the Tribal Council's quasi-official militia. They called themselves "goons" which, in a strictly tongue-in-cheek way, stood for the Guardians of the Oglala Nation. The cops and marshals might arrest you, but at least you'd end up in a jail cell. A dozen people who had started out on this long trek with packs of food had simply disappeared.

The reservation was a big place to hide a body.

"Maybe Larissa's song magic will work," he said, half-joking.

Eve's voice was totally serious. "It could. Lakota singers are powerful, and this is their land. The government has blockaded Wounded Knee for months, and food still gets in and journalists keep getting their story out."

"Maybe they have a courier," he said wryly.

"Miss the bike?" she asked over her shoulder.

"Hell, yeah. We'd have been in there hours ago and have front row seats for the fireworks if we were on a good dirt bike." He walked for a moment. "Of course, the noise would have woken every cop from here to the Montana border, but there's a downside to every great idea."

"You are right as usual, trooper," she replied. "Just keep walking."

CHAPTER 2

April 24, 1973, Wounded Knee, South Dakota

They'd been hiding out on the Northern Cheyenne Indian Reservation for five months–living in a little cabin off Muddy Creek Road for–but Rick was still awed by the size of the Montana sky. In the days, he sometimes just sat and watched the almost-solid clouds drift over like enormous sailing ships on some invisible water line. At night, the sheer number of stars and the broad, crowded stripe of the Milky Way felt like being on another world—a world much closer to the center of the Galaxy where stars were still being born—pushing and shoving to find a place in the sky.

Day or night, it was beautiful, no doubt about that, but a bit frightening as well. It made Rick feel small and powerless, a speck on the landscape. On the other hand, being a mere speck made it considerably easier to stay hidden.

When they'd left Washington, DC last Christmas, they had left four dead bodies behind them. Hector had been given a sendoff by the Dawn Riders–the motorcycle club he'd led—and Rick assumed that whoever had cleaned up all the other traces of mayhem from that affair had disposed of the bodies of his friend Dina and the two government agents or, more likely, deniable assets who'd been put on his trail by the White House. It wasn't an assumption he particularly wanted to test until a good amount of time had passed.

He had accidently tripped over a secret–something that would have blown the city apart–and now that months had gone by and it hadn't appeared on the front page of the Washington Post, he hoped that everyone would just assume it was better to let sleeping dogs lie. Of course, he wasn't willing to let the betrayal of his fellow soldiers go unpunished; but he had arranged things so his revenge would be slow, painful, and impossible to trace back to the source.

Assuming anything about your enemy was a mistake, however; so, like Eve's ancestors, they had set tripwires on their back trail to warn them of pursuit. Eve's friends and relatives were one, scattered across the Northern Cheyenne Reservation. Then there were her classmates from law school now working in legal aid clinics, foundations, and prestigious law firms back in Washington. Finally, there was the flood of gossip that Corey Gravelin gathered from his network of gay friends who worked in almost every office on Capitol Hill, most political campaigns, and even deep inside the White House.

They had waited patiently for several months; but no mysterious strangers had appeared in Lame Deer, no indictments had come down with his name on it, and there hadn't even been any news stories about bodies found in an abandoned building on the 14th Street riot corridor. Finally, Rick had managed to reach one of his housemates from the single pay phone in Lame Deer. The call was so filled with clicks, whines, and roaring static that he could barely make out that it was Steve Lord on the other end of the call. Steve apologized for the connection, explaining that his roommates' attempts at "blue box phreaking were still in the alpha stage of development."

Rick had said, "I understand," even though he didn't have the slightest idea what "phreaking" was. He'd learned long ago that his housemates were so far out on the technological frontier that asking for an explanation could lead to a long lecture on computers, electronics, or physics that usually left him even more confused.

After a while, he simply pretended he knew what they were talking about; it was kind of like jazz–impenetrable but pleasant to listen to all the same. Steve and his other housemates, Scotty Shaw, and Zeke Pickell–known as "Epsilon" or "Eps" because he was short and no one could seriously call anyone "Zeke"–had become his friends under the pressures of the deadly attacks of the past Christmas.

Rick wasn't all that happy about it. He had never wanted friends after most of them had died in one terrible week of battle deep in the Ia Drang valley. It wasn't just that they had all proven to be tough and resourceful under pressure but they'd also accepted that the nightmares and demons in his head were just as much a part of his wounds from Vietnam as the scars patch-worked down his right side.

The fact was he was screwed. The guys had become as close as anyone he'd served with and Eve was... Well, as much as he'd fought against it, he loved her; and the tough and caring woman was now an essential part of whatever it was that made up Rick Putnam.

His own family was totally screwed up, thanks to his mother's drinking, and now that he apparently had a new family, he'd just have to hope everyone lived forever.

Or he'd die first. But that felt a little macabre, even for him.

Steve had reported that he and Eps had managed to break into both the FBI and CIA computer systems whereupon they "took a walk around the files and cleaned things up a bit." They had decided they couldn't go back to the Capitol Hill place they'd shared last year. It wasn't that there were any blood or bullet holes left–the nameless agency had removed that evidence literally overnight–it was that none of them wanted to run into the sort of people who could make blood and bullet holes disappear that easily.

Now that their computer analysis had made them

reasonably sure no one in the CIA or FBI was on their trail, the three had slipped out of their bolt-hole in the all-woman Evangeline Hotel and begun to customize a house Scotty had found in the northwest part of Washington DC Steve said that they were holding a room for Rick and then was silent, letting the howl of the electronic storm fill the line.

It took a while for Rick to work out the problem.

"Oh, I'm in, but I think Eve will be getting her own place," at which point he was sure he heard Steve sigh in relief. Rick knew it wasn't a problem of old-fashioned values. It was just that none of the three were quite ready to deal with a real live woman 24 hours a day.

Rick and Eve had already concluded that any danger stemming from the events of last Christmas had diminished to a reasonable level. President Nixon was being attacked on all sides, congressional investigations were popping up like mushrooms, and the constant pressure of prosecutors and grand juries was producing a steady stream of confessions and convictions.

Rick doubted that anyone was still worried about a motorcycle courier who knew a little too much, and the people who had known anything about his involvement in the discovery of presidential High Treason were either very close friends or very definitely dead.

Eve had an offer of a job as a paralegal in one of Washington's most prestigious law firms. The whole "paralegal" concept had just been invented, and no one was quite sure what she was actually supposed to do; but she thought it would give her a chance to do some legal networking while she slogged through the months it would take to study for the bar exam.

When two hippies had run out of gas and money right at the end of the gravel road that led to their cabin, it felt as if the fates were giving them a not-so-subtle hint. The hippies gladly accepted about half what the VW Camper was worth and caught the Gray Rabbit the next time it came through on its way to California.

The day after the Gray Rabbit–a beat-up school bus with the seats pulled out and replaced by mattresses–disappeared into the west, a sparkplug blew out of the VW's cylinder head, and Rick stopped wondering why he'd gotten such a great deal from the glassy-eyed couple. A tattered copy of *How to Keep Your Volkswagen Alive–a Guide for the Compleat Idiot,* a matched set of barked knuckles on both hands, and a heli-coil on the busted sparkplug got the bus on the road and Rick and Eve on their way back to the East Coast.

The VW seemed happiest at about 50 miles per hour, so they'd taken side roads that wound through the desolate but beautiful landscapes. An enormous coal truck smashed past in the other lane and the van felt like it was going to overturn in the windblast. Rick fought the large flat steering wheel until the VW stopped rocking.

"Damn, there are a lot of those monster trucks out today," Rick said after he'd coaxed the bus back into its lane. "Why didn't I see any coal mining on the reservation?"

Eve looked out her window and regarded the brown and almost treeless landscape for a long time. Then she turned to Rick and he could see that tears were beginning to show in her eyes. Her voice was desolate, "You probably will. The reservation is in the dead center of the Fort Union Formation–the biggest soft coal find ever–and our friends in the Bureau of Indian Affairs have already leased out half of the land to Excacoal."

She shifted in her seat and put her feet up on the dash. "Some of us are ready to fight. After all, these guys will be tearing away everything that makes this place our ancestral home–the center of our religion for that matter. But the tribe is so poor, people are just thinking of jobs and not what it's going to do to the land. You've got kids who aren't getting enough to eat, and you could feed them right if we just let them rip away everything that makes us Cheyenne."

Eve was silent for a long time after that. Rick just kept driving. Every once in a while, he'd drive with his knee, letting the chugging bus drift far into the left lane while he lit a cigarette. The landscape had begun to change, pines covering more of the bare ground with its occasional clumps of brown grass as they ground their way up a long slope.

It was when they'd passed the sign announcing that they were entering the Custer National Forest that Eve seemed to make a decision. "We're going to make a detour."

Rick didn't really care where they were going, he was happy just to be moving, but it did seem appropriate to ask. "Do I get to know where we're detouring to?"

She took the cigarette from him, took a drag, and handed it back. "Wounded Knee. We'll turn right up ahead just past Broadus and head south."

"OK, cool." He glanced at her briefly. "I know your movement buddies are there, but what can we do? I do appreciate that they've tied up most of the U.S. Marshals and FBI agents who might otherwise have been looking for us but–"

"They're in trouble, and they need my help. So, I'm going to help them. I don't think they've got a lot of time left." She looked out the side window again. "You don't have to come."

"If you're going, I'm going." After a pause, he added, "After all, I promised your dad I'd keep you out of trouble."

She swiveled on the seat and shot her bare foot into his hip.

Rick sighed. "See, that's what he warned me about. He said you were always in fights with the boys when you should have been at home making him dinner."

"He didn't say that!"

"No." Rick grinned. "I think that was your grandfather, actually." Another kick landed, and he groaned theatrically. "Hey, watch it. The shrapnel in that area is property of the U.S. Army. I'm responsible for returning it in good condition. So, do me a favor."

"What?"

"Put your foot on the accelerator. Yep, just like

that." He pulled his left foot off the dashboard. "Now, hold on to the steering wheel."

"What are you going to do?"

"I'm going to take a nap, so I can drive all night. You did say that we had a time factor, right?" With that, he stepped into the clear space between the front seats and walked back to the rear.

Eve was left stretched out with an arm and a leg on the left side of the bus and her butt still on the passenger's seat. She gave a short yelp and scooted into the driver's side.

"Damn you, you could have killed us."

"Nah." He began to pull out the rear sofa and flatten it into a full-length double bed. "Plenty of time for that when we get to Wounded Knee. Wake me when you get tired."

"No need to wake you," she said. "You'll be up in about three hours. You always are."

"Yes, Vietnam, my personal alarm clock." He stretched out on the cushions and pulled a small pillow from the cabinet on his right. "But a man can hope, can't he? I've got to stop fighting that damn war someday. Play that tape we picked up. Maybe that will soothe my mind."

He could hear her rattling through the cassettes stashed on the dash. "Umm, you want that guy from Asbury Park or...dammit, I can never pronounce this band."

"Lyn-erd Skin-erd. That's the one." He put his hands up in the air and called softly, "Play Free Bird!"

The music and the steady rhythm of the four-cylinder engine under his head put him to sleep quickly.

Three hours later, the nightmares began.

CHAPTER 3

April 26, 1973, Wounded Knee, South Dakota

As they approached Wounded Knee, they knew that they were moving into a 360-degree kill zone where a combined force of federal and state law enforcement agencies were trying to ensure no one got in or out. They dropped into a ravine where there was covering brush and a few small trees. In the center of the gulch, even the soft light from the stars disappeared.

Rick concentrated on setting each foot firmly before he shifted his weight forward, aware that any lurch or stumble would be magnified by the heavy pack. He heard a muffled rattle as a rock moved under Eve's boots. They had stopped talking a long time ago.

He stopped and, when she bumped softly into his

back, found her hand and slipped it inside the back of his jeans. Her fingers immediately burrowed deeper–searching for warmth. He took a long slow breath, and after a quick rub that promised more, she took a firm grip on one of his belt loops.

He returned his attention to the path and slowly rose from the slight crouch that had kept his tall frame below the rim of the ravine. It was bitterly cold and, though the remnants of a blizzard that had hit a few weeks before had melted in the sunlight, the tough grass was bright with ice.

The ground on each bank sloped down until the gully merged into the surrounding flatland. At that junction, probably better watered than other areas, was a final thicket of brush and stunted trees. They continued their slow careful progress until he reached the edge of the brush and could see the expanse of open prairie again.

Ahead and to both sides, he could make out the blocky forms of pickup trucks and 4-wheel drive Suburbans parked behind what he recognized, even in the dim light, as sandbagged revetments.

The dim glow that had begun to spread across the eastern horizon gave his night-adjusted eyes enough light to see the long slope toward the trees and low buildings of Wounded Knee where a few campfires still glowed. Burned to embers by now, most likely.

Not a great location for a defensive battle, he thought. The Indians were dug in on the low ground and surrounded by a bowl of gentle hills. The FBI and the marshals were on the high ground, good for observing, aiming, and sniping. A smile touched his mouth as he realized it was the opposite of all those old movies. Usually, the cavalry was filmed looking up and seeing mounted warriors outlined against the sky.

He kneeled and Eve moved around his pack to rest her chin against his right shoulder so her mouth was next to his ear.

"How do we get in? Just walk past all those guys?" she whispered. "I mean, after all, you're the expert."

He couldn't help but notice how warm her breath felt as it brushed his ear.

"I guess that's the plan," Rick said without much enthusiasm. "It's not a particularly good plan, but it's all I've got. The truth is we're depending on the song. I hope she wasn't just translating this week's Top 40."

Eve tightened her hand on his shoulder and whispered sharply. "Don't make fun of medicine. It makes you sound like a jerk. Anyway, the magic won't work if you don't believe, and magic may be the only thing we've got going for us."

Rick swept his gaze across the open land, trying to pick out and memorize a path that would avoid as many of the bunkers as possible. "I guess it's like a rifle. If you don't think it'll work, you won't clean it."

He adjusted the heavy pack straps where they had cut deep into his shoulders during the long night. "And then it won't work. You're dead, but you will have won your argument."

Suddenly, Rick felt a sharp point prick his neck

on the left side, and a hand slid over his mouth. It was big and roughened, and it sure as hell wasn't Eve's.

A man's voice whispered into his ear, "Do not move."

The sharp point rotated until Rick could feel the cold length of a knife against his throat. The voice, so low it was hard to pick out from the sounds of the night breeze, continued, "Just relax fella. I'm on your side. Could you please pass that along to your girlfriend? I'd hate for her to take a sudden fright and wake up all those nice cops out there."

"She's a lot more likely to leave her hunting knife between your ribs," Rick said in a voice only slightly louder than his regular breathing. He reached back on his right side and touched her cheek. He slowly rotated his head and whispered in her ear, "Eve, stay quiet. We've got company."

He could feel her stiffen, but she didn't make a sound.

"Good." The hand and the knife both withdrew. Rick looked to his left and could just make out a man kneeling by his side–a thin guy in a denim jacket with a bandanna headband holding down long, straight hair and the line of a hunting rifle poking above his shoulder.

There was a flash of white teeth in the darkness as the man smiled. "We can relax for a bit. The best time to head into the Knee is in about 20 minutes–just before dawn when the ground fog rises."

"You the welcoming committee?" Rick asked.

"In a manner of speaking." He could hear a smile

in the other man's words. "I come out most nights to find lost sheep and guide them into the Free Oglala Nation. Let me introduce myself. Pete Talltrees. Pawnee out of Oklahoma."

Rick felt a strong grip on his hand and gripped back. "Rick Putnam. BMW out of Washington, DC." He could hear a smothered laugh. "And this is Eve Buffalo Calf, Northern Cheyenne from up near Lame Deer."

"Good morning, ma'am."

"A bit chilly but it should improve," said Eve quietly.

"Yes, it should," the man responded. "Back to you, Rick. Where'd you serve?"

"You knew I was in 'Nam?"

"Sure. I could tell by the way you moved." Talltrees settled back on his haunches. "You're no hunter, but you've been jungle-trained. I've been following you for a fair piece. I was ready to move in earlier, but you seemed to have it under control. So who were you with?"

"Seventh Cavalry." Rick paused then continued, "Which might not be too popular around here, I suppose."

There was a low, almost soundless chuckle. "Are you kidding? Toby Braveboy was walking point when the Seventh was hit at Ia Drang. Nice Cree kid."

"I'm sorry."

"Huh?" Rick could see Talltrees shake his head. "No, Toby survived. Managed to make it to the riverbank and sink into the mud. They picked him up three or four days after the NVA pulled out. Except for the fact he tried to stay in the shower for a couple of days to remove the smell, he was fine. Why? Were you there?"

Rick felt the familiar chill run down his spine. "Yeah. I came in on the third day and saw how hard the other units had been hit. I just assumed he'd been KIA."

"Well, it was a meat grinder from what I could see," Talltrees said. "Of course, I did my best to make it a barbecue. I was up top, dropping napalm from a Skyraider."

"Now, that makes me want to shake your hand again," said Rick. "Wait, did you have a feather painted on the tail of your plane?"

"Yeah, I figured it couldn't hurt to have a little medicine on my side." Rick could see the man's head turn toward him. "Why?"

"You came in over my position on Day Four about six inches off the trees and pulled straight up, dropped a full load of DuPont's finest so close I could read the warning signs on the cans." Rick grinned. "Felt like I was going to get cooked when it went off, but you hit square on a machine gun nest we hadn't seen at all. Got a nice long look at your feather as you climbed out. Never thought I'd be able to say 'thank you'."

"Not a problem," the whisper came back. "Now you owe me one. We'll make it a drink once this is over."

Talltrees stood up. "And it's going to be over a bit earlier than planned if we don't get that food on your backs to the people inside."

Rick and Eve stood, stiffly after the long break, and settled each other's heavy packs. Talltrees said, "Stay extremely frosty."

"What do you mean, 'frosty'?" Eve asked. "I'm damn near frozen already, but I don't think you mean I should relax and take it easy either."

Rick said, "In the war, 'stay frosty' meant to move carefully, listen hard, and watch in every possible direction because you were deep in Injun country. Umm…I mean hostile territory."

Talltrees chuckled. "No, 'Injun country' is exactly what we'll be going through. Sadly, it's not Indians you need to worry about. Don't stop and don't run. Just keep moving as quietly as you can. I'll be making a little noise but it's an operational necessity. You might call it a bit of psyops. Let's go."

They set off in a single line, Talltrees in front and Rick in the rear. The day was getting brighter and, as promised, a ground fog was rising from the frozen ground. After ten or fifteen minutes, Rick realized that Talltrees, who was walking point, was singing a very low chant. He couldn't be sure, but it sounded like the one the young woman had sung when she had sent them off.

The fog thickened and the sharp edges of the prairie landscape faded into soft-edged blurs. Sounds came through the mist with almost preternatural clarity. Rick could hear snoring over to his left, the chunk as a truck door opened, the scrape of a cigarette lighter.

In contrast, he felt that the three of them were

drifting through the landscape. Silent. Sure-footed.

A tent appeared out of the mists. A man was sleeping with his head outside the mosquito flap. Rick almost stopped, but Eve reached back, grabbed the strap of his backpack, and pulled him on without a pause. They passed close enough that Rick could see the man's "high and tight" military haircut and a day's worth of stubble on his face. His eyes never opened, and he was soon behind them, lost in the grey fog.

Talltrees kept softly chanting, and they walked another mile or so before he stopped, bent down, picked up a small stone, and threw it ahead of him. The sound of a rifle safety being released was clear, distinct, and right in front of them.

"Walter," said Talltrees softly, "it's me. Don't shoot or you'll ruin today's groceries."

The response was a muffled laugh.

Talltrees waved them forward and around a bunker dug deep into the frozen ground. A young man wearing a surplus Army jacket and a red bandanna waved as they passed. "Save some for me."

The full force of the sun struck, dissipating the fog, as they walked into the tiny hamlet. Slit trenches and bunkers were everywhere. Massive walls made of I-beams and packed earth protected some of the rickety wooden buildings.

There was something familiar about the layout, the seemingly random but effective defensive works with their complete and overlapping fields of fire. It was a shock when Rick realized it was a replica of fortified Viet Cong villages he'd studied as part of his headquarters duties.

Looking around, he realized why. Most of the men he saw waking, making breakfast, or standing guard were clearly veterans. He could tell by the casually careful way they held their weapons, the bits and pieces of uniforms they wore, and the watchful eyes that scanned the surrounding hills.

CHAPTER 4

April 26, 1973, Wounded Knee, South Dakota

"Light 'em if you got 'em." Pete Talltrees waved them to a halt outside the little white wooden church in the center of Wounded Knee. He looked back as Rick began to probe inside his jacket. "And if you got 'em, give me one."

"No problem." Rick gave the soft pack of Winstons a snap to make the cigarettes jut out and offered them. Talltrees took three with an unapologetic grin.

"Real cigarettes are like gold around here," he said. "They cut off all supplies weeks ago, and the people who are sending backpackers like you don't seem to consider tobacco an essential."

"Are you kidding? Everyone knows it's one of the five basic food groups: sugar, grease, caffeine, salt, and nicotine." Rick took a cigarette for himself and lit both his and Talltrees' with his Zippo. Talltrees watched the up-down snap of the lighter with amusement. "Neat trick. All you Zippo freaks are alike. Do you do the one where you keep snapping your fingers?"

After a deep draw of smoke, Rick shook his head. "Nah, I'm a purist. Just the one trick."

"He's kind of a limited guy." Eve took the cigarette from his mouth. "One trick and he does it over and over and over. Says it's his personal juju. Protective medicine."

Rick got another cigarette and, a bit self-consciously, lit it with the Zippo. "How it started is a long story, but it seems to be a good-luck charm of some sort. You ever have anything like that?"

"What do you think I am? Some sort of primitive redskin?" Talltrees grinned and pulled a strap out from around his neck. A small leather pouch was tied to the strap. "Owl feathers. Takes the sharpness from the eyes of my hunters and lends it to me for a while. Had it looped around the joystick on every combat flight."

He tucked the pouch back in his shirt. As he did, Rick caught a glimpse of a thick leather thong and just the top of an elaborately beaded bag. He looked away. Everyone was entitled to secrets.

Wounded Knee had been through a war. The peeling white paint of the buildings bore mute testimony to that. All the way around, there wasn't a square foot without the splintered gouges of ricochets and even the fist-sized holes of .50 caliber machine gun bullets. The prevailing color of the land was mud-brown, either worn down by booted feet or humped into bunkers, trenches, and foxholes. Rick thought it was fortunate that the temperatures hadn't climbed much above freezing, or the whole area would have been a sea of sludge.

Everyone looked dirty, tired, and very easily irritated. Rick felt hostility like a force pushing against him. He figured some of the glares were due to the sight of a white guy with an Indian girl, or resentment of his stock of store-made cigarettes. Then he remembered the flu bug that they'd heard about from the women in the cooking area when they had dropped off their backpacks of supplies.

The women had complained that after all their effort to make at least one meal a day; at least half the camp threw it up right after eating. Concentrating on the camp odors for a moment, Rick could smell vomit mixed with the campfire smoke and the ever-present stench from the open pit toilets. There was just a hint of cordite from the gunfire of the previous night.

Rick leaned toward Eve and said quietly, "All in all, a delightful place to spend a day."

A sharp crack echoed from the surrounding hills.

Reflex dropped both Rick and Talltrees to the ground instantly. Rick rolled on his side and swept Eve's feet out from under her.

"Over there." Talltrees pointed at a puff of smoke drifting slowly away from a patch of disturbed earth on the eastern ridge. "The marshals are just keeping us on our toes."

Rolling over to his back, he blew a lungful of

cigarette smoke straight up. "Most of those guys were Green Berets. If I didn't know better, I'd say they aren't trying very hard to kill us. It's either that or they've forgotten everything they learned in sniper school."

He gestured at the church. "The only guy we've lost so far was hit inside the church. Poor bastard had only been here a day, and a bullet came through the wall and hit him square in the head as he lay on the floor. Cherokee kid from North Carolina, I think."

"My attitude is that any bullets fired within earshot are a punishable violation of my personal space." Rick looked over at Eve. "You OK?"

"Oh, I'm just ducky wonderful, trooper." She pulled up one arm and then the other, looking at the dirt on her heavy canvas coat. "Could you find a drier place to drop me next time?"

"Hey, better yet, next time some moron fires at us, I'll just let you stay upright." Rick smiled. "Of course, with my luck, they'd miss the little target and hit me anyway."

She kicked his shin without getting up. "Short jokes? It's not enough that I'm tired, filthy, and under fire? You have to start with the short jokes?"

Talltrees got up on one knee and did a careful scan of the surrounding hills. "You lovebirds can continue this discussion here if you want, but I'm going to move to a less exposed position. Like I said, I think they were just trying to keep us alert, but there's no point waiting for one of them to remember how to aim."

Rick stood and lifted Eve to her feet without any indication of effort. They followed Talltrees toward a building in the center of the little town.

It had been the general store and gift shop before the takeover, but three months of occupation had turned it into a single large room surrounded by bulletproof barriers of steel I-beams and packed dirt. Inside, the wreckage of tacky tourist items was mixed with the inevitable trash and garbage that gathers when too many people are stuck in a small space for too long.

"Reminds me of Marine Corps encampments," Rick said. "Never saw one that wasn't surrounded by a layer of crap. Everything from ammo boxes to newspapers just tossed over the wire."

"And don't forget the wonderful smell." Talltrees walked farther into the room where cots and mattresses could be seen. "That ineffable scent of gasoline and crap that means that somewhere a lowly PFC was torching those oil-drum latrines."

He gestured to the sleeping area. "You two better get some sleep if you're walking out of here tonight." He kicked a wooden chair upright, sat down, and leaned it against the wall. "I'll take the watch."

Eve looked surprised. "Keep watch? I kind of doubt those guys in the tanks out there are going to sneak up on us in the middle of the day."

"They're not tanks." Talltrees tilted his hat over his eyes. "They're armored personnel carriers. I don't think anyone would trust those people with real firepower. They'd probably miss and take out the state capital."

"Anyway," he added, "they're not the only dangerous people around here these days. Some clever bastard in the FBI decided to tell the press all about how many spies they have in here with us. Now everyone is on the hunt for informants."

Almost to himself, he said, "Wonderful. A bunch of sick, starving folks with guns and a raging case of paranoia."

Clearly having made a decision, he looked up. "I'll be going out with you tonight. I've spent as much time as I can in this dump."

CHAPTER 5

April 26, 1973, Wounded Knee, South Dakota

They're right over there in the grass.
Get down. Down!
Freeze. Hug the ground. Shit, there's blood all over.
Footsteps approaching
Don't breathe
He's cautious
The heel and toe make distinct sounds as they crush the elephant grass.
Hands grab his backpack and flip him over.
Fuck!
A bayonet!

Rick was fighting the man crouched over him even before he awakened. He grabbed his attacker by the shirt with his left hand, spun him around, and pulled him down to cover his chest. His right hand came up, fingers crooked to strike at the eyes.

"Cool it, paleface!" A harsh voice yelled from the other side of the room. "Cool it or I'll stick a knife in your motherfucking girlfriend!"

Rick froze but didn't release the trembling man lying on top of him. Across the room, a tall man was holding Eve with his left arm across her chest and a large knife in his right hand poised at her waist. He had long straight hair held back by a blue bandanna across his forehead.

Rick turned his head and spotted two more rough-looking men. The chair where Talltrees had been keeping watch was empty.

The man pinned to Rick's chest complained, "Help me, Flick, this motherfucker is crazy! Shoot–"

His protest turned into a wordless gurgle as Rick shifted his grip to the man's throat and slowly levered himself to his feet, pulling the man up with him as if he weighed about as much as a bed sheet. Then he carefully stepped off the insecure footing of the mattress and put his back against the wall. Assessing the situation, Rick addressed the man holding Eve and ignored the others.

"Mind telling me what the hell is going on?"

"Sure, but let go of Henry first before he pisses himself."

Rick put his hands up–palm out. Henry moved so fast to get away that he stumbled and fell on the filthy floor, but even the fall didn't stop him from his non-stop bitching. "You honky mother-fucker. You're a goddamn spy, and we're going to show you exactly what we do with spies."

The man he'd called "Flick" said, "Shut the fuck up, Henry."

Then he said to Rick, "We do have some questions to ask. Are you going to come quietly or do I have to carve up your squaw first?"

Rick saw the anger build in Eve's eyes at the insult. Then she winced as Flick pressed the tip of the knife into her side and a small red stain blossomed on her shirt.

Rick wanted to kill the son of a bitch–that is, if he could get to him before Eve did–but he tried to convey calm as he brought his arms down, and began to dig for a cigarette. "First of all, she's not 'my' squaw or 'my' anything else. I've never seen her before. Hell, she wasn't even here when I went to sleep. Second, I'm not a spy. Why would I hump a load of supplies for 30 miles when I could just as easily watch everything you do through an 8 power scope like all those U.S. Marshals out there?"

Flick shoved Eve to the floor and stepped over her. "Yeah. Yeah. We're not buying that crap. We know you two came in this morning with that asshole, Talltrees. For now, both of you just shut up. You'll get a chance to talk to the Security Committee before we shoot your ass."

Henry had recovered from his fear and was looking for payback. He stepped forward and aimed a large cowboy boot into Rick's stomach. Rick tightened his abdominals and let the kick hit. A stomp kick like that was probably good enough for a bar fight, and Henry didn't expect anything but a doubled-over victim ready for a knee shot to the head.

Rick grabbed the boot with both hands when it was on the rebound with the large muscles of the leg relaxed and sharply twisted it almost a full 360 degrees. Henry threw himself into the air in a vain attempt to relieve the torque on his knee. He failed, there was a crunching sound, and Henry screamed.

Rick released the boot. "OK, now there's no need for this sort of mindless violence." He stepped back to the wall and raised his hands–palms out again. "Everybody just relax, and let's talk about this."

It looked like the two men closer to the door were willing to be convinced of the value of non-violence, but Flick was another matter entirely. He put the knife between his teeth and whipped off his denim jacket, revealing a sweatshirt with the sleeves cut off. Rick could see that Flick worked out and wanted everyone to know it.

Rick wasn't impressed. The bulges and veins on Flick's arms were a telltale sign that he'd lifted for bulk and looks. Rick's own workouts were programmed for flexibility, speed, and functional strength.

Flick grabbed his knife and dropped into a fighter's crouch. "Shit, man, you've just hurt one of my boys. White boy, I don't think we've got anything to talk about."

"You know, I was going to leave in just a couple of hours anyway." Rick stepped away from the wall to give himself some room. "How about we reschedule this little dance? I'm free tomorrow. I swear I'll come back just to keep the appointment."

The knife swept across in a horizontal slash. Rick kept his arms and hands out in front of him and arched his back. He could feel the blade pass by his abdomen, but it didn't touch him. Flick took a shuffle step forward and brought the knife back at head height.

Again, Rick evaded the stroke but the blade was almost instantly jabbing up, and he had to jump back to stay out of range. "Come on. Come on. We can all be friends, right? Red Power. Off the Pigs. The People United Can Never Be Defeated."

"Fuck you, man." That and another slash was Flick's response.

Rick felt fire streak across his forearm–he'd felt a lot worse–but he grabbed his arm and moaned as if he were completely blown away by the pain. He noticed that the two guys at the door were coming in to watch the fun–that meant he only had to keep Flick busy for a few more moments and Eve would be safely away.

Flick was silent except for slow, deep breathing. He shuffled in again, flipping the knife between his hands. Rick kept his attention focused on his opponent's eyes. The knife itself would just be a distraction.

He saw Flick's eyes narrow just before the next strike, the knife reversed and coming down from over the man's shoulder. Rick stepped in, crossing his hands to block and then grab the wrist. He covered his moves by stumbling forward, trying to make it look like a clumsy mistake.

He jerked Flick's arm, guided the knife past his torso on the right side, and pulled forward and down. Flick was pulled over his balance point and fell to the floor, flipping over on his back.

As soon as he came around, Rick landed on top of him with both knees–trying to drive his breath out. Flick was strong enough to prevent that and began to bring the knife over for a strike to Rick's back. Moving as fast as he could, Rick caught Flick's wrist when it was still outstretched. They were almost motionless as both locked their legs to gain leverage as they strained to control the knife. Rick was pressed so close that all he could see was the tattoo of a buffalo and a box-like group of small black scars on Flick's upper arm.

In one of those rare, still moments he'd found in the middle of chaos, he admired the artistry of the buffalo tattoo, eyes, horns and even the tangled mane picked out in shades of brown. While this was going through his mind, he had gained the leverage he needed and was banging Flick's knife hand on the wooden floor.

Suddenly, Rick felt something hard poke his waist, and a male voice said, "OK, we've all enjoyed this but it's time to leave. Don't fucking move or I'll blow your nuts off."

Rick froze and–inches away–saw a smile growing on Flick's face. Very slowly, Rick released his grip and looked back. It appeared that he'd guessed wrong. One of the two men he'd thought would run away was holding a small revolver on him.

Irrationally, Rick thought it should have been a

long barrel Colt like in movie westerns, but this was just a Smith and Wesson. He figured it wouldn't be very accurate with that short barrel. Then again, it didn't need to be exceptionally accurate when it was inches from his belt.

"Now, that's not fair." Rick stood up and raised his hands. "This was supposed to be a knife fight."

"You know there ain't no rules in a knife fight."

"You watched that movie, too?" Rick smiled. "Wasn't Newman great?"

The gunman in front of him said dryly, "Yup," and smashed his knee into Rick's crotch. Rick felt fireworks explode in his head, his stomach twisted in a violent attempt to escape, and he crumpled to the ground, conscious but not terribly interested in the rest of the world.

CHAPTER 6

April 26, 1973, Wounded Knee, South Dakota

Rick felt as if wires were blasting raw electricity through his whole body. He found it fascinating that, although his body had taken far worse punishment, the systemic shock of a good kick to the balls–while never fatal–was still something you couldn't just shake off.

He didn't think that there were any simple ways to escape the general store and figured that he couldn't really improve his situation inside without killing someone. Consequently, he was willing to be dragged along after Flick by the two men who had held back in the doorway. Henry was left in the store, sobbing and trying to keep his knee from moving.

Eve was nowhere to be seen. For a second, Rick

felt the virtuous glow of self-sacrifice before he admitted that keeping her at liberty significantly raised his chances of getting out of this alive and so was a lot more self-serving than self-sacrificing. Flick noticed her absence as well and growled at the two men who were supposed to be guarding the door but they just shrugged.

"Never mind her," Flick said. "Paleface here is number one priority. We can always pick the girl up later–maybe have some fun with her. Just don't lose this guy too." Then Flick headed deeper into Wounded Knee; the other two each grabbed one of Rick's arms and followed.

Dusk had fallen over the town, the sun a glowing ball just above the horizon throwing long shadows and leaving people, houses, and the scrawny trees black against the sky. When a gunshot cracked from the hills behind them, Rick noticed that the three men didn't even flinch.

Well, he'd seen a lot of guys like that on the day his battalion had arrived at LZ Albany, so exhausted by days of constant gunfire that a new salvo only registered briefly in their eyes–a quick check to see if they were going to die in the next second or so. Then their attention flickered back to their wounds, their friends' wounds, or the cleanliness of their weapon.

He was feeling better but decided there was no point in letting that become apparent. He checked the two men holding his arms: young with long hair and already-lined faces.

He couldn't be certain, but Rick decided they

weren't veterans. Something was missing, some aspect of harsh adulthood lacking from their faces. They looked young, stupid, and mean. Rick also noticed that their clothes looked like they were straight off the store shelf. He could still see the creases where the western shirts had been folded.

Ahead, Flick had his jacket back on, and he'd added a tall western hat to the bandanna. Striding along, his silhouette looked determined and dangerous, but Rick thought he saw hesitation in the way he kept looking around. He also noticed that their little group made some unnecessary turns to avoid running into other inhabitants.

This confirmed what Rick had been thinking. Despite his bravado and willingness to brawl, Flick wasn't much of a leader. Rick suspected that no one would give Flick any real power, even in the chaos of a revolutionary movement.

The man holding his right arm suddenly wasn't, and there was a muffled thud from a step behind them. Rick instantly spun to his left and smacked his right fist into his left hand, driving the elbow into the man's nose. He let the momentum of the spin carry him around and drove his right fist into a solid blow deep into the man's genitals.

It seemed fitting that this was the gunman who had shown such familiarity with Butch Cassidy and the Sundance Kid, and Rick watched him crumple to the ground with a feeling of vengeful satisfaction. Rick kicked him sharply in the temple–trying to put him out without killing him.

The precise ratcheting of an old-fashioned lever-action rifle came from the front. Looking up, Rick saw Pete Talltrees standing by the side of the trail with his hunting rifle aimed right between Flick's eyes.

Talltrees spoke quietly. "Now, I was planning to take a walk with this fellow tonight, and I don't think he'd be in any shape for a hike after a conversation with you and that bullshit Security Committee of yours."

Flick stepped forward, digging in his pocket. Talltrees stepped forward as well, gently knocked the tall hat off the other man's head, and pressed the muzzle of the rifle into his forehead just below the blue bandanna. "I'm telling you, friend, that pissant little gun in your pocket better stay right where it is, or this conversation is going to become a lot shorter than I'd like."

Flick's hand stopped moving.

Rick could see that Talltrees had things well in hand, so he turned back to the man he'd just hit and bent down and checked for a pulse. It was nice and steady. Then he patted the man's pockets and found the revolver in the man's jacket. Rick spun the cylinder, pocketed the cartridges, and threw the gun into the bushes. Then he checked for a pulse and a gun on the goon that Talltrees had taken out first.

Talltrees smiled. "OK, it looks like this is going to work out just fine for everyone. However, I would recommend that you find another place to be in the next few minutes because I'm going to go visit with Lemuel Sharp Eagle and the rest of the real Security Committee. I know that imitation is the sincerest form of flattery but I doubt they'll feel flattered."

Flick's face twisted with anger, and he started to say something, but Talltrees cut him off. "Vernon, if you open your mouth, you're going to lie. I really have a problem when people lie to me. It pisses me off and then I'll have to shoot you, and it'll bother me for the rest of the night."

He leaned back from his firing position, and the muzzle pulled away from Flick's forehead. A circle appeared, first white and then filling with red. "Now, take your buddies or leave them to wake up and proceed on their own, but get the hell out of here. I really, sincerely, do not want to see you again."

Flick looked at Talltrees for a second and then stepped to the side so he could see the two men lying on the worn dirt path. Neither looked interested in going anywhere.

He bent down, picked up his hat, and backed away. A dozen feet later, he turned, put the tall hat back on, and stalked off angrily. It looked impressive, but Rick could hear his booted footsteps break into a run after a few steps.

Talltrees lowered the rifle and rested it on his hip. Rick noticed that he didn't engage the safety.

"Well, I think this could be the first time that the Indians have saved the cavalry," Eve said as she walked up from behind Rick and poked a cautious toe into both men on the ground.

Rick laughed. "Hardly. I'd say that his little trick with the Skyraider definitely counted as a 'save.' This is just a well-timed repeat performance."

He turned back to Talltrees and stuck out his

hand. "Not that I'm not grateful, you understand."

The men shook hands and grinned at each other. Then Talltrees' face turned serious. "This isn't the best time of the night to start, but I think we should get out of here. No one thinks much of Vernon Crane–well, except for himself and I'll add in his mother, since I'm in a generous mood–but he hangs with some dudes who are damn near as dumb as he is, and they'll be back."

"Vernon?" Rick asked.

"Yeah, with a name like that he named himself 'Flick' a long time ago." Talltrees bent over and threw a pack over his left shoulder, keeping the rifle free. "Or so I've heard. I asked around about him a couple of days ago. Don't quite know why."

He shrugged and gazed off into the orange glow of the setting sun. "Guess I just felt something wrong about him. Anyway, what I heard was that he grew up here and went to Dakota State but took off one day leaving all his stuff in the dorm. No one saw him until he showed up here a few weeks after Wounded Knee's 'liberation'."

"Where was he?" Rick asked.

"The guy I talked to said Vernon got religion one day and took off with a couple of other people to join up with the..." he paused, "the Radical Labor Party Committee or the Unified Committee of Radical Workers or some damn thing. Anyway, uncles ran most of the others down and brought them home, but no one cared enough to worry about Vernon."

He turned and used the rifle to point down a path

almost invisible in the dim light. "Enough history. I think it's time for us to split the scene and leave it clean, so let's exit stage left."

Eve bent down over the man Rick had knocked out. Shifting his body slightly, she pulled out a small pack. Opening it, she rummaged through the contents. "Well, we're in luck. Food, matches, compass, and first aid kit–this guy was clearly ready to take off."

She stepped over the motionless body and said to Pete, "Listen, Snagglepuss, give me a minute to clean and wrap up that scratch on Rick's arm before it goes septic. I can't imagine that Vernon owned anything that wasn't filthy."

She pushed Rick back against a tree trunk and began to pull off his jacket. "Then big strong guy will be in great shape to carry this bag of supplies."

Rick smiled, "What are you going to contribute?"

"You mean, besides my natural beauty and enough common sense to know when it was time to find a guy with a nice big rifle?" She patted Rick's cheek before she set to work on his arm.

"Not a damn thing."

CHAPTER 7

April 26, 1973, Wounded Knee, South Dakota

Darkness had spread across the enormous sky by the time they reached the western edge of Wounded Knee. Talltrees put up his hand and motioned them to kneel.

"OK, we're going to walk out nice and quiet, at least at first," he said. "I know the marshals think they've got everyone bottled up in here because they've got the starlight scopes and thermal imagers. But they're wrong, as usual."

He slid his rifle onto the sling over his shoulder and pulled off his backpack. "Most nights I just take an extremely cold shower to bring down my thermal signature and go out on my belly, but tonight there's too many of us."

He took out a rectangular metal box with a glass

cover on one end. "Strobe light. I've been saving this for a party, but this place is seriously lacking in recreational drugs. Anyway, I don't think I'll be back, so I might as well go out in style."

Talltrees put the box on the ground and rummaged again in his pack, pulling out three plastic packs of red and silver emergency blankets. He tossed one to Rick and one to Eve. "These will keep some of your body heat from radiating. Make sure you keep the silver side against your body or you'll reflect."

He looked at the box again and shook his head—grinning teeth flashing in the darkness. "Might sound strange coming from me, but I always felt the A-Teams were just too dependent on their high-tech toys. SEALs now, those sneaky bastards are another story with all that 'Whispering Death' crawling in the mud. Luckily, I haven't heard any SEALs on the radio scanners, just a bunch of Green Berets reliving their glory days in Laos and Cambodia.

"I think I'll keep the strobe for later and go old-school here." Talltrees pulled a glass bottle out of the pack and handed it to Rick. "I don't want to be carrying this if someone puts a lucky shot through my pack."

The label said Boone's Farm Strawberry Wine, but Rick could smell the gasoline even through the screw top. He smiled. "This wouldn't be napalm, would it?"

"Nah. Too hard to ignite." Talltrees tore a piece of fabric from the T-shirt under his heavy coat, twisted it into a string. "Just your ordinary, everyday

Molotov cocktail which is, as I'm sure you know, an excellent source of bright light. Only problem I had was having to smell that damn strawberry crap as I was pouring it out. I'd rather drink the gasoline."

He motioned to Rick who handed back the bottle.

Talltrees unscrewed the cap, inserted the twisted cotton, and let it soak in the gasoline. "Barring air support, I'd say we are as prepared as possible. Now let's cause a little eyestrain to anyone watching. Wrap up in the blankets and get ready to move fast. Anyone got a light?"

"Thought you'd never ask." Rick lit the Zippo on his jeans and set the flame to the cotton fuse. Talltrees stood and hurled the bottle far to the left. The burning cotton cut an orange curve in the blackness.

They could hear the glass shatter and, with a *chuff,* a ball of flame blossomed in the open grass. They were already well out of the circle of light, and then Talltrees headed to the right at a fast pace. Rick could see their bulky shadows striding across the sparse grass and dry soil of the prairie, but he knew that, for a distant watcher, the bright gasoline flame would make everything around it as black as pitch.

Two shots came from the hillside and then several more. Rick heard one ricochet off a rock near the burning gasoline, and none of the others sounded close to them at all. "Figures," he thought, "that flame would have burned a hole in the scopes that would take minutes to clear. By that time, we'll be well out of sight."

He concentrated on following Eve who was right

behind Talltrees. He had to focus because the Pawnee would run, stop, cover up with a blanket, and then run again in a fast-moving choppy movement that Rick figured would put them deep into the background clutter of any scope that didn't have to have its phosphor tubes pulled and replaced.

After a couple of hundred yards, they came to a clump of brush. Talltrees held up a fist and then flattened his hand and swept it down. Even Eve knew that much battlefield signaling. They stopped and went flat.

Talltrees reached carefully under one of the bushes and pulled it up and out of the ground, revealing a gap in what had looked like a solid wall. Clearly, he'd cut himself this passage long ago and kept it hidden. He motioned them into it. After they had passed, he pulled the bush in behind him and carefully reset it in the dry ground, brushing the soil around the roots to smooth out any traces that it had ever been moved.

Then he motioned them to move close and whispered, "From now on, complete silence. This is the best way out because it goes right under some of the biggest bunkers and comms centers. The positive is that it's so close they tend to overlook it, but it's got a strong negative: any noise will bring a real cluster-fuck down on our heads."

Talltrees took the lead again, and they crawled for 20 or 30 yards before they stood up–still keeping their heads below the level of the bushes. Rick realized that they were moving into one of the ravines like the one they'd come through on the way in. A trail of sorts–really just a series of openings carefully cut between the thickets–was enough to get through but kept them completely concealed.

Between the quarter-moon and the stars, Rick could see enough to keep his movements relatively quiet. He did notice that he made more noise than the other two. He decided it must be genetic and tried to place his feet where Talltrees had stepped.

"That Pawnee bastard Talltrees stuck his nose in! That's what happened!"

A conversation, or more properly an argument, had risen from whispers to angry shouting. The angry voice clearly belonged to Flick Crane and he was about six feet over their heads where the perpendicular wall of the ravine met the flat grassland of the prairie. Rick and the others stopped and went down on their knees and then flat on their stomachs, slowly rolling to one side or the other to get off the trail and put as much of the sparse vegetation over them as possible.

"Don't tell me to shut up! This op is fucked and I'm going to tell the whole fucking Inner Circle when I get back to the Big House that you screwed it up. Why the hell did you tell me to whack the white guy anyway?"

Talltrees began to belly-crawl slowly toward the voice and the other two followed. When they came to the dry and crumbling side of the ravine, they could hear a second voice, much lower and calmer. This close, both voices were clear even though Flick had stopped shouting.

"You know this perfectly well, but I will repeat it

again." The second voice was high with an accent and a very slight lisp. It sounded like someone who had fought a speech impediment for a long time but couldn't quite overcome it. "Your job was to keep those redskin revolutionaries looking for internal enemies and FBI informants. All you had to do was kidnap and kill some outsider. Then we would have 'found' his body and used it to destroy the radicals' credibility in the eyes of the tribes."

There was a dry chuckle. "And to keep suspicion away from the real informants. For God's sake, the FBI has turned the U.S. Marshals into the worst snipers ever because they're afraid that they'll waste one of their own guys."

"Listen, Salazar, I'm doing my job," Flick said. "But I'm afraid you stepped in it too. Everyone is so worried about that little Pine girl gone missing that the women are watching every man in the village like fucking hawks."

There was the scrape of a match, a pause, and a contented exhalation. Rick, without nicotine for what felt like hours, was intensely jealous. The smoke drifting on the still night air didn't help.

"That situation has been resolved permanently." All humor had disappeared from the voice with the accent. "Do not discuss that again. We are discussing your failings. What about your second objective? What's his name, that Pawnee pilot?"

"Talltrees."

"Right, you were ordered to retrieve the medicine pouch that Talltrees is carrying," Salazar continued. "It's turning out that that could be extremely important."

Flick defended himself. "I was planning to snatch that after I buried the white guy in a shallow grave. How was I supposed to know that Talltrees was his buddy?"

"Yes, and he kicked your ineffectual little gang of idiots right out of camp." With a sigh, "No matter, all this ends tonight. In just a few moments, you'll see the correct way for a truly civilized nation to deal with what is, essentially, just another peasant uprising. We have them every generation. Afterward, you can go in and remove the pouch from the pilot's body. You can manage to rob a dead Indian, am I right?"

"Why does Stephen care about these goddamn Indians anyway?" Flick seemed to have forgotten that he was a "goddamn Indian" himself. Rick wondered what it took to destroy that much of someone's identity. "It's like the freaking Communist party in there when it's not just about stealing everything they can find. It's not like they've got anything to steal neither. This place is a dump."

"There is tremendous wealth here, even if it's not easily seen." A brief squawk of radio static. "Now be quiet. I've got work to do."

Rick jumped as he felt a hand on his ankle. Turning carefully, he saw Eve beckoning him. He slowly pushed himself over to her, avoiding any sound of rolling pebbles or scraping sand.

It took some time, but he finally reached a spot a few feet back along the steep ravine wall. Eve reached up and carefully, almost reverently, began to wipe loose dirt off a patch of something just slightly lighter than the surrounding earth.

Slowly, in the dim light, Rick could make out a smooth surface, rounded and pale. Then her hand moved down just a few inches and started again slowly brushing off the dirt and revealing another round object, much smaller than the first.

They lay together in the darkness for a long time as she carefully uncovered the outer edge of the two objects from the dirt that had obscured them. At first, all Rick could see were rounded shapes with irregular ridges and swirls along the sides. Suddenly, things clicked, and he realized he was looking at two skulls, one of an adult and the other an infant.

He reached over and gently held Eve's wrist. Placing his lips against her ear, he breathed, "Who were they? A mother and her baby?"

Eve nodded. She pivoted slowly until her lips were against the long hair over his ear. "The first Wounded Knee Massacre. Many women tried to escape with their children when the Army turned the Hotchkiss guns on our people. Soldiers followed the ones who managed to get away for miles through the snow and killed them."

She reached out and gently took his hand. Guiding it to the larger skull, she brought his fingers to an area that was cracked and fractured. Eve said, "She was shot, but she tried to hide her baby under her body far back in this ravine. That's how many of the witnesses survived, babies and young children. The soldiers threw the others into a mass grave."

"I can feel her here." She took a deep breath. "She was brave and loving, a good mother. I'll ask her to help us."

Eve reached for Rick's hand. She brought it to her mouth, and he could feel her lips move as she sang silently. He bowed his head and, well, he wasn't religious, but he felt there was another presence in the ravine with them. It wasn't emotion but rather a feeling of...a quiet dignity.

Slowly, he felt the presence begin to..."turn" wasn't the right term but was the closest he could come. His attention was being drawn...down.

It was too dark to see anything, so he began to run his right hand along the ground beneath him. The feeling grew fainter when he moved away from the earth wall. The area where the earth wall met the floor of the ravine felt...Again, words failed to describe the sensation adequately. Perhaps "significant" or "meaningful" caught a bit of it.

Exploring with light, almost weightless, fingers, he found loose rocks, some as large as six or eight inches across, piled in what felt like a methodical fashion at the corner where the sidewall met the ravine floor. He remained on his stomach but braced himself on his left hand so that his right could slowly, cautiously grasp one stone at a time and lift it straight up without a sound. Then he lowered the rock to a patch of soft earth and reached for another.

In the dark, his senses were drawn into his fingertips, and his concentration was so acute that, when he touched smooth skin instead of coarse sandstone, he couldn't quite still an involuntary shudder. His hand jerked back a fraction of an inch–just enough to lose contact with whatever had been revealed.

For a frantic moment, he thought it was a snake, but after a couple of deep, slow breaths to quiet his hammering heartbeat, his fingers touched the object again. It was cool and still and not alive.

Then his questing fingers found what could only be an eye, the lid closed and the lashes soft, almost invisible. He slowly reached over to Eve, tapped her on the wrist to get her attention, and, softly grasping her hand under his own, brought it over to the small face.

He had no doubt that it was a face, a child's face.

Eve gently moved her hand, and Rick could feel her head snap up as she also realized what lay under the pile of rocks. He had to move quickly to place his finger on her lips and avert a sound. Eve froze and he could see a gleam of moonlight as her eyes widened in alarm.

Rick realized that the presence in the ravine had...withdrawn. He could feel something, but any urgency or direction was gone. It was as if he had found something that he was intended to be found and now the presence had no more interest in them.

Slowly, silently, they continued to reveal the small form. The body was cool but, somehow, not quite as cold as the surrounding earth and rock.

Eve touched his face and turned his head so she could speak into his ear again. "It's a girl." Her voice was rough, filled with tension and sorrow. "She's only six or seven, just a baby."

He touched her chin and, gently turning her head, whispered in her ear, "Should we carry the body with us?"

The answer came as soft as a breath. "No. She's been so badly hurt, but I think she's safe here." Rick could see her gesture upwards. "The mother, the Old One, is watching over her just as she is watching her own baby."

He could feel Eve move as she bent down over the child again, gently move her head to the side and, his fingers still touching hers, could tell that she was working at something under the chin.

Eve sat up again and breathed into his ear. "She was wearing a bag around her neck on a piece of string. Medicine of some kind. We'll bring it back. Another mother is looking for her child and she'll recognize the bag." She reached over and tucked the bag into the chest pocket of Rick's jacket. "Can you cover her back up? I just can't."

She took his hand and brought it to her cheek, so he could feel her silent shaking and the tears streaming down her cheeks. She rested her head against his hand until the silent weeping began to slow.

With the same care he had used to uncover the tiny face, Rick picked up and replaced the rocks. He wondered if they were doing the wrong thing, if they shouldn't uncover the girl and take her...where?

Slowly, he felt the presence change from watchfulness to approval. He placed the last rock over the closed eyes and brushed gently on the loose dirt to smooth away any evidence that anything had been disturbed.

He noticed that the normal night noises of wind and wood had returned. He hadn't realized that it had been silent for the last few minutes, as if the land around them had been waiting, grieving.

The mood was broken by the sharp and metallic sound of a military radio coming from the top of the ravine. Someone had turned it up or taken off headphones because it was unusually clear and very familiar, the commands and queries of the military in Vietnam transposed intact to a different land. As he listened, he began to pick out the speakers, the clipped no-nonsense voices of the FBI and marshals contrasting with the more laconic and relaxed tones of AIM security, sounding like they never finished half the words, just got tired in the middle and trailed off.

Abruptly, the familiar lisping voice came over the band, now resonant with authority and strong enough to cut through all the other chatter. "Ready. On my count: Five, Four, Three, Two, One."

CHAPTER 8

April 26, 1973, Wounded Knee, South Dakota

For a moment, Rick thought he was back in a nightmare as the soft chuff of mortars firing echoed all around him. Looking back toward Wounded Knee, he could see a blaze of white light, 40 or 50 parachute flares in a ring around the hamlet.

Then the guns opened up.

Above him, close, he could hear the sporadic hammering of an M-60 machine gun being fired by a professional who knew enough to keep the barrel cool. All around, he could hear other machine guns joined in song by the sharper sound of M-16s on "full rock and roll" and the single coughs of hunting rifles and sniper guns. Hundreds of rounds were being fired. Nothing he'd heard or read had ever mentioned this kind of furious onslaught by the hundreds of police, marshals, and FBI agents who had been surrounding the miserable hamlet for months.

Any shots coming from Wounded Knee were lost in the barrage. Rick suspected people there were trying to screw themselves deeper into the ground.

Then he noticed something odd. The sound of the machine gun over his head was altering slightly. It was hard to be sure, but it seemed as if the operator was swiveling and firing bursts in radically different directions. At this distance, any target within Wounded Knee was within a few degrees of arc. What were they shooting at that required cranking the sights over that far?

Then he knew. A series of loud thwacks as bullets, many bullets, hit the rim of the gully above his head. For a second, he simply pressed deeper into the cold earth, but then he realized that he was protected in the cut while the firing was directed at what appeared to be a bunker on the top of the ravine wall.

The machine gun in the bunker fired back along the path of the incoming rounds. It was clear to Rick that they were firing at the surrounding hills and not at Wounded Knee. He wondered why the hell they were firing at their fellow law enforcement officers.

Whoever it was wasn't interested in a long battle; in just a few minutes, he heard the clattering of the M-60 being broken down and a quick scurry of boots fading away.

The rate of fire slowed as the ring of illumination flares sank to the ground. It didn't stop by any means, but it slowed.

He felt a firm tap on his shoulder. It was Talltrees. The pilot was on his knees, and he motioned for Rick to alert Eve and start moving again. They could move a bit faster with the continuing racket of gunfire to mask any sounds they made; and, after what Rick guessed was about a quarter mile more, the ravine ended in a vertical earth wall studded with rocks. The trees had grown taller as the ravine cut deeper into the prairie, so they had a solid canopy of leaves overhead. Talltrees removed his rifle from his shoulder, handed it to Rick, and slowly climbed, testing each rock for stability, until his eyes reached what was the ground level of the surrounding prairie.

Rick and Eve waited silently as the lanky Pawnee completed his careful survey and disappeared over the edge. It was a good fifteen minutes before his head reappeared, silhouetted against the Milky Way as he waved for them to follow. Rick handed up the rifle as Eve climbed quickly, using the same rocks and ledges that Talltrees had tested and confirmed were safe.

Rick could feel the injured muscles pull in his right side as he climbed but told himself he was making up for the weightlifting sessions he'd missed.

The prairie was in full night now, dark and quiet. It was a very different scene when they turned to look back. A few illumination flares were still hung up in trees over Wounded Knee, and the night was filled with light: red tracer rounds from machine guns in the bowl of low hills poured like liquid fire into the village and muzzle flashes marked the bunkers of the surrounding forces.

There were no answering flashes from the Indians. Their meager stocks of ammunition and a healthy sense of self-preservation doubtless kept them low and protected behind earth berms, steel bunkers, or just pits in the ground.

Talltrees tapped them on the shoulders, motioned for them to follow, and set off cautiously toward the west. Again, they passed tents and pickup trucks without being spotted although Rick suspected it was the distraction of the firefight behind them rather than any Lakota medicine song.

Slowly, the clamor of battle quieted, a combination of distance and diminishing gunfire. Rick thought that even the federal authorities had to run low on ammunition eventually after an exhibition like that.

Talltrees stopped so suddenly that Eve had to sidestep quickly to keep from walking into him. He sank to the ground and Rick and Eve gratefully joined him.

But Talltrees wasn't taking a break. He had gone into a prone firing position with his rifle on his shoulder and locked on a target. Peering through the darkness, Rick couldn't see any threat until someone struck a match and lit a cigarette about 30 yards ahead and slightly to the left.

Footsteps approached, at least two pairs of boots crunching on the dry soil. There was no time to find better cover, so Rick put his head down to hide his pale face.

"Hell of a night." A cigarette-roughened male voice.

"About damn time we finally unloaded on those bastards." This one sounded younger, smoother. "Gave them something back for what they did to Lloyd."

"Yeah, that was a damn shame. Think he'll ever walk again?"

"I haven't heard anything since they medevacked him out."

The sound of boots came closer but further to the right. There was a decent chance they would remain hidden. Rick slowly turned his face away from the voices.

"So what've you been up to?" the older man asked.

"I was on radio duty like always." There was a short pause. "I gotta tell you something was weird tonight."

"Strange?"

"Yeah. Command HQ came on a couple of times and asked about incoming fire on our positions from up here in the hills."

"Up here? Jeez, who the hell had their firing marks that far off?" A short laugh followed by a smoker's cough. "Man, someone is going to get their butts kicked for that. They're sure it wasn't the Indians?"

"Well, that was the strange thing. Command actually raised the AIM security team in Wounded Knee on the negotiation frequency. The Indians said that all their people had strict orders not to fire back because of the risk of exposing themselves. The odd thing was that they said they were taking incoming from the same locations. Command said the Indians thought it was someone out to piss off both sides."

"Well, that's fucking freaky."

"Damn right. Command warned about it on the open net and said they were giving the Indians firing coordinates."

"Firing coordinates?"

"Yeah. They know where we all are, so they could determine where the extra firepower was coming from."

At the sound of a long inhalation of smoke, Rick closed his eyes and tried not to think about lighting up. The voices began to move away.

"Ah, I don't believe it. Had to have been Indians in the hills making trouble."

"Probably." Another laugh. "And if they wanted trouble, they sure as hell got it."

"Hey, did you see that article in Sports Illustrated? They called the Mohammed-Norton fight 'Bury My Heart at Wounded Jaw'."

The voices faded as the two men walked toward a circle of tents about a quarter-mile away. When there had been nothing but the normal sounds of a desert night for 15 minutes, Talltrees slowly got to his feet and waved to them to continue the trek.

CHAPTER 9

April 26, 1973, Wounded Knee, South Dakota

There was a flickering light on their back trail.

At first, it was so faint that Rick had to watch it out of the corners of his eyes. If he stared at it directly, it would disappear in the illusions of shape and motion produced by the light of the stars. After about 15 minutes, it became clearer, and he stepped forward, tapped Talltrees on the shoulder, and pointed out the lights.

They all stopped, and Eve took a swallow from her canteen. After a minute, Rick could hear the chainsaw whine of a dirt bike engine, maybe two. They weren't revving high enough to be going all out, at least not yet.

Talltrees listened, then nodded, and walked over to Eve. He bent his head down and spoke softly to her for a minute or two. She looked up into his eyes, nodded, and then spoke to the tall Pawnee in a voice that was also too low for Rick to hear.

But Talltrees seemed to sag, and Rick knew she'd told him about the child's body they'd found in the ravine. Eve put her arms around Talltrees' shoulders, squeezed hard, and then walked a few yards farther and sat on a boulder facing the other way.

Talltrees came over to Rick.

"I can't fucking believe it. A kid?"

Rick just nodded.

"What do you think happened?" Talltrees sighed deeply. "No. It doesn't really matter--I guess the only real question is who?"

"I don't really know but you heard those guys up above the ravine?"

Talltrees nodded.

"Well, that's where we found the kid and...I don't know, one of them just sounded..." Rick paused, "it sounds strange, but that one guy just made my skin crawl."

"It's not stupid. I've been having the same feelings for a while now." Talltrees looked irritated. "I can't explain it but the FBI, the marshals, even Wilson's goons–they're all just on the wrong side. These new guys are different. Worse."

The tall man shook his head. "We don't have time to figure these assholes out. I'm betting that whoever they are, they're the ones sending those bikes after us."

He jerked his chin toward the exhaust sounds, now noticeably louder. "I think they're hunting me.

We're going to have to split up."

"Do you want me to set a false trail?" Rick asked. "Just take Eve with you."

"No, thanks for the offer, but I can feel the target painted on my back. It's like they have a radar-lock on my ass."

Talltrees laughed softly and then became serious. "I need to ask you to do something for me. Something important."

He reached into his shirt, pulled out the heavy leather pouch that Rick had noticed the other day, hesitated for a second, and then handed it over. It was about 18 inches long and three inches wide and carefully stitched closed with rawhide. In the darkness, Rick couldn't tell much more about it, but from the supple leather, it felt extremely old but carefully preserved.

"Put it around your neck and hide it under your shirt." Talltrees watched as Rick placed the pouch against his chest and buttoned his shirt. "I probably should have never come here--should have taken my responsibility more seriously."

He shook his head as if shaking off all regrets and doubts. Then he placed his hands on Rick's shoulders, held him in a firm grip, and looked deep into his eyes. "You are carrying one of the most sacred objects of the Pawnee and the Cheyenne tribes. I, Peter Talltrees, the son of World War II veteran Herbert Talltrees, and grandson of Pawnee war chief Many Tall Trees who fought against the Seventh Cavalry, was given this because I had proven myself as a warrior and as a man. I became an Arrow Man in a long and beautiful ceremony, and I regret I cannot perform it for you."

He took a deep breath. "You are now an Arrow Man as well–even if only for a short time–and I deem you fit because you have also proven yourself brave in battle and honorable in life. Others may disagree, but I am here and they are not. More than a hundred years ago, my people defeated the Cheyenne in open battle and took the four Sacred Arrows as spoils of war. After the Cheyenne gave the Pawnee one hundred horses, which was a fitting ransom, one was returned immediately. The second was taken from us in battle by the Lakota and given by them to the Cheyenne. These are the last two Arrows, and I need you to promise that you will bring them to the Arrow Men in the Northern Cheyenne Reservation as quickly as possible."

Rick nodded solemnly.

"The four Sacred Arrows were given by the Creator to Sweet Medicine, first leader of the Cheyenne. They are part of the magic that lies at the center not only of the Cheyenne but of all the First Peoples. The ancient and true leaders of the Cheyenne sought out the Arrow Men of the Pawnee earlier this year and asked if we would help them in this battle. They told us that there were strange and powerful forces moving against them, and our elders decided to forget the past and unite against a common enemy. With these Arrows, the medicine of the Cheyenne will be restored, and they will have the power to unite and reject the false offers of those who would tear their land like wolves and leave only poison and dust."

He paused and laughed softly. "And with so few of us left, who knows when the Pawnee might need friends among the Cheyenne? OK, Private First Class Rick Putnam of the...BMW people, I think that's what you said, right?"

"Yes." Rick had never thought anyone would take his little joke seriously.

"OK, the Arrows are men's business, and no woman can see them or speak of them. When you get back to the reservation, send word to Charlie Walksalone–he's the Outside Man of the Council of 44–and he'll gather the Arrow Men and perform the appropriate ceremony. Will you do this?"

"Yes, I will," Rick answered.

Talltrees seemed to slump in relief.

Rick looked back at the headlights behind them. He could hear more and bigger engines now. "Who is following us?"

"I honestly have no idea. I left Oklahoma with two others, but we lost one almost before we started, killed after he left a bar. It's sadly not all that uncommon these days for an Indian to die in a bar fight, but my father later told me on the phone that when they found his body, it looked like he'd been tortured. Cigarette burns all over."

"Shit." Rick shook his head. "That's two of you. Where's the third?"

"Disappeared several days ago from right inside Wounded Knee." Talltrees unslung his rifle, checked the action, and then patted his pockets to confirm his spare ammunition. "That's why I felt that being out on patrol with the marshals shooting at me was a safer way to spend my nights. After I brought you two in, I heard that Flick had recruited his own 'Security Squad' and was out looking for trouble. When I heard his voice outside the general store, I took off out the back. Sorry, I didn't have time to wake you."

He grinned. "I was about to come back in after you when Eve found me. Damn, but she's a tough woman. Made it quite clear that she was going to kick my worthless ass if I didn't. If you have any sense at all, you'll keep her around."

"I may not have much sense, but even I can tell how much that girl is worth."

"Good. Then I listened to those guys on top of the ravine. That guy with the creepy voice you mentioned?"

Rick nodded.

"Well, there is no way I'm going to be able to just vanish if that bastard already knows enough to be hunting for the pouch." He looked back at the headlights, "I'm going to lay a false trail but they're going to catch up. Damn dirt bikes are just too fast. Now, you take Eve and get the hell out of here. Hump to the south and then back west. There's an area of large rocks where you can kill your trail. I'll go straight and see how long I can outrun these bastards."

Talltrees patted his rifle. "And when I can't outrun 'em, we'll see how well they can shoot. If I'm real lucky, I'll get away but at the least, I'll thin the herd a bit and give you two a running start. When you get to Elvis Iron Crow's house–you know, where you started out–tell him that I said to give you anything you need. He was my crew chief back in 'Nam. Could make those old A-1s move like a bat out of hell."

Rick said, "What should I tell him about you?"

"If he doesn't see me in a couple of days, say I wished him well, thanked him for his work in the war, and to call my father so he can come and collect the Roadmaster." He laughed—a soft sad sound. "Nice car but no top end. You might suggest he tune it up."

Rick gripped Talltrees' hand. "I sure as hell don't understand all this, but I owe you my life already so this is just payback. I hope I'll see you at the ranch, and I can give everything back. I would think that a man with an eagle feather on his ass and the protection of an owl should make it if anyone can."

"Maybe." Talltrees turned and began to jog to the west. "Di di mao, ground pounder, and let a flyboy do his job."

Rick walked over to where Eve was sitting. She stood up and very pointedly did not look at what was strung around his neck.

"Time to go," she said.

About a half-mile south, Rick spotted the boulder field on his right, potato-shaped rocks that had been tumbled smooth by long-gone glaciers. They turned west and started moving from rock to rock without touching the ground. They took their time in the darkness because a slip would mean a twisted ankle at the very least. Occasionally, Rick would have to jump a larger space, turn back, and pull Eve across.

The pace was maddeningly slow, and they hadn't gone far when the crack of a rifle shot stopped them. As they stood and looked north where the sound had come from, four more shots, spaced evenly. Rick could almost imagine Talltrees methodically pacing himself through the process: loading, setting his weight, aiming, calculating all the factors, firing, and starting all over again.

A sporadic crackle of shots responded, quite a few weapons and, from what Rick could tell, of different calibers. Pete's pursuers must have gone to ground and started counter fire. The steady pace of the rifle began again. Talltrees must have been able to find more targets by their muzzle flashes.

Rick turned back to see Eve regarding him gravely. She said, "Pete's a brave man. We need to make his sacrifice mean something."

Rick nodded, and they continued their steady, rock-by-rock progress. After a few minutes, the gunfire stopped. They looked to the north, waited a moment and then Eve took the lead, jumping to the next boulder.

In another half hour, the boulders ran out at a dry wash that drained to the west. They took a swallow from their water supply and, using the firm footing of the sandy soil, picked up their pace to the point where Eve was just short of having to jog to keep up. They hadn't gone more than a couple of hundred yards before they heard the whine of dirt-bikes; but, from the way the sound carried in the desert night, it was clear that they were far on the other side of the boulders.

Hours later, the rising sun behind them lit the small butte with a notched top that was their locator for the Iron Crow ranch. The sparse grass that had covered the ground for most of their walk was giving way to taller, almost waist-high stalks.

Keeping the sharp-sided mountain on their left, they headed on as the rising sun threw their shadows for miles ahead on the flat land. Rick found himself hunching his shoulders just slightly, feeling pressed down and exposed by the immense sky.

They crossed a dirt road, two paths cut into the grass, and he could see trash layered in the ditches–years of plastic, metal, and other modern debris that would outlast the road itself. Future archaeologists would probably wonder why the inhabitants had decorated their paths with such bizarre items.

Suddenly, Rick's mental wandering stopped as he heard a shrieking mechanical howl–close, far too close. He threw himself backward into Eve, and they both fell into the ditch with the trash. Enough filthy slush was at the bottom to make the garbage moist and even more disgusting.

He didn't wait to signal, but took off on a belly-crawl into the grass, moving at a slant from the road so the path he crushed in the knee-high plants would be harder to detect. He could hear the scrapes and panting that meant Eve was right behind him. When the cycle exhaust rose to a crescendo, they froze, Rick rolling on his back with his face only inches below the waving tops of the grass.

Two cycles raced by. Rick was glad to see they

were moving too fast to pick out their trail. The riders were young men without helmets. Again, Rick noticed that their identical pearl button snap shirts and boot cut jeans were new and unwrinkled. One man's jeans still had paper tags from the store stapled to the waistband.

He rose as the bikes' dust settled, only to be pulled back down by Eve's firm grip on his collar. A second later, he realized why. Another engine, a car this time, was coming. It was a sedan, bouncing and shaking in the rough ruts. It looked like a big four-door rental car. He figured those inside couldn't have spotted anything. It was taking all their attention to brace themselves against the shuddering and wallowing of the car's soft suspension on the rocks and washouts.

This time, he didn't move after the dust settled. He looked at Eve and saw the weariness and sadness in her eyes. "We're too exposed to continue," he said. "Let's find a good hide and get some rest."

She nodded with relief. Crawling slowly and cautiously, he led her to a small solid clump of brush and stunted pines. Burrowing inside, they rolled together and immediately fell asleep.

It felt like only seconds had passed when the bushes around them were shaken violently. Rick's eyes snapped open, Eve's wide stare only inches away. They heard panting, and the brush shook again.

They rolled on their backs and looked up. A buffalo's head was right above them, nostrils wide, and eyes furious. Well, at least Rick assumed they were angry–admittedly, he hadn't much experience with buffalos.

The buffalo jerked violently against the branches, but they were apparently too strong for him to get any closer. The head lowered until the broad muzzle was only inches from Rick's forehead. He could hear inhalations as the nostrils opened and closed. The head was twisted to one side. Rick realized it was because, up this close, the animal could see only out of one eye at a time. The large brown eye seemed to regard him without any particular approval.

Without thought, Rick reached up and laid his hand on the short curls of hair under the eye. The massive head didn't move. The curls were soft and tight. He dug his fingers in and scratched hard to get under the heavy coat. The buffalo moved his head slightly to bring other areas into reach, and they kept it up until Rick had given him a thorough scratching on both sides.

Snorting abruptly, the head pulled back, and they could hear the animal's heavy hooves crunch away through the grass. They could hear other buffalo moving around them as they followed the lead bull.

In the silence, Eve looked closely at Rick. "Pretty damn brave for a white boy."

"You think?"

"I know."

"Hell, every dog I've ever known has loved to get a nice deep scratching. How different could a buffalo be?"

"About two thousand pounds and a fair amount of mean different. I think he was trying to tell us to get our butts out of this comfortable little bed and back to work." Eve started to wriggle backward out of the brush. "Anyway, he may be my sacred animal totem–I'm quite sure that this wasn't accidental–but he still had fleas."

CHAPTER 10

April 27, 1973, Oglala, South Dakota

Larissa burst through the back door as she dodged the fresh wash hanging on the line in Iron Crow's back yard. She was holding a shotgun as if it were a second child and scanning in all directions. Without looking at them, she said, "Hurry up and get inside!" As soon as they were in the kitchen, she slammed the heavy wooden door and shot the bolt.

"Trouble?" asked Eve.

"The Goon Squad has been here three times already." The young woman set the safety and laid the shotgun on the kitchen table. "That's to be expected. You did hear about Wounded Knee?"

Rick and Eve shook their heads.

"Oh, shit." She turned to pull down the heavy cups and checked to see that the percolator was hot.

"I hate to be the one to tell you. AIM decided to surrender. One of the nicest kids in the entire Pine Ridge reservation died in that big firefight and it just took the heart out of them."

She started pouring coffee so strong it looked like diesel fuel. "Of course, only those who aren't guilty of anything are going to stay behind to surrender. Everyone else will walk out like you did. We should be seeing them over the next few days."

"Come on, have some coffee." She gave Eve a critical look. "Damn, girl, you look like you slept under a bush. Did this white boy try to take advantage of you?"

Eve sat in one of the arrow back chairs and took a grateful sip. "No, he was a complete gentleman."

"What the hell's the matter with you, boy?" Larissa asked as she handed Rick a cup. "Out in the prairie night with the prettiest girl in two states not enough for you?"

Rick sagged into a chair across from Eve and smiled weakly. "There was a chaperone."

Larissa raised an eyebrow at Eve who said, "Nothing will put a chill on the desire to fool around more than the appearance of a one-ton spirit guide with bad breath. Father Buffalo was very clear that we should be up and moving."

"Well, that I can understand." Larissa headed out of the kitchen. "So we should get you two on your way. Your bus is in the barn under a pile of hay bales. I'll get Robbie started on clearing it out."

Larissa stopped as she became aware of the silence that filled the kitchen. She turned slowly, her face already hardened, braced for unpleasant news as if she were facing into a winter storm.

Rick said, "We came out with Pete Talltrees. He gave me a message for your father."

"He's not coming?"

"Pretty sure he's dead."

Larissa slumped against the kitchen counter, all the energy gone from her body. "Dammit. Dammit. Dammit."

Eve nodded agreement. "A brave man and a good one."

Larissa looked at Rick. "Who did it? Goon Squad?"

"I don't think so." Rick shook his head slowly. "I think they were outsiders, not from the reservation. In fact, I doubt they came from the West at all. I think they flew in from the East. Except for Flick."

Larissa burst out, "Flick Crane? That asshole has the nerve to show his goddamn face around here? After what he did to little Ann Marie, the whole Swift Bird family is ready to rip him apart, and I think they'd be going easy on him. Personally, I'd like to bring back 'burning at the stake' just for him. But Flick wouldn't be man enough to take on Pete Talltrees."

"No, he sure wasn't," said Rick. "Flick was working with that bunch of strangers I was talking about. The other night these outsiders were firing at both sides, Indians and marshals. That's what really caused the firefight. Then they came after us, and Pete split us up and led the hunting party off in another direction. If Flick was there at all, he had plenty of help."

He took a deep breath. "There were a lot of them out last night on bikes and trucks. When they caught up to Pete, we could hear his rifle fire for a while. But there were a lot more of them, and eventually Pete's rifle stopped. I don't think Pete had a chance."

Larissa bowed her head and was silent for a time. Then she looked up and said slowly, "Well, that might explain the guys who came by twice yesterday. I thought they were agents or marshals except they didn't flash their badges or show off their guns. These fellows just came up to the door and asked if we'd seen anyone pass by on foot. Strange folks, now that I think of it."

"Clothes all brand new?" asked Rick.

Larissa's head came up. "Yes! How did you know?"

"Sounds like the same people who've been following us. I think they flew in and just bought jeans and shirts to blend in." Rick took another sip of coffee. It was so strong that he swore he could feel it in his fingers and toes.

Larissa snapped her fingers as she remembered something. She said to Eve, "You got a message yesterday. It was bounced around from your parents and then people down here just spread the word on the party lines. Hell, everyone always listens anyway."

She pulled a slip of paper out of her jeans and handed it to Eve. "It's from someone named Kristee. Said she's in DC and in trouble. The number is right there."

Rick unzipped his jacket and began to bring out his pack of Winstons. He stopped cold when his fingers brushed the small leather bag. The warmth from the coffee seemed to drain out of his body.

"One more thing." Rick brought out the bag and handed it to Larissa. "Do you know who this belongs to? A little girl who may have been reported missing in the past days or weeks?"

Larissa stared at the medicine bag, turning to see all sides. "Yeah, this is Beth Pine's. Her parents put the word out to look for her three days ago. Where did you find it?"

Rick looked at the girl, already showing her fear, and said, "Eve, can you do this?" She nodded solemnly. Rick stood and said to Larissa, "I need to speak to your father. In private."

Larissa waved a hand. "He's out in the garage. It's just past the barn." There was a pause, and then she said softly, "Damn."

She looked at Eve and shook her head, begging for a denial. Eve nodded slowly, stood up, and took Larissa in her arms. Rick shut the door on the silence.

The weathered and split boards of the two-car garage matched the old barn and looked like they both would blow away with the first winter blizzard. Rick knocked, and a deep voice said, "Come in."

Rick swung open the right-hand door and found himself inches from the muzzle of a shotgun. Behind the trigger was an old man with intense brown eyes in a deeply lined face so tanned it looked like burnished leather. He was wearing denim coveralls that showed a lot more grease and oil than denim.

Rick slowly raised his hands. "Hello. We didn't meet when we stopped on our way into Wounded Knee, but my name is Rick Putnam. I've got a message from Pete Talltrees."

"OK."

"Do you mind if I come in?" Rick gestured to his shirt pocket; "I'd really like a smoke, especially if you're going to keep that thing pointed at me." Rick lowered his hands and dug for a cigarette. "So, if you're going to shoot me, just hang on for a minute." The Zippo flared on his thigh, and he lit the Winston.

The brown eyes behind the shotgun glanced at the lighter, and then returned to Rick's face. "Seventh Cavalry? Tell me, who were you up against at Ia Drang?"

"I was told later that it was the 1st and 66th Regiments of the Army of North Vietnam, but at the time, I only saw a shitload of gooks with real uniforms and way too much ammunition." Rick took another drag, "I do remember a fast mover with an eagle feather who passed by. I believe that was your plane, Sarge."

The gun muzzle dropped. "It's good to meet you…"

"Rick Putnam."

"Rick. Right. Elvis Iron Crow." They shook–Rick felt a strong hand weathered and callused from years of hard work–and the older man placed the shotgun in a rack custom-mounted on the left-hand door.

The inside of the garage was very different from

the weathered and dilapidated exterior. Clean and well lit, with a long tool bench down the length of the right wall and a rack of power tools down the left, it would have fit right in at Pit Road in Daytona or Gasoline Alley in Indianapolis. Rick noticed that, on the inside, the garage walls were strong with no gaps. Obviously, there was an element of camouflage in the construction.

There were two hydraulic lifts but only one was in use. The car up in the air was painted a scalding red and looked dangerous just sitting still.

"GTO?" asked Rick.

"Yeah, that's The Judge." Iron Crow ran his eyes lovingly over the length of the sleek body. "Moves like crazy once you get it out on some blacktop." He laughed and turned back to the tool bench. "Of course, there's not all that much blacktop out here on the rez, so I'm rigging the shocks and springs to give it more ground clearance. Car like this can't really go fast on dirt, but at least I can keep it from killing the passengers before they can get it on a highway. Now, tell me about Pete. Where did you see him and when is he coming out?"

Rick didn't say anything. After a second, Iron Crow gave a long sigh. "Yeah, that's what I was afraid of. Just figured there might be a chance. What happened?"

Rick told him the story of the past two nights. The old man rested against the tool bench; the dark eyes never left Rick's face, and the lines in his face seemed to deepen, every vestige of the humor Rick had seen just moments before fading into stone.

"He told me to give you a couple of messages," Rick concluded. "Said thanks for all your work in 'Nam and to tell his dad to come by and pick up the Buick."

"The Buick, huh?" He turned back to the bench and began idly to put a set of wrenches in order by size. "He didn't have any damn Buick. He found a '55 Roadmaster somewhere in Saigon and had it dragged out to Bien Hoa. Presented it to me and expected me to fix it–said it was perfect except for the bullet holes across the driver's side door.

"But hell, there are hardly any parts anywhere for those old Buicks. Sure as shit weren't any over there. It never got off cinderblocks, but he used to get in, lean back and smoke whenever he was waiting for assignment. Said he could hear the radio playing. Frank Sinatra, usually."

He placed the last wrench down on the bench with utmost care and turned back to Rick. "Whenever he took off on a particularly dangerous mission, he'd tell me to make sure his Dad got the Buick. I'd say it would be waiting for him when he got back."

"OK..." Iron Crow paused, swallowed, and then continued. "OK, clearly he was telling me to treat you the same way I treated him. What do you need?"

Rick felt that saying anything sympathetic would be a mistake. Iron Crow would grieve alone. "He gave me something to deliver."

"What?"

"Can't say."

"Who's it going to?"

"Can't say."

Iron Crow gave a short laugh. "Well, that's helpful. Can you at least give me an idea how far you need to go?"

"About three or four hundred miles tonight," Rick waved at the GTO. "I'm more used to motorcycles than this kind of big iron. I'd probably put that right into the ditch on the first turn. You know of a bike I can borrow?"

"Hey, you're forgetting that out here you could easily go a couple of hundred miles before you'd have to turn at all, but, yeah, I think I've got a two-wheeler back here somewhere." Iron Crow headed toward the back of the garage, pulled aside a pallet filled with crates of motor oil–Rick noticed the pallet was on wheels–and revealed a hinged steel panel closed with a hasp and padlock.

The older man looked back and smiled. "We used to steal ponies to prove our courage. Now the young men like to 'borrow' a good motorcycle. From the outside, the walls just continue. No one notices that there's a separate space back here."

He reached in and flipped a light switch, then duck-walked through the low opening, Rick following. On the other side was a small narrow space, as clean as the rest of the garage.

Two motorcycles were up on rocker lifts. One was a classic Harley, a Sportster with the chrome touches and leather fringe of a classic. The other wasn't anything Rick recognized, a mean-looking orange and black with one big cylinder pointing straight ahead, and the other straight up.

"What's this?"

"This is Ducati's answer to the Japanese superbikes." Iron Crow rubbed his hand along the bench style seat. "Top speed of 125 and enough torque to pull the front wheel up in fifth gear. I put a custom race fairing on it, and some tank padding for your chin in case you want to get flat at top speed, but the rest is stock."

"Never seen one before." Rick crouched to get a better look at the engine. "Pretty slick."

He stood up. "How does it handle?"

Iron Crow stood on the rocker pedal and lowered the bike to the ground. "Here, see how it feels."

Rick threw his leg over the seat and grasped the front grips. "Nice. More solid than I'm used to with anything Italian."

"Yeah, that's the part that Ducati really got right. This is the first inline twin 750 Ducati made and, by rights, it should be a piece of crap." He leaned down and buffed an invisible speck of dust off the front fender. "Taglioni, their chief engineer, is a goddamn genius. It's not only faster than hell, but it has great handling, good brakes, and these Pirellis hold on the road like glue."

Rick grinned. "OK, I'm sold. Can I borrow it for a couple of days?"

"Sure. But I think we're going to have to do a bit of logistical planning if you're going to make it to Lame Deer in one night."

He waved his hand as Rick began to shake his head. "I know. I know. I don't know anything.

Nevertheless, that's where you're going, and from what I hear, you had better hurry. Tribal Council is meeting tomorrow night."

Iron Crow began to calculate in his head. "That's about 300, 350 miles as the crow flies and more like 400 if you'd prefer to stay on asphalt. Are you going to leave your passenger here? Less weight, more miles per gallon."

"I don't weigh enough to worry about." Eve's voice came from the other side of the wall. "Anyway he's going to need someone to keep him from falling asleep."

The two men looked at each other. Rick shrugged and Iron Crow laughed.

"I'm not even going to try and argue this one," he said. "Now, my boy used to race before he joined up." He saw the look on Rick's face. "No, he's in the Navy on a submarine somewhere. Good sonar op from what I hear. Maybe it's because of his spirit animal–cetan nagin–the night hawk."

"That means we've got a full set of leathers he left up in his room." He measured Rick with a look. "Don't think they'll fit you, but they'll slide right on your eavesdropping friend out there."

There was a disgusted snort from the garage.

Iron Crow continued, "You've got the leather jacket, and I think I can fit you into some of my chaps over your jeans. Don't argue. The Black Hills will get damn cold tonight. Do you know what route you're going to take?"

"Figured I'd just go back the same way we came down." Rick tapped his forehead. "For once this bear-trap memory of mine will be good for something besides the nightly 'Midnight Movies' replay of Vietnam."

"Total recall, huh?"

"Cinemascope and 3-D Surround Sound. You?"

"I was a REMF, remember? I just had to patch up the bullet holes, clean the crap out of the flight suit, and refill the tanks." He paused. "Speaking of which, this bike may be 'super' but it ain't magic. You're going to need gas."

"Guess there aren't too many all-night stations up in the mountains."

"No, there aren't and if someone is on your tail, as I assume they are, the ones that are open are going to be the first places they'll look. No, we'll have to do it the way they chased buffalo in the old times. The hunters would have fresh horses waiting for them along the way, and they would jump from one horse to another without touching the ground. Now, at the big rodeos, they call it Indian Relays, and the tribes compete over bragging rights." He laughed. "You wasichu think you invented the Pony Express. Hah."

Iron Crow crouched and duck-walked back to the garage. Rick followed.

Eve was seated cross-legged on the oilcans. If Rick didn't know better, he would have sworn she looked smug.

He certainly knew better than to mention it.

CHAPTER 11

April 27, 1973, Pine Ridge Reservation,
South Dakota

The road ran straight until it disappeared into a horizon smeared with red and orange interleaved with bands of blue. The bike felt as solid as a rock, but Rick knew the odds–the first 30 minutes on a new motorcycle were the most dangerous–so he kept the speed down to 60. Since there were no other cars on the road, he was bending curves from side to side–trying to find the limits.

"Hold on," he said over his shoulder. He felt Eve's arms tighten around him as she curved to his back. He slammed on the brakes and let the heavy machine slide to a stop.

"That was interesting," she said. "Was there a

reason for that, or is there a stop sign 20 miles ahead?"

"Just finding out what she wants to do in a crisis."

"She?"

"Yeah." He took off again, letting the rear tire throw a bit of smoke this time, and then pulled the engine all the way up to the red line before shifting. He blew past 60 miles per hour in second gear and came off the gas. He took it up to fourth gear still trying to get used to the odd one-up, four-down gear shift and let the engine settle to a steady purr. "Funny. All my other bikes have been male. This one is undeniably a woman."

"I'm waiting for the bad jokes. Hard to handle? High maintenance? Or simply Italian?"

He laughed. "No jokes. It's just a feeling. Be glad she hasn't told me her name yet."

"What did I do wrong?" She put her chin on his shoulder. "Fall for a man who identifies the sex of his transportation. Just promise me you won't leave me for Gigi here."

"Gigi? That's her name?" he asked in mock surprise.

"Why not? No crazier than anything else we've done."

"OK, Gigi." Rick drew back on the throttle, "Let's see what you can do."

The coarse brown grass that stretched in all directions seemed to divide and blur like water around a speedboat as the needle crept up to 75, 90, 100, 120. The V-twin engine was loud but nowhere near straining, and the bike felt solid on the flat and well-maintained blacktop.

Rick bent forward to bring most of his body behind the small racing-style windshield, resting his chin on the pad. As he did, he could feel Eve shift back a bit and tighten down. Her head was resting sideways on his back like on a pillow. He could feel the tiny increase in speed as her helmet moved out of the wind stream.

Riding a bike with a racing fairing felt like being inside a cylinder of oiled glass knifing through the buffeting turbulence of the air around them. There was just enough force against his chest from the air blast through the cowling to hold his torso up, and the position wasn't nearly as tiring as he expected.

A yellow highway sign came into sight, breaking the endless stretch of road and the rolling grass on both sides. He brought the speed down to 75, still concerned about how well his reflexes were meshing with the temperamental machine.

"With Gigi." He smiled at the thought,

The sign showed a curve to the left, the first since they'd left Oglala. As they bent into the turn, the sun came out from behind a bank of clouds on the horizon and blazed red into his eyes. They were heading just enough south of west to put it right in the center of the highway ahead.

Shapes appeared in the distance. Rick blinked and squinted, trying to focus through the shifting haze of red sunlight and deep shadow.

He couldn't be certain but kicked down a gear and opened the throttle just in case. In his experience, it was generally a bad idea to slow down when going into an unknown and possibly dangerous situation. Speed and quick reflexes were a better combination than caution and disk brakes.

As the Ducati surged and the speedometer crept over the 100 mph mark, he heard the crack of a rifle–clear even inside the bubble of calm air.

Then another.

He didn't feel any pain, and the bike didn't slow. He figured they must have missed.

"Hang on!" he shouted and twisted the throttle to the stop. Eve's arms and legs locked against him. The engine was screaming well into the red zone, and the bike's torque–even in third gear–felt like a rocket sled.

The shapes became pickup trucks on either side of the road. He had a brief glimpse of men swiveling–trying to keep the motorcycle in their sights as it flashed by.

The sun finally set, and the road cleared, straight and empty.

The empty part was good, but the straight road meant that he would soon be, effectively, a motionless target for the men behind him. Even this bike wasn't going to outrun a bullet.

He backed off the throttle enough to gain some steering traction and began to cut curves across both lanes of the road, counter-steering against the intense forces of inertia that pushed the bike back into a straight line. After a couple of swooping curves, he touched the rear brake and dropped down a couple of gears, adding some more uncertainty to his path. He could feel Eve pull even tighter against his back, trying to make them one body and one movement.

Ahead was another yellow sign. Grinning like a fool, he cut into the apex of the right turn from one edge of the road to the other and back out. When the bike was again upright, he took it up to 110.

"You OK?" he asked over his shoulder.

"Now you ask." Her voice was calm. With her mouth so close to his ear, she didn't have to shout. "I couldn't see much and this helmet is blocking most sound. What happened?"

"They were waiting for us."

"Be nice to know who 'they' are."

"Yeah. 'Who are those guys?' might have worked in the movies but it's a pain in real life."

"On the other hand, let's not stop and find out. OK?" She loosened her grip and shifted into a more comfortable position. "I'm willing to live with uncertainty."

"No argument. I've never felt the need to meet someone who was shooting at me."

"They were shooting?" He could feel her body stiffen, then slowly and consciously relax. "You didn't mention that little fact. I'm covering your back, you know."

"You and a ten-gallon can of gas," he said. "Hey, could you reach back and check the cords? Hate to lose it."

"At this speed? No, no, and hell no." Her helmet twisted, and her right arm slid back from his waist. "Seems to be there. By the way, we're being followed."

"I know. That's what these mirrors are for."

"Don't be a jerk." She put her hand back around him and settled back into her tuck. "So now what?"

"Now we dance."

She gave him a squeeze. "OK, trooper. Go ahead and dance."

He kicked down into fifth gear and opened the throttle.

It was full dark when they reached Oelrichs, a T-intersection with a small gas station decorated with half-buried whitewashed tires–apparently to keep cars from driving on a tiny strip of grass and flowers.

It was closed.

As they turned north, Rick could see lights behind him–still comfortably far away but they'd been closer every time he looked. This road was busier than the stretch from Oglala, and he'd had to bring his speed down to 75. It seemed to be the unofficial speed limit on these endless stretches of desert highway.

After the fast dash across the flatlands, it felt like cruising. He straightened his back and alternated stretching his legs in front to relieve the stiffness. Eve took her hands from his waist and began twisting from side to side.

"Feeling a bit stiff?" he asked.

"Well, the parts of me that can still feel, feel stiff. I've lost all contact with quite a few parts of me." She wriggled into position against his back. "On the other hand, the last time I could feel my bottom, it hurt, so by and large, I don't miss it."

Her voice turned serious. "What's next? You may not have noticed but those guys are still back there."

'Yeah, and I'll bet there's a pay phone at that last gas station," he answered. "So they could be moving people in ahead of us. It's time to do something sneaky."

"Oh, good." She pulled in a little tighter. "'Sneaky' is my second favorite way I've seen you act."

"What's your favorite?"

"I can't remember, but I think it had to do with the parts of me that I can't feel any more."

Suddenly, headlights flared in front of him. He snapped his eyes to the white line at the right side of the road to keep from being blinded and used peripheral vision to track the oncoming car. The idiot had his high beams on. Rick flicked his own high beams with his thumb, but there was no dimming of the lights bearing down on him, and now, he could see the bastard was crossing into his lane.

"Hold on!" he shouted and swerved over to the right almost into the gravel on the verge. The lights moved right as well. There were only seconds left.

He snapped off his lights, braked for a second, and cut left. The rear tire skidded and almost broke loose, but he dropped down in the gears, opened the throttle, and felt the rubber grab the asphalt. They were still moving to the left when he snapped past the oncoming pickup, and there was no time to get back before they hit the edge of the raised road.

The ground dropped out from under his wheels, and he locked his knees on the tank to make his body one with the bike so it would fly straight. A sudden jerk and a snap from the front end and then they slammed down–bottoming out the springs on front and back–and bounced up again–throwing him into a standing position on the foot pegs.

He thumbed the lights on but saw only a rushing picture of short grass ahead. They hit again, and this time he brought his weight down hard on the saddle and kept them from going airborne again. Carefully, he worked the brakes and slowed enough to bring them around in a wide turn so that they were heading north again.

He flicked on his high beams and then cut the lights off again. They were off the road and in some sort of field, flat ahead, and that was all he needed to know. He put the bike in first and took off.

They hurtled through the blackness, the seat bucking under them. He could hear an involuntary sound from Eve when they took a particularly violent jounce, but otherwise she was silent, her hands linked tight over his stomach.

As his eyes grew accustomed to the dark, he could make out a dirt road cutting across their path, raised a bit higher than the surrounding fields. He slowed and pulled up onto it, then yanked the heavy bike to the right so it was pointed back toward the highway.

On the right, he could see headlights and hunting lights flicker as the pickup made a U-turn, bouncing hard into the ditches on either side of the road. Lights still off, he picked out the highway and–after a throbbing pound over a set of cattle guards at the end of the dirt road–pulled onto the asphalt and made a sharp left.

After they had picked up speed, he clicked the lights on. He could feel some of the tension go out of Eve's arms.

"That was fun," she said. "Please don't ever do it again."

"I'll do my best, but we've got to lose these bastards. We need to stop for gas in Hot Springs."

"Oh good, a rest stop. I'd like to stretch my legs." Her helmet moved as she looked down, and her hand disappeared as she reached down to her side. "Good thing I'm wearing leather pants. I think that was barbed wire we went through back there. I'm bleeding, but the pants took most of it."

"Is it bad?"

"It's not good." She tucked behind him. "Maybe we can have nightmares together when this is all over."

"Sounds like a terrible idea." He checked his mental map of the road ahead. "We'll take a look at it in about five minutes."

When they'd passed by here on the way south, he'd only seen one bridge breaking the monotony of mixed grass prairie and farmland, a flat two lane crossing the Cheyenne River. They could stop there, but only if he bought some space between them and their pursuers.

He took the bike back up above 120 mph, and they slashed through the night.

CHAPTER 12

April 27, 1973, Black Hills, South Dakota

Rick turned off his headlight as they approached the bridge. He shifted all the way down into first, the engine screaming in protest, but he didn't want to use the brakes and have the rear light broadcast their location. Finally, he put the Ducati in neutral and dragged his feet until it stopped just before the bridge.

"Time to get off," he said.

With a muffled groan, Eve swung off the back of the saddle seat and promptly fell to the ground. She waved her hand and said, "Keep going. My legs are asleep."

He could hear the pain in her voice as he killed the engine, got off on the other side, pushed the bulky machine off the road, and into the thick fresh grass that spread around the water. As soon as he had the bike below the road, he rested it against the concrete of the bridge and headed back to Eve.

He tried to run, but the best he could do was an aching shamble. Eve was standing by the time he reached her, and he threw her arm over his shoulder and almost dragged her off the road. The sound of engines was coming fast, but the white cones of headlights still flickered high on the trees next to the riverbank so they weren't in sight yet.

With a last effort, Rick put his arm around Eve's waist and dove into the grass. Then he rolled them both until they stopped, his dark jacket and chaps on top of her white and blue leather racing suit. They were close against the bridge, and he could feel the intense heat of the Ducati's exhaust pipes on his neck.

The engine sounds hit a crescendo as their pursuers passed, and he heard eight sets of wheels banging off the expansion joints on the bridge. As he waited for the sounds to die, he counted off the pickups he'd seen so far–two at the bend near Oglala and one coming head-on just a few miles back. Now there were four, all going faster than even the liberal standards of South Dakota's highways could allow.

These guys were being reinforced.

Eve reached up and knocked on his helmet. "Hello? Earth to Agent Putnam."

He grinned and rolled away from the bike.

"Thanks." She started undoing her helmet. "Ravishing me on the riverbank was a nice thought, but I'm afraid sex is simply going to have to wait until I'm sure I still have the proper equipment."

"Probably shouldn't admit it but I can't feel anything at all down there."

"I knew there was a downside to all this running around on motorcycles." She made a little sound–a moan bitten off by willpower. "OK, this is a rotten time for the feeling to come back in my leg."

Rick inspected her right leg as well as he could by the flickering light of the Zippo. The leather had absorbed most of the damage, but the barbed wire had torn a shallow gash in her calf, and several inches of the white leather were dark with blood. He got a small bag of supplies from the web of bungee cords that held the gas can on the backrest of the bike. Rummaging, he pulled out a small brown bottle.

"Hydrogen Peroxide. Brace yourself."

He flicked the Zippo on his leg and held it in his left hand while he poured the clear liquid on the cut with his right. Eve hissed. He wrapped a roll of gauze bandage over the leather pants and taped it down.

"Had a tetanus shot lately?"

She laughed, rolling into a seated position. "I thought you met my father. I've been vaccinated against every bug known to man. I'm just worried that it will scar my million-dollar legs. I don't suppose you have any White Oak Bark in that bag?"

He pretended to look. "Don't think so."

"How about Mugwort?"

"Nope."

"Scullcap? Knitbone? Gravel Root?"

"Nothing but aspirin."

"That'll do just fine. I'm not all that sure that any of the other crap works anyway."

He pulled a canteen from the back of the bike and handed it to her with the aspirin. Then he climbed up and scanned the road. He saw some headlights in both directions, but nothing moving fast enough to be active pursuit. He ducked back down.

"We'd better get moving," he said, snapping the Zippo to check his watch. "We're supposed to reach our first fuel drop in ten minutes. Hate to keep him waiting."

"God forbid." She stood and started to undo the braid wrapped in a bun at the back of her head. "Just let me get this hair out from under the helmet. It's been giving me a headache that's even worse than the one from your off-road driving." Eve loosened her thick braid and tucked it into the back of the leather jacket.

"I'll try to keep that to a minimum from now on," he said as he yanked the bike upright and–holding by the grips–began to pull it backward. The bike's weight and the awkward position he was forced into made it slow work. Eve came around the front of the bike and started to reach down to the front forks to help push.

"Whoa!" he warned. "One slip, and you're holding on to a red-hot engine. Push from the center of the handlebars."

They moved a bit faster with her help. "I did that once on my old BMW. I was so cold that I put my hands directly on the exhaust pipes."

She grunted with effort and said, "How did that work out for you?"

"I totaled my winter driving gloves, but it was worth it. My hands were warm for at least five seconds."

"It's going to be damn cold when we go over the mountains."

"Yeah. Just keep your hands in my jacket pockets, or, if you're really cold, you can put them inside my jeans."

He could see the flash of her teeth as she smiled. "Wouldn't that be distracting?"

"Trust me. If it's that cold, it won't matter."

There were no cars in sight when they reached the highway. Even so, he didn't turn on the lights until he was a mile from the bridge.

They pulled into a long-closed gas station just outside Hot Springs. A beat-up sedan parked next to the restrooms flashed its lights. If it hadn't, Rick thought he would have definitely passed it as just another abandoned wreck that littered this part of the country.

He took a cautious circle around the station, checking for anything suspicious. Then he came up beside the driver's window and cut his lights. A passing semi howled toward them and in the light of its high beams, he could see a young man with a weathered face and a large burn scar on his left cheek. The man looked at him and asked, "Seventh Cav?"

"PFC. Putnam. Charlie Company," Rick answered.

"Corporal Leon Bent Horn. Black Knights. Third of the Fifth." He reached over the seat and passed a gas can through the window. "Careful with that. Hot engine is how I got this." He pointed to the scar on his cheek. "Au Shau Valley on the Laotian Border. All those damn gooks trying to kill me, and I spill gas on my own damn jeep."

He laughed, coughed, and lit a cigarette.

Rick carefully opened the tank and filled it from the can.

Eve asked, "Seen anyone strange tonight?"

"Stranger than a Cheyenne girl out riding with a white boy?" Eve stiffened but didn't say anything. Bent Horn looked at her closely. "Nothing that weird, but there were a bunch of cowboy Cadillacs with guys standing up in the beds." Rick closed the gas can and handed it back through the window. "Most were carrying long guns." He looked up at Rick. "Don't suppose you'd know anything about that, would you?"

"Hell, no." Rick slapped the tank closed and said, "I'm just taking a quiet ride in the mountains. Appreciate the top-up."

"Don't slow down to see the sights on your way through Hot Springs. If I were you, I'd stay frosty." Bent Horn tried to start the old beater, but it failed with a chorus of bangs and a cloud of blue smoke.

Rick banged on the car roof for a 'thank you.' As they pulled away, Eve turned around and gave the driver the finger. Then she smiled sweetly and waved goodbye.

They could hear Bent Horn laughing and coughing even over the sound of their engine.

CHAPTER 13

April 27, 1973, Black Hills, South Dakota

Hot Springs had seen better days. Tattered billboards advertised the health advantages of a plunge in the warm springs and a restful night at the Hide A Way Cabins. The buildings looked authentically Western and authentically aged.

Despite Bent Horn's advice, Rick figured that a high-speed run through town would only result in a police chase. His spare driver's license would take care of a ticket, but a radio call and a spike strip somewhere ahead could mean a significant delay. They cruised at the speed limit through the dark town looking at the neon of the honky-tonk bars, and the hookers smoking under the streetlights.

"Some of those girls could qualify as an Old West attraction all by themselves," Eve said over his shoulder.

"Just adds to the authentic feel."

"Authentic feel? That's one way of putting it."

Rick laughed. "Well, you have to have entertainment for the lonely traveler." He stopped at the corner a block away from the intersection with Main Street. Several sets of headlights blocked their route. "However, I'm not at all sure we're lonely."

He backed the heavy motorcycle carefully until there was enough room to make a slow turn into an alley behind the stores and bars on Main. They cruised slowly, the Ducati held to a low rumble. After several blocks, they pulled back onto Main Street and looked to the left.

"Damn." Rick muttered. "Looks like they've picked up some bikes. Should have figured they would after I blew past those guys near Oglala."

"Can they ride as well as you?" Eve asked with a mock innocence. "If you are indeed the best motorcycle driver in the world, I can't see a problem."

"Well, then, it's time for the world's best motorcycle rider and her driver to make tracks." Rick headed out of town, waiting until he was a mile past the last streetlight before opening the throttle and returning to the dance.

Headlights appeared in his mirrors only a couple miles out of town. For a while, he could pretend they were just innocent travelers or one of the infrequent big trucks taking the shortcut to Belle

Fourche.

Then more lights appeared, and he could pick out the motorcycles pulling out ahead and the big lights mounted on the roll bars of the pickups. With the part of his mind that wasn't dealing with wrestling a big bike at top speed, he wondered who the hell these people were and where they were getting the money.

They came up behind a semi struggling up the long hill through the grasslands, flashed their lights, and swept past in the empty left lane. As he pulled back in ahead of the truck, the Ducati engine suddenly changed its song and began to labor, slowing by the second.

Eve leaned on his shoulder. "What's wrong?"

"I don't know," he said. "It could be a lot of things, but I think it's the gods giving me a smack on the head for a bad case of over-confidence."

"You really have to watch that. No one likes to be taken for granted."

"I'll light a cigarette for them as soon as I can stop without getting killed," he promised. "But there isn't anywhere for about 20 miles to pull off. This prairie of yours gives 'flat' a bad name."

He could feel her twist to the left to look back past the semi. "It looks like a fair number of vehicles coming up fast. I don't think they're tourists."

She snugged herself back against him—out of the wind. "I do hope you have a plan."

"It's more of an insane idea."

"Oh, goodie. I've loved every one of those so far." She tightened her grip. "I'm ready when you are, trooper."

Rick kept the bike struggling as fast as it could go, but it felt like one of the cylinders had just stopped working. As the semi they'd passed began to creep closer to their rear wheel, he turned off the lights.

"Really, why do you even have lights on your bikes?" His jacket muffled her voice. "I mean all you ever do is turn them off."

"Right now, that truck is providing plenty of light. It's going to get interesting when the first of those guys behind us catch up." He studied his mirrors for a moment. "And here they come."

He backed off the throttle and their speed dropped quickly as the crippled engine stopped straining. Behind them, the trucker flashed his high beams and blew his air horn. Rick raised his left hand with a thumb pointing to the right, hoping the trucker would realize that he was pulling over and not slow down.

Ahead, he saw the light beams as the first of the motorcycles pulled into the passing lane. Carefully, he pulled over onto the shoulder, bumping in the loose gravel, and slowed just enough to let the truck catch up and hide them.

Giving the straining engine a bit more gas, he nearly matched the truck's speed, falling back slowly. The Ducati was handling the bumpy gravel well. He strained to spot "gators," long strips of rubber that had fallen off truck tires, before they knocked his bike off the road.

When he came to the back of the trailer, he goosed the throttle and moved back into the travel lane. They were only a few feet from the rear of the truck, the road illuminated by the truck's taillights. The windblast dropped, and the engine sound dropped.

Eve raised her head. "Wow. Where'd the wind go?"

"We're drafting the truck," Rick said. "Without wind resistance, I can lay off the engine and let the truck pull us."

He checked the mirrors. "And without lights, I'm hoping that the idiots in the pickups won't see us. No one really looks at the back of a truck. You just eyeball the distance and relative speed. The way these guys are moving, I'm betting that they cowboy into the left lane way back and blow right by us."

"Interesting bet. What happens if the truck hits the brakes?"

"Well, you see that bar hanging down on the back?"

"Yeah."

"Well, that's called an ICC bar. It's solid so cars don't go under a truck if it's stopped or something—some people call it a 'Jayne Mansfield' bar."

"Why?"

"Because that's how she died. She was driving way too fast in a convertible and hit the back of a parked truck. You could say she lost her head in a dangerous situation."

Her fist struck his side. "That's disgusting!"

"But true."

"Yeah, well try and avoid it."

"Will do."

They stayed in the cone of quiet air behind the truck as the pickups came up. As soon as Rick could pick out their headlight beams on the truck door in front of him, he pulled right as far as he could and turned the lights back on. He was betting that his taillight matched the trucks and his headlight would wash out the shadow of his bike thrown by the headlights behind them.

His attention was on the foot or foot and a half between his front tire and that steel bar under the truck's rear. He knew there wouldn't be time to react if the trucker hit his brakes. He would try and go by to the right, but he didn't think they'd make it.

As he heard the pickups getting closer–their engines roaring flat-out–he pulled the bike up closer, inches away. He could see the truck's rear door bouncing up and banging down against the non-slip ridges of the top step. He risked a glance at his left mirror and saw he had been right. The pickups were already in the passing lane, and they pounded past without a pause.

He slowed, letting the bike fall back, but stayed in the cone of calm air.

"That was fun," Eve said.

"I'm glad you enjoyed it. My hands are sweating inside my gloves." Rick took a deep breath and slowly let it out. "Hopefully we've appeased the gods of luck. I think I'll just take it easy back here until we reach the next turnoff. We're going to take the slower road. We need to fix whatever is wrong before our friends realize they've missed us."

It turned out to be as simple as a loose sparkplug

wire. Rick jammed the wire down tight, restarted the bike, and heard the reassuring rumbling hum of the highly tuned engine. He turned off the bike, pulled out a cigarette and his lighter. Then he looked at the sky, said, "OK, this one's for you," and hit the lighter with the usual down-up flick on his jeans. Lighting the Winston, he said, "Well, I hope that satisfies the Fates and Furies."

Eve pulled the cigarette from his lips and inhaled hungrily. "It would be even better if you did it twice."

He smiled and lit another. For a few moments, they just smoked and looked at the Milky Way stretching over their heads.

Then Rick started to refasten his helmet strap. "We need to make tracks. I get the feeling that they're not all that bright, but these guys won't go the wrong way forever; and we've still got a lot of tough road to cover before morning. We're going to have to go over the Needles Highway."

"Great. I was disappointed we missed it coming south. I've always heard it was quite pretty. All those sharp turns and exciting drop-offs."

"Should be even more fun in the dark."

The drive past the Custer Battlefield was quick and uneventful. As the road wound upward, there were more trees, pines and scrub mostly, and more turns. Rick was pushing the bike hard but far from its limits or his. They were doing about 90 on the straightaways and only slowing enough to hit the apex on the turns, using both lanes and then pushing the speed right back up.

The next fuel drop was at a cluster of abandoned tourist cabins on the banks of Legion Lake. Rick pulled the bike in slowly, stopped at the beginning of the weed-filled driveway, and swung the front wheel slowly, raking the headlight across the peeling paint, broken glass, and trash. A single headlight flashed twice from next to one of the beat-up cabins.

Rick returned the signal, cut off his lights, and rolled slowly forward. Slouched against an old Harley Electra Glide was a young man with long, straight, black hair and a bandanna tied biker-style over his head.

Rick stopped and, for a moment, no one spoke.

"Well, is one of you going to break down and say something or do you intend to just stare at each other?" Eve swung her leg off the bike saddle and bent to touch her toes. Straightening, she said, "Apparently you are. Why don't I just leave you to it? I need some privacy."

Walking carefully between two of the cabins, she called, "With any luck, you'll have said 'Hello' to each other by the time I get back."

The young man's face broke into a smile as he watched her disappear. "Man, it can't be easy living with that chick."

"Nope, not easy. Definitely worth it, however." Rick stuck out his hand. "Nice to meet you."

"No names? That's cool. I'm Johnny." The younger rider shook Rick's hand, then produced a rubber hose, gave it to Rick, and stuck the other end in his gas tank. "You can take everything in the main tank. I can make it home on the reserve."

Rick sucked on the tube and shoved it into his tank when it began to siphon. Then he spat out the inevitable mouthful of gas. "One of these days, I'll get this to work without having to drink all this damn gas."

"Yeah, that's why I let you suck on it. You headed up over the Needles Highway?"

"Could be."

"OK, I don't need to know. *Howah*, it's colder than hell up there so watch out for ice."

"The Park hasn't salted it? They own that road, right?"

The younger man spat. "Own it, shit. The Lakota took it from the Cheyenne in a fair fight back there on Battle Mountain. The government even said it was ours in the Fort Laramie treaty–until they found gold."

"Any gold left?" Rick bent the tube over and pinched it so the gas stopped flowing and handed it back carefully. "I'm just wondering, you understand."

That got him a sharp look and then Johnny laughed. "You're OK, white boy."

"He's better than that." Eve came back from behind the cabin, buckling her helmet. "And I think we Cheyenne have a pretty good claim on these hills ourselves, so back your Lakota ass off."

"Huh." Johnny slung a leg over the Electra Glide, "You got a *kili* woman there, *wisachu*."

"She isn't mine." Rick closed the tank and re-started the engine. "She very definitely belongs to herself."

"OK, don't freak out." Johnny leaned over and whispered to Rick, "But, if the road don't kill you, she probably will."

Eve got on, and they pulled out.

When they were far enough away not to be heard, Rick asked, "So what is a *kili* woman? *Wisachu*, I've already figured out."

"It's hard to translate but 'tough chick' is pretty close."

"Well, that's accurate."

"Damn right." She tucked into his back. "Now, put some spurs to this thing, trooper. We're burning starlight."

The Needles Highway at night wasn't the beautiful drive it was in the day. Driving was like cutting through dark cold water. Outside the cone of the headlight was pure black. Rick was forced to keep the big bike below 40 to make the tight turns and blind corners.

Twice, he slammed on the brakes as deer eyes flashed yellow in the headlights. They just watched the bike come at them as he locked up the rear wheels and cursed. When the Ducati had finally stopped, they turned and ambled off the road. Once, red eyes flickered on the edge of the road–the sign of a predator–but they saw nothing as they sped by.

They had the road to themselves and could take the straight sections of the narrow tunnels and ridgetop passages at speed. The cold air was slowly burning through their clothes, forcing them to crouch lower behind the small windshield and draw their legs into the tiny area of protection afforded by the race fairings. They kept talking, even telling stories at one point, making sure they stayed awake, and gauging how badly their dropping core temperatures were affecting judgment by the slurring of their speech.

They were about two-thirds of the way across the mountain highway when their pursuers found them again. Two Harleys coming in the opposite direction, headlights blocked by solid rock until they were only yards away.

The riders snapped their heads to the left when they saw the Ducati. One shouted, "That's them!" and the other reached into a jacket pocket, but Rick and Eve were past the next turn and out of sight.

Rick's heart was pounding; it was just luck that he'd been in the right lane. He tapped Eve's wrist, she loosened the sudden death grip she'd taken on his waist, and the pain in his side subsided.

Again, he wondered who these guys were. They clearly had enough people to run a search box with men in front of them as well as behind, and they kept showing up with reinforcements in new vehicles. It would make sense if they were state police, U.S. Marshals, or FBI, but these guys had been firing at the government bunkers back in Wounded Knee.

Private investigators?

The CIA playing an inter-agency power game?

He shook his head to clear out the questions and picked up speed. Whoever they were, they'd be on his tail as soon as they could make U-turns on the narrow road–which wasn't going to be quick with those huge Harleys. He was sure the Ducati was faster on a straight but on the turns, he'd be forced to drop down to their speed. He had to do something about them before someone new showed up.

"I've got an idea," he said over his shoulder.

"About damn time."

"You know you could get off and walk if you wanted."

"No, thank you. What's the plan, trooper?"

"We're going to need to gain as much time as we can on them." He dipped deeply into a turn. "Wait, I'll explain when I get to a straight and I'm not trying so hard to keep us on the road."

"Better talk fast. 'Straight' is a relatively scarce commodity up here." She pulled closer to his back. "Right up there with 'warm'."

After fifteen minutes of pushing the bike deep into turns and powering out, staying carefully off the brakes by going up and down the gears almost constantly, they reached what Rick knew from his single glance at a map was the last of the narrow tunnels blasted through the granite spires. Now he knew there was time to talk, and he outlined quickly what he planned to do.

Rick slowed down at the tunnel exit, made a wide turn, and parked the bike facing the way they'd come, just to the left of the tunnel mouth. Behind him, the road split, the main road branching off to the left and a parking lot opening to the right. There was a needle of solid stone dead ahead—only yards from the tunnel exit.

He pulled off his helmet and put a gloved finger

to his lips. There was no sound of their pursuers, no deep rumble of the big V-Twins echoing off the sides of the stone tunnel.

"OK, let's do it," he said.

Eve began to dismantle the gear bungeed to the bike's luggage rack, pulling off the gas can to reach the backpack. Putting it on the ground, she opened the drawstrings on top and began taking out supplies. At the bottom was a metal box–the strobe that Pete Talltrees had given them. She handed it to Rick.

Rick had unlocked and flipped up the bike's seat, revealing the battery and, tucked in a small compartment to the side, a small tool kit and a roll of electrical tape. Slamming the seat down, he unrolled the cold plastic tool bag and used the screwdriver to remove the taillight screws. He used the tape to attach the red plastic taillight housing to the front of the metal box Eve had put on the ground.

He flipped a switch on the back of the box, and a blazing red strobe light exploded off the tunnel walls. Satisfied, he turned it off and wound a couple of the bungee cords around it, then handed one to Eve.

Eve had another bungee ready and quickly taped it to the on-off switch. She stepped back next to the tunnel and waited.

Rick jogged back to the Ducati. Moving as quickly as he could, he scavenged a can of peaches from the backpack, opened it with a small opener stashed in a side pocket, dumped out the contents, and placed the can on the ground on the right side of the bike. Then he opened the oil plug on top of the engine, got a good grip on the handlebars, and slowly tipped the heavy machine over until hot engine oil poured out and filled the can. He knew the can was only big enough to bring the oil level down halfway on the dipstick–there would be enough for the engine. There wasn't any visible strain on his face, but he grunted as he raised the bike back up.

Setting the bike up on the center stand, he took the can and threw about half the oil on the road back in the tunnel and then as widely as he could in a straight line leading to the wall of stone. The smell of hot oil was an affront to the crisp mountain air.

As he headed back to the bike, he heard the first faint echoes. They had only minutes.

Sorting through the tool kit, he fitted the heaviest socket wrench with an extender, making it into a foot-long rod; then he twisted the spare sparkplug into its thin-wall tool and jammed that into the open end of the socket. Finally, he pulled a one-inch washer from his pocket, something he'd made in Elvis Iron Crow's garage. It was threaded on the inside so it fitted on the end of the sparkplug. Now, he had a foot-long steel club with about a pound of metal on the end and all that weight concentrated on the narrow edge of the washer.

The motorcycles were getting louder. Rick reached over, stuck the motorcycle key into the ignition with his right hand, and grasped the end of the bungee cord with his left. Eve crouched and picked up her bungee cord.

They waited.

The tone of the motorcycle exhaust deepened as the two riders entered the tunnel. He picked up the bungee and, standing, pulled the boxy strobe toward him and up to head height as Eve mirrored his motions.

The bikes were coming quickly–headlights flickering off the rock walls–but Rick waited until the last second. Then he turned on the bike's ignition, blazing the high beam of the headlight directly into the tunnel. Eve pulled the strobe's switch, and the red light began pulsing in the center of the tunnel.

Rick could hear the squeal of tires on the asphalt for a second and then silence as they hit the oil. The first rider was already down and sliding when he came out of the tunnel. His partner, fishtailing desperately to stay upright, slammed into him, and then his bike was down. Both slid across the open space and smashed into the rock wall.

Dropping the strobe, Rick grabbed his makeshift club and ran over to the pile-up. The men were moving, the first one screaming in pain as he tried to pull his leg out from under his bike. The second rider reached inside his jacket and Rick hit his right forearm as hard as he could, trying to put the edge of the washer right on the outside of the man's arm.

He heard a crack as the bone broke.

Now they were both screaming. Eve turned away, looking pale.

Rick said, "I've got to keep them from shooting at us–"

"I know, damn it!" Eve interrupted, "It's rough to see, but it's no worse than a Sun Dance. Finish up and let's get out of here."

Rick circled and eyed the first rider. He probably had a broken leg and his left side was shredded where his jeans and denim jacket had scraped off on the pavement. Deciding that there was no point in taking chances, Rick pulled the biker's right hand out and carefully broke his trigger finger with the weighted washer.

"You mother-fucker!" the rider shrieked. "Stephen will fucking kill you!"

Rick pulled the ignition keys from both bikes, throwing them over the edge of the parking lot. He twisted the first rider's helmet so he could see his face. "Weren't you going to kill us anyway?"

"We just want that fucking piece of shit medicine bag, god damn it!"

The second rider was slowly trying to get his left hand into his jacket. Rick pulled open the heavy leather and took an automatic pistol from the man's belt. Checking that the safety was on, he put it down, and slid it over to Eve.

In a matter-of-fact voice, he asked, "Right-handed or left-handed?" The man gritted his teeth and glared at Rick. Rick shook his head and said in a mock-regretful tone, "OK, but that means I'll have to make sure. Sorry."

Then he broke the forefinger on the left hand.

Turning to the rider with the broken leg, he patted him down, removing a Colt Python from a shoulder holster.

"Jeez, you sure you've got enough firepower? What the hell are you? A lost LURP unit?" Rick asked as he cocked the hammer, and then held it muzzle-down between the two men. "And who is Stephen?"

The rider with the shredded jacket said through gritted teeth, "I ain't telling you shit, squaw-fucker."

Rick reached over and gently tapped his broken finger with the pistol.

The biker screamed and twisted.

As he did, Rick saw where the torn denim had revealed bare shoulder. He grabbed the arm, dug out his Zippo, lit it on his thigh, and held it so he could examine the shoulder. Then, he turned, yanked the jacket off the other man's shoulder, and tore his shirt away.

Both men had four black scars in a box pattern. Rick said, "What the hell is this? You guys in a fraternity or something? Or were you just branded so your boss could keep track of you?"

"You and your prairie nigger girlfriend are dead. We'll kill you the way we did your buddy on Pine Ridge." The biker's eyes blazed with fury. "Took that fucker a couple of hours to die."

Rick grabbed the man's chin and twisted his head so he could see his face. He held the pistol against his temple. "What did you say?"

"Your buddy, the tall fucker with the rifle." The biker tried to spit in Rick's face, but the spittle ran down his chin. "We wasted his ass but not until we crushed his nuts and took off every inch of his skin."

Rick's hand trembled as he fought the urge to kill the man. Slowly, he released his grip on the Colt and stood up. He raised the gun and aimed at the man's left eye.

For a long moment, he just stood.

Then he turned, lowered the hammer, and violently hurled the gun into the darkness. He said to Eve, "Give me the other one, too. These miserable bastards are not going to show up in my nightmares."

She handed him the second pistol, and it followed the first over the guardrail.

She looked at him gravely as he turned away from the two men and the twisted wreckage around them. "I would have killed them."

"Sorry." Rick headed back to the Ducati. "Look at the bright side, maybe they'll freeze to death before anyone gets up here."

"Maybe." Eve turned to follow. "But probably not."

Rick looked back and grinned at her. "Yeah. God knows they don't deserve it, but I'll call for an ambulance as soon as we find a phone."

"That's what I thought."

"I've already got enough ghosts." He picked up the oily peaches can and threw it high into a crevice in the rocks. "Let's get this place cleared of as much of our stuff as we can and get the hell out of here."

CHAPTER 14

April 28, 1973, Deadwood, South Dakota

Headlights flashed in back of the small wayside rest stop. Rick swept his headlight over an old sedan with the trademark faded blue of a cheap Earl Scheib paint job. When they got closer, he thought how much the driver resembled his car: both looked hard used and badly battered but still running.

An older man, he had thinning hair under a Dodgers cap and heavy glasses with lenses like the bottom of a bar glass. From the lines on his face, Rick suspected he'd seen the bottom of more than his share of bar glasses.

"You must be Iron Crow's buddy." The man's voice was low and scarred by years of cigarettes. "I don't suspect you need to know my name if you don't mind."

Rick felt Eve swing off the back of the bike and he pulled it up on the center stand. "No, I don't mind." He got off and bent to touch his toes, trying to get some flexibility back in his tired body. He grunted when a spasm of pain shot through the webbed scars on his side. Eve had disappeared into a wooden outhouse in a clump of pines.

"Gas can is back in the trunk if you don't mind. At my age, you don't need to be carrying heavy things around." He placed an unfiltered cigarette between his lips but began to cough before he could get it lit. "Hell, at my age, it's damn hard just to get out of the car."

With a fair amount of swearing, the driver managed to light his cigarette with the car lighter. Then he turned off the switch and handed Rick the key. The car kept running, coughing and rocking, the engine dieseling even with the power off.

"This car just doesn't want to quit," Rick said as he headed toward the trunk.

"Nope. Just too old and stupid to know when it's time to take a rest. And don't you dare say it's just like its owner."

Rick called from the back of the car. "Wouldn't think of it."

The old sedan was still gasping and popping when Rick had finished refilling his tank and put the can back in the trunk. He gave the old man the key. As soon as the key was in the ignition, the engine stopped, and the night was quiet.

The old guy laughed, relaxed in the cracked

leather of the driver's seat, and turned to the serious enjoyment of smoking. As he tapped the ashes out the window with one hand, he offered the pack to Rick with the other.

"Thanks." Rick dug out his Zippo and did his trick to light the cigarette. The driver watched curiously.

"Cute trick. Looks like an old habit."

"More of a good luck charm." Rick inhaled the rich smoke. "It seems to keep me alive."

"Hey, if you find something like that, you don't ever want to give it up."

Eve emerged from the outhouse. Rick noticed that the warped wooden door even had the classic crescent moon shape cut in it. She gasped for air. Clearly, she'd been holding her breath.

"Bad?" Rick asked.

"Only if you like to breathe. Damn. They had a stick in there, so you could push everyone else's crap aside." She took another deep breath. "I think that's a new record for all-around stench."

The old man laughed. "You've been off the rez too long. You'll be asking for paper next."

"Are you kidding? You haven't used a true New York City restroom like the one in Penn Station. Makes this seem like a field of clover."

Rick headed in the other direction. "I guess I don't really want to sit down all that much."

When he returned, Eve was leaning against the car smoking. Her face was closed and serious. "What's up?" Rick asked.

"I'll tell you on the road." She snapped the butt off into the asphalt parking lot and pulled her helmet on. "Dawn's coming, trooper. We need to push if we're going to–" She stopped suddenly then simply said, "We need to get going."

For a second, Rick thought she was worried about the old man but then realized she was trying to avoid talking about "men's business." He buckled his helmet, pulled the bike down from the stand, and backed it up far enough to avoid the front of the car on the way out. Eve waited until he got on and then settled on to the rear seat.

Rick tossed a salute at the driver. "Thanks. Much appreciated." The man responded in Cheyenne. Eve answered sharply and whatever she said reduced the old man to a combination of coughing and laughter that rendered him helpless.

As they pulled away, Rick asked, "What did you say?"

"You don't want to know. Let's just say I was defending your...honor."

"Humph." Rick turned the lights on after they'd pulled back on the main road. It was only 4:30, but there was already a dim glow on the eastern horizon. "Well, there are no mountains from here on out, straight and boring all the way to Montana. I'll use the spare tank to get us there so there will be no stops."

"There should be someone to meet us," she said. "The old guy was telling me about the phone call he got from his cousin in Lame Deer just before he came out to wait for us. Apparently, all kinds of strange people are hanging around outside the reservation, and whoever is behind them has some serious clout."

Rick got the Ducati up to a comfortable rev zone in fifth gear. Even after all tonight's riding, it was still difficult to believe they were doing 115.

Eve continued, "The Sheriff's Departments of both Powder River and Rosebud Counties have let them put up roadblocks on the main roads."

"'Let them'?"

"That's what I said. Old Buck said the deputies weren't actually helping, but they aren't making them move their trucks out of the road either."

Rick thought a moment, "Any idea where the roadblocks are?"

"Right on the border of the reservation. The Tribal Police may not get a lot of respect, but they aren't going to let a bunch of strangers set up shop on their territory. So, do you have a plan?"

"Not yet, but there's a whole lot of miles still to go. We'll think of something."

Rick stopped the Ducati and looked at the small bridge across the Tongue River as the first knife blade of gold light lit the top of the hills far to the west.

No cars, no pickups, and no armed men waiting.

Eve unzipped the top of her jacket. The temperature was beginning to rise. "Well?" she asked.

"I can't see anything." Rick kept sweeping the land ahead as it emerged from the dim of the early dawn. "But aren't 'eagle eyes' supposed to be your contribution to this partnership?"

"No. I bring legal advice and the hard-earned

wisdom of the Ivy League. The great jungle warrior here is the big white guy at the front of the bike."

"Well, big white guy doesn't see anyone."

The main road would have led them through Ashland and almost certainly a checkpoint, but they'd cut off to the south and taken a bone-rattling ride down a road that was no more than used motor oil sprayed over dirt and gravel. Rick thought it was a miracle they hadn't blown a tire.

Now, they were looking at the small bridge that crossed a small creek and entered the reservation through the town of Birney. It would be only an hour's run up to the tribal council office at Lame Deer.

If there wasn't anyone waiting at the bridge.

Rick toed the bike up into first gear. "Well, to quote a great general's last words, 'Hurrah boys! We've caught them napping!'"

"Gee, and here I'd always been taught Custer's last words were, 'Where the hell did all these fucking Indians come from?'"

"Makes a lot more sense that way." Rick opened the clutch and the Ducati leaped forward. "Here goes nothing."

The rough surface of the road cut the bike's speed. Rick couldn't get above third gear without feeling the front wheel going airborne and losing its grip. When men with rifles came out from behind the trees right before the bridge, he knew he couldn't get up enough speed to cut through them.

He slowed and stopped only yards away. Facing them were five young men, wearing jeans, denim jackets, and shirts still stiff from store shelves, and carrying identical AR-15 rifles. At least Rick assumed they were the civilian version. As far as he could see, they looked like military issue M-16's.

Rick would have bet good money that they all had identical square scars on their upper arms.

"Hey, assholes!"

The five men jerked and spun as they heard the loud voice coming from behind them. At least a dozen young men with the round faces and long hair of native Cheyenne were walking across the short bridge. There were some hunting rifles and at least one AK-47, but most had shotguns at their shoulders. Several were wearing M-65 field jackets, and Rick could tell by the careful way they moved as a group that they all had combat experience.

The one who had yelled was wearing a policeman's jacket with a baseball cap. He called out, "Tribal Police. Place your weapons on the ground and step away to the side of the road. I'm Sergeant Frank Kaline, and these men with me are an authorized posse under the laws of the *Sotaeo'o* and *Tsitsistas* peoples. You have no right to be here and you need to leave."

Two of the men standing in front of Rick moved slightly, beginning to bring their rifles to their shoulders. Instantly, three of the men in the front line of the posse dropped to prone firing positions to clear sight lines for the men in back and a dozen weapons shifted aim. The sound of safeties snapping off rippled through the still air.

The two men froze.

"Maybe, you didn't understand me," Kaline said. "So I'll translate it into 'white trash' for you. Put those fucking weapons down and move the fuck over to the side of the road. Now!"

Slowly, the men placed their rifles on the road and began to back away.

Suddenly, one reached into his jacket and turned toward Rick and Eve. A shotgun blast hit him in the right shoulder, and he continued the spin as the pistol in his hand flew into the brush. Kaline said without looking back, "I sure hope that was you, Herb."

The man who had fired the shotgun racked the pump. "Yep."

"Good. That was birdshot, right?"

"Rock salt."

Kaline grinned. "Shit. That'll sting." Then his face became serious. "To my knowledge that was the only non-lethal load any of us are carrying. I might be wrong, but I'd say the rest of you should consider the odds before you do anything as stupid as your buddy there just tried."

The man who'd been shot was bent over and moaning, a high, whistling sound of pain, but no blood stained his new denim jacket.

"Whoever you are on the bike," Kaline continued. "Get moving before any of us gets a good look at you. In a couple of minutes, all of us are going to forget any of this happened, and it would be helpful if you were out of sight by then."

Rick opened the clutch and rode across the bridge into the reservation. It was smooth paved road on the other side, and the Ducati was up to cruising speed in less than a minute.

As they approached the outskirts of Lame Deer, Rick slowed to the speed limit for the second time since they left Oglala. As they passed the intersection where Sweet Medicine Road crossed Cheyenne Avenue, a man stepped out from a copse of trees on the left and waved them down.

He was tall and thin, dressed in jeans with a silver belt buckle, a faded red checked shirt with pearl buttons, and a battered Resistol hat that might have once been white but now was the same dull red as the ever-present dust. His face was weathered and lined, but Rick thought he could have been any age between 40 and 75.

Rick slowed; the man held up both hands with the palms empty and then gestured for him to pull the motorcycle over to the left. Rick asked Eve, "What do you think? Do we stop?"

"Hell, yes." Her response was unequivocal. "He's definitely a Cheyenne, but I've never seen him before, and I know everyone on the reservation at least by sight. That makes him important."

The tall man spoke to Eve first, a soft murmur of words in Cheyenne. She nodded once, dismounted from the motorcycle, and walked over to the shade of the trees where she took off her helmet and sat resting against a tree trunk--pointedly looking away from the road.

Once she was seated, the man turned to Rick and continued to speak in Cheyenne. Rick shook his head and said, "I can recognize 'whirlwind,' the name Eve gave me, but the rest is beyond me. Could we change to English?"

The man laughed, lines around his eyes showing that this was a familiar reaction. "That's a good name for you, Whirlwind. After all, you beat the wind to get here."

"It was fun." Rick took off his helmet and rubbed his hair vigorously. "I haven't had the chance to dance on a hot bike for way too long."

"You see it as a dance?" The man's face was thoughtful and approving. "That's good. It's fitting that what you have carried has been returned in a dance."

Rick kept his face blank and didn't say anything. The other man seemed pleased. "You have the patience of a Cheyenne. Most white men just can't wait to start talking. I guess you still need proof that I'm the right person to hand off your burden."

He stuck out his hand. "I'm Charlie Walksalone, and I'm one of the Arrow Men and a member of the Council of 44."

Rick pulled off his motorcycle glove and shook his hand. It was a firm grip with the calluses of a working rancher. "Pleased to meet you. I believe I have something to give you." He paused a second, "That is, if you can say who gave it to me."

Walksalone's smile disappeared and a deep sorrow filled his eyes. "Peter Talltrees was a good and brave warrior. They found him a few days ago. It obviously took a long time for them to kill him, but from the way they took their anger out on his body, he died in silence. I know that he declared you an honorable warrior worthy of carrying the Arrows. He broke our traditions, but he would never have done that if he hadn't felt you had a clear soul and an honest mind." He chuckled briefly. "That and Pete was a Pawnee, and they never get anything right."

He continued in a sober voice. "Now I need to ask you. Will you give me what you carry willingly and expecting nothing in return?"

Rick didn't know exactly why but he answered with the respect he'd been taught to give a senior officer. "Yes, sir, I will."

Rick unzipped his leather jacket and pulled the leather loop over his head. He had never actually looked at the pouch he carried. It was decorated with dots and loops in colored paints and sewn with rawhide strips whose varied hues indicated they were from different animals. It felt both very old and recently made, an impossible combination that seemed to make sense.

He sat on the motorcycle looking at it for a moment and then handed it to Walksalone. The older man took it carefully. He studied the pouch closely on both sides, held it to his chest with his eyes closed for a long moment, and then ritually raised it to the four directions, ending up holding it above Rick's head.

Again, he spoke in Cheyenne, and Rick listened to the graceful flow of the unknown words. It sounded like speaking and singing combined as if they had never been parted, and it went on for a long time.

Finally, Walksalone put the loop around his own neck, and the pouch disappeared under the red-checked shirt. "You have given our medicine back freely, but out of respect for the medicine we must pay a respectable ransom. The first Arrow was returned for a gift of 100 horses."

The man's smile returned. "How are you fixed for horses?

Rick laughed. "Man, all those horses in Washington? I'd have to graze them on the White House lawn."

"OK, how about a hot shower, a hot meal, and an inconspicuous lift back to your bus in Oglala?"

"That would be more than enough."

"Well, it will be a start." Walksalone called to Eve, and then turned back to Rick, putting his hand on his shoulder. "We still owe you. Someday you must ask us for a service, a serious one that is worthy of what you have returned to us. Remember, you must do this."

Rick nodded.

Walksalone laughed and clapped his hands. "All right. Let's get you two washed, fed, and on your way. You're going to have to excuse me, though. I have some serious business with the Tribal Council. We need to talk about coal leases and exactly where we're going to tell Excacoal they can shove them."

"Come here, granddaughter!" He gave Eve a hug and a kiss on the top of her head. "You and your 'whirlwind' have done well. Now, it is the old men's time to fight."

CHAPTER 15

May 20, 1973, Washington, DC

"OK, that was Kanawha, and here's Jocelyn." Rick was leaning far over the horizontal steering wheel of the VW bus and peering to the right trying to pick out the road signs in the gathering dusk. "Wait a minute. Jennifer? That's not fair. You can't have two 'J's in a row."

In the passenger seat, Eve smiled. "You can't expect the city planners to be consistent all the time."

"Hey, this is Washington. A 'foolish consistency' is practically mandatory." Rick sat up and began to haul the bus into a right turn. Even after all the miles they'd put on it, it still felt heavy and unwieldy. "Ingomar. Do you know why it's named

'Ingomar'?"

"You asked me the same thing about Tunlaw and I told you it was 'walnut' spelled backward," Eve said.

"That was half an explanation at best," Rick replied as he straightened out on the quiet residential street. "Why not just name it 'walnut' and shove it back about five streets, so it fits the alphabet? And what does Kanawha mean?"

"It's a river in West Virginia and it's undoubtedly named after the original inhabitants once they were safely killed or driven away." Eve began to pack away the cigarettes, snacks, and other detritus of a long road trip. "I will, however, admit that 'Ingomar' has me stumped. Some sort of Viking?"

"A Wagnerian dwarf was my first guess." Rick shook his head. "No, I had to look it up to solve the riddle. He was the hero of a play named, obviously, 'Ingomar.' Well, 'Ingomar the Barbarian,' to be precise. It was apparently a monster hit before the Civil War, and cities and counties all across the country are named after him. And one street in Washington."

He smiled ruefully. "Only my roommates would send me a coded letter where I had to break the code first and then answer a series of riddles to find the address. I think it's on the 2100 block of Ingomar, but it could easily be on the other side of the city completely. Or in Nebraska, for that matter."

He slowed the bus and continued down what was now a single-lane street with cars parked on both sides, and houses perched on high banks at least a story above the street. It felt like a ravine. "But I think it's right along here."

It had been a long and, thankfully, boring journey from Montana. After a night's sleep back at the cabin on Muddy Creek Road, they'd been stuffed into plywood boxes in back of a pickup truck with bales of hay on top of the boxes. They had air mattresses to cushion the bumps, but the two-day ride back to Oglala was dusty and claustrophobic.

They picked up the VW Camper from the Iron Crow family and took the old Lincoln Highway east. The first coast-to-coast paved road, it was slow and relaxed with old restaurants and tourist courts that seemed to have never left the 1930's.

In Gettysburg, they'd stopped and walked through the battlefield. The numbers of dead and wounded there had struck Rick as incredible–50 thousand in just three days. He could see why there were so many monuments and memorials. The nation had lost a generation.

It was an educational experience for Eve as well. The cavalry companies and battalions that she knew from their part in the Indian wars were born in a very different conflict, learning their trade by killing each other. Although, as she pointed out, at least it was a fair fight, and damn few women and children were involved.

Standing on Little Round Top, even she was silenced as she considered the courage of the Confederate soldiers who assaulted such an unassailable position. There, they were met by the equal courage of the men from Maine who fought until their bullets ran out and then attacked with their bare hands.

All the way, they watched for strange men with peculiar scars dressed in just-bought clothes. It was easy to do since just about every car and truck would pass the VW as it struggled up hills, but no one slowed to stay behind them or waited at the next turnoff.

There was plenty of time to talk while driving and during the slow lazy evenings when they'd find a secluded spot, camp, cook dinner on a little hibachi, and watch the sun go down. They went back over every event, beginning with the "security arrest" in Wounded Knee and the coordinated fire on Indian and law enforcement positions the night of April 26, and how it had broken the AIM occupation.

There had been no police reports in the newspapers about bikers found injured on the Needles Highway or police seeking a couple on a motorcycle, but they did hear on a local radio station that there were services for a Vietnam Veteran, a pilot, who was found dead on the Pine Ridge Reservation.

The reporter said that the police suspected it was suicide, just another case of chronic depression. Rick had not forgotten Pete Talltrees–the man had saved his life twice–and the image of his maimed body haunted his waking hours much as the battle of Ia Drang still occupied his nights. Promising Talltree's ghost that he would find his tormentors and exact revenge was the only remedy he found for his anger and grief.

Eve called home and learned that the Tribal Council had refused to honor any of the mining leases, even ones that had already been signed. She didn't mention the Sacred Arrows, but she did pass along her father's "appreciation" to Rick.

As the days passed, they'd stopped talking about anything serious, turning instead to pointing out the struggling roadside attractions they passed and to a great deal of comfortable silence.

Eve grabbed the panic bar, as he suddenly swung left into a driveway almost hidden between two cars. It ran about 20 feet and then made another left turn into a two-car garage under a brown and yellow house with wooden siding.

"You could shout a warning or ring a bell or something when you're going to do something crazy," she said as she bent to collect her things from the floor. "How do you know this is the right place?"

"'This is it.' That's what Joseph Smith said when he founded Salt Lake City. Like Smith, I was guided from above," Rick said as he opened the door and embraced a tall man in shorts, sandals, and a long, bushy beard. "Steve here was waving flashlights at me from the porch."

Steve grinned and waved a pair of orange cones. "Technically, they're Runway Marshaling Wands. I figured you might need a bit of guidance. We gave you the wrong house number just in case."

Eve jumped out of the car and came around for her own hug. "In case of what? Your letter being intercepted by some random bunch of geeky spies?"

"Well, yeah." Steve leaned back and looked at

her. "I'm with the National Security Agency now. You know, 'We Read Your Mail So You Don't Have To.' You two are pretty well off the radar but there's no point in taking chances."

"So, you've decided to sell out to The Man?"

"Damn right." Steve indicated his usual uniform of shorts, t-shirt, and sandals, "Just like I went corporate with GE. The advantage with NSA is that they have ALL the good toys and one or two programmers who can actually teach me something."

Rick had pulled open the side door of the camper and started handing out duffle bags and backpacks as Steve continued. "Anyway, every once in a while, we do something useful. A couple of Arabs were going to set off car bombs in Manhattan to welcome Golda Meir last month."

Rick asked, "Really? I didn't hear about it."

"And you won't." Steve laughed. "We 'accidentally' overheard them talking about it on an open phone and passed a quiet word to the FBI."

Rick pulled out the last bag. "Well then, I'll agree that it's not a complete waste of your time. I was afraid you were just hanging around listening in to homegrown radical types. You know, hotheads like the Vietnam Veterans against the War or the Democratic Party."

"Well, I'll have to admit that we listened in on most of what went on at Wounded Knee," Steve said. "Heard quite a bit about you and your little ride through the mountains. It was odd, most of the conversations were on a frequency that the standard radios issued by the FBI and U.S. Marshal can't receive."

Eve started up the back stairs with her bags. "Would have been nice if you'd given us a head's up."

"You didn't sound like you needed any help," Steve answered. "You'll be glad to know that the two thugs you pulled the motorcycles out from under are doing well and expected to recover in a couple of weeks."

Rick shook his head, "Only a 'couple of weeks'? I should have hit them harder. Did you pick up any crosstalk between the people who gave us a hand?"

Steve smiled. "Probably. Even the NSA has damn few people who can keep up with idiomatic Sioux at all, and none if they start talking fast. Whoever they were, they had good communications discipline, not a word in English. Well, except for once..."

Rick felt a chill. "What did you hear? Those people don't need any more trouble."

Steve said, "I don't think that 'Holy Shit, You weren't kidding about that crazy-ass white boy. He just came through here like a bat out of hell–had to be doing 140!' is going to interest anyone. Well, perhaps the Montana State Highway Patrol."

"They are extremely low on my enemies list." Rick closed the bus and walked to the rear to check if it was visible from the street.

Steve walked with him. "Don't worry about anyone spotting it. The bus is completely concealed from anyone driving or walking. Anyway, the bus won't look like this for long; we've got a new handheld paint-gun, and Scotty is dying to use it. I think he's planning fluorescent daisies or something."

Rick, laughing, grabbed a couple of bags, and threw them to Steve. "Yeah, like THAT won't be noticed around DC"

Steve caught the bags and headed for stairs hidden around the corner next to the garage doors. "Noticed, yes. Identified is a whole other question. Come on in. We've got a complete quorum of the 'Friends of Ingomar' tonight."

Eve called from the top of the stairs, "'Friends of Ingomar'? Do we get t-shirts?"

"Naturally. Eps drew them up and had them screen-printed." Steve looked back and smiled. "Don't worry, we ordered a child size for you and an extra-gargantuan for your boyfriend."

"'Child size'?" Eve exclaimed. "I'm insulted. I am the perfect height. Tall enough to see over the judge's desk and small enough to go all wide-eyed and plead for judicial clemency when necessary."

CHAPTER 16

May 20, 1973, Ingomar Street NW, Washington, DC

When Rick entered the kitchen, he spotted his two other housemates sitting at a table made out of a wooden cable spool. Eps looked up from a small multi-colored cube that he was fooling with. "Hey, where you been?"

Scotty Shaw, the butt of countless "beam me up" jokes, was busy on their remote computer terminal, a boxy thing that took up a small suitcase and was usually referred to as the 'trans-luggable.' He had the kitchen wall phone cord stretched over his shoulder and the receiver jammed into a pair of black rubber cups. The green glow of the 5-inch display lighting his face from below made him look like a round, bespectacled Christopher Lee. He waved a hand without taking his eyes off the screen and continued typing.

Rick knew that, from this bunch, it was a welcome easily as warm as one of those screaming celebrations when a unit came back from 'Nam. "You guys haven't changed much," he said. "It's like I never left."

"You were gone?" Scotty didn't look up but a small smile crossed his face.

Eve dropped everything she was carrying and ran across the room to give Eps a warm hug. Turning to Scotty, she said, "OK, nerd boy. Get away from the computer and give a girl a welcome home hug. God knows it's not something that you get every day."

Scotty smiled and stood, gingerly wrapping his arms around her. "Or every year, for that matter."

Rick looked around the kitchen with its yellow walls and blue-painted cabinets. There were bamboo roller shades on all the windows for privacy, but he knew the evening sun would still light up this room with a warm glow. "OK, who is going to show us around?"

Scotty sat back at the terminal. "Eps, why don't you do the upstairs, and I'll do the 'bat cave.'."

"Bat cave?" Eve asked.

"You'll see."

Eps led Eve and Rick into the living room with Steve bringing up the rear. Rick asked over his shoulder, "So when did you finally leave the Evangeline?"

"Yeah, none of us need a whole lot of outside stimulation–much less exercise–but eventually being stuck in two rooms gets a bit old," Steve said. "We weren't on the lease for the house on Capitol Hill. You remember, the owners were on long-term diplomatic assignment and didn't care who lived there so long as the money was deposited in their account. Must have been twenty different people living there at one time or another. I don't envy the FBI agents trying to work their way through that tangle of turnovers."

"I imagine all the excitement ended that happy arrangement?"

"Yeah, it's something about gunfire and explosions," Steve grinned. "It can really piss off the neighbors. I think a group of trainees from the Naval Investigative Service are living there now."

"And the owners think those idiots won't cause any problems?"

Steve shrugged. "Sure, you and I know they were too dumb to get into any other intelligence service and are better at keg parties than catching crooks. I guess it sounds comforting if you're trying to be a landlord from a couple of thousand miles away."

"So how did you find this place? The Delaney Network?"

"Is there any other way?" Tom Delaney lived in an aging mansion not far away that he had subdivided into an amazing number of living spaces ranging from the top-floor suite where he lived to rooms only large enough for a single bed and a desk. The kitchen had three refrigerators–all padlocked– along with a fourth stashed under the back deck. It was rumored that he was already a millionaire from a clutch of other group houses, and he acted as the unofficial rental agent for Northwest DC

"We're technically living over in Columbia Heights. A delightful Hispanic couple gathers our mail and forwards it to a private mailbox in Tacoma Park. Then it's just three more transfers to the Ace Check Cashing storefront in Adams Morgan where an agile young man affiliated with the Black Mafia–"

"Those guys who shot up Kareem Al-Jabbar's place on 16th Street?"

"Yeah, I wasn't thrilled about that, five women and two kids murdered just for being Hanafi Muslims." Steve grimaced, "But, as I said, this kid is only affiliated insofar as his older brother is Black Mafia. Justin himself got a track scholarship to Brandeis, but his brother's influence keeps him safe while he's still at home."

Rick nodded. "How about the phones?"

Steve shrugged. "They've just finished installing computer controls on all the primary Telco switches."

"Much more secure that way, no doubt," Rick said dryly.

"No doubt. Of course, that means we own the entire phone system, but we are gentle overlords. I believe our phone number is listed to a 95-year-old woman in one of the projects in Southeast. We made sure she would override us in case she has to call for an ambulance, but everyone else she might talk to has already passed on so the line is usually clear."

At the other end of the room, Eps snapped his fingers for attention. "If the chatterboxes in the back could join the rest of the group, we are heading upstairs to the sleeping quarters." He started walking backward and beckoning like a Japanese tourist guide. "OK, we are walking now, stay together, and mind the steps. We are walking now."

The stairs went straight up from a small foyer in front of the main door, splitting the first floor between a dining room and the living room. There was no dining table in the dining room; instead, three long tables covered with electrical parts, soldering irons, and technical manuals were shoved up against the walls. The living room held a couple of old sofas, two armchairs, and a television.

From the condition of the furniture, Rick assumed it had been acquired in the usual way: driving around the neighborhood on the day trash was picked up in search of treasures that others had abandoned.

Upstairs, there were four bedrooms opening off a square hallway and a large bathroom. Eps led them to the left and turned with a flourish. "We saved you the best room. Please note the spacious closets and the rooftop deck with solid walls, perfect for getting that 'all-over' tan."

Eve sniffed. "I suppose that's your room over there with the window that looks out on the deck?"

"Well, yes, but, as you know, I am a perfect gentleman." Eps put his hand over his heart as if wounded.

"Yeah, who owns every item of high-end camera equipment in the B&H catalog."

Eps looked indignant. "Never. I only buy from the

guys with the long sideburns at 42nd Street Photo."

It was, in fact, a nice room with a small bathroom, a double bed, two closets, a battered desk, and windows on two sides, indicating there would be enough moving air to survive the sweltering Washington summer. The deck was built over the entrance to the double garage and screened by evergreens from the street.

An extremely fat orange cat yawned from a nest in the bedcovers. Eps reached over to pick it up. "This is Max, our watch cat."

Rick asked, "Watch cat?"

"Damn right." Eps tickled the cat's stomach and whipped his hand away before it was mauled. "We've conditioned him with food. Anyone but one of us comes in at night, and he goes off like a fire alarm."

"I thought you couldn't train cats."

Eps snorted. "Of course you can. People just don't try because of all the mythology about dogs. We started with toilet training–on a real toilet, natch– and just kept going." He put the cat back on the bed and pulled a small metal object from his pocket. "Watch this."

He clicked the little gadget and the cat looked up and fastened his gaze on the small man. "OK, Max. Orders."

He double clicked, and the cat stood up. Eps said in a flat voice, "Flip."

The cat gravely took a step forward and did a complete back flip. He was rewarded by a triple click and lay down again. Eps gestured with the metal object. "This is a 'cricket.' Actually, it's the same thing American paratroops used on D-Day to identify each other. The clicks are associated with food in his mind. We haven't actually given him treats for tricks in weeks, but he hasn't figured that out yet."

Eve regarded the cat with suspicion. "Does he answer to everyone or just you?"

"Well, just me at the moment." Eps looked guilty. "You might find it a bit difficult to persuade him that this isn't his room. He's had it to himself for a long time. So, if you want to be alone, just–" Eps reached over to a pile of sheets and towels on a chair, picked a bath towel, and threw it over the cat. Bundling him up, Eps took the cat outside to the porch, and released him, jumping back inside and slamming the screen door inches ahead of a vicious claw.

"Yeah, he looks adorable. Is he safe outside?"

"He's safe," Eps answered. "I'm not so sure about any other animals in the neighborhood."

The cat gave them a long look, then stalked over to the front side, jumped on the wall, and used a tree like a spiral staircase to reach the ground.

CHAPTER 17

May 20, 1973, Ingomar Street NW, Washington, DC

The rest of the tour was a perfunctory "Bedroom. Bedroom. Bedroom, Bathroom, Linen Closet." One of the things Rick had learned about his roommates was that they wasted remarkably little time on anything that didn't interest them.

They trooped back downstairs. Steve was sitting in a wooden rocking chair on the front porch smoking a pipe and reading a book. As they went into the kitchen, Rick noticed him stand as a woman and a young girl came up the walk.

Eps never cooked so his description of the kitchen was only a succinct, "Kitchen," and then he passed them off to Scotty. "And now as promised, the mysteries of the 'bat cave'."

Scotty shut down the terminal, yanked the receiver from the cups, and hung it up on the wall receiver. "OK, down we go."

Next to the back door was a walk-in pantry and, to the left, a slightly battered brown-painted door that Scotty indicated, saying, "Rick, why don't you open the door to the basement."

Knowing it would be impossible, Rick dutifully twisted the knob and tried various combinations of pushing and pulling. The door remained closed.

Stepping back, he said, "Wow, I'm stunned, the door won't open. Who'da thunk?"

Scotty pointed to the molding above the door. "Reach up there. Feel that chain?"

Rick found a small chain like one from an overhead light but with only three of the little metal balls and gave it a pull. He heard a solid *tchunk* on the other side, and the door swung open. He could see that its other side was braced with layers of plywood.

Scotty crouched down to floor level, reached just inside the right side of the door, and flicked a switch. Bright lights blazed in the basement. Still in a crouch, he pointed up. "There is another switch mounted up there where you'd expect to find one."

He waggled a finger at Rick and Eve. "Do not flip that switch."

Eve frowned. "Why not?"

"Take my word for it. Just think of our redheaded friend's penchant for explosives and do not flip that switch."

Scotty stood up and pounded on the plywood

that backed the door. "This is cross-grained. It would take someone with an axe a long time to get through it, and that's not counting the chicken wire we laid underneath."

Eve shuddered. "I'm not sure I like the way you guys tend to worry about people with axes."

Scotty started down the steps. "Well, we're actually thinking about the police or your friends in the CIA but, yeah, we do tend to have friends who like to play with axes. All part of the fun of belonging to the Society for Creative Anachronism."

Rick followed Scotty down. "I thought all that hacking and slashing was an outdoor sport."

"Well, for the newbies, sure." Scotty reached the bottom step. "It's another matter when you're playing at the Master level. We've had the Black Knight of Gaithersburg come through here twice during Insurrections."

He pointed back up at the door, which was swinging closed behind Eve. "Well, 'through the house' technically, but never through that door. Broke his axe haft the last time, which made him a prime target for Eps and his over/under crossbow."

Eve just shook her head.

The room at the base of the stairs was small or at least seemed so with the computer equipment lining the walls. Lights blinked, enormous reels of tape spun back and forth, and some sort of device chattered and spat punch cards in a corner.

Rick noticed it was perceptibly cooler.

"You put in central air?" he asked hopefully.

"Nah, just a couple of wall units out back with a

redundant power supply and air ducts to this room," the big man said. "We can all stand a little heat and humidity, but Gidget here is a PDP-6 mainframe, and she needs her environment cool and dry at all times."

Rick whistled. "Extremely cool. Where did you get it and what are you going to do with it?"

"Well, it was over at the Pentagon and they wanted the PDP-8 and so they declared the PDP-6 outdated. You know how they like new toys, so we literally became trash collectors." Scotty rubbed a speck of dust off one of the monitors. "Showed up in a truck wearing overalls, and they handed it to us on the back loading dock. We had to take a wall down to get it in, which was a bit tricky since that particular wall was holding up the rest of the house, but she's all ours now."

"And I repeat, what are you going to do with it?"

"Do with it?" Scotty looked genuinely puzzled. "I don't know that we'll do anything with Gidget. It's enough to have her here and let her teach us new stuff." He waved his hand by his head as if brushing away a bothersome fly. "I'm sure we'll find something useful for her to do at some point."

Scotty led them to another heavily reinforced door. After another lesson on secret latches and booby traps, they entered the garage. "Now, you'll be able to park the van and a bike or two in here but only on the right side."

He walked over to a tarpaulin-covered shape against the left wall. When he hauled on a rope that ran over a complex series of pulleys, the heavy canvas rose to the ceiling.

Underneath was a sleek wooden shape made of black-painted wood that looked like some sort of boat. After a minute or so walking around, Rick looked through a Plexiglas panel in the front and exclaimed, "This is a goddamn airplane!"

Scotty's smile grew to a grin. "A Bowers Fly Baby, homebuilt, open cockpit, single-seat prop plane constructed from the finest aircraft-grade spruce plywood. I bought if off a friend who had spent three years building it and one hour flying. Turned out he was afraid of heights."

Eve stroked the silky-smooth surface of the painted fuselage. "What a shame. It's beautiful."

Scotty's eyes sparkled as he released a lever and pulled a wing out from the side until it locked into place reaching almost all the way across the garage. "Yeah, it was a real downer, but I hear he's gotten into spelunking now. You know, exploring caves."

Eve laughed. "That's much safer, I'm sure."

"Probably not but he's having fun," Scotty said. "I learned to fly when I was a kid, so I just renewed my liccnse and put in enough flight hours to solo. I'm going to go out to Warrenton next weekend; they've got a glider port–well, it's just a smooth field–and they only charge five bucks for each takeoff and landing."

He reached under the wing, released a catch, and folded the wing back. "See, under here? I've got a complete custom trailer already hooked up." He turned to Rick. "All I need is someone with a car to pull me out there and then act as ground team."

"Ground team?" asked Rick.

"Well, you never really know where a plane like this will end up," Scotty admitted sheepishly. "It's not as bad as a glider, but it's still a good idea to have someone following you on the ground in case the engine quits or something."

"I'm in."

Scotty walked over to what looked like a pile of aluminum rods and nylon sheets along the far wall. "And, in return, I'll teach you how to fly one of these. A hang glider."

Eve put her hands on her hips. "Are you trying to give me ulcers or just kill my boyfriend? Because I'm telling you right now, I love you a lot, but if he dies, I'll remove your skin with a potato peeler and dump you in salt water."

Scotty looked worried for a second and then laughed, hoping it was a joke. "These are relatively safe. It's a Rogallo wing, and it's held in shape by the air itself. Of course, they're still in development, so I guess they're a little dangerous."

Eve stared at him silently.

"OK, they're quite dangerous," said Scotty. "But only if you don't follow the safety rules."

Eve headed for the door back to the stairs. "I think the only reasonable safety rule would be to never get in one, but I know I can't convince the trooper of that. You boys keep playing with your dangerous toys. I'm getting some tea."

Scotty looked at Rick. "So?"

Rick scoffed. "Of course I want to fly it. It's the coolest thing I've seen in months."

Scotty smiled. "There's only one thing more to show you."

"Let me guess. A back way out."

Scotty stopped and stared at Rick. "How did you know that?"

Rick laughed, "After you blew up that Vietnamese hitter and took off through the sewers? Give me credit for learning a few things about the guys I live with."

"Well, to my surprise, you are correct." Scotty turned and walked through the computer room to a door in the opposite wall. The door opened to reveal a small closet with shelves on three sides filled with spare computer parts, old cans of paint, metal springs, and other things that someone clearly felt might be useful for some project someday. Bending down, he tugged a small bolt fitted into the concrete floor and pulled on a handle concealed underneath a shelf.

The entire wall pivoted in the middle and revealed another basement.

"Welcome to our next door neighbors, the Nordheimers. Nice people, and they sleep soundly," Scotty said in a low voice.

Pointing to a workbench on the back wall of their neighbors' basement, he said, "That workbench is another door leading to a short tunnel and then to the Porters over on Hamilton Street. Their basement window looks the same as the day it was first installed, but the entire frame now swings out into a window well. That puts you a block away, probably outside any cordon, and we figure it should give us enough of a head start to be useful."

He pointed to the neighbor's side of the door. "See, we cemented the cinder blocks onto the doors and mounted this section of the wall on heavy-duty bearings."

Rick whistled softly. "You're pretty proud of this aren't you?"

"Well, the original idea came from the Jews in the Warsaw Ghetto. They held off the German SS for three months by connecting every building underground, so they could move without being seen." He closed the door and snicked the bolt back in place. "No one is shooting at us–but it never hurts to be prepared. Speaking of which..."

Scotty carefully closed the wall and reset the bolt that kept it from accidentally swinging open. Then he bent and, pushing aside a box marked "Pyrotronics, Inc. Anaheim California," pulled out a paper bag. The bag held what looked like a regular sleeveless undershirt but seemed to Rick to be strangely stiff. Scotty looked at the tag and handed it to Rick.

"It's an extra-large so it should fit."

Rick held it up. He could see heavy, stiff fabric patches in front and back. "What the hell is this?" he asked. "I don't usually wear undershirts, anyway."

"Well, you might want to wear this one from time to time." Scotty pointed at the patch in the front. "That's a new material DuPont has just invented called Kevlar. It's not on the market yet–still being tested–but it's supposed to stop bullets."

Rick swung the shirt and examined it more

closely. "This stuff stops bullets? Hell, the 'chicken suits' in Nam were a hell of a lot bigger, and they wouldn't stop shit. Everyone just threw them away."

"Yeah, well, that's because they were just metal plates–essentially the same thing knights wore in the Middle Ages. This is completely different. You can thank Dr. George Emory Goodfellow for that."

"Who?"

"The doctor who treated the wounded after the Gunfight at the OK Corral. He was one of the foremost experts in bullet wounds at the time."

"Probably had a lot of practice," interrupted Rick.

"Undoubtedly," Scotty agreed. "The point is, in several cases, he saw that multiple layers of silk were quite effective in stopping bullets. Eventually, all the leading mobsters of the 30's wore the silk vests he invented."

The big engineer turned and began searching on a higher shelf. "That worked until law enforcement developed the .357 Magnum cartridge. A classic case of the seesaw between offensive and defensive technology. Really, it's a lot like the English longbow at Agincourt–"

Rick could tell they were heading for a lengthy tangent. "Whoa. Back to this super t-shirt or whatever it is."

Scotty gave up on whatever he was looking for and motioned Rick back into the larger room. "It's not a t-shirt. It's a ballistic vest. Like Goodfellow's vests, it's made of dozens of crisscrossed layers of Kevlar, which is similar to silk but far stronger strand for strand. A single layer won't stop a bullet, but when they're combined–"

He suddenly brightened as a thought struck him, and he reached over the top of the computer cabinet. "Here it is."

He turned with a small revolver in his hand and said, "Put it on, we'll give it a test."

Rick thrust the shirt behind his back. "The hell we will."

"Really? OK." Scotty looked disappointed but put the revolver back where he had found it. "None of us are willing to be the test subject, but I thought that your physical strength would make you better able to absorb the shock."

"Forget it," said Rick firmly. He held out the shirt and examined it again. "What's the deal? It only covers my chest. What if I get shot somewhere else?"

"It's all about probabilities," said Scotty. "That's the area where it's the most likely to save your life. If a bullet hits you in the head, you're dead; if you are struck in the arms or legs, you'll probably survive the trauma. Protecting the chest area is calculated to give you a survival rate approximately 60 to 75 percent greater than without it."

Rick shook his head ruefully. "Why is this somehow not all that comforting? I think I'll just continue trying to avoid people with guns."

"You can, but your track record on that is far from perfect. I'd suggest having it around in case you change your mind. I'd like to see if it works." Scotty checked his watch and headed for the stairs. "Let's go up. I think our new housemate should be here."

CHAPTER 18

May 20, 1973, Ingomar Street NW, Washington, DC

Everyone was in the living room when Scotty and Rick came back upstairs. Eve was on the sofa, holding hands and talking animatedly with a woman Rick had never met. She was average height, skinny, with mouscy brown hair and a face that could almost have been called pinched. Her brown eyes didn't stay on Eve but darted around the room as if someone might attack her at any time.

It took a moment for Rick to realize that there was a little girl next to her, sitting so close that she almost disappeared behind the woman. Rick supposed that they were mother and daughter. There was a resemblance in the hair and angular features but, more than that, they had the same darting eyes always looking for trouble. He wasn't very experienced with children, but he guessed she was seven, maybe eight, years old.

When Eve paused long enough to notice he'd come in, she said, "This is Kristee, my college roommate. She's from Wolf Point which makes Lame Deer look like a big city."

Eve reached around the woman to poke the little girl in the ribs. "And this little hellion is Sage." The girl squirmed even further behind her mother to escape Eve's finger. Rick noticed that, even when she giggled dutifully, she never stopped her constant scrutiny of everyone in the room.

"Hi guys. I'm Rick," waving a greeting as he sat on the floor with his back against the sofa where Eve was sitting. Eve put one hand on his shoulder, still holding the woman's hands with the other.

"Rick was out at the reservation with me," said Eve. "And then we did a little detour into Wounded Knee on the way home."

Eps was sitting in one of the old recliners. "Wounded Knee? Cool."

"What were you doing there?" asked Scotty from the other chair. Steve was lying on his back on the other sofa. His eyes were closed, but Rick didn't think he was asleep.

Rick just jerked his head back to indicate it was Eve's idea. "Everything had to be carried in on foot at night, so we volunteered to make a food delivery," Eve said. "It was…an interesting experience."

"I'll bet," Steve said without opening his eyes.

"Kristee and I met at the University of Montana.

We were both in Kyi-oh. She was a fifth-year senior but she kept an eye on me in my freshman year," Eve said, squeezing the other woman's hands a little tighter. "Ho-wah, I was so lonely that year. You saved my life."

Eve stopped for a second and cleared her throat. "She left me a message at the Iron Crows, and I called her before we left for Lame Deer. She said that...maybe she should tell her own story. At any rate, she's a computer tech, so I told her to get in touch with Steve, figuring he could find some work for her."

"Which I did. She starts at Riggs with Eps tomorrow," Steve said. "The guys agreed we could put them up here for a while."

"Long as you want," Eps broke in. Scotty smiled and nodded in agreement.

"Eve said you needed help and that's good enough for us. On the other hand, if we knew what the problem was, we might be able to work on a solution."

The room was silent. After a moment, Eve whispered, "Come on, honey."

Kristee's voice was low with a smoker's rasp. "I think we'd better get this girl to bed first," She said as she wrestled the little girl out from behind her back.

"Come on, tough stuff. Stop your hiding back there and get upstairs. Put your pajamas on, brush your teeth, and then I'll be up to tuck you in."

It took a while, but Sage finally dragged herself up the stairs, one loud step at a time.

Rick was surprised that Eps and Scotty, who were usually blissfully unaware of social tension, filled what could have been an awkward silence with a long and involved story about a recent Spacewar tournament they'd hosted on the Riggs Bank mainframes. In the end, it turned out that MIT had won, but later Scotty proved that they had tweaked his game program and made gravity a variable instead of a constant. Steve joined in and the three discussed how they planned to introduce reverse gravity in the next game.

The conversation was animated but stopped when Kristee returned from her post at the bottom of the stairs, satisfied that her daughter was, if not in bed, at least out of sight. Eve had gone to make coffee but quickly returned and ordered Eps to come with her and do whatever one did with what she called their "unholy" collection of beakers and distillation coils to make coffee.

She emerged with a cup for Kristee and handed another to Rick. "I think it's coffee," she said. "It could be almost anything."

"Hey, who needs kitchen equipment that only does one thing?" Eps came out with his own cup. "That's a great setup. Just this afternoon, I made a batch of rocket fuel with it."

Rick who was just about to take his first sip stopped, thought for a second, and then drank. It tasted like coffee.

Kristee carefully, gingerly, put her cup down on the battered table beside the sofa. Eve settled in beside her. "OK, no more stalling. What's the problem?"

"Well, you remember Gary."

"Unfortunately," Eve replied.

"Yeah, you never did like him." Kristee sighed. "But he was my boyfriend since forever, almost before I can remember. Then, when I got pregnant, he did the 'right thing' and we got married. My God, I was fifteen! What were our parents thinking?"

Eve laughed. "It was a different world back then."

"That's for sure. One day, I'm going to sleep with 17 stuffed animals and the next, I'm standing in my pajamas in the bathroom at Gary's parents' place and so scared I'm throwing up. Seven months later, there was Sage."

She smiled and nodded her head toward the stairs. "It's funny. She ruined all my plans, and I'd guess you could say she pretty well screwed up my life; at the same time, she's the best thing I've ever done, and I wouldn't give her up for a million dollars. How can something be so good and so bad at the same time?"

Eps said, "It's like Madame Curie and radium. I mean, her research into radium enabled her to become the first woman to win a Nobel Prize, but it also ruined her health and eventually killed her."

Steve and Scotty smiled in agreement, but Eve glared at them. "It's not even remotely like Madame Curie and radium." She turned back to Kristee who was smothering a laugh. "Go ahead, sweetie."

"You know, on a bad day, I think that having a child is a little like radium poisoning but…well, back to the story. So there I am, a high school junior with a baby. The high school decided I could continue, but I couldn't come to class. They got this weird little phone device that Sophie McAllen would carry from class to class and plug in. I could hear everything, and if I pushed the button on top, it lit up a light and that was me raising my hand."

The thin woman made a face. "It was so lame. I mean, I wasn't contagious. No one was going to catch a baby from me!"

Everyone laughed. "Anyway, that's how I got through junior and senior years. It wasn't so bad; we'd listen to a lot of classes while Gary and I were just sitting around the kitchen table smoking cigarettes and feeding Sage. Hell, she probably learned more than I did."

"Anyway, Gary dropped out of school and worked nights stocking at the Valu-Mart. I thought he was an idiot–"

Eve nodded vigorously.

Kristee waved a dismissive hand at her. "I know, I know. So somehow, I managed to graduate by remote control and went to Missoula."

"I can remember passing Sage around at the Kyi-oh meetings like a talking stick," Eve said and then seeing the blank looks on the men's faces explained. "'Kyi-oh' is an Indian student organization. Mostly just social–keeps us from dying of homesickness–and at the meetings, a 'talking stick' is passed around; if you're holding it, it's your turn to talk and no one can interrupt."

Steve said, "Do you think we could get one? We–"

"–could really use–," Scotty interrupted,

"–one in this house," Eps finished.

Scotty and Steve nodded in solemn unison.

Eve laughed and then turned serious, "OK, that's all ancient history. Where's Gary, and why do you and Sage look like hunted rabbits?"

Kristee said slowly, "That's a pretty apt description. I feel like I'm always trying to make sure I've got a good deep hole to hide in."

Steve raised his hand and opened his palm to indicate the house. "This is as good a hole as any."

"Better than most," Scotty added.

Thinking of the basement, Rick agreed.

Kristee looked at the guys closely as if she couldn't quite believe they weren't kidding.

"Anyway," she said to Eve, "if you remember, you never saw much of Gary. He came with me, of course, and got a job at the checkout counter at Olsson's. Then he kind of disappeared."

"Yeah, I didn't really miss him." Eve said. "I always thought you could do better."

"Well, if you look around Wolf Point, you won't see a whole lot of prime husband material," said Kristee with a bitter smile. "I figured if he was ambulatory at least one night every weekend, I was ahead of the game."

"OK. OK. Point taken. What happened to him?"

"Well, the two of us had joined another group besides Kyi-oh, a political discussion group that used to meet in the Humanities Building in the evenings. I never paid all that much attention; it was just a way to get out of that stinking room over the

Chinese restaurant and sit with Sage for a while."

Kristee shook her head slowly, "But Gary...he got real serious. It was as if he was hypnotized or something. Afterward, he would just talk and talk and talk about politics and religion and, you know..." she made air quotes..."'The Revolution.' So finally, he was given some sort of scholarship or grant or something and came to Washington for what they called..." more air quotes "...advanced training'."

Rick had been watching Scotty as his face became more and more concerned. Scotty asked, "Advanced training? That's what they called it? What's the name of the group?"

Kristee looked at him. "It's a weird religious-political mishmash. Originally, it was a bunch of radical left-wingers, and then it got religion and became the Children's Crusade formed by this guy who calls himself Stephen Cloyes and based near here, out in Warrenton. Why?"

Scotty's face relaxed, and he exhaled a long breath. "I've heard the same phrase, but it was another group. One I used to belong to until I ran out of money for all that 'advanced training,' and they kicked me out."

"And you are lucky they did," Steve said. "We almost had to resort to drastic measures."

"Yeah," Eps chimed in, "We were all set up for electroshock therapy."

Scotty shot them a look. "I wasn't aware of these plans."

"You would never have known anything about

it," Eps said cheerfully. "A couple of thousand volts while you slept and–Shazaam! A deluxe brain wash-and-wax with a mental tune-up thrown in while you wait. We had the contact electrodes built into your pillow."

Scotty looked suspicious. "Are they still there?"

"Um, Possibly. Why?"

"Probably nothing. Some strange dreams."

"I wonder if there is some residual Gaussian pickup from the house wiring." Eps looked excited. "We could raise the voltage and–"

"Boys, discuss your mad scientist experiments later," Eve interrupted. "Kristee still has the figurative talking stick. Go ahead, sweetie."

Kristee jumped off the couch and walked quickly to the stairs. "Sage! I can hear you rutching around up there like a calf after it's been roped. Get your pjs on and brush your teeth, now!"

There was a muffled complaint from the top of the stairs. Kristee pointed one finger and said, "Move, little girl," in what could only be described as a "mom voice." Loud footsteps stomped off in the direction of their bedroom. Kristee waited a few seconds and came back to the sofa.

She sat with her feet up, wrapping her arms around her knees and pulling her face out of sight. Rick thought that she was compressing herself into as tight a ball as possible like someone who expected to be hit. Eve put a hand on her shoulder and massaged gently. Kristee raised her head and took a deep and shaky breath before speaking.

"I finally graduated and...well, I was married, and

married people live together, right?" Eve nodded. "So you helped me pack up Sage and everything we owned–which wasn't much–in Dad's old pickup, and I drove out here.

Dad wasn't big on the idea but there wasn't anything for me in Wolf Point. Dad ran a hunting lodge, and I'd been working there all my life, but business is bad and..."

She hid her face again behind her knees. Her voice was soft and muted. "Since Mom died, Dad hasn't been interested in running the lodge, or seeing his granddaughter or, much of anything, really."

No one spoke and, after a long moment, Kristee said, "Mom got to see Sage, but the cancer took her like a month later."

Eve put both arms around her friend and squeezed. Rick looked at his housemates. Their frozen faces demonstrated what he already knew. They were even worse at handling emotion than he was.

After some sniffling and a deep breath, Kristee said, "So we came out here. The Crusade has a big place. I think it used to be owned by millionaires or something. It's got one big house and about a dozen smaller places that used to be for cars or servants or something. Now it's all just bunkrooms for the... Well, the people who truly are way deep into this thing call themselves 'Crusaders'." She shook her head. "I never bought the whole thing. The leaders– the Inner Circle–are just creepy."

This caught Rick's attention. "What did you call

them?"

"Crusaders?"

"No, the people in charge."

"The Inner Circle." Kristee looked puzzled. "Why?"

Eve and Rick exchanged a look, and Rick said, "No real reason. I've just heard something like that before."

Eve cut him off with an eyebrow and then pulled Kristee a little tighter. "Never mind, Kris, get on with the rest of your story."

Kristee leaned her head on Eve's shoulder. "Well, the whole setup was fucked-up from the beginning. Sage and I were put up in a big bunkhouse building way out in the back–in the woods, really–with the other mothers and children. Gary wasn't allowed to stay with us. He was only allowed to visit once a week."

She shook her head. "What was really strange was that it didn't seem to bother him at all. I mean, we might have stayed in Montana for all we saw of him, but he said it was fine. He had to concentrate all his energy on praying for strength and preparing to fight to bring about God's will. Or whatever.

"I mean they kept changing what they believed in. They made me go to special 'women's classes.' What a load of crap. It was like you'd taken Jesus, Saint Augustine, and Che Guevara and mashed them up with bits and pieces of Sun Dance and Blessing Way rituals and cooked them in a pot for a couple of weeks. And when you'd finally learn something like how awful capitalism was and that capitalists were The Real Enemy, they'd go and yell at you because 'everyone knew' that capitalists were their best buddies and radicals and anarchists were The Real Enemy."

She glanced over at Eve. "Most of the guys obviously didn't have a clue what it really meant. However, when Stephen preached, wow, it all made sense and you just felt like you would be...I don't know. Wrong? Evil? If you didn't dedicate your life to making it all happen."

Scotty nodded and, when Kristee looked at him quizzically, said, "Yeah, that's what I thought about 'Cosmic Wisdom' where I took all those lessons. When I listening to them, it all seemed to make sense, and it felt important. But afterwards," he shook his head, "it just didn't cohere into a logical whole."

Eps said, "Dude, that's what we kept trying to tell you."

Scotty looked at the smaller man skeptically. "You think that there are billions of tons of 'dark matter' out between the stars. That's not exactly a sign of an excess of logical consistency."

"Wait a minute! If you take Einstein's equations out to their logical endpoint and then factor in the latest computer runs from the telescopes in Hawaii–"

Steve held up his hand. "Guys. Remember the rule. No quantum mechanics around civilians–it just scares people. We'll take dark matter up at lunch on Wednesday like we always do." He broke off and said quietly, "I see a child's size-4 foot at the top of the stairs."

Kristee didn't even get up this time. "Sage! Bed. Now!"

Loud stomping noises came down the stairs. In a softer voice, Kristee called, "I'll be up in a couple of minutes to tuck you in, kiddo."

CHAPTER 19

May 20, 1973, Ingomar Street NW, Washington, DC

Rick's muscles were stiff from too many days in a microbus, so he slid down until he was lying full-length on the floor. Eve stretched out a bare foot and rubbed his shoulder. Most of her attention was on the thin woman still tucked into a defensive knot on the other end of the sofa.

"OK, now we know how you got to DC but why did you leave the happy little family out in Warrenton?"

"It was bad enough to be stuck in the back and expected to cook and clean in the Big House." Kristee's face tightened and her eyes appeared to darken with anger. "The women would have to do household chores all morning. Then we were supposed to stick around our bunkhouse in the afternoons and evenings when the guys would take classes and do some sort of weird martial arts training. I think they said it came from Brazil, but it just looked like trying to dance and fight at the same time to me.

"In the beginning, it wasn't so bad. Sage had other kids her age to play with, and I could hang out with the wives and girlfriends, so I wasn't all that lonely even without Gary."

Kristee paused so long that Eve prompted her with a low "but?"

"Yeah, there's always a 'but,' isn't there?" Kristee's face twisted into a quick smile and then returned to its previous introspective impassivity. "When Sage got to be old enough to go to school, first grade, Gary told me that it wasn't allowed."

Rick spoke from the floor. "'Wasn't allowed'? Since when is first grade not allowed?"

"Beats me." Kristee shook her head. "I should have known something was wrong. All the kids went to kindergarten, but the following year, the girls were just left sitting at home. Sage is a real tomboy and usually hung out with the boys. She just wouldn't let it go. Kept bugging me every morning when the bus left."

She took a deep breath. "And she was already almost a year behind because of all the moving around, so I talked to Gary and said we were going to send her to school. That's when we had our first real fight. Just screaming at each other, banging doors, throwing dishes, the whole thing."

Kristee laughed without humor. "I guess having our first fight after seven years wasn't that bad, but we hadn't seen each other for almost four of them."

Her voice sobered as she spread her hands out and shrugged. "I packed, put Sage in the truck, and left. I wasn't really leaving him. I just wanted to get her into school, so we rented a room over a biker bar in Leesburg. In the end, Gary calmed down and even helped us settle in. He still lived at the mansion, but he'd come by and play with Sage on the weekends sometimes.

"I put Sage into first grade and worked the day shift in the bar in exchange for rent. The tips were good, so things were OK. I figured Gary would come to his senses at some point and we'd get back together. Hell, I liked the guy. I still do, for that matter."

She shook her head as if she couldn't believe what she was about to say. "But then they came and got us."

Eve broke in, "'Got you?' What do you mean, 'Got you'?"

"One evening, Sage and I were watching TV, and Gary knocked on the door and said he'd come to hang out, but when I opened the door, Gary wasn't standing there. It was these guys, kind of like Stephen's foremen or lieutenants or something. They just walked in, didn't say a word to me. They grabbed Sage, packed up all our stuff, and drove us back to Stephen's."

Steve asked, "Didn't you say something?"

"Hell yes, I was screaming bloody murder, but

they didn't pay any attention." She rubbed her cheek. "And that bastard Flick backhanded me three times, real fast and told me that he'd smack Sage next if I said another word. Then we were down the stairs, through the bar, and into the truck."

Rick sat up slowly. "What did you say his name was?"

"God, he was such a horse's ass. He didn't like his real name or whatever, so he made everyone call him Flick like he was a tough guy." She pursed her lips and then said, "And since he was the best fighter they had, no one argued. Why?"

Rick looked at Eve who gave an almost imperceptible shake of her head. "Oh, it's a strange name, that's all." He swiveled on the floor and leaned back against the sofa again. "So what happened?"

Kristee sighed. "Well, it was even worse than before. Sage and I had to stay in our room anytime we weren't doing chores, and one or another of Stephen's tough guys was always keeping an eye on us. I think Gary didn't like it, but they were just as angry with him for letting us leave, so he was on lockdown, too. Then it got weird."

"You mean it wasn't weird already?" Eps asked. "What would be your definition of 'weird'?"

"OK, it got weirder." Again, Kristee responded with a hint of humor in her voice, which disappeared fast. "I started hearing stories from the other girls. Stuff about how girls were taken to the Big House for 'special training' when they turned nine, and, well . . ."

She paused and looked off into nowhere, seeing something that wasn't in the room.

A muffled thump came from the top of the stairs.

Eve got up and ran up the stairs, returning with a struggling, pajama-clad Sage over her shoulder. "I think the grown-ups–if you can call us that in this house–have talked quite enough tonight."

She knelt down in front of Rick. "Could you help me? I think these feet need tickling."

Over screams of protest that dissolved into giggles, Rick obliged. Glancing over at Kristee, he was glad to see that she had relaxed her defensive tucked-in position. She was even smiling a very small smile.

Eps stood and went to the battered stereo on the bookcase by the stairs. "Well, I guess it's time for this place to quiet down but, first, we have something special prepared."

He selected an album, pulled the record out of the cover without showing the front, and placed it on the turntable.

He called over his shoulder, "Everyone up. We need to clear some space."

Rick stood. "Wait a minute. You guys have taken up dancing?"

Scotty just nodded solemnly, but Steve took a notebook filled with graph paper from where it was leaning against his chair. "Well, just the one song, really. We saw it twice, and between us, we managed to get it all written down."

He handed the notebook to Rick. It was covered with strange symbols, squares, triangles, and things that looked like stick figures. It was meticulous and dense with intricate lines and dots.

Rick studied the notebook. "What is this?"

"Labanotation. It's a way of recording dance." Steve came around, looked over his shoulder, and pointed at the first figures. "See, this tells you where the hands are, here are the feet, and then you can see how the weight moves in a curve to the left, resting on the ball of the foot as the hands clap–"

"Enough tech talk," Eps said as he dropped the needle and stepped over to Scotty. "Come on. We have five seconds, four, three . . ."

Steve joined the line and, as the drumbeat started, all three began to sway in unison, their arms coming up from their hips as they swiveled from side to side.

"L.A. proved too much for the man."

"Too much for the man." The three men responded together, hands out, fingers wagging, dead-on imitations of the Pips.

Eve clapped her hands, her eyes sparkling. This side of his normally staid friends astonished Rick, and he noticed that Sage had cuddled up against her mother with a big smile on her face.

Spinning, swaying, clapping–the three had every step, every gesture, and every word down perfectly, even the "pull the cord" motion on the "whoo hoo."

When they finished to a round of applause, whistling, and foot stomping, they motioned everyone to join them as the turntable recycled to the beginning of the song and started again.

Dancing wasn't one of Rick's strong points, but Eve had the whole sequence down the first time. By the third time, Kristee joined one end of the line and Sage, concentrating furiously, was in the center with Steve and Scotty coaching on each side, matching them move for move, laughing, and scampering to catch up whenever she missed a step.

CHAPTER 20

May 21, 1973, Ingomar Street NW, Washington, DC

The gunshot broke the silence with the flat crack of a bullet that's heading straight toward you.

I'm on the ground before I even realize I've moved.

"Incoming! Sarge, where do we dig in?"

No answer. I look to my right where Sgt. Rickard is standing.

He's looking down at his stomach.

Crap! Where did that fucking hole come from? His guts are falling out.

Sarge begins screaming, a terrible high sound.

Shit, he's not even taking a breath.

There's another round.

Ten.

Twenty.

Fuck! Where are they coming from?

More bullets are smacking into the mud around me with vicious snaps.

Where is it coming from? It has to be back there. Way up in the trees.

Fuck. We just cleared that area!

In front of me, Spandau suddenly loses all his bones and flops straight down.

Wait, he's sitting.

No, he's down.

Shit. That guy from C Company.

I can't breathe. My fingernail breaks as I scrabble in the dirt.

I need a hole.

I look around. Man after man after man just…falls.

I'm trying to scream.

A warning.

A call for help.

Nothing is coming out. My throat is locked.

All around me, the men keep falling.

Jones spins, Brant…Lardner…Bout…disappear in the grass.

More fall.

There.

There.

My chest is burning.

I can feel the scream coming up from my chest.

"Whuff!"

A blow in the stomach chuffs out Rick's air and doubles him up. He reacts by whipping his hands forward and grabbing, looking for a strap or a belt that he can use on his attacker.

Needles slash into his arm.

Rick opens his eyes. Max, the house "watch cat," was sitting on his crotch with a paw up and his claws out. A deep warning growl came from his chest.

"Good morning, trooper."

Rick put his hand over the bleeding scratches on his arm and continued to focus on the cat. "This animal is a goddamn menace."

Eve walked over, picked up the heavy orange cat, and began to scratch under his chin. "So are you. Anyway, you hit him first."

"He attacked me." Rick was beginning to come down from the terror and adrenaline of the dream. "I was just sleeping peacefully."

"No. You were screaming, and it was heading up to that wonderful fire-siren sound I've come to know and love." She put the cat out on the porch where it glowered at Rick through the screen door. After a long moment–Rick was sure the cat was vowing revenge–Max stalked off to his tree and disappeared. "So I used Max to quiet you down."

Rick examined the four deep gouges in his arm. He didn't think they'd be fatal. "Couldn't you have just woken me yourself?"

Eve didn't turn from the mirror where she was examining the woman's version of a man's suit she was wearing. "No, I've found it's risky if I'm not already in bed with you. Then I can hold on to your chest until you realize we're not in a rice paddy. Twice last week, you took a swing at me when I woke you up to switch drivers. There's not a lot of space in a VW Bus to dodge, you know."

"Damn. I didn't know that." Rick looked at her with real pain on his face. "I'm sorry."

"No reason to apologize, trooper. You're still fighting the war in there, and I've just learned to take a few safety precautions." She turned to look at him, and he could see her smile. "Like siccing a cat on you. I figured Max could handle himself."

She tossed him a washcloth, and Rick used it to wipe the blood off his arm. "Sure, when I'm asleep AND on another continent. I'm calling that cat out, best two out of three. Let's see how tough he is when I'm awake."

He sat on the side of the bed and wound a clean gym sock around his arm to stop the bleeding. "I need to pick up some weights, don't I?"

"And a motorcycle. I don't think you can get any real relief in a VW Camper."

"It lacks a certain something. Maybe because it can't go over 55 miles an hour and the only real danger is when a strong wind tries to turn it over or blow it off a bridge. But I think I can solve the motorcycle situation today."

Eve finished her critical self-examination, pulled up the grey pinstriped skirt, and began to tug at her panty hose. "I HATE these damn things. Yes, you do need your weights. You couldn't sleep for hours. I could tell by your breathing."

"Well, so much for being considerate and letting you sleep." He headed for the bathroom. "You ready for the first day at the law firm?"

"I'm not putting these glorified socks on for

nothing. Damn it!" Rick looked back to see her bend over, inspect a hole, and begin to peel off the panty hose. "That's three pairs this morning," she complained as she hurled the most recent pair into the trash. "And that's my last pair. You're going to have to stop somewhere so I can pick some up on our way downtown." She went back to staring at her clothes in the mirror and making minute adjustments.

"Why can't you break with tradition and just wear the clothes you're comfortable in?" Rick asked as he was loading up his toothbrush.

"Because, as an Indian and, even worse, a woman, I've already got two strikes against me. I'm not going to let the other paralegals get any advantage. These aren't clothes, they're armor, and the slightest chink will give them a chance to put a knife in me."

Through a mouthful of toothpaste, Rick said, "Man, you women fight rough."

She turned and began to examine her back and sides. "You have no idea. I had to fight my way into the measly five percent of my law school class that they 'set aside' for women. I'm going to have to go into government because no reputable law firm will allow a woman to take the lead on a case–" She turned to the other side. "And now I'm going to be the punching bag for every legal secretary at Marsden Angle."

Rick spat and rinsed his mouth from the faucet. "Why?"

"Because I'm a 'paralegal,' and no one knows

what that is." Eve walked to the bed and began examining two pairs of dress shoes. "I'm not a secretary, and I'm not an associate, and I'll be doing some of the work of both. Hell, they only invented 'paralegals' last year. I have no idea what I'll be doing, but I can guarantee that every woman who's spent years fetching coffee and getting hit on by her boss is going to hate me."

Rick leaned against the bathroom door. "Speaking of 'getting hit,' what is going to happen with Sage and Kristee?"

Eve picked up one pair of high heels with a clunky, thick sole. "Well, you heard last night that the guys have found a job for Kristee. She's going to do maintenance on the mainframes with Eps over at Riggs. They've already gotten her security clearance and an ID badge."

"What about Sage?"

Eve threw the clunky shoes on the bed and picked up a black, conservative pair. "You know, the guys have genuinely taken to her. By the time I got down for breakfast, Eps had already showed her all the 'cool' features of the house and Scotty was teaching her chess using Lucky Charms for pieces."

She turned around and held out both pairs of shoes. "You pick."

Rick turned and headed for the shower. "I may be dumb enough to go three rounds with a professional 'watch cat' but I'm not dumb enough to do that. Why don't you just go all the way and ask me if that dress makes you look fat?"

"Does it?" Eve spun back to the mirror and Rick escaped into the shower.

CHAPTER 21

May 21, 1973, Washington, DC

"I'll see you tonight," Eve said as she slid down from the high VW Camper seat.

"Should I pick you up?" Rick asked.

"The traffic down here in rush hour is horrible. It's not worth it. I'll just take an L bus." Eve turned and considered the brick walls and glass doors of the squared-off building on 16th Street. "Plus, I don't know when I'll be getting out. The saying is that 'the lights never go out at Marsden Angle' because someone is always working. Usually, some desperate associate."

She turned and gave Rick a smile, "And now, one desperate paralegal." She slammed the bus door shut and turned to walk into the building. Rick thought that no one else would notice the slight touches as she made sure her clothes were exactly right or the way she re-gripped her leather briefcase just a bit tighter as she opened the door.

The VW chugged away from the curb and slowly picked up speed, just making second gear before he hauled the flat steering wheel around to turn onto H Street. Across Lafayette Park, about a hundred demonstrators were outside the White House. A quick glance told Rick that the protesters were vets, but their signs were about missing benefits, not stopping the war. They looked bedraggled but determined.

Rick wondered how his former housemate, Corey Gravelin, was doing. He'd been the one chosen to hold the film with the evidence of presidential crimes, the film that had cost Rick two friends and nearly his own life. From what he'd seen in a cursory look at the headlines for the past few weeks, it looked as if the White House was in full meltdown. There were days when Rick was sure that the president was the only person left in the place; the rest were either in jail, in disgrace, or in deep conversations with prosecutors.

Couldn't have happened to a better bunch of people as far as Rick was concerned.

He felt a sudden intense pain as he remembered the friends who had died only a few months before because of secrets that the government was willing to kill for to keep out of the press.

Dina Scholten had been the first to break through

the emotional walls he'd constructed after his return from Vietnam. They were a part of his dogged attempts to keep his nightmares under control, but she'd showed him that he could have friends–he was going to have the dreams anyway. Dina and Hector Rodriguez, one of the few other survivors from his platoon, had both died because they'd helped him after a government hit squad marked him for elimination.

Rick shook the tension out of his shoulders and brought his attention back to the living–the dead would show up tonight anyway. There would be plenty of time to talk to them.

First, he had errands to run. He didn't want to park the VW in any of the underground parking garages–to be honest, he wasn't sure it would make it out again–so he drove slowly in search of a parking spot–finally locating one a block north of M Street.

He walked over to the American Broadcasting Network on 18th Street, enjoying the tentative warmth of an early Washington spring day. After the brutal cold of the Montana winter, it felt great. It was a shame that it would be followed, all too soon, by sweltering humidity. In Washington, when the real summer hit, the colors drained out of everything. Even the trees, green now, would turn gray in a month or so from the amount of moisture in the air.

Today was one of the days when Rick could understand living in Washington. The azaleas were blooming, the sunlight seemed to caress rather than burn, and every office worker had found a reason to get out and enjoy the city.

As he turned up the short walkway to the door on 18th, it opened and Larry Summers, the security guard and fellow vet, said, "Hey man, I know you were scared of that next game of chess but running away for six months is taking the game a bit too seriously."

"Scared? Hell, I was out getting my ass beaten by a bunch of 10-year-olds so I'd dumb down enough to give you a fair game," Rick said, as they exchanged a "black power" handshake. "How's it going?"

"Same old," the slim black man responded. "The Watergate thing is so crazy they had to put on another courier. The White House seems to leak a new story on the hour. Don't quote me, but I swear I saw Mayweather actually smile the other day."

"Jamie?" Rick stepped back in mock surprise. "I didn't think he knew how."

"Yeah, well, the tension is getting to everyone." Last week, Ken Garrison punched out Evans over a story."

"Garrison?" Rick shook his head. "He's the nicest guy in the place."

"Well, he knocked Tom flat and just walked out."

"And as the sole officer of law and order on duty, did you respond appropriately?"

"Sure did. I held the door and saluted him as he passed by." Larry grinned. "Evans always treated me like one of those little blackface jockeys rich people have on their lawns."

"Oh that's just wrong." Rick said, "For one thing, you're way too tall."

Rick expertly dodged a half-hearted punch and headed down the hall past the newsroom, shaking his head at the idea of the unflappable Garrison taking a swing at anyone, much less the man who would decide if any of his stories made air. The tension here must really be amazing.

Since it was still only mid-morning–hours away from the Global Report's six o'clock deadline–the newsroom was almost empty. The writers were seated with their backs to him, diligently examining their newspapers. This might have been a bit more impressive if they weren't both reading the sports section.

A single desk assistant was on duty, a heavy-set black man whose name Rick didn't know. He was clearly not enjoying tending to the wire machines. As Rick watched, he grabbed the rolls of copy and distributed them, making sure to slam them on each desk with enough force to make them look like crushed beer cans.

"Hey, dude! Where did you disappear to?"

On his right, Don Moretti was leaning against his doorway smoking a cigarette. He flicked ashes on the linoleum floor and asked, "Did that imitation can of film work out for you? You never came back after that."

The film can had been part of a desperate plan to rescue Eve from the fixer someone had sent to make sure that any evidence the president had taken bribes from South Vietnam stayed lost and forgotten.

Since the agent and a Korean woman who worked for him had ended up dead, Rick wasn't about to discuss it.

"It was perfect," he said.

When Rick didn't offer any more details, Moretti took a long look at his face, nodded slightly, and took another pull on his cigarette. "Glad to hear it. You know, it's amazing how much I learn just talking to you."

"It's because you're a trained journalist, Don." Rick continued toward the rear of the building, "You'll have to excuse me. I'm going to see if Casey Ross is around."

"Looking for your old job back?" Moretti asked. "They were pretty pissed when you just disappeared, but the last two guys missed air."

Rick stopped and turned around. "Missed air?"

"Yup. Apparently they never learned to tell time." Moretti turned back into his edit room. "That or the drugs burned out that part of their brains. They didn't even realize that it was a problem even after everyone started to scream at them. It was not a pretty sight. You might have a chance after all—compared to these guys, you're a Rhodes Scholar."

"It's not a very high bar," Rick said and heard a snort of laughter from the editor.

Nothing had changed at the Assignment Desk.

The wire machines kept up their steady rhythm, the phones rang constantly, and the editors were in much the same positions as the last time he'd been there. It did seem as if the hanging haze of cigarette smoke was a bit thicker, but Rick supposed that could just be his over-exposure to fresh air.

Casey Ross was bent over his typewriter with a telephone jammed against his shoulder. He glanced at Rick and wordlessly pointed at the empty desk next to him, never losing his concentration. Rick nodded to the other two editors and carefully made his way through the tight spaces between the desks, chairs, and wire machines.

He made it to the empty chair and dropped into it. Since it was comfortable and out-of-the way, he decided to stay for as long as possible. He lit the Zippo on his thigh, fired up a Winston, and settled back, happy to observe.

From the steady cadence of the conversation, Ross was repeating an argument he'd obviously had many times before. "Geri. It's a great story. We both know that. But New York simply isn't interested." Ross paused and made a face while listening to the other side of the conversation.

"Geri, Geri. Don't get all upset. Yes, strip mining is a serious issue, and no one is more interested in environmental stories than I am. But, with everyone lining up for gas, they want stories on where to get more energy, not the problems that might cause."

This time, Ross lit a cigarette while he listened. "Strip mining" had caught Rick's attention, and he began to listen to the conversation, pretending to leaf through a copy of the Christian Science Monitor,

Ross was clearly trying to wrap it up. "Geri, Geri. Stop for a second, will ya?"

After a short pause, he began again. "Look, you keep researching the story, and I'll keep trying to get the show interested. Hey, you could even try to sell it to the morning show. However, for today, you concentrate on tonight's story like a good girl. Mayweather is doing the news, but you'll cover the dinner the Nixons are throwing for the returned POWs. I mean, you'll have Bob Hope, Jimmy Stewart, and John Wayne–there's got to be a terrific piece to be made out of that."

After a series of quick "Yesses" and an "Absolutely," Ross hung up the phone and dropped his face into his hands. "God, why did we let broads into broadcasting?"

Rick stopped pretending to read the paper. "Who was that?"

"Geri Hardin."

"Where did she come from? I thought Carol Ann was the only female reporter."

"You mean Romper Room's 'Miss Peggy'?"

Rick snorted, and Ross said, "Hey, far too many years ago, that's where Carol Ann started. On the other hand, Geri was in Saigon. She went there to be with her boyfriend, of course, but she ended up stringing for us; and, I hate to admit it, she didn't do bad at all. So when she got tired of death and destruction, and found out her boyfriend was screwing half of the girls on Tu Do Street, she dumped the guy, came back home, and got a job as a reporter."

Ross took a final drag on his cigarette and crushed it out in the overflowing ashtray on his desk. "And if you're about to say that she slept her way into the job–"

"I wasn't."

"All I can report is that it wasn't with me," Ross finished. "Now let's turn to the subject at hand. Meaning you."

The desk editor stopped and Rick assumed he was looking for an explanation of where he'd gone and why, something Rick certainly wasn't about to give him.

"Well, I'm looking for some work. I don't think Cosmopolitan Courier is going to hire me. Not until I pay for their bike at least. So I need to keep a low profile for a bit. You know how hard I can work, and I just figured I'd check."

Ross studied him for a moment. "So no explanation?"

"Nope."

"OK. Do you still have a bike?"

Rick shook his head. "I will in a couple of days. I had to leave it…well, I left it with a local biker gang, and the negotiations to get it back are going to be ticklish."

"I'll bet." Ross smiled and then looked at one of the TV screens that were playing silently on the wall over the wire machines. After a moment, he pointed at the TV marked "Network" where a commercial filled with quick cuts of smiling faces was running. "As you can see, the network, in its infinite wisdom, has decided to start a morning show so we can get our collective butts soundly beaten by the Today Show."

He swiveled back to face Rick. "Here's the thing. I have to find a desk assistant to cover an overnight shift–1:00 a.m. to 9:00 a.m.–and all the prima donnas we've got on staff think they're too good to work at night. I believe they think that a lack of sleep will hurt their chances for that anchor job that's just around the corner."

Ross shook his head. "An anchor job is never going to happen to anyone in this group of turkeys. However, we still need to staff these hours. You game for a little midnight madness?"

"Sure. What do I have to do?"

"What does any desk assistant do?" Ross said, putting his hand on the phone but not picking up the receiver. "Roll wire, get coffee, and run scripts. It's not like it requires any skill."

He picked up the phone and said into it, "One second." Then to Rick, "So, you're our new semi-official overnight D.A. Since you've never given us any information about yourself, we'll make it freelance. And, as a bonus to the worst possible hours, you get to be off the streets, something you appear to be interested in."

He held up his hand. "No, don't say anything. It'll either be a lie or an effusive expression of thanks, and the former will embarrass you and the latter, me. You'll start on June 19th when Brezhnev is at the White House. Now get out of here." He waved dismissively and turned to the phone.

CHAPTER 22

May 21, 1973, M Street NW, Washington, DC

M Street was crowded. The pace on the sidewalk was noticeably slower than usual as sauntering replaced the usual Washington speed walk. Rick knew it wouldn't last. In a matter of weeks, walkers scurrying to get out of the winter cold would be replaced by walkers scurrying to get out of the summer heat. Rick could believe the old story about how the British used to pay their diplomats stationed here a "tropical duty" bonus.

"Will you buy a candle to support disabled children?"

Rick looked at the ugly brownish candle being thrust at him by a ragged teenager with hair falling out of a tangled ponytail. She had the glazed look of the convert in her eyes and, whether she'd been converted by New Hope, the Children of God, the Jesus Freaks, the Healthy Happy Holy People, or the Soul Rush followers of the Guru Maharaji Ji, he knew that none of that money was going to children, disabled or otherwise.

Looking past her, he could see four or five knots further down the sidewalk where other cults were selling pamphlets, wind chimes, or pictures of their particular Beloved Leader. A dozen Hare Krishna Dancers were spinning ecstatically on the corner of 19th Street, banging tambourines and finger cymbals, faces turned to the sky.

Rick looked back at the girl with the candle and said, "Disabled children? Come on, that's not even original. What dumbass religion are you working for?"

Now that he was paying attention, he could see that she was very young, maybe thirteen and quite possibly younger, and looked like she could use a bath and a good meal. She had tears in her eyes.

Feeling like a complete jackass, he reached into his jeans and pulled out a twenty-dollar bill. He'd read somewhere that giving alms was actually about the soul of the giver and not the need of the recipient.

Anyway, he liked to watch their faces.

This girl suddenly looked like a normal kid as her eyes widened, her shoulders relaxed, and a smile blossomed. Rick realized that she'd been tensed up for the contempt or rejection she undoubtedly got from most passersby, and he'd stepped right up and delivered.

She started to say something, then stopped. She was looking around him at the snarl of cars crawling along M Street. Instantly, the childish expression of appreciation was replaced by an almost feral look of fear and submission. She mumbled something and darted away.

Rick took a couple of steps into the recessed doorway behind him. Less visible to the street, he watched as the girl darted between two parked cars and stood at the edge of the M Street traffic with her hand up. A battered blue Econoline van pulled up, and the passenger rolled down the window.

Sitting in the passenger seat was Flick Crane.

Rick turned and went inside the store. Embarrassingly, it was the Erotic Bakery, a favorite for bachelorette parties and gay birthdays. Stoically, he pretended to admire the phallus-shaped cakes while watching the van through the window.

As he watched, the girl proudly handed Flick the twenty and then dug through the pockets in her oversized bell-bottom jeans, producing a small pile of grubby bills and some change. At the sight of the coins, Flick spoke to her sharply, and she flinched, as if she thought he was going to hit her.

She shook her head and seemed to pull into herself, trying to become smaller and to move as far away from the van as possible without actually moving her feet.

Flick snapped another question, and the tangled ponytail bobbed as she checked the contents of the canvas newspaper carrier's bag on her shoulder. She nodded, and Flick made a dismissive gesture, clearly telling her to get back to work. As the van pulled away, Rick could see him hold the twenty up to the driver and throw his head back in a laugh.

"Can I show you one of these or would you rather see the men's cakes we have over there?" A sweet-faced college-age girl was looking at him across the bakery counter. Rick took a quick look at the lifelike baked replicas of the female anatomy she indicated and said, "Oh, no, thanks, I was just...umm...browsing."

"OK, something for a boyfriend, then?" She bent down and searched the display case for a second. "We do have some marzipan penises here somewhere. I've been told they're delicious."

"No, I was just looking. Got to go." Rick escaped before she could stand up again. He could feel the heat rising in his cheeks and smiled, amused at his own reaction.

On the sidewalk, he turned right and headed for the VW, thinking about how Kristee had said Flick was an enforcer for this weird religious-political cult in Virginia.

Whoever they were, he knew they had been involved in the Wounded Knee shootout, but why would they go halfway across the country to cause trouble? Why had they been willing to kill to stop the Arrows from being delivered to Lame Deer?

Before he reached the VW, he stopped and snapped his fingers. Shaking his head, he turned and walked down to the Union Trust Bank at Connecticut and L Streets. His favorite bank manager– well, actually, the only bank manager he'd ever liked, or even remembered–was sitting at his desk at the door. Rick assumed he was placed there because he still believed in the concept of customer service, and the real managers didn't want him to corrupt the rest of the staff.

The graying head came up as soon as Rick came through the door. "Why Rick. You've been away forever! It's good to see you."

"And it's good to see you again, Mr. Nicholson."

Nicholson came around his desk and gave Rick a warm handshake. "Please call me Jeremy."

"Yes sir, Mr. Nicholson."

The older man shook his head with a smile and asked, "Do you want to go downstairs?"

Rick nodded, and Nicholson led the way to an elevator just inside the front door. It opened immediately, and they went down a floor to the safety deposit boxes. Rick signed the card, produced his key, and they unlocked the two locks on Box 213. Nicholson led Rick to an empty room and closed the door.

Opening the box, Rick looked at the neat stacks of cash inside. He'd taken quite a bit with him to Montana, but there was still about $10,000 left, neatly stacked in blocks of 20 one-hundred-dollar bills. He took a brick and put ten folded hundred-dollar bills in his shirt pocket. Then, he undid his belt, unbuttoned the top button of his jeans, and slipped the remaining bills into a pocket from an old pair of jeans that he'd sewn in the same place as the outside rear pocket so that the thread was hidden. The money was held tight against his butt.

Nothing in that pocket had ever been found in a casual search. Rick figured if he lost the money because he'd taken his pants off, it was either an extremely serious police search or he deserved whatever happened.

He re-did his jeans, closed the box, and returned it to its niche in the wall of boxes. He knew that anyone who saw a scruffy biker with all that money would automatically assume it was stolen. In fact, it wasn't a result of how much he'd received but how little he'd spent.

When you wore the same boots, jeans, and t-shirt every day, you only needed so many clothes. Group houses were incredibly cheap, especially if you shared food costs, and until now, his motorcycle had been the property of Cosmopolitan Couriers.

He just didn't spend much money.

He kept a checking account and a credit card under each of his identities, Rick and Jim Putnam, which he normally only used to cash his paychecks. He wrote checks every April when he paid state and federal taxes for both identities, far less hassle than trying to avoid paying.

He was quite content with this way of life. He had the money to buy whatever he wanted, and, luckily, most of what he wanted couldn't be bought with money.

Nicholson was speaking to another customer when Rick emerged from the elevator, so he waved "thank you" and left.

CHAPTER 23

May 21, 1973, Georgetown, Washington, DC

Rick piloted the bus down M Street in Georgetown. If anything, Georgetown looked worse than before he left. The Summer of Love and Woodstock had plowed head-on into Altamont, and the human debris from that disaster was everywhere.

Kids ranging from college age down to eleven or twelve years old were drifting up and down the sidewalks, smoking cigarettes in doorways, or trying to catch some sleep in the afternoon sun. Rick thought that it must be tough to find a safe place to sleep at night, so a nap during the day could be a real lifesaver for these wanderers.

DC Metro police were cruising Wisconsin Avenue on their Vespas, blowing horns at the sleepers or, for those too tired or too stoned to react, parking the little scooters and walking over to deliver a sharp rap on the sole of the foot. The kids would pick up their backpacks, plastic bags, and surplus Army gear and rejoin the slow drift to another place to sleep.

The more alert were working the tourists for coins at the corner of M and Wisconsin. Through the open van windows, Rick could hear all the variations of "Got any spare change?"

He remembered a panhandler in Manhattan who'd given him a two-minute standup comedy routine before hitting him up for cash. Afterward, he had pursued Rick down the sidewalk and insisted that there must have been a mistake. Rick said the twenty was no mistake. His performance was better than most he'd seen at the improv clubs.

By comparison, these kids were barely trying.

As he crept along in the solid mass of traffic, he had time to notice the predators. They looked like the kids, but their faces were a little sharper, a lot more awake, and far more calculating.

Repeatedly, they'd come up to a kid, usually one who was alone, offer a cigarette, and then start a quiet and serious discussion. Rick knew that the pimps worked the bus station over on New York Avenue, so he figured these were the various cults out to "save" these poor young souls.

Most of the kids just took the cigarette and stared blankly in the general direction of their benefactor. Others had that desperate look of someone well past the end of their rope, and they listened intently.

Rick remembered what it was like. One year, he'd hitched down to the Daytona motorcycle races with just enough money to buy an infield ticket. Most of it was fantastic: the almost-solid sound of 100 race-tuned engines at maximum revolutions, swooping riders almost parallel to the asphalt in the turns, riders drafting and fighting for position. Other parts weren't quite as enjoyable: camping in the grassy area next to the track with hundreds of drunken Pagans, Warlocks, Banditos, and a mixed bag of Florida Outlaws, Mongols, and other hangers-on.

The worst was when he tried to take a nap under the boardwalk and got worked over by a platoon of Jesus Freaks. It felt as practiced and planned as an NVA ambush. Before he was fully awake, they'd offered him water, food, and cigarettes; and one particularly attractive girl was sitting on his backpack. They had never stopped smiling as they told him how happy they were, how miserable their lives on the street had been, what incredible love and affection they had for each other, and the glorious sense of joy when they accepted Jesus Christ as their Lord and Savior.

They'd all gathered around him in a warm huddle. Later he learned that this was called "snapping," so completely filling the potential recruits with love and warmth that they would suddenly "snap" into the group.

Rick just felt awkward and uncomfortable. He ducked down and out of the embrace, retrieved his backpack by tumbling its rider onto the sand, and escaped.

His childhood with an alcoholic parent had given him a thick armor against anyone who used love as a weapon. Even so, he could still feel the powerful pull of that promise of unconditional love and acceptance.

As he made the left turn to Wisconsin, Rick thought he'd given his trust to the Army and his loyalty to his country, and, even though he still had a positive attitude toward the U.S.A., his allegiance to any group much bigger than a dozen was pretty well used up.

He hauled the VW around an immediate left turn and into a narrow alley where Cosmopolitan Couriers had their garage, office, dispatch center, repair shop, and parts department. Parking illegally across from the entrance, he took a deep breath and went inside.

It was a mess. Well, it was always a mess, but this was extreme, even for Cosmopolitan Couriers. BMWs were lined up along the back wall three deep, and the left side of the space was filled from floor to ceiling with boxes marked with what looked like part numbers.

The only open space was the front desk where the dispatcher worked and the bottom of the stairs that ran up to the second floor. Cesaro, the immigrant mechanic who did all the repairs and maintenance on the bikes, was carrying one of the boxes down those stairs and staggered over to place it on the growing pile.

The dispatcher, an older man with an enormous mustache–Rick had never known his name–was hard at work. A multi-line punch-button phone was blinking silently, slips of paper were lined up precisely on the desk, and he was coolly giving commands into a large stand microphone.

Snarls of distorted radio noise that, as far as Rick was concerned, could have been Martians discussing the weather, came over. It must take practice to learn Martian, since the dispatcher calmly responded with new orders, directions, or advice.

Down the counter, Boyce Gassel, one of the co-owners of the courier service, was shuffling a pile of bills and invoices, muttering to himself. He didn't look up so Rick walked over, leaned on the old wooden counter, and said, "Hey Boyce."

Boyce's eyes flicked up for a second and went back to the papers in front of him. When his head snapped up and he scowled, Rick knew that he had realized that a man guilty of the sad and ugly death of one of his beloved bikes had dared to show his face.

Without warning, Boyce stood up and took a swing at Rick. Luckily, the counter shortened his reach, and Rick, who had expected something like this, stepped back out of range.

Boyce's face was bright red and he spoke in a low, venomous whisper, "You shitty little son of a bitch. How dare you walk in here after dumping Number 115 into a Metro dig? You were fired the instant that bike hit the bottom and don't even try to get your fucking back pay."

Remaining out of reach, Rick said, "I feel terrible about that bike. Seeing it down there was like a death in the family."

He held up his hands in a placating gesture,

"Look, I'm here to pay you back."

Boyce grabbed for Rick's shirt but missed. "You bastard! That was my baby! It was the first Beemer I'd ever owned! This whole company is built around it, and you think you can destroy it and just pay me some fucking money?"

The dispatcher cradled a phone on his shoulder and said, "Bullshit, Boyce. You say every busted bike was your first bike. By now, I've got to believe you went and bought a hundred bikes at once."

Boyce glared at the older man and then turned back to Rick. "OK, so 115 wasn't the first. It was still one of my babies."

Rick nodded. "I understand that. That's why the first thing I'm doing, now that I'm back in town, is trying to make it right. I'll pay you full price for the bike."

"Are you kidding? That was a vintage jewel!" Boyce's voice was still furious, but Rick thought his face was a bit less flushed. "There is no amount of money that can make up for the loss."

Cesaro was passing behind Rick, carrying another box. "No way, Boyce, 115 was $1540 new and counting the parts and depreciation, it's worth $893.54. Maybe $900, but no more."

Boyce scowled at the mechanic. "What about having to hire a truck to lift it off the spikes where this bastard left it? What about my mental anguish when I saw it lying broken in that pit?"

Cesaro put the box on the pile and headed back upstairs. "I don't know about your anguish, but you know damn well that the Metro crane pulled it out and dropped it right in the bed of our pickup truck."

"Traitor!" Boyce shouted after Cesaro's departing back.

Rick pulled the ten hundred dollar bills from his pocket and fanned them out so Boyce could count them. "I figured that $900 was the price, but I'll add in a bit for your anguish. I've got a thousand here. Will that make us good?"

Boyce leaned back and began to pound out a rhythm on the counter with his hands. "You're not thinking you're getting your old job back, are you? Because that's not happening."

"Nope. I just want to make things right."

Boyce's hands suddenly went to a crescendo, stopped, and he thrust a hand forward. "OK, give me the thousand, and I'll let you walk out of here alive."

Rick was amused at the idea of Boyce beating him up; but he was already looking over his shoulder for too many people, so he stepped forward and held out the money. Boyce snatched it out of his hand and began counting.

Rick glanced around and asked, "What's going on? Are you shutting down the business?"

Without looking up, Boyce said, "Hell no. We just lost the lease on this place. Fuck! You've made me lose count. Wait a second."

The dispatcher chuckled, "Only you could get lost counting to ten."

Boyce glared at him but kept counting. When he was finished, he tapped the bills into a neat stack, pulled an enormous roll of bills from his front pocket, undid the rubber bands holding it together, and added Rick's money. Rolling it back again, he looked around and said, "No, we just lost the lease. Some idiot is going to try to create a jazz club in here. Can you imagine? I mean, it was a stable before we showed up, and we've never gotten the stench of horse shit out of the floor."

Rick nodded and asked, "Where are you going?"

"Up to Adams Morgan, where it's still happening. Georgetown is over, man."

Rick laughed. "Are you kidding? The only things up there are Columbia Station, the Omega, and the Ontario Theater." He shook his head, "And the Ontario's been showing nothing but chop-socky and porn since their little art-house experiment failed."

Boyce had already turned back to his papers, "It's going to be the next big thing. Now get your sorry ass out of here before I change my mind and beat you up."

Rick gave an OK sign to the dispatcher as a "thank you" and headed for the old double doors left over from the place's stable days. "I'll see you around, Boyce."

"Better not. I said I wouldn't beat you up, but my baby is calling for revenge, and I might just run you down if I see you on the streets."

"I'll lie awake nights worrying about you."

CHAPTER 24

May 21, 1973, Georgetown, Washington, DC

Gas lines were new.

There didn't seem to be any real reason for their existence–no one could point to any real shortages–but Rick heard every possible cause as he listened to the radio while he waited two hours to get to a pump: tankers parked out in the Chesapeake Bay waiting for higher prices, the president's price controls, or the worsening Arab-Israeli tensions. All he knew was that he was glad he had the VW. At 50 miles an hour, it could go all day on a single tank of gas. A motorcycle should be even better.

Rick sighed. A motorcycle would be better for many reasons. It felt like an eternity since he'd danced. Of course, there had been the night road race through the Black Hills a couple of weeks before, but the effect of that had faded. So, when he finally put the allotted ten gallons in the bus, he decided not to drive back to Ingomar Street but to find the Dawn Riders instead.

Their old clubhouse on H Street looked abandoned, the faded sign "Motor Mouse Couriers" now off-kilter, swinging by a single chain. Of course, it had looked abandoned when it was in operation, so Rick parked the bus, pounded on the garage doors, and walked around back. The gang's mechanic and de facto leader, Hector Martinez, had died last year helping to save Eve's life and, without him, it looked like the old clubhouse was closed.

It wasn't very surprising since, as far as Rick could tell, Hector had been the only member with a real job.

Rick got back in the VW and thought for a few minutes. Then he headed to an area of strip clubs, bars, and tattoo parlors in Upper Georgetown. A part of Cleveland Park, it had always been the best place to find a large group of bikers, assuming that anyone in their right minds would want to find a large group of bikers.

If they weren't watching the girls dance in Act 4 or the Good Guys, they'd be listening to local rock bands in Clancy's or the Keg. In any case, they'd be drunk and ready to fight.

Of course, there weren't all that many times when they weren't either drunk or ready to fight so no point in putting things off.

It was dark by the time he parked outside The Keg, making sure he was well away from the pools of light cast by the few unbroken overhead lamps. Turning off the engine and killing the interior light, Rick reached down between the driver's seat and the door and pulled out the lug wrench that came with all VWs. An 18-inch steel rod with a socket at one end on a 90-degree angle, it wasn't terribly useful for getting tires on and off. Rick had replaced it with an X-shaped universal wrench after the first flat tire, but it tended to be a handy item to carry around.

He slipped it into the right-hand sleeve of his denim jacket so that the socket was hidden by the cuff, and the rod lay along the outside of his forearm. It was only a precaution but, in his experience, bars like this were the places where you took precautions.

Prepared, he got out and walked over to Clancy's. "The problem with strip bars," he thought, "was that they had to light the place enough to see the girls (which was bad enough) but that meant you could see the cheap and chipped nature of the place and the unsavory faces of the clientele. Dark bars were always better. You could at least pretend you were in the kind of sophisticated place you saw in magazine ads."

He bought a beer and walked through the crowd, pretending to ogle the two tired, depressed, naked women slowly swaying on the platforms but actually looking for Dawn Riders. He didn't see any, but there were still three bars to go.

As he strolled over to The Keg, he could hear the sound that always meant a fight was starting. A rising confusion of shouts, threats, foot scraping and–well, it was just the sound of a fight. Rick had been a bouncer during college, and the sound was a messenger of trouble. He reached into the jeans pocket and pulled out his Zippo, wrapping the fingers of his right hand around it. While he didn't intend to get in a fight, in his experience fights in bars often didn't give you a choice.

Even from a distance, he could tell they were all bikers, their "colors" proudly displayed. As he walked closer, he recognized one as the Dawn Rider he'd exchanged insults with outside the old clubhouse back in December. Now, a couple of Pagans, easily recognized by the flaming sign of the Norse Sun God on their colors, were about to kick the snot out of him.

Pagans were one of the toughest gangs on the East Coast. Rick didn't buy the rumor that the "secret" knock on their clubhouse out in Prince George's County was to bang on the front door and then step aside before the .45 hollow point came through at chest height.

It wasn't that he doubted the Pagans would do something like that; he just didn't think they'd want to bother replacing the door all the time.

True or not, the Pagans were not people you wanted to mess with. On the other hand, Rick did need to get in touch with the Dawn Riders. As he watched, the confrontation made its inevitable progression from threats to insults, and the first fists were thrown. He knew the next step would be weapons and decided to see if he could even the playing field a little.

Walking up behind the Pagan on his left, an overweight guy with a Fu Manchu mustache and body odor that was almost a physical presence, Rick tapped him on the shoulder, and, as he turned, hit him with a classic rabbit punch, the Zippo-filled fist striking at the place where his jaw met his neck.

The Zippo kept his fingers from collapsing inward and put all the power of hours of weight lifting directly into the fat guy. First, his head snapped away from Rick, and then his massive body followed. He spun completely once and fell over the battered hedge that was desperately attempting to add a little class to the bar.

"Well, that's one who won't remember me," thought Rick. He turned to the other two just in time to see the Dawn Rider dropping to the ground without being touched. The Pagan looked a bit surprised as well.

Rick raised his arms, primarily to conceal his face—he really didn't want these guys to be able to identify him later—and advanced. His opponent was a tall guy in a dumb-looking leather cowboy hat. When he grinned in a manner Rick was sure he thought wolfish, he revealed about four remaining teeth.

Clearly, the entrance of a new fighter had changed the rules because the biker reached into his back pocket and pulled out a large set of brass knuckles, which he quickly fitted on his left hand.

"Must be my lucky day," Rick thought.

He moved forward, careful not to trip on the Dawn Rider, and dropped his right fist a little. As he figured, the Pagan immediately launched a looping left at his face. Even without the brass knuckles, it could have done considerable damage. With them, it could shatter bones.

If it landed.

Rick snapped his right arm up and blocked hard at the man's forearm, leading with the tire iron in his sleeve. There was a snap as iron won the contest against bone. As the man's face clenched in pain, Rick jammed the leather cowboy hat down over the biker's eyes, spun him quickly, and launched him between two parked cars with a foot in the small of his back.

Neither Pagan was going to do much of anything in the immediate future, so Rick slid the tire iron up the pant leg of his jeans and let the sharp end drop into his boot. Then, he turned to the Dawn Rider.

To his disgust, the man had fallen into a puddle of his own vomit but, since he'd apparently passed out before the fight even started, didn't seem to be injured.

Stinking but not injured.

Rick rolled him over on his back, stepped on his toes to keep his feet braced, and pulled him upright. Then he stepped forward, flattened his shoulder into the man's gut, and carried him into the bar.

Inside were the usual dim lights, loud noises, and pungent aromas of a biker bar. Rick did notice that there were no stools or chairs, only large, tall tables that he suspected were firmly nailed into the floor. When he saw that the windows had all been replaced with glass brick, he knew that the management had taken all the precautions they could against seeing their property destroyed in the nightly warfare. One of the bartenders glanced over at him and noted the body on his shoulder. He nodded but prudently stayed behind the battered-but-sturdy wooden bar.

Rick spotted other Dawn Riders across the room near the stage where a young band was pounding out some almost tuneless Metallica cover song. He went over. "Anyone in charge here?"

An older man with a braided beard took a drink of beer, belched, wiped his mouth, and said, "That sort of depends on what you want."

Rick heaved the man off his shoulder and placed him on his feet. Amazingly, he managed to stay erect. "I believe this is one of yours," he said. "I found him outside with a couple of Pagans debating whether to take him apart or just stomp him flat."

The bearded man looked at the weaving figure with a total lack of concern, "Yeah, that's 'Brains.' As in 'Shit for.'"

Brains finally lost the battle with gravity and fell backward into the arms of a brother Dawn Rider who, as soon as he felt the vomit on his shirt, allowed him to complete his trajectory to the floor.

The first man pulled on one of the little braids coming down from his beard. "Pagans? So you're saying we've got a beef with them, now?" He dug a booted toe into the side of the man on the floor. "All because of Brains having 15 or 20 too many beers?"

Rick laughed, "I don't think so. 'Street fighter' here passed out before he ever threw a punch."

"Why are you being so helpful?" The leader

peered at Rick's face in the dim light. "Oh yeah, Hector's friend. The Army buddy who got his ass killed." He held up a hand as Rick began to say something. "Don't say anything about it. Hector never did a damn thing he didn't want to do, and I sincerely do not want to know what exactly happened on 14th Street.

"I'm 'Preacher,' and I guess I'm about as much of a leader as this sorry-ass chapter has. I think Hector called you 'Zippo' so why don't we leave it at that, because I don't want to know any more about you. For one thing, people with guns come around looking for you, and, for another, I just don't give a shit."

"Fine with me." Neither man offered a hand to shake, but, when a muscular waitress who looked like she could go several rounds with Muhammad Ali brought a new round of beers to the table, Rick was given a bottle. He assumed it was originally for the biker on the floor.

Preacher looked down at Brains, now wrapped around the base of the table and snoring loudly. "So, I'm assuming you didn't just show up to save this poor idiot from having his skull broke. My guess is you want your bike back."

"Yep."

Preacher took a long drink of beer, belched, and finally said, "Well, I would be happy to get that piece of shit rice-grinder out of my sight. Of course, you realize there is rent due?"

"Why don't we consider Brains here as a down payment?"

"Why not? Because he ain't worth shit." Preacher sighed, "But I guess that's the burden of being chapter prez. I've got to worry about the worthless ones."

Another Dawn Rider raised his beer in a mock toast, "Because, we sure as shit don't."

The rest of the bikers laughed as Preacher just shook his head.

Rick asked, "Where can I pick up the bike? I stopped by Motor Mouse, and you've clearly moved on."

"Well, when your club president, who also happens to be the guy who pays the rent and holds the lease, gets his ass killed...well, yeah, we figured it was time to wander."

"I had the same feeling," Rick said.

"We noticed." The biker said dryly, "It took a while but we found a new place. It's down in Southeast, right behind Pier Nine."

Rick was surprised. "The gay dance club?"

"Yeah, we're trading a bit of security for the use of a row house in the back. As it happened, two of our members were working as dancers in the upstairs lounge anyway." Preacher shrugged. "Apparently, black leather works as well on the dance floor as it does on the road. As the Buddha said, 'whatever floats your boat.'"

"I'll drink to that." Rick raised his bottle. As he drank, he looked around the crowded bar. The two men he'd left in the parking lot were being helped through the front door. They didn't look like they had clear memories, or any memories at all, but it was probably time to leave.

"I'm out of here." He put his mostly full beer on the table. "When can I pick up the bike?"

Preacher wiped the foam off his mustache with a hairy forearm. "Well, let's see. What day is today?" He looked around at the other Dawn Riders but got only blank looks.

"It's Monday." The voice came from the floor at their feet.

Preacher looked down at the recumbent Brains, "That's what we keep him around for. Stupid as he is, he usually knows things like that." His attention turned back to Rick. "Tuesday is a big club night so we'll be around. In the meantime, we'll try and remember where we stuck that Japanese piece of shit."

"Sounds like a plan." Rick stuck out his hand. Preacher just stared at it.

"Jeez, it's clean and everything, too." Rick held up his hand and examined both the front and back. "Forgot how friendly you guys are."

"You're lucky we don't kick the crap out of you."

Rick turned and said over his shoulder as he left, "Nah, you're lucky you didn't try."

CHAPTER 25

May 22, 1973, Ingomar Street NW, Washington, DC

"Not another 'twisty little passage'!"

"I'm afraid so. What shall we do?"

"Rub the lamp?"

"OK. Hmm. It says, 'Rubbing the electric lamp is not particularly rewarding. Anyway nothing exciting happens.'"

"Rats."

Across the living room, Sage and Scotty were hunched over the tiny green screen of the Data-Comp, Sage giving commands and Scotty patiently typing them in. When he had come in, Rick had asked what they were doing. He still wasn't quite sure, but they were playing a game on Scotty's mainframe computer.

Rick had settled into one of the battered recliners, shut his eyes, and pretended to take a nap.

"Scotty! I got it." Sage seemed to have an intuitive grasp of the game and was more often right than wrong. "The 'twisties' aren't the same. Look, Go North."

"OK." Rick could hear the click of the keyboard.

Sage squealed, "See! These are 'little twisting passages' not 'twisting little passages'! Let's make a chart."

"OK. Where's the graph paper?"

His roommates had been watching the little girl for only a day, but Rick could tell that a bond was forming, particularly between Sage, Eps, and Scotty. Rick mused that it was probably because, in so many ways, the guys were more like brilliant children than adults. Steve was in slightly better contact with the "real world"; but, basically, they all saw life as a series of opportunities to play with toys, and the fact they were frighteningly smart let them get away with it.

Rick closed his eyes and listened as Sage excitedly celebrated their escape from the maze.

Yes, sir. I'm here.

I'll tell your wife you loved her.

Captain, just hang on, the medics will be here any second, and we'll get you out.

Fuck. I can't see shit. That fucking elephant grass has got to be six feet high.

Where are they, sir? Well, they're everywhere.

Up in the trees, hiding behind those damn anthills.

Hiding in the grass.

Shit! That one went right by my head.

Oh, Captain, your foot. Shit. Shit. I'm going to take off my shirt and bandage it.

I'll wrap it and the medics will be here any second now.

Yes, sir. Mabel. That's your wife's name. Mabel.

No sir, I won't forget.

What's that? Say again, sir.

You want me to do what?

No sir, I won't do it.

No, we don't have any more morphine.

FUCK!

Ah, Christ. Maybe my shirt will stop the blood. No, using the shirt already.

Yes, sir. You took another wound. It's in your gut.

Sir, I'm not fucking going to kill you.

Someone will be here soon, and you'll be OK.

No sir, I don't really believe that either.

OK, Come on. Loosen your fingers. Got it.

Shit. It's all covered in blood. Well, it's an M-1911 so it'll still work.

Are you sure, sir?

Fuck! Two shots right into his chest. How the hell is he still screaming?

Sir, it will be all right. I'll tell Mabel you loved her.

Just close your eyes. I can see the medic coming.

Damn it! Damn it! Damn it! There's fucking blood and brains everywhere!

It was a direct order.

Fuck! Where did that one hit?

Ah, shit. My fucking arm. Damn, that hurts!

Hide.

I'll just slide under the Captain. He won't mind.

When Rick opened his eyes, all he could see were Sage's eyes, big, wide, and scared. She was staring at him from the other side of Scotty who was slowly leaning his wide frame in an attempt to block off her view. As he leaned, Sage bent so that her eyes never left Rick.

Without looking at Rick, Scotty kept up a quiet, continuous, if one-sided, conversation. "OK, Sage, we're almost to the Giant's Cave. What should we do about the bear? No ideas? Well, let's try killing it. OK, it says, 'your bare hands against his bear hands.' Get it? A bear has 'bear' hands."

Slowly, Scotty's chatter got the little girl's attention, and they went back to the game.

"He's pretty good at that."

Rick turned his head and saw Kristee standing next to him watching her daughter. "I just walked in at the end of that. Sounded pretty horrible."

Rick rubbed his face with both hands. "Well, it's a lot less horrible now than it was when it was happening. I'm sorry if I upset Sage."

Kristee thought for a minute. "Eve told me about what you keep going through, and I explained it to her." She laughed, a short exhalation of breath, really. "Well, as much as you can explain to an 8-year old kid. I said you'd had some hard times and when you were dreaming, you went right back into them."

She moved over and sat in the other recliner. "I

said there wasn't anything wrong with you, that you were just stuck fighting some bad guys."

"I don't know that I'd agree that 'nothing is wrong with me,' but I appreciate the effort." Rick watched as Sage became more excited about the game on the computer. "It's not bad enough that I have to go through this crap all the time. I really hate making everyone around me participate."

"Well, don't feel like the Lone Ranger," Kristee said. "I don't know too many people who get through life without a scratch." She sighed. "That's why I had to get Sage away from the compound."

Rick rolled his head over to look at her and waited for her to continue, but her thin lips were locked in a straight line, and she didn't take her eyes off her daughter.

Eve popped her head out of the kitchen. "Hey, if any of you want corn, I need help with shucking. It's not local, but it's better than canned."

Rick and Kristee levered themselves out of the broken cushions of their recliners and walked to the kitchen. The back door was open, and Eve's voice came from outside. "Come on out here so we don't make a mess."

Eve had taken a seat on the low stone wall that marked the rear edge of the property and the outer wall of the tiny back porch. She said, "Pull up a step and make yourselves at home." A Safeway paper bag with at least two dozen ears of corn sat between her legs. She tossed an ear to each of them, and they settled down to ripping off the leaves and picking out the threads of silk.

Eve looked up and peered through the kitchen window. "Good, I can see Sage, so I know she's not sneaking up on us. Ergo, Kristee, you've got no excuses. Give with the rest of the evil that lurks in Christian Cuckoo Land?"

There was a pause filled with the sound of ripping husks and the "pop" when the ear came off the last bit of the stalk. Kristee began to talk, not like someone who was scared or unwilling, more like a witness in court trying to bring clarity to events that were confused, jumbled, and colored with intense emotion.

"Well, I told you how the Crusaders hauled us back to the mansion. I guess that was in 1972 around Thanksgiving. I was furious but hey, I'm a woman, I'm not that big, and my biggest concern was keeping Sage from being hurt.

"So we were back in the bunkhouse. The other women were told to keep an eye on us and make sure we didn't 'wander off.' I had to go to a special class they called 'Spiritual Service,' but it was really just a bunch of crap about obeying your husband– after Stephen, of course–and how a woman could only be happy if she was in a state of 'Spiritual Submission.'"

Eve said angrily, "Sounds more like 'spiritual slavery.'"

Kristee looked up and then concentrated on picking out the silk threads. "Yeah, you'd think I'd have realized that, but, hey, all the women's lib stuff wasn't around when I was growing up, and the Children's Crusade's pitch wasn't all that different from the crap I'd heard at Holy Word Baptist every Sunday."

She finished the ear of corn, laid it in the neat pyramid growing on the step next to Rick, and snapped her fingers at Eve who threw her a new ear. "On the other hand, I didn't buy into it any more than I'd ever bought into all that Baptist bullshit about 'surrendering to your husband.' I waited, watched, and planned. I memorized all the shifts of Crusaders guarding the area, explored the woods in back of the bunkhouse when I could sneak away, and waited for a chance."

Her voice dropped to almost a whisper. "Then Sage was scheduled to begin her special training. They made her swear not to talk about it with anyone, especially her parents. That almost had me grabbing her and taking off for the front gate, I tell you."

Kristee shook her head. "Man, I'm glad I didn't. The place is about a mile from the nearest anything, Gary had the keys to the pickup, and it would have put them on alert. The thing I worried about most was that they would just take Sage and send me away. I don't know what I would have done then."

Her voice cracked, and she pulled a bandanna out of her back pocket, held it out to find the little cloth label, and then swiped at her eyes with one edge and blew her nose on the other. Shaking her head as if to banish an unpleasant dream, she continued. "But they didn't, and I was the meekest, most obedient believer in the Children's Crusade you've ever seen. And then, in February, everything changed."

Rick put a cleaned ear on the pile and asked, "Around the end of February?"

"Yeah." Kristee looked bewildered. "Why?"

"Just wondering how it matches up with something else. Go ahead with your story."

Eve threw new ears to the two on the steps and looked in the bag. "We're almost done."

Kristee ripped the husk off with a particularly vicious twist. "Suddenly, everyone was running around, all the men anyway, and then most of them grabbed weapons, piled into the cars and pickups in the Common Pool, and took off. No one would say where they were going or why, but I heard some talk about a mission or a calling or something like that."

She tossed the husk away and started on the silk. "I didn't think I was ever going to have a better chance to get the hell out of there, and, as far as I knew, they could all be coming back any time. I'd already filled a knapsack with whatever food I could put together and taken all the money from our family stash.

She continued faster. "So, the first night, I woke Sage up at 3:00 a.m., dressed us both in just about every piece of clothes we owned. I had us wearing two socks on each hand. I mean it was cold, not as bad as a Montana winter but still . . ."

Eve said, "Nothing is as cold as a Montana winter."

Rick agreed. "Damn right, last winter almost made me feel like Vietnam wasn't that bad."

He paused. "Almost."

Kristee finished her last ear and dusted off her hands. "We went out through the back woods, and I used every hunting trick my Dad ever showed me. Walking on rocks, stepping in each other's footprints, climbing trees and moving from branch to branch. Everything. Lucky it was a full moon. After we were about a mile away, I saw the outside lights go on at the Big House, and I knew they were coming after us."

Eve asked, "You ran?"

Kristee shook her head. "That would have just gotten us caught. No, as soon as I knew they were hunting for us. I headed for a downed tree that I'd found weeks before. You see, in addition to exploring the woods, I'd been digging a hunter's hide between the base of the tree and the root ball it had torn when it fell. It wasn't much bigger than the two of us, but it was dry and warmed up pretty good if we snuggled together. They came by twice but never saw us. We stayed there for two days before we made a break for the fence."

Eve nodded her head. "Smart girl."

Kristee laughed bitterly. "Ya think? Would a smart girl ever have gotten herself in a fix like that? No, I've been making nothing but dumbass moves my whole life."

She paused, and Rick could see the muscles clench as she set her jaw. "Well, that ended that night. Had to be ended. Sage is never going back there."

"No, she isn't," promised Rick. "Then what happened?"

"We walked north for several miles after we got over the fence. Then I noticed that this house had a sign on the lawn that said, 'No Crusaders Allowed.' I figured we had to take a chance and knocked on the back door. The woman who answered welcomed us, let me use the phone to call you, and put us up for a couple of days."

Kristee smiled at a memory. "Man, you should have heard her when the guys from the mansion knocked at the door. She told them to get the hell off her property and backed it up with a 12 gauge. Mrs. Lewitinsky was one tough lady, and she had no time for the Children's Crusade. Turned out neighbor Peter had 'donated' about 40 acres of the back part of her farm to his property. She went to see one day, and there was a new fence. She said that no one would help, not the police or the county court clerk. They showed her a bunch of papers she swore she'd never seen before and said they couldn't do anything about it."

Kristee stood. "So we made it to the city, stayed at the Evangeline Hotel for Women for a couple of days, and then looked up Steve after you told me about this place."

"And you can stay here as long as you want." Eve hopped down and hugged Kristee fiercely. "This is home for you and Sage."

When she released the other woman, Eve brushed angrily at her cheeks, scooped up the husks, stems, and silk into the paper bag and handed it to Rick. He put it in the trashcan at the bottom of the stairs while the two women gathered up the corn and carried it into the kitchen.

Rick strolled out to the sidewalk and spent a while just watching the street—men coming home from work, kids in the yards, and women sitting on their front porches. Finally satisfied that nothing was out of place, he headed up the stairs and into his home.

CHAPTER 26

May 22, 1973, Ingomar Street NW, Washington, DC

"Are you listening?"

Rick grunted and placed the bar in the supports of the weight bench. He picked up a small towel from the floor and wiped his face. "Yes. I am listening. It's responding that's hard when I've got the weights going."

In the afternoon, Rick had stopped by Sears and picked up a set of free weights, an essential part of his pre-sleep routine. As he took a breather between reps, he thought about how much more intense his exercise routine had been before he had a roommate.

Then he looked over at Eve, sitting on the edge of the bed with a small table pulled close to hold the spread of papers and folders she was reading, occasionally highlighting a line with a thick yellow marker or making a tiny note in pencil. He thought of the comfort of her strong arms waking him out of the endless nightmares that ruled his nights and the sheer wonder of feeling that body almost buzzing with life as she slept in his arms. An interrupted routine was an exceedingly small price to pay.

The rest of the house appeared to agree: he hadn't heard anything about Eve finding her own home since they'd gotten back. He figured part of it was the hassle of having to live with Kristee and Sage without Eve to act as mediator.

"You were telling me about your boss. Tommy Finkle?"

"Franklin." Without looking, she tossed her pencil in his direction. "I knew you weren't paying attention."

Rick caught the pencil out of the air and gently lofted it back on the bed so it rolled slowly and bumped her side. "What I don't understand is exactly what he expects you to do."

"That's the worst part." Eve picked up the pencil and went back to reading. "We're the first paralegals that Marsden Angle has hired. The woman who directs the program said that it depends on the lawyer we get assigned to."

Rick lay back and began another set of slow presses. "And what does your guy, Franklin, want you to do?"

"I don't know. The first day, I was told to meet him in the library." Eve shook her head. "It was the strangest thing. I walked in there and looked for him. My first thought was 'who left a pile of dirty shirts in here?'"

"Dirty shirts?"

"Yeah. It was Tommy Franklin, with his feet up on the table, glasses up on his forehead, and slouched all the way down in his chair. I swear the man is a walking wrinkle." She laughed, "I'd bet he thought I was a complete idiot staring at him with my mouth open, except I don't think he paid the slightest attention to me until I walked up and introduced myself."

Rick smiled despite the pressure of the weights. "Anyone who doesn't notice you can't be all that smart."

Eve grinned back. "Thank you, sir."

She turned back to the pile of papers she was working on, "But all he said was 'Can you shepardize?' and, when I admitted I didn't even know what it was, he just tossed a case transcript to me, and told me to find out."

"Isn't that some kind of dry cleaning?" Rick said as he racked the bar and wiped his face again.

"That's Martinizing, you dope. No, it's going through these massive books called, oddly enough, Shepard's Citations and finding out if every case mentioned in the file has been overturned–which is bad–or cited–which is good."

Rick raised one edge of the bench, locked it down, and began to do extremely slow sit-ups. "So, what's your case?"

"I have no idea." With a laugh, Eve swept the

papers off the table. "I'll figure it out tomorrow."

After a short pause, Eve walked around the table and began to file the papers neatly into their folders. "The biggest problem I have is Tommy's clients."

"Why?"

"Well, he's representing tobacco companies. I spent half the afternoon measuring ads for the sides of buses to make sure that the Surgeon General's warning was no bigger than it absolutely had to be." She put the papers in her briefcase and pushed the table against the wall. "But tobacco companies aren't the real problem; they're bad but they're not evil."

"The Shangri-Las." Rick interrupted.

"Very good. No, the problem is that he's the point guy for the coal companies. You remember the guys who want to strip mine my home and built monster power plants on it?"

"Didn't sound like a great way to preserve the place for future generations to me." Rick hit a hundred sit-ups, got off the bench and, putting his feet on the bed, began slow pushups. "But I thought that had all stopped when we made the run with the...uh, when we made the run to Lame Deer."

Eve began to undress. Rick immediately stopped with his arms at full extension and watched.

She laughed. "Aren't you going to end up with sore arms doing that?"

"Worth it. Definitely warrth it."

Eve continued, enjoying the attention. When she was nude, she did a slow turn like a model. "So you approve?"

Rick's arms were just beginning to tremble, but

he kept his gaze on her and said, softly, "You are the most beautiful thing I've ever seen."

"Well, I think I had better cover up before you get all stiffened up."

"Too late for that."

She laughed and disappeared into an enormous T-shirt with a Daytona Bike Week logo on the front.

Rick resumed his pushups.

When her head popped out, she was obviously thinking about work again. "No, the leases haven't been canceled. They could still be overturned." She sat on the bed and bounced her way up to the pillows, pulled up the blanket, and tucked her feet in. "And, of course, the leases are technically controlled by our friends at the Bureau of Indian Affairs."

"Friends?" Rick asked.

"I was being ironic." Eve settled back against the pillows with her hands behind her head. "The BIA has been controlling Indian lands and selling off the natural resources ever since the Indian Wars. We're supposed to be getting the money, but somehow there never seems to be much left."

"I wonder if we could prove that." Rick finished and stripped off his shorts and t-shirt as he headed for the shower.

Eve whistled appreciatively. Rick said over his shoulder, "Stop that. You know you are not going to be happy until I get this sweat off. Give me two minutes."

"I am not going anywhere, trooper," she promised.

However, when Rick had showered, he came back to find her sound asleep. He slid into bed and wrapped an arm around her, drifting off almost immediately.

About three hours later, he awoke, shouting warnings about snipers in the treetops. Eve pulled him close and hugged him fiercely until he quieted.

CHAPTER 27

May 22, 1973, Ingomar Street NW, Washington, DC

The kitchen was a whirl of housemates. Steve was headed to a secret location in one of the least discreet cars in the world: a bright-red 240Z convertible. Rick whistled approvingly when he spotted Steve sliding into the car outside the house, Steve yelling back, "Onc of thc pcrks of selling out to The Man."

In contrast, Eps and Kristee were walking down to Connecticut Avenue to catch the bus. Kristee only fussed a little bit over Sage, who was going to spend the day with Scotty tend lwas clearly delighted about it. She started pestering the laconic programmer before her mother was even out the door. "Can we try the Volcano today?"

"Only after we make sure Gidget is OK."

The little girl didn't pause for a second, flying down the basement stairs, and asking if she could load the DECTAPE. She was disappointed for a moment when Scotty told her she was headed for another day at the cardpunch but cheered up when he said he'd teach her some FORTRAN.

Scotty paused at the door to the basement for a moment and said to Rick, "The cool thing is she has no preconceived idea that she can't program FORTRAN so she just does it. It's an interesting experiment."

He might have said more, but a plaintive "Scott-eee" came from the basement. He hurried down the stairs but not before Rick could hear the extra locks snap into place.

Rick was left alone with a cup of coffee and a fresh pack of Winstons. As he raised the coffee mug, he could see ripples. His hands were shaking, a remnant of the night's warfare. He put the cup down, extended both hands in front, and concentrated, willing the nerves to calm. It took almost 30 minutes before he could pick up the now cold coffee without a tremor.

I need to get that bike today, he thought. I'm like a heroin addict quitting cold turkey.

The Washington Post was blessedly free of Watergate coverage–at least on the front page–but there was an article on Wounded Knee entitled "Indians vs. Indians."

Rick shook his head as he read the first paragraphs. Clearly, AIM had brought in the tribal elders, described as "...cultural remnants. Seven old men, worn and toothless, who still clung to the lost glory of the Sioux nation."

Eve had described the elders as men of tremendous wisdom and integrity, but the government agents who had met with them had dismissed them out of hand. Their preferred leaders were modernized Indians like Dick Wilson, the elected tribal chairman of Pine Ridge, ready to assimilate, willing to work with the coal companies, and a giant fan of Richard Nixon.

It was also clear that the reporter felt the same way.

"Catching up on the news, trooper'?" Eve blew into the kitchen in a fury of controlled energy: getting coffee, checking her briefcase, kissing Rick on top of his head, checking the briefcase again, and finally, sitting down across the wooden drum table with her cup of coffee and a contented sigh.

Rick watched her with fond approval.

She looked up from her first sip of coffee. "What are you grinning about?"

"It's not a grin," he said. "I think it would be better described as a 'smirk.' It's the outward expression of feeling incredibly lucky."

"Lucky?"

"Yeah, you are one of the smartest, toughest, and sexiest women in this town, and for some unfathomable reason you seem to enjoy hanging with me."

She looked at him for a long moment. "OK, I'm going to assume that was a compliment. You know, you could be a little more succinct–we're not in court."

"I love you."

"Umph." Eve swayed a bit as though she'd been hit. "Take it easy, trooper. I knew that one day, all my sledgehammer work would put a crack in that 6-inch steel armor around your heart, but I'm not prepared to deal with it today."

Eve reached across the table and squeezed his hand. "I'm not going anywhere. Ever."

She pulled the front section of the Post out from under his hands and made a show of reading through the articles in a calm and businesslike manner. Rick would almost have bought the act if he couldn't see the pulse in her neck racing.

"So, Wounded Knee ended and nothing was settled." She sipped her coffee, "I'm shocked. Shocked."

Rick didn't take his eyes off her, but he let his mind wander. "Any word on the coal leases up in Lame Deer?"

"Not really." She turned the page with an efficient snap, "The vote in Council was to terminate the leases, but it's being slow-walked by the BIA bureaucrats. The coal companies are putting on all the pressure they can: offering jobs, schools, cash, hell, anything, to get people to change their minds. My uncle says their slogan is 'Moving Forward to Prosperity.'"

"Good line. Was that one of Tommy's?"

"Of course."

Rick leaned back in the chair and lit a cigarette.

Eve stuck two fingers out from behind the paper, he placed the cigarette between them, lighting another for himself. Blowing smoke rings, he mused, "I wonder if there's a way to convince people that it's not actually going to be 'Forward to Prosperity'? I mean, from what you've told me, it's another crappy deal in a long history of crappy deals."

"Right."

"I can see the attraction of keeping the land for future generations." There was a pause as Rick took another drag, "but it's always struck me that can be trumped by promises of enormous profits, spiffy new houses, and pickups made of pure gold. What if we could prove that the deals suck financially as well as environmentally?"

Eve began to fold the paper, her face closed in concentration. "Hard to do. The contracts are a maze of incentive clauses, set-asides, and interlocking shell companies. They were impossible for me to crack."

"For you? When did you see them?"

"When the boys left the BIA, they didn't go empty-handed." Eve stood up and began to gather her things. "We've always known that the BIA was screwing us. I mean everyone is making out like bandits except the people who actually own the land. So they smuggled dozens of boxes of documents out right under the FBI's nose."

She laughed. "One of the last groups went out in a convoy guarded by the FBI and Metro Police. The guys were howling with laughter because the cops were essentially guarding all the documents stuffed into the trunks of those rusty reservation beaters."

Rick said, "Then it should be easy. We can get the documents and work the numbers."

Eve shook her head, her face now serious. "The FBI has been going nuts, trying to get those papers back. When we tried to give some to one of Jack Anderson's reporters, they put his ass in jail."

She blew out a sigh. "The papers themselves are radioactive, the boys are moving them continuously, and they are damn hard to understand. I don't know how we'd do it quickly enough to make a difference in the final vote on the coal leases."

Both were silent as they considered the problem. A muffled giggle came from the basement and then Sage could be heard saying, "You forgot to put in the macro for the DECTAPE before you did JOBSTART, silly."

Rick and Eve looked at each other and smiled.

CHAPTER 28

May 23, 1973, Southeast Washington, DC

Rick spent much of the day just cruising DC, checking to see what had changed and who was still around.

Down at Connecticut and H, where the Metro dig took a hard right and headed north, they'd finished the tunnel, and trucks were lined up, dumping ton after ton of dirt into the vast gulf. After each layer of dirt came a small army of miniature bulldozers, steamrollers, and the strange little machines known as "jumping jacks." The operators hung on grimly to the engine on top and an enormous footplate rammed endlessly into the earth. Rick wondered how their forearms felt after a day of this.

The homeless woman who sang to the passersby

was at her usual position down from the Mayflower Hotel, and the guy with no legs was stationed on his roller board near the department stores on F Street. Rick had heard that Eddie the Monkey Man– apparently he used to have a monkey help drag quarters out of people's pockets–was in reality quite well off and spent winters in Florida. It seemed to be a tough way to make a living.

He spotted Ronald, the semi-mythical scam artist near the Union Trust Bank. He'd taken Rick for 75 dollars a year or so ago with a long and involved story about needing his car repaired and a bit of brilliant "cold reading" that convinced Rick he was a neighbor Rick had seen but never spoken to.

Later, he read in the Post that he was far from alone; the guy had cashed in on everyone from congressmen to DC judges, often working right outside DC Police Headquarters on C Street. Rick shook his head, thinking you had to admire real skill regardless of the use it was put to.

On Capitol Hill, a new group had moved into their old house on North Carolina and C Street. A battered Yamaha two-stroke sat in the back yard, and a bushy-haired guy was tearing down the carburetor of a red VW bug at the curb, carefully placing each tiny part on a sheet of newspaper. Rick couldn't see much improvement in having the NIS as tenants.

He still had time to kill before he expected the Dawn Riders at their clubhouse, so he drove up the 8th Street strip, looking at the flashing neon of the drag clubs and the restrained elegance of the more refined clubs. The lesbian bar was still closed up like a fist, green paint covering the shuttered windows and the heavy wooden door as if to say, "Hey move along. Nothing to see here." Then the door opened as two women left, and he caught a flash of the bright lights and the pool tables in back, so he knew it was still in operation.

As he swung west to Pennsylvania Avenue, the sun was backlighting the Capitol Dome in a deep gold, and Rick knew it was time to head over to the Pier Nine. The nightclub was really a large warehouse like so many others in the almost abandoned triangle of Southeast Washington trapped between I-395, South Capitol Street, and the Anacostia River. The Washington Star newspaper was still operating down there, as was the Washington Navy Yard behind 15-foot walls. The rest was decaying public housing developments, vacant lots, and some of the hottest gay clubs in the city.

Pier Nine had been around for years and was one of the few places that would tolerate straights. One night Rick had raced another bike off the light on Calvert just before the guaranteed police-free zone of the bridge over Rock Creek Park. When his engine hiccupped and died, he realized that he'd forgotten to turn the little gas cock under the tank from Park to Run.

The other rider and his girlfriend were waiting for him in front of the Windsor Park Hotel. When the guy stopped laughing, he told Rick that he was an off-duty DC cop and invited him along for "a little clubbing." They'd wound their way through DC To his chagrin, Rick was beaten consistently even when he had fuel–the BMW had never been a speedster–and wound up at Pier Nine.

The bar was two stories with straights allowed on the first floor; the second floor was "gays only." Rick sat at a table, watched the crowd, and listened to the music–Love Unlimited, The O'Jays, The Chi-lites. The pounding beat drove a frenetic mix of men seeking men, young girls seeking excitement, drag queens in full regalia, and straight couples looking around to make sure they had the steps right. Rick had to refuse a couple offers to dance and one to go upstairs, but mostly he was left alone to nurse a beer and enjoy the scene.

The sun had just gone down as the VW sputtered into the parking lot, ringed by battered chain link fencing. Pulling around to the back, Rick saw an old townhouse, the sole remaining structure from what had obviously been a whole street of homes. Now, it stood alone in a dusty froth of newspapers and vines. The backyard was packed earth and held a dozen Harleys and an opening cut through the fence to allow easy access to the club.

Rick parked the bus, locked the doors, and walked toward the clubhouse.

"Hey, look who's here."

The voice came from behind. Rick didn't turn around or hesitate; hopefully, the caller was talking about someone else.

As three burly men in grimy leather vests with the Pagan's MC colors on the back stepped from the shadows, Rick knew that wish wasn't going to come true. He stopped and backed so that he was braced against a Chevy station wagon, watching as five bikers formed a semi-circle around him.

The man in the center was easily six–and-a–half-feet tall and looked strong and fit without the beer belly that seemed to be required for outlaw bikers. "Thought we might find you here since you were hanging out with these chickenshits at the bar," he said. "Bronc and Slider said they'd have loved to be here, but Slider's arm got itself broken and Bronc's not making a lot of sense since you rabbit-punched his ass."

"He never did make much sense." That was from a small but stocky biker on the giant's left.

"Yeah, but now even his nonsense don't make sense," said a blond biker with an American flag bandanna on his head and barbed wire tattoos circling both biceps. Rick noticed that it took a fair number of barbs to cover the distance–unquestionably a weight lifter.

The back door of the townhouse banged open and a couple of Dawn Riders came down the stairs and crossed the yard. Rick recognized Brains–the one he'd rescued from a beating–and Preacher, the club president.

OK, it would be three against five. That's not bad, he thought.

"Hey guys." Brains said. "Don't knock over any of our bikes while you're dancing with this fool, OK?"

"Yeah," Preacher agreed. "If any of the paint on my custom is scratched, I'm coming out to Waldorf and collect, understand?"

The two walked around behind the Pagans–Brains waved sardonically to Rick–and kept walking around the corner of the nightclub, heading for the front door. Rick called after them, "Appreciate the help."

"No problem," Preacher said as he disappeared.

Rick pulled his pack of Winstons from the breast pocket of his jacket and dug the Zippo out of his jeans. Lighting up, he looked around. "Anyone else want a smoke?"

All five of the men in front of him shook their heads. The big guy in the center grunted a laugh. "Nah, those things are bad for your health. Haven't you heard?" As he spoke, he pulled a set of brass knuckles out of his back pocket and began to fit them on his right hand. The others followed suit, the blond guy putting on gloves with suspiciously thick padding over the knuckles, another unwrapping a motorcycle drive chain from around his waist. The stocky guy just tilted his head to loosen up his shoulders, but a thin guy with a Fu Manchu mustache to Rick's far right started doing a flashy whirl with a butterfly balisong knife. Rick added up his options and decided he was going to get stomped–there wasn't much to do about it. Didn't mean he had to go quietly.

He asked the man playing with the knife, "How long did it take before you stopped cutting your hand with those mutant scissors?" The gods must have been smiling on him because at that moment the knife bit into Fu Manchu's hand and went flying away. One of the other bikers had to duck to avoid it as it flew past his head.

"Shit!" the thin biker exclaimed and sucked a finger as he went to retrieve his knife. The biker who ducked roared, "Will you stop that stupid Bruce Lee crap? You almost stuck me."

The skinny guy started to respond, but the tall guy in the center said, "All of you just shut the hell up."

Turning to Rick, he adjusted the brass rings over his fingers. "We're here to fuck this bastard up. Now, why don't we get down to business?"

As the bikers closed the semi-circle around him, Rick slipped the Zippo into his right fist, and resigned himself to the pain he could see coming. It's not as if it was going to be worse than in the MASH unit in Vietnam or even during rehab in Japan, he thought.

What happened next was almost surreal. The biker to his far left suddenly whirled, stumbling off into the parking lot.

Blondy was stepping toward Rick, fist cocked. Then his fist went down and up behind his back. Rick could hear a snap that almost certainly meant a dislocated shoulder. The blond guy knelt down, cradling his arm.

The leader was a bit more alert than his companions. He half-turned to his right and swung at a figure standing there.

"Rick. Move left, please." The command came in a calm and familiar voice. Rick stepped left and the leader smashed headfirst into the side of the Chevy where he'd been standing. The man was strong; he managed to stay on his feet until Rick gave him a gentle push backward, and he toppled to the pavement.

Rick crossed his arms and relaxed against the car, content to enjoy the show as Corey Gravelin, another of his housemates at the Capitol Hill house, demonstrated his considerable skill at aikido on the remaining Pagans.

The weightlifter spun in a front flip, smashed to the pavement on his back, and lay gasping for breath. The knife fighter advanced, slashing and stabbing. Corey just stood there, slipping the blows with soft, sweeping arm blocks until his opponent lost control of the knife again, and it flew off into the darkness.

For a second, the Pagan hesitated, confused as to how this had gone so quickly from five-to-one to one-to-two.

Corey inspected an invisible speck on the sleeve of his silk shirt and said, "Do you really want to have your ass kicked by a skinny little fag like me?" Rick could see that Corey's smile was turning evil, "Because I will personally make sure that it becomes public knowledge in every clubhouse, biker bar, and Harley dealership in Prince George's County."

The Pagan thought this over for a second, then spun around, and dashed off between the cars. A minute later, Rick could hear the sound of a heavy Harley V-Twin being kicked over to the accompaniment of pleas and curses. After five tries, the engine caught, the big machine pulled out, and rumbled away.

The guy who'd been sent spinning into the parking lot came back, stopped to assess the scene, and put his hand up in a peace sign. "Peace out, dude. I'm just going to help my brothers here get on their rides; we are out of here. Cool?" Corey nodded and the four Pagans staggered off to their bikes. The leader had to be supported by two of his gang, and the rumble of the engines announced their departure as well.

Rick started to shake hands with his friend, but Corey pulled him into a strong embrace. "You know, despite the fact that I have to rescue you at an inordinate rate, it's damn good to see you," Corey said. "Why didn't you let me know you were back in town?"

"Hello. No one knows where you live these days," said Rick.

"And you think that's an excuse?" Corey began to dust off his immaculate trousers. "Are you up in Northwest with Tom Swift and his Electric Housemates?"

"'I think they are my hosts, Tom guessed.'" Rick joked.

Corey groaned, then asked, "What are you doing down here? Got sick of Eve and decided to switch sides?"

"No, Eve is still very much in the picture. I came down here to collect something I left with the Dawn Riders." Rick motioned with his chin to the clubhouse. "Not that they're much use."

Corey laughed. "Yeah, they are one of the wussier gangs, but they look impressive; and, a lot of the time, it's better to look like you can fight than actually fight. Anyway, Preach told me you were 'playing with some Pagans' when he came in for a drink just now."

"Don't tell me that," Rick protested. "I really don't think I could bear to thank him. It's just too much to ask."

They began to walk toward the awning that marked the front door of the club. "How is it going with the President's personal bank account?" Rick asked.

"Much better than I thought," Corey answered. "The pressure on Nixon is building; we're concentrating on the Republicans now, and Dina's idea about using the documents as protection was a good one. The White House had its fingers burned badly the last time they went after one of us "lads" on the Hill. Anyway, with what we've got on Wilbur Mills and Wayne Hays, the House leadership isn't about to make a lot of noise about anyone's sexual peccadilloes."

"Wait a second." Rick put a hand on his friend's arm. "Let me ask you about something before we go into the Land of Hearing Loss. What can you tell me about some guy named Stephen Cloyes? He runs a strange outfit called The Children's Crusade."

"Outfit? That's a full-out cult." Corey shook his head. "We've been watching Cloyes for several years, but he keeps switching sides—he was a communist, then an anti-drug crusader, and now he's trying to present himself as a devotedly conservative mainstream religious figure. Maybe the

Congressmen and Senators believe him–who knows–but whatever he believes at any particular moment, all of those kids selling candles and begging for spare change are supplying a lot of money, enough to have friends all over the Hill.

"With all those 'friends,' Cloyes is almost bulletproof even though . . .." Corey broke off and shook his head in disgust. "I don't know why everyone always puts gays in the same category as the gutless bastards who go after young kids."

Rick felt a chill go down his back. "What's that got to do with Cloyes?"

"You mean Wilton Calderson, formerly of Crockett's Bluff, Arkansas?" He grinned at Rick's puzzled look. "Yeah, that's who the holy Mr. Cloyes was before he arrived in DC"

He paused and his voice lost all humor. "I don't know anything for certain: no one will investigate, and all his people are too brainwashed to talk; but there have been stories for the past several years...stories about kids being separated from their parents and..."

He coughed and continued, "Well, there's been nothing firm, but I don't like the guy."

"You've met him?"

"Yeah, he came up to meetings on the Hill a couple of times. Some of the Congressmen are even dumber than they look, and he's a fast talker with a lot of money. He has a nasty bastard for a deputy that keeps hanging around the Energy Committee. Can't remember his name but he's about as cuddly as an SS Sturmfuhrer." He looked up at Rick, "Why?

You're not thinking of becoming one of the Saved? I hate to break it to you but I don't think they'll let you in. I mean, you hang out with gay people. You're doomed."

"Ha, Ha!" Rick shrugged. "No, the Crusaders just keep popping up here and back in Montana."

"Well, I'd recommend staying away from them. You've heard of Synanon out in California–started out getting people off drugs and proceeded to turn them into zombies? Well, these guys are just as bad–they just haven't had a movie made about them."

Corey put his arm around Rick's shoulders as they walked into the club. "Of course, you've never taken my advice before. Why start now? Let's find Preach and get your psychological crutch back."

CHAPTER 29

May 24, 1973, West Virginia

At 6:00 a.m., Rick could see the sun lighting up the clouds in his rear view mirrors.

He knew he was somewhere in West Virginia but not much more than that. Most of the night had been spent relearning how the Kawasaki handled.

It handled like a rocket–all raw power and a tendency to go its own way.

Coming off the light on River Road in Gaithersburg, he'd decided to see what would happen if he really cranked it off the line, expecting a dramatic tire burnout. Picking himself up from the road 15 feet past the light, he walked to the green bike with new respect. You had to respect a machine that would lift the front wheel up and over your head at three-quarter throttle.

Respect it or hate the bastard.

Later, when he'd achieved, if not mastery, at least a grudging partnership with the little beast, he dropped it down to third gear while he was going 90 on I-270, and–standing on the pegs–the insane torque of the three-cylinder engine pulled him up until he balanced on the rear wheel.

Last year, he'd only ridden the bike once. On that crazed ride, all his attention was on the two men pursuing him. Now, the strange gearshift with neutral below first instead of between first and second like every other bike, the "rhumba" that it made on turns, and the fact that it was built to go faster than it was built to control, all were things he noted and mastered.

Filling the tank in the only gas station open in New Market, he could see where someone had painted the original white tank the neon green of the Kawasaki factory race team. He could understand the desire to bond with Team Kawasaki– their riders were tearing up the tracks–when they finished a race.

Turning to face the sun, he headed back to DC, choosing the rural four-lane of Route 211 over I-81. Interstates just weren't fun, no matter how quickly they got you places. Anyway, school was out, he'd learned the way this bike behaved, and it was time to give it a real workout.

A Corvette fell in behind him as he came up the sharp curves of the small ridge before the Shenandoah River. Rick was glad to see that it was the 1970 model, made before they'd gutted it with emissions controls.

They tested each other out on the curves, taking turns in the left lane, and then the big-block Chevy opened it up on the long straights leading up to the mountains. Rick thought the driver looked a bit surprised as the Kawasaki blasted past him and pulled out to a commanding lead.

Before the tight curves of the climb to the Skyline Drive, Rick backed off the throttle and let the car catch up. He wasn't interested in winning–the point was to dance, and, like any type of dancing, it was much more fun with a partner.

The sound of the car's motor suddenly doubled in volume, and Rick smiled as he looked back to see flames shooting out both sides of the low-slung sportster. The driver had just flipped the lever on an illegal exhaust cutout.

Definitely worth waiting for.

They were both running close to their limits as they pushed through the switchbacks. Rick was almost touching his inside knee to the asphalt on the turns, and he could hear the wheels of the Corvette right behind him as the driver fought to find the perfect balance between speed and traction.

After three tight turns, the Corvette slid into the groove and held it through a hairpin turn. Rick fell in behind and rode the draft while he looked for the right moment.

It came on a sweeping right around an arm of the mountain–a 200-foot drop on the outside. Rick pushed the Kawasaki down into third gear and feathered the throttle to keep it from lifting the front wheel. Pulling out to the left, he lowered his head almost to the tank to cheat the wind, and pulled past.

It felt like slow motion. He stayed locked into what he knew was the best position at precisely the top possible speed and gained on the car by inches. Coming out, the road swooped immediately into a left; instantly, Rick was on the inside line and pulling away.

It was a moment of pure speed and balance. A crystalline clarity of mind he so desperately needed.

He knew that if they were on the road, the state troopers would be waiting at the summit. He slowed the bike, sat up, and turned in the seat, giving a thumbs-up to the driver. He waved and Rick could see the wide grin that split his face–he knew there were no losers–it hadn't been a race. The big car's engine suddenly sounded stifled as the exhaust was redirected through the mufflers.

At the top of the ridge, Rick pulled off and parked the bike. The sun was full, and he could see the trees give way to fields and roads and parking lots. The white spire of the Washington Monument was a tiny point on the horizon.

He lit a cigarette with the snap of the Zippo and sat back and relaxed, shaking the vibrations out of his arms and hands. It had been a great run. He managed to smoke two cigarettes before the memories of head-high elephant grass, blood-soaked mud, and the incessant, terrifying buzz-zip of incoming rounds returned.

CHAPTER 30

June 4, 1973, Raven's Roost, Virginia

Two steps and a hundred-foot drop.

Rick tried not to think about what was beneath him and to concentrate on what was in front of him. The Shenandoah Valley stretched away under a perfect blue sky. The fields were all shades of bright green, the tree lots and forest a uniform darker green, and the river a wriggle of blue at the bottom of the mountains.

The breeze picked up just a bit, and the blue hang glider on his back lifted slightly. He looked up and, once again, went through the pre-flight check: kingpost, control bar, harness, tension wire left, tension wire right.

It all looked good.

Time to review the flight plan. In the middle distance was the landing zone: a dirt road that showed its orange dust just past the river and what looked like a postage-stamp-sized green meadow.

Of course, it was over two miles away, but it still looked damned small.

He ran through the lessons learned in last weekend's trial runs on the gentle slope of a cow pasture west of Frederick. Rogallo wing hang gliders were still so new that there weren't many skilled pilots around to give lessons. He'd spent the day with Eps and Steve, the three of them taking turns reading from the spiral-bound book of instructions and shouting guidance and encouragement to whoever was flying. The fact that each participant's idea of the proper guidance tended to be different added to the fun.

The flight where Rick finally got it, he ended up making an almost perfect landing on an exceptionally startled cow. Luckily, the cow went left; Rick went right and safely skidded to a stop in a fresh cow patty.

They'd discussed whether to continue on the small slopes, but they could already tell that the only pilots who truly flew were those who jumped off a damn mountain. There wasn't a learning curve–it was cow pasture or goddamn cliff, your choice.

This led to today's flight. Two miles out, a thousand feet down. They were flying off the western side of the Blue Ridge where you could catch the lift from the constant westerly breezes as they flowed over the mountains.

That was the theory.

Doing this for real was frightening. Rick reminded himself that the trick was to set a series of three actions: the first two were easy, and the third just happened.

That's how a firing squad worked, after all.

He took a deep breath, pulled the kite up to a level position, feeling the lift of the wing like an umbrella in a storm, and took two steps forward.

It was just as terrifying as expected. Even as he realized he was falling to his death in possibly the stupidest mistake of a life filled with dumbass mistakes, he remembered the steps he'd tried to hammer into his brain all week.

Pull in on the bar and dive.

That was tough because while his rational mind knew he needed air speed to keep the wing filled and avoid a stall, every muscle in his arms wanted to hit the brakes, slow down, stop rushing toward those trees.

Stalls were bad, he thought, because a low airspeed stall was the difference between flying free under a beautiful blue wing and falling with a useless mess of lightweight nylon, aluminum tubes, and guy-wires on his back. Try to avoid that.

So he kept the bar tucked into his torso, watched the trees rush toward him, and counted to three. Then, he slowly pushed out on the control bar, felt the wing rotate around his center of gravity, and then the blessed lift as the wing filled with air.

It was pure joy.

He swooped through a heart-stopping change

from the vertical to the horizontal and had to remember to pull the bar back just a bit so he wouldn't lose that precious airspeed.

Damn! He was flying.

The wind seemed to fill his brain; he could hear the whoosh through the posts and guy wires, feel it create the firm support of the wing above him. His eyes were open, but he couldn't see.

Pilot blindness.

OK, he'd read about this. The world around you was suddenly all new, intense sights, sounds, and sensations flooding in; your brain simply couldn't process it all, and sight went first. He worked to stay calm, to listen to the wind, feel the lift, and, suddenly, he was hundreds of feet above the ground with the beautiful greens of the river valley laid out before him.

The little piece of ribbon at the sharp tip of the front was steady and swinging a bit to the left. He moved the bar a bit to the right and felt the wing immediately soar to the left–closer to the wind.

He looked back, trying to spot Eps' rusted-out Impala SS that they'd used to bring the kite up. He was already hundreds of yards from the Skyline Drive where he'd launched, but he'd regained most of the altitude he'd lost in the takeoff, and the worn, soft-edged slopes of the Blue Ridge were falling away beneath him.

Then the wing reacted violently to the twisting of his body, and he jerked his head to the front and tried to spot the landing field. It all looked so different from when he had his feet on solid ground, but he found the blue of the Shenandoah, then the dirt road, and finally the small pasture where he was supposed to land.

As he got accustomed to the sensations, he began to take long, smooth turns. Moving the bar sideways and in toward his stomach put the kite into the turn without losing speed. He could feel the pull and swing of the turns all through his body.

It was a feeling of pure flight—easy to forget the wing as the balance of body, harness and lift surface all mingled into a single sensation. Changing direction or speed was frightening, but in a way that was very much like the swoop and lift of a bike; the proper word was "exhilarating," he decided.

With a start, he realized that the river was amazingly close. He needed to lose altitude and line up for landing. He was a bit too high so he made a wide 360-degree circle to the right, the world sweeping past him until he straightened out.

OK, it was more like a 300-degree turn but not bad for a first try, he thought. Another swing of the control bar to the right, and he was lined up on the pasture.

He slowly, carefully pushed out to pivot the wing's front up and lose speed. Suddenly, he heard the chatter of slack nylon from behind him that warned of a stall and yanked the bar back. The kite shuddered, seemed to pause, and then dove out of the stall.

He thought, "I just might live through this, but it's not going to be pretty."

Sweeping over the river, he spotted his ground

crew. Eve, Sage, and Kristee were waving from the edge of the field where they'd parked the bus. Sage was screaming encouragement.

He was about 20 feet up when he came over the fence and then, suddenly, he had to switch gears from staying aloft to getting down. He feathered the tip up until he felt the stall again–on purpose this time–and then tucked it down, dropping quickly to the long grass. He leveled out inches above the ground and pushed the bar all the way forward, using the wing as an airbrake that dumped him hard into a skidding slide on the grass.

He knew that he was supposed to land running, but everything had sped up pretty violently at the end, and he just lay on the grass smelling the richness of spring and relished what he'd done right. It seemed as if all the strength had evaporated from his body. He didn't move, listening to the sound of Sage racing across the damp grass in her pink Wellington boots.

CHAPTER 31

June 3, 1973, Summit Point, West Virginia

With help from Kristee and Eve and distraction disguised as help from Sage, Rick transformed the hang glider into a long bundle, and they carried it on their shoulders to where the bus was parked.

They used bungee cords to secure the bundle to the VW roof. Then Rick pulled a four-foot length of heavy board out of the body of the bus, set it up against the back of the sliding door, and jockeyed the Kawasaki down the ramp. The bike had just fit inside the camper with the front wheel up next to the driver and the back wheel jammed against the sofa/bed.

The plan was that Kristee and Sage would head back in the bus, and Eve and Rick would do a slow cruise, enjoying the quiet roads.

Suddenly, there was a squawk of radio static from the Citizen's Band radio tucked under the dash. Eps and Scotty had decided that channel 22 was the "household channel" so that they wouldn't have to listen to the endless "breaker breaker" of the big rigs on 19.

Eve was closest so she pulled out the microphone, keyed it, and said, "This is Turing. Who's out there? Over."

Steve's voice came out of the bus speakers. For once, his voice was clipped and terse, not exactly excited–Rick would have found that hard to believe–but certainly not his usual calm and measured style. "Turing, this is Babbage. Glad you got your ears on. How's the S-meter? Over."

Eve looked over at the little meter on the radio that measured the power of the incoming radio signal. "Wall to wall and treetop tall, Babbage. We're just packing the bird away and unloading the pocket-rocket. What's up?"

"I've got something sensitive for Bike Boy. Over."

"Bike Boy is right next to me. Go ahead. Over."

"I'm out at the farm and I couldn't help but overhear the neighbors talking–" By this, Steve meant he was working at the NSA's top-secret listening facility at Sugar Grove, West Virginia. The NSA wasn't supposed to eavesdrop on any radio, satellite, or telephone lines inside the United States, so Sugar Grove conveniently belonged to the Navy.

"Which neighbors, Babbage? Over.," Eve said.

"Sadie Crews' family?"

Eve snorted at the clumsy backward code for the Crusaders and then transmitted, "That's a 10-4 on Sadie Crews. Go ahead."

"Well, I overheard that she's coming to visit. It seems that one of their kids spotted your Beetle Box coming over the mountain and called in your '20.' Sadie's looking to pick up her little girl and she's bringing friends." There was a pause. "Turing, did you read that?"

Kristee's face had gone dead white. Eve looked coldly furious, but you couldn't hear it in her voice. "10-4 Babbage. We'll make sure the 'little girl' is ready to go. When should we set the table for guests? Over."

"Turing, it should be real soon. Repeat, real soon. I'd think you'd better stop yakking and start tracking. I'll see you on the flip, Babbage out."

"10-4 Babbage." Eve said. "Keep the shiny side up and the dirty side down. We'll see you back at the barn. Turing out."

Eve tossed the microphone on the passenger seat and turned to Rick. "I'd say this one is up to you, trooper. This bus is extremely nice but a healthy snail could outrun it." Turning to Kristee, she asked, "That OK with you?"

Kristee seemed to be unable to talk, frozen in a mix of fear and rage, but she nodded agreement.

Rick had already pulled two helmets out of the bus and was strapping one carefully on Sage, packing her long hair in to serve as padding.

Then he measured out an arm span of nylon rope from a pile of spare glider gear on the bus's sofa and cut it with his pocketknife. He ran the rope up one sleeve and down the other of his thick leather jacket so about a foot was exposed at each cuff.

His jacket covered the little girl down below her knees, and it would offer her almost complete protection. Rick took one of the bungee cords off the roof and used it to tighten the mass of leather around Sage's slim torso. The two pieces of rope dangled down from the little girl's sleeves like the snap-ended keepers the parents of kindergartners used to attach mittens.

A pair of cheap wraparound sunglasses that Rick had for riding in heavy rain was the final touch, and Sage stood, looking a lot like a strange little brown insect with pink feet. Kristee wrapped her in her arms and squeezed her hard.

Rick put on his own helmet and said to Eve, "I think you guys should just stay here. Leave the bus as bait and hide out in the woods. If we're lucky, they'll eat up time coming all the way down this dirt road, but I don't want you to be around if they get here. If you don't see them, give it an hour and then head home."

"What's your plan?"

"Well, my first plan would be to head straight for home but, like all plans, I expect that will only last until we meet the enemy. After that, I'll ad lib."

Rick swung his leg over the green bike and kicked the engine into life. He motioned for Kristee to lift Sage up behind him. As soon as Sage was settled, Rick took a firm grip on Kristee's arm and said, "I promise that she won't get hurt, and she won't go home with anyone but me. OK?"

Kristee nodded, still unable to speak.

Rick patted with both hands to make sure Sage was seated properly, giving her a small tickle in the process. Then he took the rope ends and tied them loosely with a square knot over his stomach. "OK, Kiddo. This rope will keep you from letting go but I don't want you to trust it. Can you grab your hands together? Great. Now I want you to tuck in close to my back, keep your feet right on these pegs, and hold tight. OK?"

He could feel the helmet move as Sage nodded.

"First, you can let go just once to say goodbye to your mom." He waited as the little girl threw an arm around Kristee's neck. "Now, Sage, let's see how hard you can squeeze."

He grunted theatrically as the little arms tightened around him and said in a strained and choked voice, "Yep, that's tight enough. Don't worry about me, I don't need to breathe." He was glad to feel a small giggle against his back.

He started carefully, avoiding any wheel spin on the dusty road. As they bumped across the rocks and into the potholes, he kept the speed down and gently wove back and forth–testing out how the bike handled in the dirt and how well Sage was holding on. He was glad to find that she stuck on like a barnacle, bending into the turns if she'd been riding forever.

He hadn't been riding more than five minutes when the dirt road made a left and disappeared behind a clump of trees, orange dust rising on the other side. "OK, Kiddo. I think we're going to have company."

They were on a long-established farm, and high berms of dirt and brush had built up on both sides of the track; so there was no way to get off the road and hide. A Pontiac Firebird complete with the showy bird emblazoned on the hood came around the turn about 20 yards ahead wallowing on its soft shocks.

As soon as the driver caught sight of them, the car skidded to a stop and swung to the right until it blocked the entire road. Rick slowed and checked both left and right. There was just no room to squeeze through.

He stopped the bike and put his foot down to steady it. The Firebird's doors opened, and two people got out. It was Sage's father, Gary, and Flick Crane. Both were carrying baseball bats. Clearly, shooting at Sage was out of the question.

"You OK, squirt?" he yelled. He heard a muffled sound he took to be a yes and felt a short squeeze. "OK, we're going to do something exciting so you hold on as tight as you can." Once again, he felt her tuck in hard against his back.

Flick had been driving so he was on the right side of the car. Rick kicked into gear, spun the rear wheel, and cranked it down until it was heading the other way. He drove up another 20 yards or so, made another skidding turn, and headed for the Pontiac.

Dust totally obscured the road, but Rick's eidetic memory told him exactly where the car was. He kicked up into second gear and let the bike go. He curved to the left until he could feel the edges of the road and then went right.

They exploded out of the dust cloud only yards from the car, moving fast, and heading on a diagonal right toward the left rear of the car where Gary was standing. Rick could hear Flick yelling, but he was irrelevant, blocked by the bulk of the car. Gary stood for a second and then dove behind the rear bumper.

Rick was completely focused on the high dirt bank behind the Pontiac. His front wheel hit the slope about ten feet before the car, and he accelerated. The Kawasaki's brutal power kicked in and the bike went up the bank and toward the car at about a 45-degree angle.

As soon as he knew the bike was holding on the rain-hardened dirt, Rick began to wrench the handlebars to the left with all the considerable power of his upper body. The bike went right to compensate and tilted–running for a split second perfectly horizontal about four feet up the berm like the daredevil riders in a carnival Ball of Death– only their speed kept them pinned to the bank.

As soon as they'd passed the car and the astonished face of Sage's father, Rick goosed the throttle to bring the front wheel off the ground and threw his weight to the outside. He was already forcing the bike back to the vertical when the Kawasaki's rear springs compressed and then threw them into the air, right above the road.

In the air, Rick used his weight to rotate the bike upright and pulled the front end up at the same time. They were still slightly off center when the rear wheel hit the road, but another burst of power shot the bike airborne again, and when they hit the second time, Rick had the bike under control, and they were past the car and already moving at high speed.

"Hey Sage!" he yelled. "Was that fun or what?"

He could just make out her voice screaming, "Do it again!"

Rick laughed. "Maybe some other day, squirt. Right now, I say we just take it easy and get out of here. OK?"

Another squeeze.

CHAPTER 32

June 3, 1973, Summit Point, West Virginia

A green Ford Falcon was parked on the verge where the dirt road met the pavement, but the driver wasn't anywhere in sight. Rick paused just long enough to scan to the left for oncoming cars and head right. The rear wheel spun in the dust momentarily, and then he was back on the asphalt and began pulling steadily up through the gears, keeping the power within sensible limits.

Out of the corner of his eye, Rick saw a middle-aged man trying to zip up his fly as he ran from the woods to the parked car. The narrow two-lane swooped left in less than a quarter mile, and they were out of sight.

It was a great day for dancing. The sky was clear

and, for once, humidity was low. Even though Rick was riding without a jacket, the cool air felt good. The road was a narrow, rural two lane, but the asphalt was new and smooth.

"How are you doing?" he shouted.

He could feel Sage's head come around his right side so she could look straight ahead. "This is so cool!"

Rick grinned. "Yeah, I think so, too. Now you just keep your hands together, and we're going to make some time."

His optimism was premature. The turns became increasingly tight, and the joints where concrete bridges and asphalt road surfaces met turned out to be so badly maintained that they could launch them into the air if he wasn't careful.

As a result, he had to keep his speed down to a very rural thirty miles per hour, and before long, he spotted the green Ford in his rear mirrors.

Well, what he couldn't do with sheer speed–at least right now–he could do with superior cornering. As the road skirted the right-angle edges of fields, he concentrated on hitting the apex of each corner precisely to cut time without gaining speed.

Sage was riding like a pro, clinging tight, and moving right with him as he dropped his weight into the turns and swooped up coming out.

After he scraped the pegs a bit on one particularly tight left-hander, he felt her small body shaking against his back. He worried for a moment and then heard a whisper of sound and realized she was laughing.

There was a red light where he needed to turn to get on Virginia Route 340, but he cut through an abandoned gas station instead. All that was left of the station was the front wall–everything behind it was gone.

340 was what amounted to a main road out here–two and sometimes four lanes of solid asphalt–the curves shaved down and the dips filled in. He brought the speed up, testing to see where the balance point was between speed and safety. He wasn't going to take any chances of dropping the bike with Sage tied on.

The powerful three-cylinder engine was running smoothly in top gear, and the speedometer was bumping against the eighty mile per hour mark as he came into the outskirts of Elkton and the first road across the mountains and back to Washington. He knew that he couldn't keep up any speed–340 was the Main Street of the little town, and, even though the old farming community had suffered the economic death that had struck most rural centers, there were still traffic lights, parking, and police.

"Well, if you can't go fast, get creative," he thought. He watched for the first 25-mile-per-hour sign, usually where a speed trap was hidden. When he saw one about a mile ahead, he cranked the Kawasaki to its top speed and then, right at the town line, he dropped all the way down to second gear and used the front brake to keep them to a sedate 30 miles per hour. They had gained at least a quarter-mile on their pursuer.

He could see the signs ahead indicating that he

needed to turn right to stay on Route 340. Instead, he turned into an alleyway between a battered wood frame house and a feed store. There was a big crape myrtle in the closest corner of the worn and faded front yard. He took a chance and stopped cold right behind its massive pink and red blossoms.

Sure enough, the Ford blew right past, the driver probably angry that he'd lost ground and looking for them up ahead. When he'd passed, Rick drove slowly down the gravel alley for the next four blocks, cruising slowly up to each sidewalk, bending forward to look both ways for the green Ford, and then cutting across the street fast, and going up the alley again.

When the alley ended in a "T" intersection, he stopped again and just relaxed. Twisting around, he tipped up the big helmet, so he could see Sage's face. He couldn't see her eyes behind the bug-like sunglasses, but her smile was wide and genuine. "That was fun," she said. "Are we done?"

"Nope, we've got a fairly long way to go." Rick laughed, "Don't worry, you'll be sick of riding on a motorcycle before we're done."

"No way!"

"You know, that's how I feel about bikes, but most people don't agree." He said, "You sure I'm not going too fast?"

"Faster!" was the enthusiastic response.

"OK," he said as they pulled slowly out from their hiding place behind a garage and turned left. "We'll see how fast we can go."

He was hoping that they could take Route 33

over Swift Run gap, but, when he reached the point where 340 and 33 split, he spotted a car on the right side. Two men were sitting in it, and he could see their reaction when they spotted his bike.

"Do they have all the ways across the mountains blocked?" he wondered as he headed north on 340 again. In his mirrors, he could see the car–some sort of boring, gray sedan–pull in behind him. They were still in the town of Elkton, so he obeyed the speed limits. He knew that on a beautiful Sunday like this a lot of city folks would be out for a drive, and the local police would be looking to boost the town budget.

Right then, a reflection shot sunlight into his eye. It had come from a dip in the road about a half-mile ahead.

"Has to be a cop," he thought.

He shouted back to Sage, "Hold on, we're going to play Roadrunner and the Coyote."

He could feel her giggle as her arms tightened around him.

He accelerated, daring the car behind him to keep up. He smiled as they took the bait and he saw the sedan grow in his mirrors.

Right before the dip, he stood on the brakes and swerved off the road. Then, tires smoking, the sedan shot past–fighting to slow down.

Yes!

He never thought that the sound of a siren could be so sweet, or the swirling red of police flashers could look so good.

He waited an extra minute or two to make sure

the policeman would be out of his cruiser and too busy to notice how small his passenger was. Then he motored past and managed to resist waving at the two tough-looking guys as they sat waiting for the officer to stroll up to the driver's window.

Once they were out of sight, he picked up speed again, using both lanes to make faster turns. Sage had her head sideways and seemed to be watching the beautiful mountain scenery roll by.

Most of Rick's attention was on his driving, but he started to run through his options on the straightaways.

Clearly, Cloyes was dead serious about getting Sage back. If one of the gaps through the mountains was blocked, Rick assumed they all were, and there would be cars waiting in Front Royal where the Blue Ridge fell away to open farmland.

The good thing about these rural two-lanes was that there were more options for escape, but his pursuers were undoubtedly slamming up Interstate 81 on the other side of the ridge. Even with state police patrols, they could easily be waiting for them on Interstate 66, the fastest route back to DC

Heading home just wasn't going to work.

Then, he spotted the race-prepped silhouette of Flick and Gary's Firebird far behind them and realized they just couldn't continue running either. Eventually, the big-bore engine in the Firebird would overtake them.

Wait a minute, he thought. Racing. Now that's something I hadn't thought of.

Just as in Bruce Brown's classic movie, On Any

Sunday, the couriers, who lived their weekdays weaving their bikes through DC traffic, spent a fair number of their weekends throwing the same bikes around a racetrack. This Sunday, the barely-organized insanity of the West-Coast East-Coast Road Racers Association was holding its season opener at Summit Point Raceway, tucked away on a back road before the Charlestown Racetrack and the historic reenactments in Harper's Ferry.

Working the speed and distance equations in his head, Rick realized it would be close.

Very, very, close.

He reached down and patted the little girl's hands where they were locked together over his stomach and thought, "No way in hell are you going back there, Kiddo."

The big helmet turned against his back as Sage looked up at him and she yelled, "This is totally cool!"

Yeah, they're going to take her over my cold dead body.

He turned left and headed up the winding twists of Route 211 through Brandywine State Park. Even without taking the extreme lines he had on his earlier solo runs, the bike had the advantage over the heavy muscle car on a road like this. When a combination of trees and curves allowed him to spot their pursuers, he could tell they were dropping behind.

Soon, a flurry of historic markers signaled they were nearing New Market, and he took Route 11 North to avoid the little market town and the bottleneck that would force him onto Interstate 81. With a bit of frustration, he kept his speed down until they passed the 50-miles-per-hour sign at the edge of town. The road was straight and flat from here to the West Virginia state line, so he let the Kawasaki run. He could feel Sage's arms tighten, and he began to slow down. Then he heard a scream of sheer joy over the wind's howl, smiled, and nailed back the throttle.

There weren't many cars on the road—most people just took the Interstate—and he swept past the ones that were, taking full advantage of the bike's ability to squeeze through on the centerline while the Firebird had to wait for a clear space to pass. It became a pattern, the car closing in and then falling back behind some tourist or, best yet, a tractor crawling along pulling a trailer piled high and wide with bales of hay.

The town of Winchester came up, and he blew through without slowing down. He was concerned about Sage's safety, but he knew how thin his margin would be and decided to depend on his reflexes. It was his day: they caught all the lights on the green, and the police must have been somewhere else.

The Kawasaki began to falter as they turned onto Old Charlestown Pike. Rick reached down and twisted the gas cock into the "Reserve" position. That meant he had about a gallon left, 40 miles if he was taking it easy, a lot less the way he was riding now. He worked out a rough estimate and relaxed—they should make the entrance to Summit Point with a couple of ounces to spare.

Still, he tried to take it easy on the long wide turns of the Pike, accelerating gently and staying off the brakes as much as possible. Behind him, he could see the Firebird steadily getting larger. He forgot about the scenery, the road, even Sage as he focused on the pure mental exercise of balancing speed, distance, and fuel.

The faded overhead sign that marked the entrance to Summit Point appeared on his right just as he surged over a small rise and started to fall into a left-hand turn, the Firebird only yards behind. Using both brakes hard, he burned off speed and whipped through the gate. Flick, in the heavier car, missed the gate and slammed on the brakes, throwing up a billow of blue smoke.

Rick shouted, "I'll be right back!" as he flashed by the old man sitting by the side of the gate, and then he was on the rutted dirt road that led to the paddock area where the racers rested and repaired their machines. To his right, a flock of a dozen riders swept past on the main racetrack, dicing for the lead in every combination of mismatched, ripped, and filthy leathers.

Looking back, he saw that the gate attendant had stood up just in time to block the Firebird. It would only be a momentary pause: in a minute, they would either pay him the fee or simply run him over.

The paddock road made a hard right turn ahead and rose to a single-lane wooden bridge that carried fans over the racetrack. Rick knew that this was the only way into the paddock area–high fences and suicidal racers were an efficient deterrent in every other direction.

In the center of the bridge, he stopped the bike and frantically untied the rope around his waist. "Sage, jump off, run as fast as you can to those woods, and hide," he said.

As soon as she hopped off, he pulled the bike around so it was blocking the way, got off, opened the gas cap, and kicked the machine over on its side. The fuel tank was so empty that he had to grab the center stand, grimacing as his arms brushed the hot exhaust pipes, and dead lift the machine until it was upside-down–balanced on the handlebars and the saddle. Finally, fuel spurted onto the wood and tar surface of the bridge.

Stepping back, he pulled out the Zippo, lit it, and tossed it into the puddle of gasoline. A satisfying billow of flame rose up followed quickly by thick black smoke as the motorcycle's road-heated tires caught.

Turning, he ran down toward the camping area. Sage ran up to him when he reached the trees, and he caught her in his arms without a pause. The scrubby woods blocked any sight of the bridge and, in just a few more yards, stopped in front of a sea of tents, tarpaulins, and RVs. Everywhere bikers were getting ready to race, repairing their bikes after a race, or wandering around talking about a race. The smoke from a dozen barbecues drifted up, mixing with the blue smoke of hot Castrol coming off the racetrack.

He swept his eyes across the scene, looking for the two ABN couriers he knew would be here. He spotted Kyle Sims' red hair first and then the stockier body of Sam Watkins. Both were just yards away, concentrating on an engine. Running toward them, he shouted, "Hey guys. I need help!"

Both men stood and turned to look at him with clear disbelief. Sam said, "What are you doing here?"

Putting Sage down, he slapped her helmet and said, "Sage. Hide somewhere. Under an RV or something. Now go!"

He pointed after her as she scrambled away, the big helmet wobbling, and the jacket flapping. "Listen, there are some assholes coming right behind me who want to take that kid and . . ."

How did you explain what he feared?

Might as well try honesty, he decided. "Listen, these are guys who like to fuck little kids, OK?"

The faces of his friends went from amusement to shock and anger and others turned toward Rick from the nearby tents. He raised his voice even more. "Listen. There are some real assholes about to come in here and grab that little girl. I need some guys to block them at the bridge." Bikers and fans across the paddock began to pick up heavy wrenches or tree branches, and several grabbed weapons from their vehicles. In seconds, dozens of people were heading for the bridge.

As Rick turned and started back, he yelled over his shoulder, "Oh, and I set the bridge on fire; so, if you ever want to get out of here, you might want to help me put it out."

CHAPTER 33

June 4, 1973, Ingomar Street NW, Washington DC

"You do realize this is two motorcycles you've destroyed in less than a year?"

Eve gave Rick a moderately believable scowl and returned to sipping her tea. They were sitting at the kitchen table on Ingomar Street, alone after an hour of explanation and celebration with Kristee and the other housemates.

"Yeah, well, I really never liked that little green monster." Rick was squeezing his pink ball and stretching out back muscles stiffened by riding. "It was fast as hell but, man, it was a bitch to drive. I had to spend about half my time just keeping it from heading off into a ditch or landing on top of me and pretending it was a hat."

"Are you saying that you would have set fire to it anyway?" Eve's eyes gave the lie to her scowl.

"Someday, probably. It was only a matter of time before the damn thing made a serious attempt on my life."

"You said your bikes always developed a personality." Eve reminded him, "Was it a girl or a guy?"

Rick looked at her suspiciously. There were lots of wrong answers to this question. "Well, she did do a pretty thorough job on those Saigon street cowboys and then tried several times to turn me into road kill. How about 'Lizzie Borden'?"

Eve immediately quoted, "Lizzie Borden took an ax and gave her mother forty whacks."

Rick chimed in with the second verse, "And when she saw what she had done, she gave her father forty-one." He stretched out his legs, put the pink ball on the rough wooden table, and began to massage the small of his back with both hands. "Yeah, that's a pretty fitting description. I felt I had to be ready to stop her from doing something stupid."

A pause and then Eve said thoughtfully, "At least you're learning. I don't think you even considered saying, 'Just like a woman.'"

Rick gave her his very best innocent look.

Kristee came into the kitchen and said, "Stand up, Rick."

Rick stood up, and Kristee wrapped her arms around him, burying her face in his chest. A bit confused, he shot a questioning look at Eve who just shook her head, warning him not to say anything.

Kristee began to shake, and Rick realized she was crying. Hard. He patted her shoulder.

Finally, Kristee took a long, ragged breath, and stepped back. Then she grabbed Rick by the hair, pulled his head down, and kissed him fiercely on the forehead. "'Thank you' just isn't enough." She let him go and gave him a gentle shove that sent him back into his chair.

"Um. You're welcome," Rick said in honest confusion.

Kristee turned to the stove, giving Eve a squeeze on her shoulder as she passed. Eve reached up and patted her hand affectionately.

As she made herself a cup of instant coffee, the thin woman said, "OK, I've heard it as far as you setting fire to the racetrack, but Sage fell asleep before she could tell me more. How did you get out of there?"

"Well, Flick didn't seem to be nearly as tough when he was facing a couple of dozen bike racers." Rick thought a second. "Although, it could well have been their wives and girlfriends. Hell, I was innocent, and they were sure as hell scaring me."

He shook his head at the memory. "So, after his front windshield and two side windows were smashed and the women started to rock the car, Flick decided to get the hell out of there.

I guess he might have tried to come back when everyone went back to racing but a considerable number of the women starting standing guard at the main gate. You'd be amazed how many people have shotguns in their RV's. Must be part of the vagabond culture."

He pulled another kitchen chair over with the toe of his boot, and Kristee sat down with her coffee. "After that, it was all pretty simple. We got the fire out before the bridge was damaged much, not that such a little fire could have done much to eight-inch railroad ties. Then, Sage and I watched the races until Kyle won his final heat. I mean, Sage went nuts. You should have seen her, screaming and waving as he took his victory lap. I tried to tell her that Kyle wasn't worth all that, but she wasn't about to be convinced."

Rick shrugged. "We gave the Kawasaki a decent burial by pushing it into the trees behind the grandstands on Turn 11 where all the other busted cars and bikes end up and caught a ride home in Sam's van. Someone might have been looking for us but about a hundred people left at the same time, and we were lying on the floor between the seats, so I don't think it's a problem."

Kristee looked up from her cup. "Well, that girl couldn't stop talking about getting a bike and going racing. I will hold you responsible for putting that dream to rest in a couple of years. As for everything else, well, what I've got is yours."

Eve chuckled, "Sure, that's easy. You don't have anything, girl."

"Yeah, well, it's the thought that counts."

Suddenly, Kristee reached forward and pulled the top section of the copy of the Washington Post that sat on the far side of the table. "That son of a bitch.

What's he doing now?" She stabbed her finger at the smiling picture of a slightly chubby man on the front page of the Metro section.

Rick leaned over and read the accompanying headline aloud, "'Leesburg Landowner Stephen Cloyes Reveals Plans for New School.' So that's what he looks like."

Eve grabbed the paper out of his hands and studied the picture intensely, "Wait a minute. This guy was in the building yesterday!'

Kristee asked, "The building?"

"Marsden Angle. The law firm where I work. He came to visit Tommy, the lawyer I work for." She threw the paper down on the table. "Now what in hell would he be doing with Tommy?"

Rick shook his head. "Well, does Tommy do religious cults?"

Eve shook her head. "Not unless you count contributions to Catholic Charities."

"Well, what about the tobacco companies?"

Kristee interrupted. "Stephen doesn't have anything to do with tobacco. Gary told me that his place had been a tobacco farm before he bought it, and he refused to plant a crop even though the subsidy transferred along with the property. Gary said the farm managers were pissed because it was far more profitable than the feed corn they're growing now."

Eve said, "Well, then there's coal. I've had the feeling that Tommy has been keeping me from working on the coal stuff intentionally, but Josie, the other paralegal, says he's leading the team working to implement the 1971 North Central Power Study. That's the wonderful plan by the Interior Department, the Bureau of Indian Affairs, and the coal companies to strip-mine most of the Midwest. I got my hands on a copy, had to read it in the ladies' room, and the basic idea is to dig out the Fort Union Coal Formation–all 1.3 trillion tons of it–and use that to power most of the East Coast."

She sighed. "It's a gold rush, just like when they stole the Black Hills from the Cheyenne, except this time they want to strip the entire reservation down to bedrock. If we ever get it back, it will look like the surface of the moon."

Rick said, "I thought the Tribal Council had voted against the coal leases back in May."

"They did, but the BIA doesn't really have to listen to the Council, and there are a lot of Cheyenne who need the money that working coal would bring in."

"What about those guys outside Wounded Knee? The ones who were shooting at everyone in sight."

Eve snorted. "You mean the strange guys who followed us all the way through the Black Hills?"

"Yeah. And that asshole Flick was working for them." Rick swung around to Kristee. "Hey, did you ever see a strange tattoo or maybe more of a scar when you were around the Crusaders?"

"You mean 'God's Hand'?" Kristee rolled up her sleeve to reveal the blackened scars on her upper arm. "Everyone in the Children's Crusade has one. It's a big ceremony where Stephen cuts the mark into your skin and then rubs in this mixture of ground up pages from the Bible, dirt from Indian holy sites, and his own blood. Puffs up and hurts like hell for weeks and when it heals, it looks like this."

She rolled her sleeve down. "Everyone gets it when they pass the first stage–that's Light Seeker–and become a Knight of the Holy Road. After that, the devout and dangerous become 'Crusaders,' and, at the top, there are the Masters of the Inner Circle. What a load of crap."

She looked disgusted and then shook her head violently, as if trying to banish a memory. "Gary even held me down when it was happening. Said it showed how much he loved me. What a dickhead."

Rick looked at Eve. "Well, I think with the tattoo and the reference to the Inner Circle, that's a confirmation that it was the Children's Crusade who caused that clusterfuck at Wounded Knee."

"Then they must have been the bastards who killed Pete and tried to take us down on the way back to Lame Deer. They've got to be working with Tommy to eliminate opposition to the strip mining."

She turned to Kristee. "Can you see any reason that Stephen would work with the coal companies?"

"Sure," Kristee replied, "Money."

"Money?"

"Yep. I mean the man changes his politics the way you or I change clothes. His religion is a load of crap aimed at getting little girls into his bed. In the end, it's all about the money those poor kids on the street bring in, and he's not paying the mortgage on that estate out in horse country off candle sales."

For several minutes, Rick and Eve just looked at

the thin, tough woman.

"You're not really certain, are you?" Rick joked.

Eve looked for something to throw at him and had to be satisfied with kicking him–hard–under the table. She turned back to Kristee, "Well, it looks like my boss and this religious nutcase are in cahoots."

"Is that a legal term?" Rick asked while quickly moving his legs away from the table, inches from the toe of Eve's loafers. "Why would Tommy hire someone whose brain is filled with worms?"

Rick turned to Kristee. "At the racetrack, I said Cloyes had a thing for little girls, but I will admit a certain amount of that was working the crowd. But you really think it's true?"

Kristee slowly nodded her head and then answered in low, careful tones. "The girls get separated out for 'special religious training,' they start wearing these white robes, and–" She stopped, apparently unable to continue.

Eve scooted her chair a bit closer and took the other woman's hands in hers, waiting until Kristee could speak again.

"The thing is . . ." Another pause. "I didn't . . ." Pause.

Eve spoke in a gentle whisper, "Come on honey."

Kristee took a deep ragged breath. "I think the girls are being raped by the bastards on the High Table. I was pretty sure–" She clenched her teeth and then clearly forced herself to continue. "I was sure it was happening, but I didn't do anything about it. I let Gary and all the other true believers convince me that it wasn't happening. That it couldn't be happening. In the end, I didn't protect the other girls."

She hung her head, and the words came from behind a curtain of hair. "I knew and I didn't do anything. I was just worrying about Sage, and all those little girls who were laughing and running around and being smartasses were turning quiet with holes where their eyes used to be."

Eve stroked the back of her neck and whispered, "Shh. Don't blame yourself. There wasn't anything you could have done."

"That's bullshit!" Kristee jerked away from Eve's hand. "I could have done something. Anything. I could have gone for help. I should have gotten the girls out. I could have . . ."

She had been talking increasingly quickly like an engine when you've missed a gear. Now, it was as if she couldn't get words out fast enough. She was sitting rigid and silent, unable or unwilling to look Rick and Eve in the eyes.

Eve got up, knelt by the other woman's chair and, batting aside Kristee's unconvincing attempts to push her away, wrapped her arms around her, their heads touching. Whatever they were saying was so low that Rick couldn't make it out.

Rick felt hollow. The humor of just moments before was gone along with the feeling of triumph from today's run. He busied his hands with lighting another Winston and picking up the bits of tobacco leaf that fell on the table one by one with a wet fingertip before carefully rolling them off into the ashtray.

After what seemed like a terribly long time, Kristee and Eve stood and walked to the stairs, Eve almost holding up her friend to keep her from collapsing.

Steve and Eps were watching TV in the living room with a running commentary by Scotty who was on the Digi-Comp. Rick was suddenly aware they had been laughing and talking because now there was silence.

The television suddenly seemed loud. Sonny and Cher were teasing a special guest, heavyweight boxer George Foreman. When he asked, "What am I going to do?" they chorused, "Anything you want" to a cascade of canned laughter.

The TV was switched off, and Rick's housemates wandered into the kitchen. Steve sat down at the table while Eps and Scotty rummaged in search of snacks.

"That as bad as it looked?" Steve asked.

"Worse, if anything," said Rick.

Scotty spoke without turning from the sink where he was pouring water from the metal teapot, filling it with fresh cold water, and putting it on the stove. "Sage is a smart kid. She's really getting to be useful with Gidget."

Eps had his head in the refrigerator. "I've been teaching her to play Tactics Two. The other day, she holed up on that island and pulled off a parachute assault that almost had my supply lines blown to hell. You should have heard her; she was dancing around pretending to be a gunfighter, blowing smoke off her finger."

Rick said, "You're a bunch of emotional morons, you know that?"

"Yep."

"Sure am."

Steve said, "I think that's an accurate assessment."

He turned to the other two. "Shall I consider the motion moved and seconded?"

Scotty nodded and Eps stuck an upright thumb out from behind the refrigerator door.

The bearded computer genius turned back to Rick. "OK, Sage and Kristee are officially full-share housemates with all the rights and privileges."

At Rick's questioning look, he explained. "They're part of the family, and we're going to keep them safe."

Scotty turned off the burner under the whistling teapot and said, "I guess I'll teach Sage all the other exits."

Eps closed the refrigerator and sat at the table with what turned out to be cooked bacon wrapped in a paper towel. "I'll put her through the explosives course and show her how to set the mantraps."

"Of course, there are 'other' exits, mantraps, and explosives. Why am I not surprised?" Rick shook his head, finally smiling. "Thanks, guys."

CHAPTER 34

June 6, 1973, Ingomar Street NW, Washington, DC

Two days later, a battered blue Ford Galaxy with a white top that showed every mile of dirt road it had covered in a decade of driving on reservation roads swung into the driveway and blew its horn, two short beeps. Sage and Scotty, who had been waiting in the computer room, opened the garage door, and the old beater pulled in as they closed the door behind it.

The driver was wearing a button-down blue shirt and striped tie but, when he got out of the car, they could see that they were matched with well-worn jeans and cracked and creased cowboy boots. He looked at them and grinned. "You're wondering about the outfit? Well..." He turned and pointed to where his braided hair disappeared into his shirt collar. "The pigs kept stopping me for DWI–that's 'driving while Indian'–so I put on my 'innocent white boy' disguise where they could see it. Amazing how my driving improved."

He led them to the back and popped the trunk, revealing five cardboard boxes filled with a mix of files, computer printouts, and ledgers. "I'm Ted Rousseau, and I brought the records Eve wanted. It's everything we liberated from the BIA that concerned the Northern Cheyenne."

In a demonstration of strength, he pulled two boxes up–one on each shoulder. Scotty struggled to lift the third, Sage ran to open the door to the computer room and then ran back to help Scotty whose box was giving way on one side and threatening to spill its contents all over the garage.

Once the boxes were dumped in a corner of the computer room, the young Indian looked curiously at the PDP-6 on the opposite wall. "What the hell is that?"

"It's a computer," Scotty answered dryly.

"Yeah, but who has a computer in their house?" he asked. "What the hell do you do with it?"

"Look, look. I'll show you." Sage ran to the cathode ray tube and pointed in clear pride. "Right now, we're playing Spacewar. See, these two little rockets are going around this circle. Well, that's the sun, and you have to shoot the other rocket without falling in and burning up in the sun. Eps taught me how to write the program, and now Scotty has been teaching me how to play."

She puffed out her chest, "I've been beating him all afternoon."

Scotty turned a bit so Sage couldn't see his face and gave Rousseau a quick wink. "Yep, she has been clobbering me."

Turning and pointing at the young girl, he said in a stern tone, "But our agreement was that we could play Spacewar until the documents arrived, and then it's card-punching for you."

Sage's face fell briefly and then her smile returned. "Card-punching is OK." She pointed back at the computer tech. "You're going to have to get the RIM drive to work, and my mom said you aren't allowed to use bad words like last time." She stuck out her tongue.

"OK, I can see that you have a serious labor detail going here." Rousseau laughed. "I'm going to get out before she puts me to work, and I'd like to avoid the Feebs." He turned and headed for the car, "I've had hot-and-cold-running FBI agents following me for the past month. They finally got bored and took a day off, so I grabbed this stuff from the cache and ran it over while I had the chance."

With a stuttering growl, the Ford engine came to life, and, as soon as Scotty pulled up the door, the car swung out and backed into the street. Rousseau waved at Scotty, shot a forefinger and thumb pistol at Sage, and drove down the narrow street.

Scotty looked at the front porch and raised his eyebrows. Rick, who was sitting on a rocking chair observing the street, gave him an "OK" sign. Scotty and Sage went back in, closing the garage door and bolting the heavy door to the computer room.

They could hear Rick's boots on the floor above and, in a moment, they heard his knock. Sage ran up the steps to trip the catches that opened the metal-clad door. They gave each other intentionally goofy "black power" fists and then she led him downstairs.

"How's Gidget today?" Rick asked. "I'm still not sure exactly what you're doing."

Scotty started to answer, but Sage interrupted. "It's so cool. We're going to take all these documents and transfer all the information to cards. Well, as soon as Scotty and Eps figure out a system to...trick?"

She looked at Scotty who said, "Track."

"Right. A system to track everything."

"Just the money figures from the contracts," Scotty said.

Sage barely paused in her explanation. "Right. And then we'll punch in the cards, transfer all the..." She paused and then said very slowly and carefully,"...the input data..."

Scotty nodded approval, and she smiled and rushed on, "...onto the tape reels, and then we'll create a...ooh, I can never remember this one."

Scotty prompted, "a multi-dimensional matrix."

"Right, a moldy-dimensional mattress and then we can see where all the money went as easy as pie," she finished triumphantly.

Rick had no idea what either of them was talking about, but he tried to look as if all this were perfectly clear. "Cool. Is there anything I can do to help?"

Scotty shook his head, but Sage said, "No. Steve said you weren't allowed to help after you looped the processor last week."

Scotty turned to the computer's keyboard so Rick couldn't see his face but his shoulders appeared to be shaking. Rick said, "That seems reasonable. I'll be upstairs if you need anything."

Sage ran around him and started up the stairs. "I need a snack before I start punching cards. You can pour the juice."

CHAPTER 35

June 6, 1973, Ingomar Street NW, Washington, DC

"I couldn't tell if he saw me or not."

Eve had just gotten home and was taking off her work clothes. Rick was resting on pillows against the headboard and putting about half his attention to listening to her talk about her day.

No, less than half.

Most of his attention was concentrated on Eve herself.

"He might have missed me," she continued. "I was sitting in back of the deli, eating one of their sandwiches."

"The ones with four inches of pastrami?"

She smiled as she unbuttoned her white linen shirt and carefully put it on a hanger. "Yeah, you liked those, didn't you?"

"Almost worth spending the day reading about toothpaste." Rick responded. "Not quite. But almost."

"Why?" Eve asked. "You aren't interested in finding the meaning of a word?"

"Reading studies of toothpaste advertising for eight hours is more than should be expected of anyone. By six hours, I'd completely forgotten what we were looking for."

She took off her pantyhose, balled them up, and threw them at the bureau with distaste. "God, I hate these things! They make me hot, and they itch!" She threw herself on the bed beside Rick. "You'll see, when women take over, all these instruments of torture will be outlawed."

Rick nodded solemnly. "I couldn't agree more."

"What do you know? You won't even wear a tie." She snuggled closer to him and demanded, "Ooh, scratch my back, please."

Beginning a thorough back scratch at the top of her shoulders, Rick said, "Hey what do you want? I bought a shirt with a collar, didn't I?"

Her voice was muffled by the pillow. "Sure. From the Goodwill store."

"It's the best place to get classic styling." He changed the subject but continued to run his fingernails over her back, "So, did he see you or not?"

"Who?" Eve said dreamily. "Oh. Gary."

"Right."

She turned her head toward him. "I really don't

know. He was yelling at a bunch of kids who were panhandling outside that weird computer place with the painted-over windows when I came out, and I kept my head turned the other way until I was across the street and back inside the Federal Trade Commission."

"But you're sure it was Gary, right?"

"I remember him from college. I never liked him, but he was around Kristee all the time, so I had to spend quite a bit of time with him." She shook her head and ended up face down in the pillow again. "No, it was Gary."

"But you didn't see him after that?"

"I don't think so," Eve said, "I was in the Reading Room for another couple of hours, and, frankly, the torture of reading complaint letters about mail order almost drove everything else right out of my head; but I did watch for him on the way back to the firm or on the bus heading home. Didn't see him."

Rick bent over, lifted the heavy braid, and began to kiss the back of her neck. In between kisses, he mumbled, "It's probably OK. Nothing we can do about it now, anyway."

Eve rolled over and put her arms around him, and all conversation ended.

It wasn't until much later that Rick remembered Kristee's husband.

He was alone, sitting and smoking on the second floor porch in the late summer twilight. He felt relaxed. They'd made love and then napped entwined and cooled by the breeze coming in the open windows.

After that, everyone sat down for an excellent dinner. It had been Kristee's turn, and she'd cooked a massive lasagna with chorizo sausage and seafood.

Sage was playing catch with a bunch of the neighborhood kids in the narrow street. With the parked cars and the thick trees providing shade, Rick wondered at how parts of Washington could feel so much like the suburbs when they were only a few miles from the center of the city.

Rick heard a scream of tires.

He looked over, puzzled that a car was coming fast the wrong way on the one-way street in reverse. It took him a crucial extra second to recognize the Firebird from the rear, and then he was running for the stairs.

He slammed through the front door and down the steep steps to the sidewalk. The Pontiac was already accelerating forward, tires smoking. Kristee was running right behind the bumper, screaming Sage's name and repeating, "Damn you Gary! God damn you, Gary!"

The car sped out of her reach, but Kristee–with Rick close behind–kept running to the end of the block. Then she collapsed, sobbing and cursing. Without a bike, Rick knew he could never catch the muscle car, already vanished around two turns and headed for Wisconsin Avenue.

He felt helpless and clumsy as he stood over the weeping young woman. Eve ran up and knelt next to her friend, squeezing her in a fierce embrace. She looked up at Rick, a question in her eyes.

"Yeah, we're going to get her back," he said. "No fucking doubt about it."

Suddenly, he heard the car's tires braking hard and then the slam of what he knew was a gunshot. He ran up the street and around the corner; but, by the time he turned into Harrison Street, the Firebird's rear lights were turning left onto Wisconsin. Under the yellow streetlights, he could see a body in the street.

As he ran up, he felt relief; it was clearly an adult and not a child.

Not Sage.

Suddenly Rick felt as if one of his nightmares had turned real. Gary was lying in a growing puddle of blood with most of the back of his head gone, replaced by a gaping red gash. Rick could see the horrible white contours of bone and brain, the things inside a person that no one should see.

A scream behind him and Kristee whipped past, slipped in the blood, and continued to scream as she fell next to the body, cradling the head.

"Oh, Gary, Gary. You asshole. Oh, Gary." She screamed in a mixture of anger and terrible grief. "You fucking asshole."

Rick thought, "The guy must have finally remembered he was a father and not just a follower. It could have been Kristee or Sage, but someone had gotten through to the man who had been buried under all the conditioning. He'd tried to stop the kidnap and paid the price."

He reached down and pulled the sobbing woman to her feet. "Leave him. The cops will be here in a minute. We need to think about Sage. Come on."

He felt Eve on Kristee's other side, and they both half-pushed, half-carried the incoherent woman in a stumbling run down the block. When they were turning the corner to Ingomar, he heard the sirens coming up Reno Road.

CHAPTER 36

June 8, 1973, Warrenton, Virginia

Two nights later, Rick sat in a grassy field just outside the town of Warrenton. He had already checked and re-checked all the components of the hang glider now sitting limply at an angle to his rear. All the rods and wires had been spray-painted a matte black with rustproofing primer and the once-red nylon wing had been blackened with a chemical solution that Eps swore wouldn't weaken the fabric or lower the lift-to-weight ratio.

Rick sincerely hoped his roommates had gotten that right. Enough other untried technology was being used tonight.

There was a new moon, but he could just see the starlight reflecting off the varnished wings of Scott's tiny Fly Baby airplane. Fifty feet of nylon rope ran from the back of the single-seat aircraft to a quick-release clip clamped to the balance point of the hang glider's king post above the wing. A string led down from the clip's release lever through the hole that allowed the king post to pierce the hang glider's wing. A hefty lead fishing weight on the end kept it hanging straight and would, hopefully, prevent it from being blown backward too far for Rick to reach it.

The idea was for the Fly Baby with Scotty at the controls to tow the hang glider up and above the Children's Crusade compound. Once there, Rick would pull the release and fly into the compound, land, unhook, and head for the Big House to find and recover Sage. Rick thought that it was less than a perfect plan, but attempting to crash the front gate had been ruled out by a combination of half-inch cable woven into the chain link gate and some impressive firepower in the hands of the guards.

The next night, Rick had tried going over the back fence where Kristee had made her escape only to be forced back as well. As soon as he reached the top of the fence, electric lights blazed along its length activated by a motion sensor, and he had to drop back into the shrubbery and evade a considerable amount of rifle fire from what appeared to be Crusaders perched on hunter stands up in the trees.

Along with a heavyweight flashlight and a roll of duct tape bungeed to the crossbar, Rick had his Zippo in one pocket of his jeans and a short steel rod threaded through heavy washers and securely bolted with self-locking nuts in the other.

There had been a brief discussion of whether he should carry a pistol or even a rifle, but he had nixed the idea on the grounds that either choice was too heavy for the already-stressed flight characteristics of the hang glider. The real reason was that he simply didn't want to kill any more people, but he kept that to himself, safely locked inside with those whose mutilated faces haunted him every night.

As a compromise, Kristee was tucked behind a fallen tree on the small hill that sat just outside the Crusaders' property line to the south. This morning, Mrs. Lewitinsky had listened calmly to her story, given her a long hug, and taken her into the bedroom where Kristee had picked out a hunting rifle from the late Mr. Lewitinsky's collection.

They'd consulted a topographic map of the surrounding area, picked out a location, and then she had taken Kristee out to a field far from any neighbors where they worked together to zero the scope for the approximate distance. When they returned to the house, the older woman had handed Kristee a set of keys for the gates on her property and most of her neighbors', kissed her on the forehead, and promised to leave a light on at the back door.

Steve was working at the NSA listening post in West Virginia and simultaneously monitoring almost all the radio and telephone traffic in Northern Virginia. Irritated and unwilling, Corey Gravelin was sitting in a car just down the street from the local police station. His job was to call in a report of a disturbance at the compound or bail people out, depending on how things went.

Rick had been concerned that, when attacked, the cult would simply grab Sage and disappear, but Eps had assured him that wouldn't happen. When pressed for details, he'd grinned broadly and said, "Once again, you really don't want to know."

Knowing his housemate's penchant for explosives, Rick decided he didn't.

He was startled out of his thoughts when Eve appeared at his side. "Scotty's ready. Are you all set?"

"I'm as ready as possible, considering."

"Good." Eve gave him a passionate kiss, placed her forehead against his, and whispered, "You'd better come out of this alive or I'll come in and kill you myself." She spun and ran off into the darkness.

Rick stood up and lifted the glider into its takeoff position, slightly nose-down to avoid any premature lift. Ahead he could hear the sputter as the 65-horsepower Piper Cub engine came to life. Its rough sound smoothed out quickly as it warmed, and Scotty released the choke.

There was a double flash from the darkness ahead, and Rick reached down, took the flashlight, and signaled back. The tiny plane was never designed for night flights, so it didn't have running lights or an electrical system. Scotty would be flying through the moonless night with only streetlights and a handheld compass for reference. Rick reflected that there wasn't anyone else he'd trust to get him there safely.

Eve, who was the traffic control for their makeshift airport, appeared in front of him; face lit by a flashlight, and gave him the up-down hand thumb signal that meant, "Go? No go?" When he responded with a steady thumbs up, she dashed back into the darkness. Moments later, Rick heard the sound of the airplane engine increase; and, when the sound had built to a throaty growl, he had a second to note the rope straightening in front of him, and then he was running full out across the grass.

Everything was off-kilter. The pull of the rope was all wrong with his weight on the ground instead of suspended from the king post. He had to use the considerable strength in his arms to keep the wing from pitching forward and plowing into the ground.

When he simply couldn't run any faster, he leapt into the air, flopped forward into a prone position, and simultaneously pulled back on the control bar.

Now the pull from the towrope was right on his center of gravity. The wing dipped down until he could feel the tops of the grass blades against his hands and the toes of his boots. It was low, but it was flying.

It might have just been his imagination, but he felt the little airplane in front of him straining for speed. Slowly, painfully slowly, it began to rise.

Suddenly, his wing was buffeting violently. With intense concentration, he forced it into a slight lift. After a couple of minutes that felt like years, the buffeting stopped as he rose above the turbulent air being thrown back by the airplane's propeller. He concentrated on staying in the narrow safe zone between the prop wash below him and going so high that the towrope would begin to catch on the front apex of his kite.

For a time, his mind was entirely focused on maintaining this delicate balance. When he achieved enough control to consider anything but his hands on the control bar, he looked down.

They had gained an amazing, almost frightening, amount of altitude. He could pick out the lights of Virginia highway 334 far below and thought with gratitude that Scotty had nailed their primary navigation beacon. Ahead, the airplane was only a slightly darker bit of sky. The sound of the engine was a steady purr.

Ahead, he saw the spotlights on the orange roof of the roadside Stuckey's that was their final point of reference. Their carefully calculated plan was to make a 30-degree turn to the south directly over the combination candy store and lunch counter and then fly for a steady count of 180 seconds. At this mark, he'd release from the tow cord and bank right and down while Scotty would simultaneously bank to the left and up. Scotty had said "with reasonable luck," they would avoid a mid-air collision.

He counted "one Mississippi, two Mississippi" as they flew away from the highway's lights and into a featureless darkness. Concentrating on keeping the control bar steady with his left hand and the count going at the same time, he reached out with his right hand and–after a few seconds of desperate searching–found the lead weight on the end of the release cord.

He slowly pulled his right hand back to the bar, thinking how all this coordination took patting your head while rubbing your stomach to a whole other level. It might have been a nice thing to practice at least once.

After 180 careful "Mississippis," he pulled gently and then with increasing power on the release cord. Finally, he gave it a hard jerk and felt the snap as the catch released. Without the air speed provided by the towline, he almost instantly went into a low power stall; but he slammed the control bar back against his thighs; and, with a shudder as the rear of the wing almost lost lift, he pulled into a swooping dive that gave him the airspeed to stay aloft.

He could hear Scotty off to his left and wished him luck–he was going to have to land with only Eve's flashlight and three roadside flares to guide him. Then he came up over a hill, and the brightly lit windows of Cloyes' Big House appeared about a mile ahead. It was long after midnight, but the house and the lawns, gardens, and courtyards immediately around it were all visible in pools of white cast by floodlights.

Rick concentrated on picking out a place to land, having to choose between those areas that were too well lit and those where darkness could be hiding trees, rocks, or stone walls. From their study of the available maps, they had decided that somewhere behind the large horse barn was the best of a number of poor choices. There were a number of fences, but it also contained the largest open spaces out of sight of the house.

Squinting to block the light from the house and grounds, Rick worked to pick out the white fences as he descended through the darkness. As he came into the shadow cast by the three-story barn, he could suddenly see a fence running directly across his line of flight. A wrenching turn to the right dumped the air from the wing, and he dropped a couple dozen feet in a sickening lurch.

There wasn't time for conscious thought as he snapped the wing straight and went directly into a dive, pushing out to a landing stall when he was inches off the ground. There was a chorus of startled squeals as he zipped past a group of drowsing horses, causing them to thunder off into the darkness, and then he was bouncing and skidding across the packed earth of the stable yard.

Even before the wing stopped moving, he had snapped the belts that held him and was rolling as far away from the glider as possible. When he stopped, he lay on the ground with his face down in the dirt, listening to the light aluminum and nylon frame bounce and crumple off to his left. When the glider and the frightened horses both settled into silence, he waited, listening intently for a shout of discovery or the patter of approaching footsteps.

The silence settled, and the sound of frogs and crickets returned.

CHAPTER 37

June 8, 1973, Leesburg, Virginia

A school bus.

Rick wondered, "What is a school bus doing back here?"

He was prone at the corner of a garage and looking around it to the brightly lit asphalt of the parking area behind the house. An old school bus–muddy brown paint peeling off to reveal the original bright yellow color underneath–was parked next to the back door with the engine idling.

He couldn't see anyone, but that didn't mean there weren't watchers. Most of the windows that lined the three stories of the Big House were dark, and the bright lights of the courtyard meant they were effectively one-way mirrors. Garages, horse stables, other small outbuildings lined two sides of the yard, leaving only the north end to his left open to the darkness of the Virginia night. The bus meant that at least one person was awake, almost certainly more.

Rick squirmed back a few feet on his stomach before rising to his feet in the deep shadow. He had the big D-cell flashlight in his right hand, but he kept the light off as he picked his way slowly around the south side, moving from shadow to shadow and stopping often to listen. He could hear voices from inside the house, but they were too low to tell if they were male or female, child or adult.

A concrete and brick porch followed the sides of the house except the back. Rocking chairs, ceiling fans, and hanging flowers gave it a comfortable feeling that Rick found disturbingly at odds with everything Kristee had told him about what went on there. He avoided the wooden steps where his boots would have made noise, stepping over the railing instead.

As soon as he was on the porch, he turned to the south and blinked the flashlight three times. He knew he wouldn't see anything from Kristee; he could only trust that she now had him in her scope.

The sole window not completely dark along this side of the mansion was toward the front. Glad that the cement floor turned his footsteps into soft scuffs, he moved slowly to the edge of the window and peered inside.

The room was illuminated by overhead lights from what appeared to be the central hall. The spray of light through an archway showed the outsized chairs and side tables of a formal parlor, but there were no lights on and, as far as Rick could see, no inhabitants. He waited for a full count of sixty, looking for anything to change, seeking a watcher in the darkness.

Finally, he moved slowly past two windows and hugged the wall just before the corner of the porch. Slowly kneeling and then prone, he pushed his head along the porch floor. White light spilled from the open front door and fanned onto the neatly trimmed lawn. The voices inside the house were clearer now, the querulous sounds of young girls asking questions being shouted down by the deeper voices of men giving orders. He pulled back, stood up, and turned the corner.

A voice said, "Got you now, motherfucker."

An arm came up and the hand took a firm grip on the back of his neck in a half nelson. There was a multiple snapping sound and a knife swept in from the right and rested on his carotid.

"Not so tough without your flyboy buddy?" It was Flick Crane.

"Why Vernon," Rick said calmly, "this is a pleasant surprise."

"The name is Flick."

"Yeah, whatever." Rick's voice stayed steady as his mind raced. "If my real name was Vernon, I'd change it, too."

The grip on his neck tightened, and Rick could feel the other man's knee moving in to break the stability of his right leg. He was certain he would have to fight; the odds of this dick murdering him were simply too high. He just wanted to learn something first.

"So where is everyone?" he asked. "I thought this place was a 24-hour party."

The knife pressed harder into his neck, and Rick felt a sharp burst of pain. Blood streamed down his neck, but it wasn't the explosive spurts of an arterial bleed. Flick had cut next to the artery, not through. He was clearly planning to enjoy every second of this.

"You won't need to worry about everyone else." The voice in his ear hissed. "But you might as well know that your friends in Lame Deer are going to be dead in just a couple of days. And I'll be fucking that arrogant squaw of yours after I kill your buddies on Ingomar."

"Why'd you kill Gary?" Rick asked. "He seemed like such a loyal Crusader."

"Fuck Gary. I needed him to get the little cunt into the car, but when he heard she was the next in line for Stephen's bed, he started to get crazy. So I wasted his ass just like I'm about to do yours."

The point of the knife moved from Rick's throat to rest just under his right eye. Flick's voice was like a terrible caress. "Right through your eye and into your brain. Bleeding out doesn't fucking hurt much, but a brain shot can leave you screaming on the ground for a long time."

Rick couldn't help it. His neck strained as he tried to pull his head back, involuntarily pulling away from the knife. Was there one more chance to stall, to push for more information, or would that be fatal?

He shrugged.

"It won't matter that much. I'll be dead either way. But do me a favor. Don't let Sage see me, OK?"

He could feel Flick's laugh where the man's chest was pressed against his back. "Damn, I'd not only let her see you, I'd make her cut off your dick and eat it."

"But?"

"But Stephen took her with him." The knifepoint was moving slowly, off the skin and over Rick's eye. The light reflected from the front door slashed into his eye.

Rick had gotten the information he needed, and the time for restraint had passed. Rick swung the big flashlight. Flick jerked, but the heavy light went out and flew forward. Rick was throwing away his only weapon

Rick used the split-second it took for his opponent to work this out to slam both hands up to his head, snaking his fingers under the arm holding the knife. In the next instant, Flick jerked the knife inward with all his strength.

Rick watched as the light on the point came toward his eye. Then he threw all the power built from night after night of workouts into his forearms. For a moment, the knife trembled and hung quivering and then it slowly began to move away from Rick's face.

Flick grunted and released his grip on the back of Rick's neck, reaching forward to lock his left fist around the right. Now he had twice the power behind the knife, and Rick knew that he'd never be able to push it away.

He dropped his right hand and drove his elbow into the other man's side, wrenching his body to put more power behind the blow. Flick stepped back, swiveled, and locked into position to continue the relentless pressure.

For a second, neither man could move. Then, there was a wet pop behind Rick's head, followed a half-second later by the sharp crack of a bullet's sonic wave.

Flick's arms flew away from Rick's face, and the knife spun off into the shadows. Rick spun and tackled Flick, driving his now-limp body back into the darkness in an ungainly waltz before lowering him to the concrete.

Lank hair still covered Flick's head, but the left side was concave, the skull shattered from the eye socket, and his brains sprayed across 10 feet of concrete. It was too dark to see, but Rick could feel that the reaction jet of the bullet's impact had covered his face and left side in blood as well. He pulled a bandanna from his pocket and wiped at his face; he wasn't going to get it all off, but he wanted to be sure he could see.

Even though he knew she couldn't see him in the darkness, Rick raised a hand in thanks to Kristee. As he'd hoped, she taken the shot as soon as he'd turned and Flick was motionless, silhouetted against the light.

Without a pause, Rick moved silently to the back

of the side porch and jumped to the ground. The gunshot was certain to bring other Crusaders to investigate. He could leave them to Kristee. They wouldn't stay on the well-lit porch long.

More important was what Flick had just told him. Stephen Cloyes had gone to the Northern Cheyenne Reservation and taken Sage with him. Since the man had thought Rick was moments from death when he said this, it was probably true.

It raised an entirely new set of problems–how to get to Montana, how to find Sage–but it simplified his immediate situation.

He needed to get out of the compound. Fast.

As he worked his way through the shadows surrounding the rear courtyard, it exploded with activity. Several men came running, brandishing handguns and yelling commands. One ran to the school bus and got into the driver's seat, leaving the door open.

Then, with an armed man in front and one behind, a dozen girls in white nightgowns stumbled out of the back door and into the floodlit courtyard. Rick thought that they looked odd. It wasn't just that they obviously had been awakened and rushed out of the mansion; it seemed they weren't truly paying attention, as if they didn't care what happened to them.

With a shiver he remembered how Kristee had described the girls after they were taken up to the Big House, "...quiet with holes where their eyes used to be."

Rick turned and began running around the

mansion. This time, he stayed away from the building and the lights that were beginning to go on inside the first floor windows. When he thought he was in a position where Kristee could see him against the lights, he stopped and waved one arm above his head in a wide circular motion. If she could see him, she would know to begin her slow and careful walk back to Mrs. Lewitinsky's. If not, she would leave just before dawn. That would work, but it would be better if she were available to help plan their next move as soon as possible.

He continued to move through the darkness, stopping when his feet hit the asphalt of the long, sweeping driveway that led to the front gate. He could make out a large tree next to the road and moved to stand behind it just as the headlights of the school bus flared through the darkness.

Staying close to the trunk, he waited until the bus came past–moving slowly on the dark, curving road– then ran up behind and jumped onto the back. His photographic memory placed his left hand on the handle of the rear door and one foot onto the bumper just to the right. He concentrated on pulling sideways on the handle–not down–to keep from opening the door and bent his leg into a painful crouch to keep his head below the bus windows.

It was only a half-mile to the main gate, but with his muscles strained and cramped by the battle to maintain his perch without revealing himself, it seemed far, far longer. Finally, the bus stopped, and he heard the call and response between the driver and the guards at the gate and heard the rattle and squeal as the chains were removed and the gate swung open.

The driver ground the bus into first gear and began to pick up speed.

A moving light appeared in front of the bus. Rick couldn't see it because it was coming from directly ahead of the bus, but it cast long shadows that whipped away in both directions. With a loud, metallic crash the bus stopped, the tires squealing as it slid in a slight diagonal, bumping up against the brick edge of the gate.

Rick jumped down and moved to the right away from the driver. Looking along the side of the immobile vehicle, he saw a single guard in front of him, rubbing his eyes, and shaking his head. Rick hoped this meant the intense light had momentarily blinded him. He pulled the rod with its heavy washers from his back pocket.

Staying on the grass next to the road, he came up behind the guard, grabbed his right arm with his left hand, and slammed the rod into the elbow. As the man shouted in pain and dropped a pistol from his now-limp arm, Rick moved around the man's left side, grabbed a handful of his long hair, and stepped forward, slamming the guard's face hard into the metal side of the bus. When he released his grip, the man slumped to the ground, moaning softly.

Rick jammed the steel rod under the rubber bottom edge of the folding bus door. He drove it in until the washers caught on the bottom step, lifting and jamming the mechanism. That should hold the girls until the cops arrived, Then, he ran into the darkness, his back tingling as he expected a bullet any second.

When he was far enough away to feel relatively safe, he slowed and moved back toward the road. In the starlight, he could make out the long shape of the Impala SS. He intentionally scuffed his feet slightly as he came up to alert the driver. The passenger side door opened, and Eps said, "Need a lift, sailor?"

Rick slid in and closed the door. "Let's move."

The big convertible slid into the darkness with the lights off. Rick looked back. "What the hell did you hit that bus with?"

"A bazooka."

Rick felt anger surge in his head, "What the fuck were you thinking? There are kids on that bus!"

Eps flicked on the headlights and accelerated. "Be cool, man. You can't buy a real bazooka in this country." He glanced sideways and said, "But you can mail order a really sweet training model that has everything but the explosive payload. I just put about five pounds of steel through the radiator and right into the engine block."

The redhead looked into the rear-view mirror. "Admittedly, an explosion would have been cool but, as you've so succinctly pointed out, I didn't want to hurt anyone. It's all good; finally seeing that rocket go was so cool."

"Finally? You mean you hadn't tested it?"

Eps glanced to the left, and suddenly the acceleration of the big V8 engine pressed Rick back into the cracked leather seat. "Those things are expensive. I fired into one of those 8-foot concrete pillars that hold up I-95. It dug about six inches into solid concrete exactly where I'd aimed it, so I figured the second round would do the job on the cheap steel in one of those GMC engines."

Rick could see the grin of pure pleasure return to his housemate's face. "But that was in the daytime. It was so much cooler at night!"

Rick reflected that his friends' addiction to explosives occasionally came in handy. He settled back into the seat and said, "Where's the CB? I need to reach Corey and get some local cops out here. As a responsible citizen, I definitely think there is a case of mass kidnapping going on. That and some child molestation, endangerment, and weapons charges."

"Open the glove compartment. I put the stereo and the CB in there so a thief would steal the piece of junk in the dash and leave the good equipment alone." Eps pointed forward where red and blue flashes reflected off trees not far away, "As for the cops, I'd say we don't have to worry about them showing up. Put your seatbelt on. We do need to worry about reaching the main road before they get here."

CHAPTER 38

June 9, 1973, Ingomar Street NW, Washington, DC

The morning sun was reaching down Ingomar Street when the housemates finally assembled in what Eps called "a council of war." All of them looked serious and, in Scotty's case, downright glum, but Kristee was almost beyond reason. She sat rigidly on the edge of the sofa, her hands continuously twisting and clenching in the thick material of her jeans.

Eve was sitting next to her with an arm around her shoulders. None of this had any effect on Kristee. Her face, always thin and a bit pinched, now looked like leather stretched over a stone carving.

Rick thought, "If Saint-Gaudens' sculpture in the old Rock Creek Cemetery is known simply as 'Grief,'

Kristee would be 'Terror' or 'Fury.'"

Corey came in the front door, looking as though he'd just had eight hours of sleep and a shower (although Rick knew that was far from the reality), gazed around the room and said, "Well, it looks as though all you meddling idiots made it back alive. Any injuries?"

Rick answered, "Not on our side."

Corey paused, then spoke carefully to Rick. "I would appreciate if you didn't expand on that statement. I'm desperately trying to keep my law license here."

Rick nodded, and Corey continued. "I hung around the Loudoun County Sheriff's office just long enough to confirm that the girls were taken to Social Services, based on the general mayhem at the scene combined with an hysterical phone call about child abuse that, to be honest, I'm rather proud of."

His voice suddenly took on the high, strident tones of an angry, frightened, rural housewife. "You gotta do somethin' about them girls! They're being kidnapped and raped by those bastards. I seen it!"

He coughed to clear his throat after the strain of that last sentence; when he spoke again, his voice was its normal smooth tenor. He nodded to Kristee. "They were still dithering–the authorities hate to break up even the most dysfunctional families. Then, your friend Annette Lewitinsky swept in and didn't allow anyone to have the slightest doubt of the proper course of action from that point on." He shook his head ruefully. "I'd hate to face her in a courtroom."

In a strained whisper, Kristee said, "Sage?"

All humor gone from his voice, the slim attorney said, "Kristee, I'm very, very, sorry but there was no mention of Sage at all. But there was only one fatality, a man named Vernon Crane, so please don't give up hope."

He turned back to the door. "And now, I'm sure that you are going to begin discussing something illegal or dangerous, probably both, so I'm going to go while I still have a chance of making those big salaries on K Street after I leave my, hopefully brief, period of public service."

The screen door slammed.

For a moment, there was silence.

"OK," Scotty began, "Let's gather the available facts and make a plan for further action. First, we voted Kristee and Sage into the house. That means that we will take reasonable–,"

"And unreasonable," Eps interrupted.

"–up to and beyond the point of completely fucking insane action," Steve finished.

Scotty nodded. "Precisely. We will make ALL efforts to get Sage back. The second fact is that from all available evidence–primarily the testimony of the late Crusader Flick–she has been taken to Montana where Stephen Cloyes and his minions–,"

"Thugs," Eps added.

"Brainwashed zombies," Steve finished.

"All of that and more," Scotty agreed. "Where Cloyes and his thuggish and brainwashed minions are apparently planning to engage Eve's people in some as-yet unknown but undoubtedly objectionable action to pressure them into signing the coal leases."

He reached over to the table beside him and picked up an inch-high stack of folded computer printouts. "Luckily, Sage and I got this cooking before she was taken, and the result came up overnight. We brought the lease contracts down to the most basic levels, so we could perform a true comparison and then ran them against other similar projects."

Eve looked up. "How did you get those?"

"Called up the Colstrip City Clarion and told the city editor we were representing Japanese investors," Scotty responded, "all of which is irrelevant. What is important is that the new leases will remove the topsoil from virtually the entire Northern Cheyenne Reservation, build a hundred power plants there, and the tribe will get paid only an average of seventeen cents a ton."

He paused to check a figure in the mass of paper. "In a market where local gravel is bringing in eighteen cents a ton."

Eve's face clouded over with rage. Rick said, "We are not going to allow that to happen. We've gone too far and lost too much to let these bastards win."

He turned to his housemates. "OK. I've only got the VW and, while it's a lovely piece of machinery, it's not fast."

Without a word, Eps shot from his seat, and ran out the front door. At Rick's quizzical look, Steve said, "We've got transportation worked out. You'll see when Eps gets back."

He turned to Scotty. "I can't leave the NSA. I'll do communications over-watch. I think Rick would be the natural choice to take my place at the wheel, and you two can stay on navigation and countermeasures?" The quiet engineer nodded.

Steve looked at Kristee. "Do you have enough cartridges and cleaning supplies for your dad's hunting rifles?"

Kristee maintained her desperate concentration on things no one else could see, but she nodded agreement.

"Great." Steve looked at Eve. "Can you get off work?"

"I think a better question is whether I should take off at all," Eve replied. "We know there's a connection between the Children's Crusade and Marsden Angle in general and between my boss and Stephen Cloyes in particular." She reached over and squeezed Rick's knee. "I would follow you into any battle, and you know that, right?"

Rick nodded.

"Well, I think my place in this battle is here, in the camp of the enemy."

Steve summed up. "So, you and I are going to stay here to monitor the situation, Eps and Scotty will handle transportation and logistics, and Kristee and Rick are the front-line troops. Does that make sense?"

For a moment, everyone was silent, considering other options. Then they all nodded agreement.

A two-tone horn sounded from the street.

When Rick reached the front porch, he saw a

long, rounded motorhome painted deep blue with a 1960s style white stripe. Eps was in the driver's seat, grinning like a fool.

Behind him, Steve chuckled. "He does love that beast, doesn't he?"

"That's cool, but it can't go very fast."

Steve sounded a bit hurt. "Do you seriously still think all we do is sit around dark rooms and play with computers? Dude, you are looking at Gussie, the current record-holder in the Cannonball Baker Sea to Shining Sea Memorial Trophy Dash. The Motorhome Class, of course."

Rick looked at his smiling friend, "The Cannonball what?"

"A completely unsanctioned competition which I trust you realize is decidedly different from an 'illegal' race in which contestants compete to drive from the Red Ball Garage on 37th Street in New York City to the Portofino Inn in Redondo Beach in California in the shortest time. OK, sure, Dan Gurney was fastest in his little Ferrari, but we were the only team with fresh-cooked food and clean sheets for our off-duty naps."

He sounded wistful. "We still hold the class record of 35 hours and change. We would have done better, but Scotty had to pull open the engine hatch and adjust the timing while we were driving. That dropped the average speed down to just under 90 miles per hour."

He slapped Rick on the shoulder. "Our calculations predict a run to Montana in less than 21 hours. You'll be in Lame Deer before the sun comes up tomorrow."

CHAPTER 39

June 10, 1973, On the Road

In fact, the sun was well above the horizon in the motorhome's rear window when they crossed the Tongue River and entered the reservation.

Rick was behind the wheel as he had been for most of the trip. The driver's license that proved he was James Putnam had been put to good use when they'd been pulled over by a local police car in Galesburg, Illinois, and by two Iowa State Patrol cruisers as they slowed to 50 miles per hour going through Davenport.

The rest of the way had been smooth. Terrifying, perhaps, but smooth.

The Travco could go well over ninety miles per hour on its own so long as the road was in good shape. At that speed, a suspension designed for comfort rather than speed meant that every breeze or crack in the pavement would send the rig wallowing, and only constant attention kept it from piling into a ditch.

It was even more frightening when they located a Monfort Foods truck heading back to Greeley, Colorado, and drafted behind him. With bigger engines and a promise from the company that all tickets would be repaid, Monfort drivers nailed the accelerator to the floor, always drove in the passing lane, and had Benzedrine as their co-pilot. Only two or three feet from the brightly painted Monfort Foods sign, Gussie topped one hundred miles per hour several times with the windblast slamming behind the truck so hard that the radio antenna would be bent forward instead of back.

Scotty and Eps had taken turns on the dual CB radios set into the passenger side of the Travco. One of the radios was always scratching out the chitchat of truckers on Channel 19, and the other continuously scanned through the other channels. There was a real radio scanner seeking out internal police bands which had to be reset every hour or so as they passed into a new jurisdiction. Finally, the mobile radiotelephone mounted on the center console would ring from time to time as Steve made coded reports on his intercepts of local telephone and radio traffic.

Eve called when she got home from the law firm. Scotty put her on speaker, and they listened intently. She had managed to slip a harmless mixture of dried

Cephaelis ipecacuanha root and buckthorn into the morning coffee she brought to Suzie, Tommy Franklin's secretary. After half an hour of vomiting and diarrhea, Suzie was helped from the Ladies Room to a cab, white-faced and shaking. Eve said her conscience demanded she send her a truly massive Get Well gift of chocolates and fruit when all this was over.

The result, however, was that Eve ended up at Suzie's desk all afternoon, answering phones and typing letters. Like most of the attorneys, Tommy had a silent receiver installed on his secretary's phone so she could listen in on his calls, take notes, and save him the trouble of having to tell her about it later. He had a switch on his desk phone that would cut off the extra receiver, but Eve had heard Suzie complain enough about long calls to his mistress that she figured he'd forget to use it.

Luckily, Tommy followed his usual practice, and Eve caught a couple of critical phone calls. One was from the Chairman of Excacoal complaining about the Northern Cheyenne breaking their lease agreements. Tommy reassured him that it was "all taken care of."

Later, an operator asked if they would accept a collect call from Nebraska, and Tommy immediately shouted for her to accept it. It was difficult for Eve to understand the caller in Nebraska through the static of the long-distance lines. On the other hand, Tommy's voice was clear, and Eve heard him order the man who she was sure was Cloyes to ensure that the traditional tribal chiefs would be unable to continue in office. Like any lawyer, Tommy was circumspect, but Eve picked out Cloyes referring to it as similar to the infamous Phoenix assassination program in Vietnam.

They both agreed that, without the chiefs, there was enough support for development among the younger men–and particularly those of mixed parentage–that the leases would easily survive the vote.

Eve said there had been more, but she heard Tommy's feet hitting the floor and knew he was standing up. She'd slipped the round earphone back on its hook and was typing diligently when she heard Tommy open the door a moment later. She'd spun around and asked if he needed anything, but he just shook his head and closed the door.

The conversation ended abruptly as red lights sprayed the darkness behind the motor home, and Rick had to switch off the phone, pull over, and give yet another policeman James Putnam's driver's license. Scotty and Eps conferred and declared it was time for countermeasures.

They spotted one of the blue signs with the leaning pine tree that indicated a roadside rest area was ahead, and Rick pulled the motorhome into the curving gravel drive until it was out of sight. After 15 minutes of furious activity, the blue and white Travco was roughly covered with a coat of Pepto-Bismol pink. As they packed the portable air-compressor back into its storage compartment, Rick wondered how they would ever get the paint off.

"Paint?" laughed Eps. "That's real Pepto-Bismol.

You can't beat the 'coating action' and it's guaranteed to wash off in the next rain."

Right behind the driver's seat were a long sofa and a foldout kitchen table. Whoever wasn't on radio watch would be going over everything from Triple A TripTiks to detailed topographical maps, trying to find a way around a police speed trap or a shortcut that would shave a few precious seconds off their time.

All had taken at least one break and slept in one of the beds for a few hours. Eps was usually busy at the small workspace and bench in the rear, mixing various powders and attaching fuses and impact triggers.

Kristee was unable to help with the driving: she simply couldn't concentrate enough on her driving to prevent them from slowing down. Instead, she stripped, cleaned, rebuilt, and checked her father's Winchester model 70 and his pump-action shotgun over and over on the workbench.

When her compulsive preparation finally ended, she sat for hours in one of the rear bucket seats, rigid with tension and staring through the windshield as the road rolled into the headlights.

CHAPTER 40

June 11, 1973, Lame Deer, Montana

They parked the Travco behind a small factory that put new treads on old truck tires just off Cheyenne Avenue, and Rick walked alone to the corner of Sweet Medicine and Cheyenne. As he approached, he saw that Charlie Walksalone was sitting in a battered white plastic chair under a pine tree. He seemed to be asleep, tooled boots crossed well out in front of him, the broad Resistol hat tipped down over his eyes, and his hands clasped over his chest.

He looked up as Rick walked over, eyes sharp and amused in a web of creases. Without a word, he gestured to the chair next to him; Rick sat and pulled out his cigarettes. He offered one to Walksalone, who took it without hesitation, and sparked his

Zippo with the quick up-down motion on his jeans.

"So, you're still doing that little trick?" Walksalone remarked.

"Yeah." Rick looked at the flame and felt a little sheepish about depending on such a silly thing.

"Go ahead," Walksalone said. "It's about the only thing been keeping you alive since that flashy move you pulled on that dirt road. Luck should never be taken for granted."

Rick lit both their cigarettes, and they settled back in the flimsy chairs.

Walksalone took a deep drag and blew several smoke rings. They watched the rings drifting in the still air. "No sir. Luck is a lot like a woman. If you stop appreciating either one, you can expect to find them gone fairly damn quick."

It didn't seem to require an answer. Rick put the lighter back in his jeans, and the two men sat in the shade without speaking for a time.

Eventually, Walksalone finished his smoke, stubbed it out on the sole of his boot, expertly fieldstripped the butt, and put the filter in his shirt pocket. Rick followed suit and said, "That brings back some memories. Were you in the war?"

"The war?" Walksalone seemed to find it funny. "No. At least not this last one. It's just that those filters last for thousands of years, and I find I like this country the way it is, not all junked up with *mâsêhánééstóva.*"

"Huh?"

"Craziness." Walksalone sat up straight and angled his chair slightly to face Rick. "So you've come back, Whirlwind. Have you come to ask the Cheyenne to repay the debt we owe you?"

"Well," Rick paused and regarded the sere landscape for a moment before continuing, "A little girl was taken by a sick bastard who intends to–"

"Infect her soul as well?" interrupted Walksalone. He turned his head away and spat emphatically. "Yes, I've heard about his coming. It might help you to know that the girl is still OK. He's waiting to defile her as a celebration of his success."

"How do you know any of that?"

Walksalone just shrugged. "Is the 'how' important? I could have friends in his camp, or I could have wiretaps on his phone. Let's just say that I'm certain. Do you want the Cheyenne to help you rescue this girl?"

Rick thought for a moment before answering. "No. I think we can find her and get her back. It may sound odd, but my favor would be for the Cheyenne to do something for the Cheyenne."

Walksalone's calm gaze didn't show any surprise. He nodded slowly, waiting for Rick to continue.

"This bastard is bringing his little army of fools and thugs here. I'm afraid that he intends to kill or capture all the 44 traditional chiefs and use them to blackmail the Tribal Council to agree to the coal leases."

"I didn't know that. It could pose a problem." Walksalone kept his gaze on Rick. "But not a problem for you in particular."

"Well, that's the thing." Rick shook his head in mild frustration. "I'm well aware that I'm not

Cheyenne, but I was here for months, and the land...it gets into you."

"Into your soul?"

Rick grimaced. "I'm not quite sure about souls and all that but it got into my head. And it's nice to have something in my head besides nightmares."

"So what is your favor? Do you want to come and live with us?"

"No," said Rick, but his voice was uncertain. There was another pause, and then Rick spoke with confidence. "No. If the Cheyenne owe me a favor and, mind you, I'm not actually asking for one, I'd have brought that–"

"Delivery?"

Rick laughed briefly. "'Delivery' is as good a word as any other, I suppose. I'd have delivered that just for Pete Talltrees. But I think what we have here is a 'potlatch.'"

Walksalone nodded. "That's from the Northwest tribes, but I know what it is. It's when one person gives much, and the other can never get out of debt. It's a good description of where we are."

"Well, here's what I'd like. You're absolved of any debt to me if you protect the chiefs and the tribe from the Children's Crusade and make sure that the coal leases are rejected." Rick reached around and pulled a folded set of computer printouts from his back pocket. "We crunched the numbers, and you're being robbed. The plans for the future are even worse. They're going to build over a hundred power plants on the reservation. Your land will be ripped away, your water will run green with acid, and your air will choke you."

Rick handed the printouts to Walksalone. "So, that's my favor. My friends and I will find the little girl. I'd like you to fight to save yourselves."

Walksalone kept reading for another couple of minutes. Still concentrating on the printouts, he said, "This is from a PDP, isn't it?"

"A PDP-6. How did you know?"

"What? You think I hang out here on the prairie all the time?" He laid the papers on his lap and leaned back, looking at the countryside again. "Magic and computers have a lot in common. Your friends are a bit more than just smart people."

Rick was surprised, but he nodded, and they were quiet for a few minutes. Then Walksalone said, "Can I tell you a story?"

"Sure."

"You've heard of the Sioux fighting with Custer, right?"

"Of course."

"How about Chief Joseph and the Nez Perce?"

Rick nodded. "They still teach his tactics in Officer Training School. Not that I got there, but I did read some of the textbooks."

"And, finally, do you know about the journey of the Northern Cheyenne back to their home?"

Rick shook his head.

"Well it's a long story, but I'll give you the Readers Digest version if you pass over another of those Winstons." Walksalone held out two fingers, Rick gave him a cigarette, and they both lit up.

He stretched out again, blew a single smoke ring,

and began to talk. "After Custer's death, Washington reinforced the troops in the West, and the Cheyenne were captured and marched off to the Indian Lands down in Oklahoma. Perhaps it was well-meant–although I doubt it–because there were already Cheyenne living down there. Living there still, for that matter.

"Well-meant or not, once the Northern Cheyenne showed up, there wasn't enough food for that many people, diseases spread, and it was generally a piss poor situation. They begged to be allowed to go back to their home here on the High Plains, but the federal government in its wisdom refused."

Walksalone took another long drag of his cigarette and Rick said, "Can't see that all that much has changed."

Walksalone laughed. "No, I guess not."

Then he went on. "Finally, in 1878, two of the chiefs, Morning Star who was also known as Dull Knife and Little Wolf decided it was time to stop dying in Oklahoma and headed home. About three hundred people followed them, but less than a hundred were warriors. The rest were women, children, and old men."

Walksalone stopped again, looking off into the distance as if he could still see the long lines of marching people. Rick didn't say anything.

"The Indian lands in Oklahoma are a thousand miles from here," Walksalone said slowly. "The Army put thirteen thousand troops in the field to stop them, and, when they couldn't sneak around them, the warriors straight up beat them. It was the biggest, longest, and most successful campaign by any Indian tribe in the entire history of the West."

He snorted. "'Successful' is a relative term, I guess. By the time they got to Nebraska, they were starved, almost barefoot, and low on ammunition. So Morning Star sent Little Wolf off with all the young men who could still fight and gave them the best horses and most of the weapons. Little Wolf was to keep going, fight his way back up here to the Tongue River while Morning Star would surrender with the old and weak, trusting to the benevolence of the U.S. Army."

"The Army isn't a notably benevolent organization," said Rick.

"No. No, it isn't." Walksalone took a deep breath as if he were gathering strength. "It was the dead of winter, below zero most of the time. Morning Star's band was captured and taken to Fort Robinson. Of course, the commander told them they had to go back to Oklahoma, and, of course, they said they'd rather die right where they were. The commander, an idiot named Henry Wessels, decided that they'd change their minds if he cut off their food and heat.

"Well, that lasted for six days, and finally there was nothing else to do but escape." There was a small smile on Walksalone's face. "You see, Indians aren't all that stupid, and so when the Army ordered them to 'disarm,' they turned in the worst of their weapons and hid the rest. They had about a dozen old rifles, and the rest just took kitchen knives or whatever they could find."

"So many of them had no moccasins that

witnesses said there was a trail of blood in the snow leading from the fort. The pursuit and the slaughter went on for three weeks."

"Those who were wounded were brought back to the fort; but, when Wessels asked them again if they would go back to Oklahoma, one of the women stood up and said, 'You've already killed most of us. Why don't you just go ahead and finish the job?'"

"Tough people," observed Rick.

"Yes, they are," agreed Walksalone. "Dull Knife eventually made it to the Sioux reservation to the West. Weak as they were, they had run almost all the way; and every time the troops caught up, one of his chiefs would drop back and fight until he died, and then he'd be replaced by another who would drop back, fight, and die. The warriors under Little Wolf were faster and more dangerous, so they made it as well."

Walksalone took off his hat and, pulling a bandanna out from his back pocket, wiped the moisture off the sweatband. "So that was it. Dull Knife was never allowed back here to the Tongue River. The few Cheyenne left alive made an agreement with General Miles that they would remain peaceful if allowed to stay. It's a small reservation, smaller than most of the others, but it's our home."

Walksalone put the Resistol back on his head, set it firmly, and stood up. Rick stood as well. Walksalone said, "So, Whirlwind, do you think the Cheyenne can take on a few deluded idiots?"

"Sure sounds like it."

The Indian held out his hand. Rick shook it and felt the strength of the man's grip.

"We will honor your request, and I think the printouts you've brought should persuade even the greediest that the coal deal is a bad one. Good luck with your hunt."

CHAPTER 41

June 11, 1973, Lame Deer, Montana

As Rick walked up to the motor home, he could see that Eps and Scotty had found a faucet, attached a hose, and were just finishing scrubbing off the last of the pink color. Since it was a Sunday and they were hidden from view by the tire retread facility, they decided to stay where they were. A planning meeting soon assembled on the couches and bucket seats of the "living room" area.

"OK, first thing is to find Sage, and that means we need to find Cloyes," Rick said. "My bet is that he's not going to be involved in the attack. He'll have some strong point well out of the action and direct everything by radio."

"Congratulations! Give the man a Kewpie doll!" Eps said, "Steve just found his frequency, and, indeed, he appears to be buttoned up somewhere in that humongous power plant they're building up in Colstrip."

"Sadly, Steve can't triangulate his location closer than a box a couple of miles on a side," explained Scotty.

"How long will that take us to search?" Rick asked.

"It's not really relevant." Eps answered. "Steve also said that what they're calling 'Operation Sand Creek Two' is going to happen early tonight. We don't have enough time to perform a physical search."

Kristee's fingers buried themselves in the tough vinyl of the bench seat, and the muscles on her jaw stood out like ridges of stone.

Scotty glanced at her and held up his hands in a "hold on" gesture. "There's another way. We can split up and do a triangulation on his radio signal. It will be imprecise at first, but if he keeps talking, we'll keep moving and decrease the margin of error."

Kristee exploded. "So fucking what! You decrease the margin of whatever? How does it help find my kid?"

Scotty started to speak, stopped, and started again. "When we get done, we'll know exactly where he is."

Kristee relaxed slightly. "Oh. OK."

Scotty turned to Eps. "We need two points of reference. You offload and set up a receiver here for the baseline, on top of Tire Tread City would work. Stay low so no one can see you."

Eps nodded and ran out the door. Almost immediately, they could hear the sounds of boxes scraping and slamming in the cargo compartments under the floor.

Scotty continued, "I'll get the exact frequencies from Steve and then re-configure our rooftop parabolic receiver. That should take me," he glanced at his watch, "approximately twelve minutes. Then we'll start moving the Travco and calibrating the angles."

He turned to head for the workroom but stopped and faced Rick and Kristee. "We will do what we can, but, frankly, Eps and I aren't highly skilled at direct confrontation. Once we find Cloyes, you two are going to have to take the lead."

Rick looked at Kristee and watched as her eyes narrowed in concentration. "I don't think that will be a problem."

CHAPTER 42

June 10, 1973, Colstrip, Montana

The big motor home drifted slowly through the streets of Colstrip. They passed jammed parking lots outside Colstrip Baptist, the Church of Jesus Christ of the Latter Day Saints, and the New Hope Christian Alliance, but there were still plenty of vehicles on the streets. Rick assumed that those enormous draglines didn't stop scraping up coal for anything as frivolous as a day of rest.

Scotty was manning the communications and mapping station on the dining room table. One receiver was tuned to Eps on the roof of Tire Retread World and two tuned to the frequencies being used by the Children's Crusade. A U.S. Topographic

Service map was laid out on the center of the table and taped to keep it secure.

They'd started out by driving north to complement Eps' listening post in the south. Every five minutes, Scotty would call for a halt at one of the intersections clearly marked on the map–many dirt roads and gravel tracks weren't marked at all. They would wait for a transmission from Cloyes, everyone silent but vibrating with tension.

There would be a squawk of a man's voice followed by a confirmation from Eps. With exquisite care, Scotty would pinpoint the intersection and make a dot with a note of the time and strength of the signal. Then he would call for another location.

While Rick drove, Scotty would be manipulating protractors, a slide rule, and a triangle, tracing very light pencil lines on the map. Whenever they stopped, another light line would appear.

Rick stood up and bent over the map. He could see how the lines–a single solid line from Eps' position and the cloud of light scratches that Scotty was adding–were converging on the power plant.

The map showed the plant covering almost a square mile. Rick knew there would be guards on duty even on a Sunday morning. They'd have to be fast, and speed depended on the accuracy of intelligence. He shrugged and went back to the driver's seat. If anyone could do this, these guys could.

The process continued for another 30 minutes and ended after two passes along the chain link fence with the blue and white signs that proclaimed

"Excacoal's Powder River Plant, We're Building Montana's Future."

Scotty sat back and said, "We've got it." Rick picked up speed and drove up and over a slight rise that took them out of direct line of sight of anyone in the plant. Then he pulled over, set the parking brake, and joined Kristee at the plotting table.

"OK, it's definitely right here." Scotty used the tip of his precision draftsman's pen to indicate a box immediately to the south of what was marked "Exhaust Stack #2." "It shouldn't be too hard to find–those smokestacks are easy to spot."

"To say the least," Rick said.

"Um…yeah. They are the highest points in a 50-mile radius. This is the second one."

"Really? Must be why they named it #2."

Scotty looked concerned until he realized that Rick was joking. A small smile crossed his face. "Yes, well, you should orient yourself by the tower, and this building–whatever it is–will be less than 50 yards due south."

Outside the motor home, there was a squeal of brakes and the clatter of wheels on gravel. Kristee grabbed her dad's shotgun and racked the slide. Rick squatted to look out the front window and saw the dust still blowing away from a red pickup. The door opened. "OK, it's Eps."

When the redheaded engineer jumped up into the motor home, Rick asked, "Where did you get the wheels?"

"Hot-wired the ignition." Eps shrugged. "I mean it wasn't like anyone was using it. It was just sitting there outside a church." He sat down next to Scotty and began to examine the map. "Anyway, I'll return it–at some point."

Rick and Kristee re-joined the others at the map. Rick said, "I think we have to sacrifice careful planning for sheer speed."

Scotty nodded. "I agree. There seem to be two voices on the radio–one sounds like a spokesman or a minister. I'm assuming that's Cloyes. The other man is very different, cold and almost brutal in his tone."

"That's the guy we heard that night in the ravine before they blew the crap out of Wounded Knee," said Rick.

Kristee spoke in a low voice, almost a whisper. "That would be Salazar. Vaughn Salazar. Stephen brought him in when they had a 'purge' a few years ago. I didn't run into him much at the Big House, but when I did, I hated the way he'd look at Sage."

She shook her head as if to get rid of the memory. "One of the wives said he was from Chile, did something with the military, and had to get out when Allende won the election. A nasty bastard."

Scotty looked at her for a moment and then bent back to the map. "That would fit. He just ordered the Crusaders to 'silence' the chiefs. Rick, are you sure the Cheyenne don't need our help."

"Trust me, after what I just learned about these people, they are very capable of dealing with a bunch of brainwashed assassins." Rick shook his head slowly in admiration, "The Crusaders are about to find out that they are definitely not the meanest motherfuckers in this particular Valley of Death."

"Hmm. Cool." Eps was still concentrated on the map. "Look, that fence is well-built. I don't think we can rely on crashing it even with Gussie." He patted the vinyl seat next to him absently.

"I vote that we blow the side gate over here." He jabbed a finger at the south side of the construction project. "Then you two use the pickup truck for the assault while Scotty and I create a diversion up here." He indicated an area along the north fence.

He got up, headed to the workroom in the rear, and began to rummage through cabinets. "I'll give Rick a Very gun–hot damn, we've got two. OK, both of you will have flare guns."

Scotty spoke as Eps continued to pull fireworks, long cardboard boxes, and Tupperware bowls out and pile them on the workbench. "When you've got Sage, set off a flare, and we'll drive Gussie to the blown gate. You pull out ahead of us in the pickup truck Eps borrowed, and we'll block anything coming from behind. We'll rendezvous back at Retread World."

Kristee looked dubious. "Are you sure you can draw security to the north end?"

Eps shouted from deep inside a cabinet. "Are you kidding? They're going to think it's the Normandy landings and a Rolling Stones concert rolled into one."

Rick agreed. "Corey and I used to think they were just three boring computer geeks. Boy, were we wrong."

Scotty got up and headed back to help Eps. "Yes,

you were. We're three boring computer nerds with a LOT of explosives and very few valid excuses to use them."

Eps came out of the cabinet with a handful of red-waxed sticks that Rick could only assume were industrial-grade dynamite. "I found them! This is going to be freaking awesome!"

CHAPTER 43

June 10, 1973, Colstrip, Montana

Rick and Kristee sat in the pickup truck.

Both were wearing heavy goggles with darkened glass and bandannas around their necks. Rick's leather jacket and Kristee's battered hunting vest were unzipped in the heat.

They were parked on the verge of the road about 50 feet down from the side gate of the power plant, hidden by the tall prairie grass on top of a slight rise in the ground. With the windows open, the soft breeze brought the warm smells of earth, prairie grass, and just a hint of sourness from the Excacoal mine about two miles upwind.

Kristee was alternating between checking the

action on her shotgun, counting the number of extra shells in the pockets of her vest, and flipping open the cylinder on the enormous revolver she'd inherited from her father.

"What's that?" Rick asked.

She held up the gun and examined it as if she had never seen it before, "It's a Ruger Blackhawk. My dad carried it when he was hunting. Said it could take down a bear."

"Think we'll run into any bears?"

"Probably not," Kristee said seriously. Then, realizing that Rick had meant it as a joke, "No. I don't suppose there are too many bears where we're going." She put the gun back in her lap. She had a holster in the small of her back, but with the gun's long barrel, it was uncomfortable at the best of times and not something you wanted to be sitting on in a badly sprung pickup truck. She went back to staring blankly out the windshield.

Rick looked at her face closely and asked, "How are you doing?"

"Huh?" Her head snapped around to face him. "I'm...I'm fine. Don't worry about me."

"I'm not asking about whether you're ready to go in there." Rick gestured toward the power plant. "I was thinking about your head. Sage and...well, killing Flick."

She turned back to the windshield and was silent. Finally, she took a big, shuddering sigh and said, "Sage is an ache that feels like someone has just hollowed out my insides and filled me with acid. It hurts so much, I'll do anything to make it stop."

She paused.

"But I could see what the rifle did to Flick...his head just–"

"Exploded," said Rick quietly.

"Yeah."

"I shot two people in Vietnam. One VC just popped up in front of me, and I grabbed the sergeant's M-14 and jammed it at him. It was on full rock-and-roll, and he just...evaporated."

"But I thought you were in Ia Drang. You must have shot lots of enemies there, right?"

Rick shook his head. "Nope. I spent most of my time trying not to get shot, and I didn't do a terribly good job at that." He gave a short snort of laughter. "Shit, I was the fucking company intelligence clerk. The most dangerous thing I carried was an ax for chopping away tree roots when we dug out a command bunker."

There was another silence as both looked out at the clear, high-plains day. Rick could feel the breeze coming in from his window.

"It's not like hunting." Kristee's voice was so soft Rick almost couldn't hear her. "Even a scumbag like Flick. He was a person. I still see him–" Her voice trailed off.

"It's not going away." Rick said. "Those guys I shot are featured players in my nightmares. Nobody talks about it, but killing people, even the enemy–armed soldiers who are trying to kill you–is the biggest part of the broken glass in their brains. I mean, shooting him is right in there with the screams at night as the Cong found our wounded or–"

Rick found he still didn't want to talk about his other kill.

"Really?"

"Damn right." Rick shook his head but kept looking out the windshield. "That and because Sage is in there is why I only took these flash-bangs." He hefted an army surplus gas mask bag slung over his head and shoulder. "I killed a woman last year when she was about to slice Eve and me up with a razor. Now she shows up at night too. I can see her crying as I strangled her and all the time–" Rick took a deep breath. "She was talking about how much she loved this guy who'd been trying to kill me."

He shook all over and sat up straighter behind the steering wheel. "Ah, shit. I get enough of these people at night. I don't need them now."

"So you don't get used to it?" asked Kristee in a wistful voice.

"Some people do." Rick answered. "I'm not one of them, I guess."

"I guess I'm not either." There was another pause. "But I've got to get Sage back. I have to."

"I'm right there with you on that one."

"But you're not going to kill anyone?"

Rick sighed. "If it comes down to it, I won't hesitate to kill in order to save Sage. I just hope it won't have to go down that way."

Kristee looked at him. "You know, most people would say that was a fucked-up way to go into a gunfight."

Another snort of laughter. "Well, yeah. On the other hand, most people have never killed anyone, so who gives a fuck what they think?"

Kristee patted her ammunition pockets again. "Well, we'll see if Eps' sandbag shells take down the bad guys." She touched the revolver in her lap. "But I've got this and the heavy buckshot, and I'll use them if I have to."

Rick glanced at his watch. "OK, check your seatbelt, and get your earplugs in. We're one minute from Go."

Rick zipped his jacket, pulled the bandanna over his mouth, and gripped the steering wheel tightly. "If there's one thing I know about Eps, he's a very punctual and very loud person."

"That's two."

Whatever else Kristee might have said was drowned out by an explosion under the gate that slammed the right side back against the fence and sent the left cartwheeling into the air. Rick stretched his jaw to try to clear the ringing in his ears and jammed the truck into gear.

CHAPTER 44

June 10, 1973, Colstrip, Montana

Thunder roared from Rick's left.

It was the drum solo from Louie Bellson's "The Hawk Talks" being routed through the 8-tube breadboard amplifier that Scotty had made and blasted into two PA speakers that Eps had "liberated" from Colstrip Regional High School. Bellson's signature double bass drums made an enormous muttering groan, and the snares and tom-toms ricocheted off the walls of the plant like every caliber of weaponry going off at once.

Then came three enormous slams as dynamite charges took out both of the end fence posts on the north side and rocketed a Port-a-John 20 feet into the air. From the corner of his eye, Rick could see flashes in the high grass on that side as string after string of firecrackers and fulminate squibs went off, and homemade mortars dropped flash-bang grenades into the construction area.

A moment later, there was no time for anything but taking a sharp left turn with all four tires skidding on the smooth asphalt, followed by an equally tight left. The pickup swayed and shimmied but a touch more acceleration brought it out straight, and Rick could see the small, square cinder-block building just south of the smokestack.

Rick hadn't seen it earlier. The building had been blocked by two other buildings, so he examined it now. Two stories high, it had no windows on the ground floor and only high glass-brick windows near the flat roof. The single door he could see looked steel-clad, if not solid steel, and had a lever system that rammed metal bars deep into the frame on either side.

If they've got the same bars on the inside, that's going to be tough to open, he thought.

"Kristee." He spoke as calmly as he could to combat the jitters from the noise and speed of their approach. "Load those TESAR breaching shells first. Forget the door. We'll go straight in through the wall. I figure we'll need four."

Kristee nodded and slotted the copper shells into her shotgun. Eps had told them that the special rounds hit with tremendous power, but then the slug fractured into a powder making it less likely that anyone on the other side would be hurt, a vital factor until they knew where in the building Sage was being held.

She loaded the remainder of the tube with the pink-colored shells that indicated they were the non-lethal sandbag variety. Then she leaned forward and holstered the big Ruger back of her jeans.

Rick slid to a screeching stop in front of the door and yelled, "Get out! Hit the wall while I jam the door!"

Kristee jumped, and Rick backed up a few yards, slammed the pickup into first gear, and rammed it firmly into the metal door. As he got out of the pickup, he was relieved not to see the cloud of steam that would have indicated a blown radiator. They needed the vehicle to escape.

As he came around the back of the truck, he heard a muffled boom and saw two square feet of the first layer of the cinder block disappear in front of where Kristee stood braced against the recoil of the shotgun held against her hip. She racked the slide and fired the second shot low, and then two more to take out the second layer of cinder block. A two-by-four-foot hole went entirely through the wall.

Rick could hear cement grit and pebbles rattle against his heavy, dark goggles. After a second, he pulled them off, and dropped them around his neck. His own glasses were shatter-resistant, and he wanted his eyes to adjust when he entered the building.

They split up and flattened against the wall on each side of the hole. Rick held up three fingers of his left hand while reaching into the bag with his right. Then he pulled three of the baseball-sized aluminum foil explosives, lit each fuse with his Zippo, and lobbed them into the hole. Handmade by Eps, they were called "flash-bangs" because they had remarkably little concussive power but a stunning amount of light and sound.

Blue light flared out of the hole in the bright sunlight, and a shattering crack was only slightly muffled by the wall; and Rick realized that, as he'd expected, he was deaf. He signaled Kristee by making a fist and jerking it down. Kristee revolved around the edge of the hole, lowering herself into a crouch against the inside wall.

Rick did the same on his side, desperately trying to make sense of the scene through drifting smoke and dust. He heard Kristee's shotgun and only then picked out a man turning toward them with a gun in his hand. When the sandbag hit him in the stomach, his eyes seemed to turn inward, and he looked down and fell to his knees, dropping his weapon as he wrapped his arms across his torso.

Suddenly, the smoke shifted, and Rick could see another man to his left. Just a silhouette in the dim light, he was trying to pull a pistol from his waistband. Rick launched himself up and forward, grabbing the man's gun hand just as he finally got the hammer unstuck from his belt, and began to raise it.

All those hours of working out surged power through Rick's arms and shoulders, and he grabbed the wrist behind the gun with his left hand while the right covered the hammer, preventing it from cocking. His fingers were locked as he spun to his right. The snapping feeling and the accompanying scream told him that his attacker's right arm was either dislocated or broken. He pulled a semi-automatic from the man's limp grip, removed the clip and cleared the slide, and threw it out the hole in the wall. His attacker was a young Indian in the inevitable brand-new western shirt and jeans. His face was pale with pain, and he fell back into a chair clutching his arm tight against his side.

It was only when Kristee shouted "CLEAR!" that he realized he could hear again. He pulled a couple of Scotty's plastic cable ties and immobilized the young man's ankles and wrists. Kristee's opponent was already zipped tight and lying on his side on the floor in a growing pool of vomit.

A young girl screamed from upstairs.

It cut off abruptly.

Before the echoes from the scream had stopped, Kristee was taking two steps at a time up concrete stairs along the right wall.

Rick followed. There was a gunshot and chips of concrete spat off the wall at the top of the stairway. Rick lowered himself to the stairs and climbed as quietly as he could to a small landing where the stair turned, and he could stand up and see into the second floor.

Kristee was standing stock still in the doorway at the top of the stairs. Her body was shaking.

A male voice was saying, "Mrs. Whitaker. You have my sincere condolences for the loss of your husband, but please do not increase your pain by forcing me to kill your daughter." Rick recognized the voice, the cold lisping tones he'd last heard ordering the assault on Wounded Knee, the man he'd been told was Vaughn Salazar.

The man he'd heard boasting of the rape and murder of Beth Pine.

Salazar spoke again. "Now, move very slowly, and please raise the muzzle of that weapon so that it points toward the ceiling."

Another voice cut in. Rick recognized Stephen Cloyes' baritone, but the soothing, persuasive tones were gone, replaced by strain and fear. "Vaughn, just kill the bitch and let's get the hell out of here!"

"Calm down, Stephen. We have time." The voice was cutting, decisive. It had the resonance of a military leader in contrast to Cloyes' panic. "Please, Mrs. Whitaker. Point that weapon away from me before I have to do something I would truly regret."

Rick resumed his slow creep up the stairs, moving by fractions of an inch to keep the motion of his head from sparking off the hunter's reflex attention to anything that moved. Only Kristee had spoken during the fight downstairs, so there was a chance they assumed she'd come alone.

Finally, he could see everything.

On the far side of the room, a slim, short man had his arm around Sage's neck pulling her close to his body. He had a pistol–it looked like an old German Luger–pressed against the little girl's temple.

Cloyes was standing in front of a table on the right filled with radios, chargers, and other communications equipment. Behind him, a fire door with a metal panic bar and an alarm was set into the rear wall.

Another way out, Rick realized, I couldn't see it as we drove up.

The radio crackled with static and a voice came through, speaking urgently. Cloyes spun around and listened intently, his head down and his eyes closed to concentrate on the fragmented voice coming from the speaker.

Salazar never took his cold eyes from Kristee and pushed the barrel of his pistol harder into Sage's temple. She flinched and a squeak of pain emerged from her clenched teeth. "This is your last warning. Point that weapon up and then put it down, very carefully."

Still trembling with repressed rage and fear, Kristee slowly raised the shotgun to a vertical position and then crouched to place it carefully on the ground. As she did, Rick could clearly see the bulge of the Ruger holstered at her back. Moving slowly and carefully, he reached into the bag over his shoulder, fingers seeking the aluminum foil flash-bang grenades.

"They must have fallen out!" he thought.

Then he felt the thick plastic of the Very pistol. Slowly, he pulled it out and released the safety. The flare wasn't meant to be a lethal weapon–just a signaling device–but anything was better than nothing.

Kristee stood up slowly bend softly kicked the shotgun a few feet away.

"Shit!" Cloyes spoke explosively and smashed his hand down on the radio receiver. "All the men are gone! Fucking gone. How in hell did they get stopped by a bunch of damn Indians?"

He spun around. "We've got to get the hell out of here!"

Salazar didn't take his eyes off Kristee. "Calm down, Stephen. You can catch the 2:00 p.m. flight back to Washington. I would love to take you with me, but the Company seems to want me back in Buenos Aires immediately."

He loosened his grip on Sage, and her head came upright as the pressure of the gun barrel eased. "Mrs. Whitaker is a very brave and determined woman. I hope her daughter takes after her. I'll find out when she and I are back in my hacienda.

Rick saw the pistol begin to swing toward Kristee and fired the flare gun. The room filled with white smoke and then a violent green light blossomed from the wall behind Salazar's head. The flare was jammed into some small crack in the wall, but a waterfall of green sparks and flame cascaded over the small man.

"Sage! Drop flat!" Rick screamed as he surged up off the stairs and across the room. He heard a gunshot go off almost next to his ear as he slammed into Salazar. He slid his hands up the man's right arm, pointing the gun toward the ceiling as another shot fired, and finally stripping the pistol and sending it spinning off into the smoke--carrying the tip of Salazar's finger with it.

Rick put all his rage into a solid right to the belly,

pushing the power through his hips and using all the muscles in his body. His fist sunk deep into Salazar's stomach, and the man collapsed to the floor. Rick kicked him in the crotch.

The first sound he heard through the ringing in his ears was the door alarm going off. Cloyes was getting away.

Rick ran to the door, flung it open, and then stepped back as a bullet went sprang off the metal doorframe. He heard a powerful engine start up and looked out. Cloyes was driving a black pickup from behind the building.

As the truck passed under the stairs, he heard the dusty scrape of brakes, and the truck stopped.

"You motherfucker!" Cloyes screamed. "You think you've won? Bullshit! I know where you and your girlfriend live. I'll fuck her and kill her before you can make it back to Washington."

The truck's tires smoked as it fishtailed off and around the corner of the building out of sight. For a second, Rick was frozen, paralyzed with the plans he was making and rejecting, and then he shook his shoulders and turned back into the small building.

Kristee was crumpled facedown on the floor with a puddle of blood spreading steadily from her throat.

Salazar had struggled to a sitting position against the wall, feebly trying to pat out the smoking bits of white phosphorus from the flare on his right shoulder. The strained grimace showed his pain, but his eyes never left the small figure directly in front of him.

Sage was standing with her legs slightly spread

and her knees bent. The Ruger looked like some enormous cartoon weapon in her small hands. As heavy as it was, it was rock steady, fully cocked, and aimed directly between Salvador's eyes. Tears were streaming down her face, and her nose was running, but Rick could see the furious determination as her finger began to draw back on the trigger.

"Sage," he said calmly and began walking over to her. "Sage. Please wait."

"Mom's dead," she said in a choked voice trying to keep back tears. "He killed her. I'm going to kill him. Don't try to stop me."

"I won't." Rick came up next to her and knelt down. "This guy is a worthless bastard who deserves to die. I'd like to kill him myself. But I'm asking you not to do it."

Her eyes flicked to his face for a second and then back to Salazar's face. "Why? He was going to kill me too. He told me."

"I know. This guy should be dead."

"Then why do you care about him?"

"I don't. I don't give a shit about him. I wouldn't piss on him if he was on fire." Rick glanced over. "Which, in fact, he is."

There was a tiny twitch of the little girl's mouth, almost the beginning of a ghost of a smile.

"Sage," Rick reached out and touched her hands softly. "I'm worried about you."

"What?"

"You've heard me at night?" he asked.

"The screaming? Sure, everyone on the block hears you."

Rick gave a snort of laughter. "Yeah, well, I guess that's true. I've got a question for you."

She just looked at him again.

"What do you think the nightmares are about? The worst ones?"

She shrugged. "I don't know. Soldiers trying to kill you?"

He shook his head slowly and tightened his grip on her hands, slowly pushing the gun away from Salazar. "Not the worst ones. They're about the people I've killed. They're the monsters who come back and live in my head."

The gun slowly came down to point to the floor, and she looked in his face.

"If you kill this scumbag, you'll have to see him in your dreams every night for the rest of your life." Rick took the Ruger from her hands. "He deserves to die, but he doesn't deserve to be inside your head. Not for one minute. Not for one second."

Sage collapsed into his arms and sobbed. Rick held her with one arm and raised the Ruger with the other. "Señor Salazar, Sage doesn't deserve the pain, but I can stand to have another asshole hanging around at night, so I would strongly advise you to stop reaching for your gun."

CHAPTER 45

June 10, 1973, Colstrip, Montana

Rick and Sage stood on the hot asphalt and watched the blue and white motor home coming toward them. Sage had pulled away from Rick after a long bout of tears, and Rick wasn't comfortable enough to put his arm around her again.

Rick had zip-tied Salvador into his chair–taking care to run the plastic ties over clothing to keep from leaving marks. He'd tried to explain to Sage that moving her mother's body would mean that the police would come looking for them; and, after a long moment's consideration, Sage carefully knelt on one of the very few patches of floor not covered in blood and stroked her mother's hair.

Rick thought he should join the little girl in some sort of ceremony, but it just wasn't something he could do. After a few moments of silence, he moved around the room trying to wipe down any surfaces that they could have touched.

Finally, Sage stood up and looked at Rick, her eyes clear of tears. "I'm ready to go now."

Without a word, Rick started down the inside stairs to the lower room, checked the two men there to make sure they were still breathing, and led the little girl through the hole her mother had punched in the wall.

The Travco stopped and Eps bounced out, followed a moment later by Scotty. Eps was ebullient. "We did it! We showed those bastards!" An instant later, Scotty tapped his shoulder and whispered in his ear.

"Dead?" Eps asked.

Rick nodded.

The engineers stood awkwardly and stared at Sage. Rick could see the struggle between sympathy, sorrow, and a massive inability to show emotion on their faces. Then Scotty stepped up to the little girl, bowed to her height, and extended his hand. "Sage, I'm really sorry about your mom."

Sage looked into his eyes and shook his hand. "Thank you, Scotty."

Scotty stood straight, relieved that he'd carried off his emotional performance properly. Eps shook the little girl's hand as well although he didn't have to bow down. Then he turned and gestured toward the motor home. "How about you hop on board? You can have the co-pilot's seat."

Sage solemnly climbed the steps and disappeared into the dark interior.

Rick asked, "OK, how much time do we have?"

"Steve is spoofing the local police channels, but it's going to be close," said Scotty.

"OK, do you guys have anything that can put a couple of bad guys to sleep without killing them?"

The smile returned to Eps' face. "A Mickey Finn? Of course. How long do you want them out, and how miserable do you want the headache afterward?"

"Why am I surprised that you have a whole pharmacy on hand?" Rick smiled and his face felt like frozen muscles were moving for the first time in a long time. "An hour should do, and you can make the headache as lousy as you like. Memory loss wouldn't hurt."

Eps' face fell and he shook his head. "Chloral hydrate will do the job, but memory loss would mean something like sodium pentothal; and that could result in an unfortunate case of death."

"Forget the memory loss."

Eps bounced into the motor home, and Rick turned to Scotty. "Cloyes got away."

The big engineer slowly shook his head without speaking.

"He said he knew where we lived, and he was going to go after Eve."

"That can't happen," Scotty said firmly. "She never took the training in escape hatches and man-traps. We'll have to call her."

Eps came out with a small vial of clear liquid and handed it to Rick. "A good slug of this should do the trick."

Rick nodded and turned back to the building. "Let me clean up here while you reach Eve."

Inside, he dosed both men and Salazar. When they no longer responded to being poked with a pencil, he cut and pocketed all the zip-ties, reclaimed and reloaded their weapons, and emptied them by firing into the walls and ceiling, careful of potential ricochets. Then he placed the weapons in their hands.

He left the shotgun beside Kristee, wiped down, and replaced the Blackhawk in her rear holster. He spent one final moment looking down at her silently and then turned and left.

Outside, Eps was completing a full wipe-down of the pickup truck. "Look, hardly a scratch! I told you we'd return it in great shape."

Far off across the prairie, a police siren sounded.

Scotty started the motorhome, and minutes later they were past the blown gate and motoring sedately down the highway heading east. Sitting in the passenger seat, Rick looked back and could see Sage lying on one of the side benches, her face to the wall. Her shoulders were shaking.

He faced front and asked Scotty, "Did you reach Eve?"

The engineer shook his head.

"Phone not working?"

A nod.

"Fuck."

The radiotelephone on the center console rang. Rick picked it up and heard Steve say, "Turn around."

"Turn this thing around," Rick told Scotty who just nodded, slowed, and began a three-point turn in a gravel pull-off. Rick spoke into the phone. "I need to get back to DC. Fast."

"I know. It's all arranged."

"It is?"

"Yeah, Langley wanted Salazar headed back to Chile bad enough that they laid on a private jet. It's sitting at Sunday Creek Airport—although I think calling a single runway with no lights and no tower an airport is a stretch."

"Two problems. I don't look much like Salazar, and I don't really want to go to Chile. What's going on down there anyway?

"The Agency has something planned with the current president–Allende–and Salazar appears to have...skills that they think could be extraordinarily useful. Where is he anyway?"

"Unconscious and holding the gun that killed Kristee."

"Shit. I'm sorry about Kristee. Sadly, it's highly unlikely that Salazar will go down for it. Tell Scotty to take the next left."

Rick said, "Steve says turn left. How does he do that?"

Scotty just smiled and pointed straight up as he put the big vehicle into a slow left turn.

"Good. Tell Scotty that it's about 15 miles to Sunday Creek Road, and there are signs he can follow from there."

Rick passed on the information and then repeated his questions to Steve. "OK, what about the fact that I'm not Salazar, and I don't want to go to Chile--at least, not right now."

"No problem, amigo. You're forgetting that I'm with 'No Such Agency' and we can boss around the CIA. Well, we can if we're careful. All the pilots know is that they are waiting for a tall guy with glasses and motorcycle boots who needs to get to DC ASAP. You'll have to land way the hell out at Dulles, but there are urgent telexes requiring you be met with a fast motorcycle on the tarmac."

"Don't forget a helmet."

"Do I have to think of everything? Don't answer–that's rhetorical–both open-face and full-coverage will be waiting with the bike. Now, Cloyes will be on the 2:00 p.m. out of Billings, and it's going to be close. I'll do some delicate screwing with his flight plan, but too much of that can irritate the air traffic controllers, not to mention the passengers who find themselves plummeting to the ground."

"I suspect you're right on that," said Rick dryly.

"Yes, indeed. Now, I've been running diagnostics on the house phone, and it's been cut or blocked somewhere, probably before they came after Sage the first time. I don't think we ever used it after that. I'm in West Virginia and, even if I was the heroic, muscle-bound type, I can't get anywhere near there in time."

"No problem." Rick said, "Just get me there in time."

"We live to serve. One more thing. Scare up a pair of sunglasses to look like a real secret agent, and don't talk to anyone on the plane. Not anyone, understand?"

"Yeah. Why not?"

"Well, I can do a lot but I couldn't get rid of Salazar's accent. Anyway, they'll expect you to be an asshole. If you act like a normal human being, they'll know instantly that you're not with the CIA. OK, the turn for Sunday Creek is right ahead. Tell Scotty I'll call him after you get airborne."

CHAPTER 46

***June 11, 1973, En Route,
Dulles International Airport***

Jones is hit.

The Staff Sergeant's been hit. Shit. I need to get to him.

Stay low. Stay fucking low. There's a fucking cloud of 50 cal. going right over my head.

OK, moving now. Hold the rifle and crawl. Just like basic.

I can't hear Jones.

I can't hear shit. There must be 20 goddamn machine guns behind those anthills.

Fuck. That was close.

Jesus! That was our guys!

Crawl!

Be a fucking joke if my own side kills me.
Don't stop.
You've got to make it.
He needs you.
Don't stop.

"Sir. Sir!"

Rick automatically tried to get away. He was stuck. A seat belt.

"You were screaming. Figured I should wake you."

Standing in the aisle, the co-pilot was looking down at him, sympathy in his eyes. Rick remembered what Steve had said and just stared back. Silent.

"Don't worry. We hear it all the time on these flights." He motioned toward the cockpit of the small jet. "The captain just wanted to let you know we'll be wheels down at Dulles in ten minutes."

The co-pilot began to work his way back to the front, and then stopped. "Oh, and just so you know. You weren't talking. Just a lot of yelling."

Rick nodded slowly.

"Yeah, a lot of guys need to make sure they didn't say anything they might regret later. You didn't."

Rick looked out the tiny window at the circles of light thrown into the darkness of rural Virginia. He concentrated on regaining his control, slowing his breathing, getting his heartbeat back to normal. When he looked up again, the co-pilot was gone.

Stepping down from the plane, he looked back and nodded at the co-pilot. The man waved and pulled the stairs up, and the jet engines began to whine. In moments, they'd be gone.

Rick turned and saw a man walking toward him from the business jet office. Tall, with weathered eyes, and a full, David Crosby-style mustache. He had a helmet tucked under his arm.

"So, are you the important guy from Montana?" the man said as he walked up.

Rick nodded.

"Good." He held out the helmet. "This is for you. Steve said you were a big guy so I picked out a double XL. Hope it fits."

"So you know Steve?" Rick asked.

"Yeah, we're sort of in the same business." He dug in a jeans pocket and produced a ring with two keys, "The bike is around front. You can't miss it—all black and damn near faster than light."

Rick took the keys, and they began to walk back to the small terminal. "Do you work for the NSA?"

"Are you kidding? Those guys might as well be in the phone book. No, I work for an operation that's actually capable of keeping secrets. It's out in the woods over there." The mustachioed man gestured vaguely to the south, then pulled the door open and waved Rick through. "But Steve's done some…favors for me. Plus, he called in my marker from our last chess game."

He shook his head. "I still can't believe that he pulled off that damned Lasker-Bauer without losing both bishops."

"I hate it when that happens." Rick said dryly.

The other man glanced over, clearly detecting the

gentle sarcasm. "Hey, chess, computers, spying, all the same. Now, there's just one thing to remember about the Vincent Black Shadow. It's one up, four down. If you can remember that, you'll be fine."

They came out the front of the terminal, and Rick noticed the interior lights go off behind them. A battered green VW bug was idling next to a mean-looking motorcycle with an L-shaped engine. "Oh, you might also want to keep in mind that this monster will hit 90 in second gear. I put a chin pad on the tank, so you could keep your head down."

Rick found a pair of light leather gloves inside the helmet, put them on, and then the helmet. By the time he had replaced and adjusted his glasses, the other man was getting into the passenger side of the VW. He yelled, "Thanks," but it was drowned out in the rattling spatter of the VW as it pulled onto the access road.

Rick kicked the spindly bike to life and heard the deep burbling rumble of the inline V-twin. It was already warmed up, so he worked the clutch and brake levers to locate the points where they activated. He'd had a borrowed bike lock up the rear wheel on him once just because the foot brake was set for a much shorter rider. The transmission's upside-down pattern wasn't a problem since it was similar to the late and unlamented Kawasaki Triple, but he still went through the gears with the clutch in until he had the rhythm.

Only then did he head out of the parking lot and onto the largely empty access lanes that led to the sail-shaped main terminal.

He was doing a series of speed and distance calculations and knew there wasn't much time to get back to the group house before Cloyes would land at National, rent a car, and drive through DC to the group house on Ingomar. He decided against the Dulles Access Road with its excess number of bored police officers and headed due north. Route 7 was a wide-open stretch of good asphalt, and he soon had the powerful street-racer up over 100 mph.

At Leesburg, he swung right on the tiny bypass road and onto the bumpy rural Route 15. In a few miles, he had to slow to make sure he didn't miss the tiny sign for the Balls Bluff Civil War memorial. Just past the place where the first battle of the Civil War was fought, he made a right onto the road to White's Ferry.

The Vincent took flight on most of the whoop-de-doos on the road that led straight toward the Potomac, and Rick had it flattened almost parallel to the road on the right-angle turn at the riverbank, holding it by sliding his boot on the asphalt. Swinging around to the riverside ramp, he saw the pilot of the General Jubal Early beginning to undo the chain that held the tiny ferry against the current.

He blipped the accelerator, brought up the front wheel, and bumped the rear over the widening water gap and into a skidding stop on the baby-blue ferry. The operator, an older man in farm overalls and a gimme cap, finished unchaining the boat, spun the attached powerboat that pushed it across the river, and said, "That stunt will cost you double price."

Rick paid the $2.50 without complaint and then added another $20. He'd have wasted at least 20 minutes if he'd had to wait for the next trip. He stood with the bike between his legs and watched the river slide past on its way to the thundering rapids of Great Falls. At the other bank, the operator lowered the exit chain before he pivoted the powerboat around by the pin in its bow to slow the ferry; as soon as Rick heard the first scrape of iron on concrete, he was off the boat and up the ramp.

River Road was unlit dirt for the next 20 miles, but Rick had ridden it many times and kept the European-style speedometer needle close to the 100-kilometers-per-hour mark even though he was airborne about half the time. When he turned onto the paved roads of rural Montgomery County, he opened up the black speedster, swooping through the curves with his off leg hanging out for balance, and a gloved hand brushing the road.

Outside of Darnestown, a police cruiser pulled out of a closed gas station with its lights going. Rick didn't even slow–there was simply no time to stop. He took the right turn onto the paved portion of River Road in a screaming power slide and brought the bike up through the gears to a frightening 180 kph. He didn't know how much over because he had no concentration to spare for the speedometer. The revolving lights receded quickly behind him and were lost to sight long before he saw the Purple Pickle at the crossroads town of Potomac.

He was certain that there would be more than one police car ahead of him–radio was the bane of a fast motorcycle–so he cut through the gas station to avoid the red light and headed back toward the river on Falls Road. Another scraping turn and he was dropping down past the Angler Inn and then a left onto the clear straights of MacArthur Boulevard.

The pipes echoed their tuned thunder off the long walls of the Naval Research Center, and then he was under the Beltway and forced back to third gear to negotiate the fast turns down to the Aqueduct Bridge. He didn't slow when he turned at the red light onto Wilson. Another stretch of River Road passed by in a blur, and then he was in DC and scrambling his way toward Tenleytown.

He parked the bike at the end of the block when he reached Ingomar, worried that the sound of the exhaust would be a dead giveaway. He pulled off the helmet and left it on the seat. The exhaust pipes were glowing red-hot where they emerged from the cylinders.

Nice bike, he thought as he ran down the darkened street using the parked cars to mask his approach.

There were no lights in the group house, but there was a black Buick Electra parked at an angle in the driveway, bumper stickers clearly identifying it as a rental. Rick moved forward quietly, reached the VW Bus, and retrieved the tire jack handle from the floor next to the driver's seat.

He stood in the driveway, watching each window of the house in turn, and trying to separate out any foreign noises from the usual night sounds of insects, the whoosh of tires on Reno Road, and distant sirens. When he couldn't identify anything as out-of-place, he walked slowly and quietly to the front and up the stairs to the front porch.

At the front door, he paused and listened again.

He checked the knob. It was locked. That set the hairs on the back of his neck on end. After Steven had explained how easily an intruder could break the glass panes in the door, no one had ever bothered to lock it again. The spare key was in its usual hiding place, the second flowerpot to the right. The idea was that putting it in the most obvious place might keep them from having to replace window glass as often. It was all very logical, but Rick did feel as though somehow logic had trumped caution. Eve had been even more insistent but was outvoted.

With steady pressure on the key, Rick undid the handle latch and pushed the door ajar. Slowly releasing the key to keep the latch from clicking, he listened again.

Nothing.

From the evidence of the rental car, Cloyes was inside. Almost certainly, he already had taken Eve. Rick simply shut off any consideration that he might have tortured or killed her–thinking of that would serve no purpose. From the silence, he assumed that Cloyes was either upstairs or standing in the living room watching the front door move in the dim light.

He had to go in.

But he didn't have to go in slowly. He yanked the door and plunged into the living room–diving down and to the right.

Pain blossomed. His head and chest exploded as the flame of a gun flared from the center of the room.

He saw Eve's face frozen in a scream in the afterimage of the gunshot. Then the incredible pain in his chest drove everything down to a flat, silent blackness and disappeared.

CHAPTER 47

June 11, 1973, Ingomar Street NV, Washington, DC

Damn. It stinks.

I can't breathe. Jeez, look at that. There's got to be a thousand dead PAVN out there.

All rotting in the sun.

Well, a stink never killed anyone—even if this feels like it could be the first time.

I'm staying right here. These tree roots are good cover.

What?

Moving west? Yes, sir.

Fucking shit.

Doesn't Captain Wales realize that LZ Albany is way the hell over to the east?

I'm safe here.
I'm not going to move
I'm just going to stay right here.

"Rick! Rick!"

Rick heard the voice but tried to pretend he didn't.

Smack!

The slap rocked his head to the left, and one eye opened in reflex. Steve was kneeling beside him and winding up for another slap. Rick held up a hand.

"Wait." There was pain across his chest, and moving his arm had made it explode into true agony. Steve looked like he was about to hit him again. "Stop. If you hit me again, I think my head is going to fall off."

Steve seemed to collapse in relief. "Good. Hitting people has always been one of my worst skills."

"I'd hate to see one of your better skills. What the hell are you hitting me for anyway?"

"You don't remember?" Steve sat back on his heels. Rick started to sit, but another wave of pain washed across him, and Steve pushed him down with a gentle shove. "Stay down for a second. I think you've been shot, but there's an anomaly."

"A what? Listen, I've been shot, so I'll just lie here quietly and bleed out."

"That's the anomalous factor," Steve said. "You're not bleeding."

Slowly, Rick brought a hand up and began to run it gently across his chest under the leather jacket. There was a hole right over the breast pocket. He slid a finger into it and found another hole in the other side. "I seem to have a bullet hole in the jacket here. That's usually a bad sign."

Steve began to unzip the jacket. "It is a bad sign. That's what I don't understand." He paused as he slowly pulled the jacket open. "Nope, you've got a hole in your shirt as well."

"Well, you know what they say, 'A sucking chest wound is God's way of telling you you've been ambushed.'"

"I would say that the ambush is a given. I'm not so sure about the chest wound."

Pain tore through Rick's chest again, and he drew in a breath and gritted his teeth. The pain rose to a peak.

Steve held up a small object. "Did you develop invulnerability recently? This is definitely a bullet but it's not inside you."

Rick let out his breath. "That's good. Isn't it?"

"Definitely good." Steve gently explored Rick's chest again. "Wait. Did Scotty give you that bogus vest?"

"You mean the Kevlar thing? Yeah. I ran out of clean shirts and put it on a day ago."

Steve shook his head. "What do you know? It's not bogus after all. At least, that's what the available evidence points to. None of us agreed with the force and deflection equations, so we never experimented with it."

"Tell you what. Keep right on avoiding those experiments." Rick managed to sit up this time but couldn't stand. He sat, propped against the wall and panting from the effort. "There are distinct drawbacks to this invention."

"On the positive side, you aren't dead."

"Yes." Rick suddenly went rigid and looked around the room. "Eve. She was here. Is she OK?"

Steve stood and put out a hand to help Rick to his feet. "She's not here. I came in through the basement escape hatch when I couldn't get through on the phone. All I found was...well, what I thought was your corpse."

"A reasonable assumption." Rick dug out his pack of Winstons, felt in his breast pocket, and slowly brought out the Zippo. There was a shiny gouge in the stained and weathered steel. "This look like a bullet scrape to you?"

Steve leaned closer. "Yes. That must have taken off most of the momentum of the bullet, the vest kept it from penetrating, and your bulked up chest muscles did the rest."

Rick turned the lighter over and examined both sides, then whipped it in the up-down motion on his pants leg. He lit a cigarette, took a deep drag, and immediately started alternating coughs and groans. "Damn! That hurts!"

Steve was heading for the kitchen. "I'd bet you have deep muscle bruises and probably some cracked ribs. You might want to cut down on the cigarettes."

"Don't be silly." Rick got the coughing under control and took a less powerful drag. "There are no problems that can't be solved with nicotine. So where's Eve?"

"I heard what I suppose was the shot that hit you

as I came in through the basement wall, and then there was quite a bit of banging and yelling–mostly Eve's voice–and a car burned rubber out in the driveway." Steve gave it a moment's thought. "It took a couple of minutes to wake you, so I'd say she was taken four to five minutes ago. Do you know who it was?"

"Yeah, it was Cloyes." Rick frowned and then looked out the kitchen window. "And I guess since it's no longer here, he's driving a black Avis rental with 'We Try Harder' bumper stickers."

Steve looked up. "Avis? That helps a lot." He picked up the kitchen phone, listened for a second, and began dialing.

"Why does that help?" Rick asked. "And why is the phone working?"

"Second question first. Remember we routed it through that old lady in SE who never used it? Well, I listened in when I was in the basement, and her grandson just got out of Jessup and apparently has girlfriends in every ward of the city. It must have been tied up for two days."

Someone on the other end of the line answered, and Steve started speaking rapidly in a technical lingo that might as well have been a foreign language as far as Rick was concerned.

Steve hung up. "We've got him."

"How?"

"Avis is helping out with Project 621B and the MOSAIC System," Steve began, and then stopped. "Listen, you don't need to know all that. What you need to know is that Cloyes–or at least his car–is heading north on Wisconsin right now."

Rick started for the front door.

"Wait a second." Steve grabbed his arm. Rick groaned. "Sorry. Listen, while you were out West, I did a little research, and Cloyes has a second place–a safe house, really–down along the river just past National Airport. The cops are still swarming all over the place in Leesburg, so he'll almost certainly head south."

Rick thought for a second. "Fastest way there is down the George Washington Parkway."

"Right, and you can cut the angle on Nebraska Avenue by taking River–"

"And catch his ass." Rick interrupted. "Thanks. Now, where did I put that tire iron?"

"You mean the one in your left sleeve?"

"Yep."

CHAPTER 48

June 11, 1973, Interstate 495, near Washington, DC

The Vincent Black Shadow sliced through the turns and down the ramp to the Beltway at the River Road interchanges. Bending it hard, he shaved a few seconds by cutting down the bypass at the Clara Barton Parkway exit and then on to the main Beltway just before the Potomac River. Steve had done some fast trigonometry in his head and calculated that the rental car would be within 300 feet in either direction, depending on the traffic lights on Wisconsin Avenue.

Rick hadn't stopped for any lights so it wasn't relevant to the equation.

Playing the odds, Rick twisted the throttle and ran

the bike up above 200 kph, weaving through the relatively few cars and trucks spread out on the three lanes of blacktop. If he sped up and didn't find Cloyes, he could always pull over down by Spout Run and wait until they passed. After he crossed the Potomac River, he put the black speedster almost flat going through the 240 degree turn onto the George Washington Parkway–never touching a brake–and then wound it back up again.

As Rick had expected, there was a Park Police car squatting on the median just after the Beltway entrance. They didn't have a lot to do at night so they picked off the unwary drivers who didn't realize that the speed limit dropped from 65 to 50 inside the national park.

Red and blue lights exploded as he passed, but he knew even a Ford Police Interceptor wasn't going to catch him tonight, and, in seconds, the lights were just dim reflections in his rear view mirrors.

He passed two cars before he spotted the black rental with the bumper stickers just after the Turkey Run Park exit. He didn't want to give Cloyes another chance to shoot him, so he flicked off his headlight. On a racing bike like this, it was more of a legal formality than a useful light source anyway. He could see the road surface by the light of the stars, and very soon he was pulling up along the other car and using its lights for guidance.

Slowing dramatically, he came up on the left side of the car, matching speed just behind the driver's head. He made out Eve's head poking up above the passenger seat and was relieved to see it snap into profile as she clearly said something to the driver. Cloyes backhanded her viciously, and she slumped back in her seat.

"That's my girl," Rick thought.

As a racing bike, the Black Shadow was fitted with an illegal thumb lock on the accelerator that would keep it from slowing down if you let go. Rick goosed the engine, jumped forward to just ahead of the black car, and set the thumb lock. He knew he only had a few seconds before Cloyes realized what was happening and attempted to knock him off the road.

He ripped off his helmet to increase his peripheral vision and let it thump off the windshield in front of the driver. Then he reached carefully to his left arm and grasped the fat, right-angled end of the tire iron. He let out his breath, centered himself for just a second so that he wouldn't put a disastrous sideways torque on the bike, and then whipped his head until he was almost facing backward. Trying not to aim but letting his eye find the target, he pulled the tire jack from his sleeve, whipped it around, and threw it straight at Cloyes.

The car's brakes screamed in the split-second Cloyes had to react. It wasn't enough.

Rick watched Cloyes' face–an eerie blue in the lights from the dashboard–freeze in terror as the chiseled end of the heavy iron rod smashed through the windshield, between the spokes of the steering wheel, and sank deep into his chest.

As he'd prayed she would, Eve grabbed the wheel and, after one terrifying swerve, brought the car under control.

Rick slowed and paced her on the right as she guided the car to the gravel verge, and, with some difficulty reaching the brake pedal, b r o u g h t i t t o a stop. Rick pulled the bike behind the car and up to the passenger-side door.

"Get on, fast!" he yelled. In the mirrors, he could see the blue and red flashes glowing off the trees.

Eve got out, swung up on the rear of the bike, and Rick sprayed gravel in an all-out racing start.

She was hugging him so hard he could see black clouds coming in from the edges of his vision. "Not so hard!" he called.

The pressure immediately lessened as she leaned forward so her mouth was closer to his ear. "Why aren't you dead?" she asked.

"Disappointed?" Rick answered. Then he quickly added, "And do NOT punch me. My chest has already taken a beating tonight."

She hugged him and buried her face into his jacket.

After a moment, she lifted her head. "I really don't mean to complain, but you do know there's no seat back here?"

"Yeah, well it's meant for racing," he answered. "Don't worry, we're going to get rid of it in a minute."

Ahead, a small green sign that said, "B.P.R." pointed to the next off-ramp. Rick guided the bike up the incline, cut right until he was hidden by thick woods, and parked on the gravel. They got off, and Eve turned for an embrace; but Rick grabbed her hand, spun her around, and headed back to the Parkway at a slow jog.

Seconds later, the Park Police car flew past, followed quickly by two more.

"OK, let's hurry." Rick said and led Eve south along the Parkway until they reached a low fieldstone wall. They tucked in behind it, and he said; "Now we have time."

He wrapped his arms around her and they kissed urgently, each seeking reassurance that the other was alive.

After another, slower, Park Police car came past heading North, Rick poked his head up and surveyed the road. "OK, it's going to be a long walk. We'll go south until Route 123 crosses over. We're going to have to hide whenever we see headlights, but we should be OK."

Eve stood up but didn't release her hold on his arm. She took a deep breath on his chest, drinking in his familiar scent. Then she shook herself, and they started walking quickly along the highway.

After a few moments, she said, "I do have some questions–the most important one being 'Why aren't you dead?' but let's work up to that. Why did you leave the motorcycle back there? Wouldn't it have been better to keep it?"

"Well, one of Steve's friends loaned it to me, and I wanted to make sure he got it back."

Eve looked back at the small green sign. "From the B.P.R. Whatever that is."

Rick smiled. "Well, the sign stands for the Bureau of Public Roads, but that's actually the entrance to the CIA's Langley Headquarters."

"And Steve's friend will find it there?"

"I think as soon as the CIA boys figure out where he works, they'll probably deliver it personally."

Eve slid her hand down and wrapped her fingers around his. "OK, the other questions can wait. I know you're alive and that's enough for right now."

Rick squeezed her hand, and the warmth seemed to run up his arm and gather somewhere inside his chest.

CHAPTER 49

June 13, 1973, Ingomar Street NV, Washington, DC

Rick's mind was pleasantly empty as the weight bar rose and fell. He was doing slow rows, bent at the waist and pulling straight up, closing in on a good hour of steady lifting. The pain in his chest muscles—while steady—was less than yesterday, and yesterday had been less painful than the day before. He was working out on the rooftop porch outside the bedroom he shared with Eve, and the deep Washington humidity felt like it had been soaking deep into his core.

Who could ask for more?

"Hey trooper." Eve stood in the bedroom doorway. "Towel off and come on downstairs. We're going to have a house meeting."

"Can't I just give you my proxy vote?"

"I don't think you're going to get a vote, but you need to be there anyway." She walked over and smacked him on the butt. "Now stop showing off for Mrs. Zimmerman, or you'll give the poor woman another heart attack."

Rick turned his head sideways and grinned at her but continued his lifts without pause until he completed a full set. Then he stood and carefully placed the weights in their rack against the house wall. Eve threw a towel at him, and he began to wipe the sweat on his face and chest. He had his head covered with the towel when he said, "You're just jealous of the poor woman. She gets to sit in her bedroom window and watch me as long as–"

A solid punch to his midriff cut him off in mid-taunt. Under the towel, his smile was slow and deep. He heard the screen door slam as Eve headed back inside.

Fifteen minutes later in dry shorts and t-shirt, he settled in his usual place stretched on the floor in front of where Eve sat on the tatty green sofa. Sage was curled up tight inside Eve's left arm, and the three engineers were seated around the room. Rick noticed that they all looked nervous–Eps looked scared.

When he looked a bit closer, he realized they were all afraid...like 15-year-olds arriving at the door to pick up their first prom date.

He began to say something, but a quick dig from Eve's sharp toes silenced him.

Eve spoke, sounding like a TV moderator throwing a question to the audience. "OK, guys. I've had a long talk with Sage." She gave the little girl a firm hug. "And she's cool with the idea, but she'd like to hear what you have to say."

Eps and Steve looked at Scotty. Scotty had the face of a man about to face a firing squad, but he lifted his chin and looked Sage in the eyes. "Sage. We all miss your mother. She was a brave woman who gave everything she had to save you." He looked at the other men and then continued. "We would all like to make sure you know how sorry we are she's gone."

Steve and Eps both nodded solemnly.

Scotty coughed to clear his throat. "None of us are very adept at this but–"

He ground to a stop, shook his head, grimaced, and began again. "Sage. We've voted, and it was a unanimous decision. You don't have any family left–here or up in Wolf Point–and, well, you could always go into foster care, I guess, or we could look for a regular family but–"

The big man stopped again and then took a deep breath, "But we'd really like it if you lived with us."

He stopped and the room was completely silent. Eve nudged Sage a little, and murmured, "So, it's up to you. We talked about this. You can really do whatever you want."

Sage looked at Eps, Steve, and finally Scotty. In a small, soft voice, she said, "I'd like to live here if it's OK with you guys."

"All right!" Eps jumped up and stuck both fists up

in a victory salute. Steve relaxed back into his chair, a big smile appearing behind his beard.

Scotty was speechless, fear turning slowly to wonder on his face.

Suddenly, Sage was off the sofa and across the room, her arms wrapped around Scotty's neck, and her face pressed into his shoulder. Her voice was muffled. "I wasn't sure you guys wanted me to stay."

Scotty didn't seem to know what to do with his hands but slowly hugged her back. Eps gave her a few quick pounds on the back. Steve leaned forward and gently patted the top of her head.

Tears began to flow down Scotty's cheeks, but he didn't attempt to wipe them away. "No way, kiddo. We voted you in and that means that you can live with us forever."

Sage pulled back and looked at his face. "Really? And I can keep helping with the computer? And you'll let me play in the Dungeons and Dragon's games, the ones you play all over town?"

"Yeah, all of that and more," Scotty promised.

Eps chimed in, "You'll even have your own password and login."

Sage looked over, a grin on her face. "Really? All right!" She spun around, sat on Scotty's crossed legs, and leaned back into his chest. She reached a hand to each side and brought his arms in around her. Scotty looked down at her with a dumb grin like he'd just won the lottery.

Rick raised his hand. "Hate to break into this but what about Social Services and the cops and everything? Granted, living with you guys would be like Snow White and the Three Dwarfs, but I'm not sure it's going to get past a social worker."

Steve shook his head, "Once again, you've forgotten how things are done. We've already done a dry run into the vital records systems–here and in Montana–and–"

Eps turned to the table behind him and typed a quick command into the DigiMatic computer remote.

"Done."

Steve continued, "We set up a program that young Eps just triggered. Scott Shaw and his late wife legally adopted Sage four years ago in Missoula after a long and exhaustive background check. Eve is her legal guardian; she's even registered for school right over at Wilson. I had a friend 'adjust' the paperwork last week and Eps here just did the final swaps on the index database."

Sage looked up and back at Scotty's face, "So you're my dad?"

The big engineer shook his head. "No, I'm not going to pretend to be your dad. You already had a dad. I'm going to be the guy who makes you breakfast and checks your homework and takes you on vacations and will never, ever leave you. Is that OK?"

Sage nodded and then looked at Steve and Eps. "Well, what are you guys?"

Steve said, "I'm the wise uncle you go to for advice about baseball and advanced calculus and–"

"And I'm the crazy uncle who'll teach you about chemistry and explosives and–"

Scotty tightened his grip on the little girl and growled, "The heck you will." Then, seeing the disappointment on Sage's face. "OK, well, maybe but only if there's an adult present–and that doesn't include you, Eps."

Sage's smile returned.

Eve was smiling. "And I'm the grown-up. If you ever change your mind or have any problems that these brainy men can't deal with–like boys–" Sage made a face. "Well, you may not think so now, but you will."

She rolled her toes over Rick gently. "And this lug is here for, well, the things he's good for."

Eve's voice sobered, "We may not always be living in this house or even all living in the same city–that's why Scotty is adopting you–but all of us are your family."

"This means you have The Deal," Scotty said, and Rick could hear the capitals in his voice. "The Deal means that we will always take you in and never tell you to leave. You'll always be loved and taken care of for the rest of your life."

Sage asked, "What do I have to do? What if I'm rude or fail in school?"

"It doesn't matter," Scotty answered. "Even if you turn into an ungrateful, nasty, horrible brat, even if you fail every class, even if you crash the car when you learn to drive…nothing you do will ever break The Deal." He looked at the other two, "Right?"

In unison, Steve and Eps said, "Right," and then Eps added, "But you still have to take your turn doing dishes."

Sage looked around the room, "Well..." She screwed up her face in mock concentration. "What if I wanted to go to The Dancing Crab and get All You Can Eat blue crabs with corn and brown paper and the wooden hammers?"

Scott said, "Then you'd be perfect." He put his hands on her sides and tossed her a few feet to land squealing on the sofa. "Let's go to The Crab."

THE END

Author's Note

I am not a member of any Native American tribe (so far as I know but the family has been on this continent quite a long time). I have attempted to be as accurate as possible with the land, traditions, and culture of the Northern Cheyenne with one major exception. I specifically stopped my research into the Arrows, the Arrow Men, and all the other elements of their religious beliefs with what was known (to white anthropologists) around 1905.

From what I've gathered, the tribes are all undergoing a tremendous and joyous rebirth of traditions and religious customs at the present time; and, frankly, while I thought it was acceptable to use outdated and probably incorrect reports of someone else's religion as a plot point, I didn't think it was the same when an outsider goes poking around in current beliefs. In addition, from several online posts, I gathered that these matters were not to be discussed with outsiders, and I decided to be incorrect rather than intrusive.

So, if I've made mistakes, I apologize, but if I was just way out of date, that was intentional.

I've also taken liberties with the day-to-day events in and around Wounded Knee in April 1973. I found a lot of contradictions in the various histories so I made my own timeline—*Warrior* is a thriller, not a serious history.

As for the other "religion" in this book, I would like to ask all the bikers to chill out. Sturgis was not a big deal in 1973 (a one- or two-day hill climb) and the parade of massive motorcycles through the Black Hills really hadn't begun.

–Terry Irving

Acknowledgements

I wrote this book right before my publisher, Exhibit A, vanished into legal limbo and, while I did receive an advance for it, I'm fairly certain that no one there actually read it. Two years later, when I set out to publish it myself, I received some major help in editing and proofing from Barbara Flanagan—one of my wonderful Reading Ronin. The cover by the incredible Nick Castle, is as good as the original *Courier* cover and I want to thank him for allowing me to keep using that gorgeous *Courier* cover after Exhibit A went belly-up and it became a Ronin Robot Press book.

Now, as I write this, I am crowd-funding Ronin Robot Press on Pubslush.com and I'd like to sincerely thank the following people who have given me a helping hand as I try to fight my way through the puzzle palace of publishing. So far (the rest will have to be thanked in *Taxi Dancer*, my next book,) the List of Honor includes: Sandy Irving, Page Godwin, George Rivera, Tom Tarvin, Barbara Flanagan (again!) David Guilbault, Christy Birmingham, Bruce (Fang) Davidson, Turner Bridgforth, Sharon Gibson, Robert Early, Charlie Seymour, David Bohrman, John Wulff, Ken Tillis, Pat Alder, Katie Sullivan, Jesse Lakes, Sam Foley, and Bill Pastuszek.

Special thanks to the absolute #1 Fan of All Time: Don Critchfield, who shall now appear as a really cool character in *Taxi Dancer* and not the guy who gets killed off in the first chapter. Any writer with a brain in their head would give anything to have someone like Don in their corner.

Thank you all for your encouragement and thanks to all the people who have bought *Courier* and *Day of the Dragonking* and even the more than 3,000 people who have downloaded these books for free because you read them, reviewed them, and told your friends about them.

Ronin Robot Press

Did you enjoy this book?

Well, there's a lot more books to discover.

An entire world of exciting new books from Terry Irving and Ronin Robot Press. Sign up to be one of the few, the proud,

The RONIN READERS!

Get the latest news first in our bi-weekly Newsletter! Read what Terry's writing right now; give him comments, criticism, and advice (all of which he really needs.) Read chapters from all the other new authors and get your hands on new books before they go public.

(Type bit.ly/roninreaders into your browser.)

GOLD FOR SAN JOAQUIN
By Cliff Roberts

Framed for his family's murder, the family homestead burnt to the ground, and the people meant to protect him seeking to shoot him down as an outlaw. Young Jacob Thorn must give up his childish ways and become a man. They killed his father for his family's gold. To protect their greed and power, they will stop at nothing to kill Jacob and the truth. On the run and desperate, Jacob enlists the help of his father's best friend after the man leading the hunt for young Jacob kills the sheriff and his deputy. Chased into a corner, Jacob cheats death with the help of his father's friend and decides it's time to stop running and start taking the fight to his enemies. Using the tactics his father taught him from his cavalry days, he goes in search of revenge on behalf of his family and vindication for himself.

COURIER
By Terry Irving

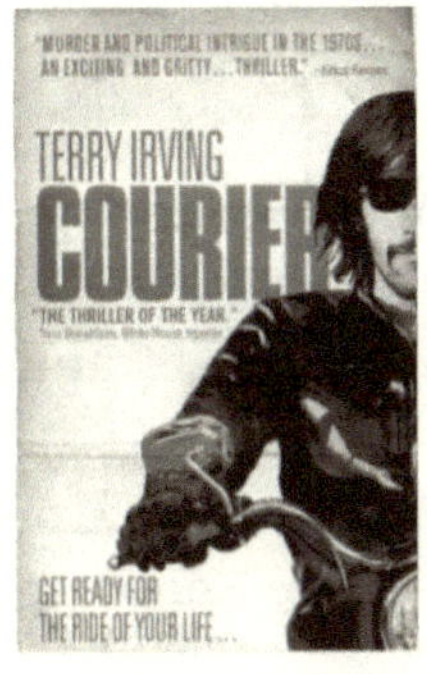

Rick Putnam is running for his life. A Vietnam Veteran riding a motorcycle for a national news network, he's picked up something too hot to handle. So hot that a reporter and a camera crew has already been killed and a rogue CIA kill squad is on his tail. Stick with this charismatic character as he fights his way all the way to 1600 Pennsylvania in his battle for the truth.

"An action-packed tale of murder and political intrigue set in the politically turbulent 1970s... Irving portrays [courier Rick Putnam] as a classic pulp-fiction hero: a chiseled, chain-smoking ex-soldier who's always ready with snappy quips...Irving's story is relentlessly paced, punctuated by bursts of action and violence, and driven by artfully unfolding suspense...An exciting and gritty...thriller."

–Kirkus Reviews.

"Rick Putnam is a recent Vietnam vet in the early 1970s who works as a courier for a Washington, DC television station while trying to put his life back together after being injured in the war...*Courier* is a tense story set in the days before social media, when news professionals still need to develop film in a dark room and splice footage together. Author Terry Irving clearly knows the inside of the news business in a different time..."

–Reviewed by Kathleen Heady
for *Suspense* Magazine

"The year is 1972, mix the White House, the Watergate burglary, the war in Vietnam and murder in Washington and you've got a terrific story...Kudos to one of television's best producers for writing the thriller of the year!"

–Sam Donaldson,
former ABC News White House reporter

"...Welcome to Terry Irving's fast-paced thriller from a bygone age. The Vietnam War is winding down, a wounded vet takes a job as a motorcycle courier at a network's Washington news bureau, and finds himself caught up in the backwash of a harrowing conspiracy. Terry Irving knows the landscape. I was there. So was he."

–Ted Koppel,
former anchor for ABC Nightline

"To call Terry Irving's book a "page turner" is a gross understatement. As a journalist who covered Vietnam developments in Washington, and the Watergate scandal, this book is entirely believable, scary, and thrilling. Irving is in the top tier of political-mystery writers. And as a (ABC) network producer, he draws on a vast inside knowledge to keep readers glued to every page. If you like politics and a good mystery, you will love this book."

–Bill Greenwood,
former White House Correspondent

"With all the power and speed of a motorcycle courier trying to beat a deadline, and the cyclist's fine balance of thriller thrust and inside-the-newsroom detail, Terry Irving's new novel, *Courier*, will keep you entertained from start to finish."

–Dave Marash,
former Nightline Reporter

DAY OF THE DRAGON KING
Book One: The Last American Wizard
By Terry Irving

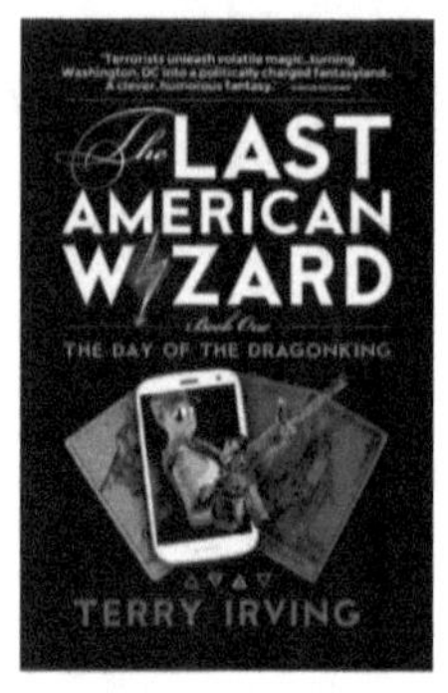

What if this world is just "magic" and somehow it is replaced by a stronger magic? In *The Last American Wizard,* the world Steve Rowan has known ceases to exist. He can no longer rely on anything he thought was real and his life as well as everyone else's is now being controlled by a deck of tarot cards. A deck in which he plays the fool. The epicenter of this magical change...Washington D.C., of course.

Steve Rowan has witnessed an airliner crash in front of his home, but he appears to be the only one who can see it. He soon finds himself to be the 'Fool' from a deck of Tarot cards. He meets up with Ace, a SEAL, who in this new world is the Ace of Swords. Each person they encounter has taken on the persona of another card. As they fight their way through the deck, they come to realize that computers and the Tarot Cards now control the fate of the world. Everyone they encounter wants one thing, the death of the Fool. Steve is attacked by Illuminati and Masons, elves, gnomes, and too many mythical creatures to mention.

Steve and Ace are abetted by a smartphone

named 'Smart Money' and the voice in the phone, Barnaby. Ultimately, it will be up to the brains of the "Fool" to secure the cuter of Washington D.C.

"Terry Irving has written a science fiction/fantasy thriller that will have you laughing one moment and racing through adrenaline-pumping action the next. *The Last American Wizard* will twist you in knots while expanding your imagination. You will never look at magic the same again."

–J.M. LeDuc, author of Sin
published by Suspense Publishing

"A clever, humorous fantasy…Mystically powered terrorists unleash volatile magic on the world, turning Washington, D.C., into a politically charged fantasyland ripe for human sacrifice.

A trio of suicide attackers with magical abilities bring down a 747 by summoning a dragon to rip it from the sky, using the hundreds of lives lost as a sacrifice to initiate the Change. The country morphs into a new landscape of swords and sorcery. Now computers and other machines are coming to life, and regular people have started to turn into mythical creatures and forgotten deities, creating a chaotic world easily seized by whoever–or whatever–set this shift into motion.

Hope appears in the nation's capital where, along with transforming Democrats into potbellied elves, Republicans into cantankerous dwarves, and Tea Party members into trolls, the Change has granted struggling freelance journalist Steve Rowan the abilities of the Tarot Arcana's Fool card, making him a powerful, yet unreliable, wizard. Realizing his potential, he is "hired" by the trivia-obsessed sentient computer Barnaby and coupled with the attractive, no-nonsense female Navy SEAL Ace Morningstar to uncover the puppet masters behind the plane crash.

Irving (*Courier*, 2014, etc.), a producer of Emmy Award–winning news television and a journalist well acquainted with the Beltway, makes good use of clichéd Washington stereotypes by mashing them together with fantasy tropes, breathing new life into political satire….

Like many first books in a genre series, the novel foreshadows a greater enemy behind all this madness while barely hinting at its identity, offering a wonderfully bizarre consolation prize as its denouement."

–Kirkus Reviews

The Author

Terry Irving (seen here in both 1969 and 2010) is a four-time Emmy award-winning writer and producer. He has also won three Peabody Awards, three DuPont Awards and has been a producer, editor, or writer with ABC, CNN, Fox and MSNBC.

Exhibit A Publishing released his first novel, *Courier,* on May, 1, 2014 and subsequently went out of business on June 7, 2014. Terry denies all responsibility. Courier went on to win several awards, sell close to 10,000 copies, and form the nucleus of Ronin Robot Press.

Courier was re-released in January of 2015, and Warrior, the sequel, in July 2015. *Day of the Dragonking: Book One of the Last American Wizard* was released on April Fool's Day 2015 (you need to read it to understand why I thought that was appropriate.) Last, but not least, *Taxi Dancer,* the first in a series featuring private eye Angel Pearl and set in 1930's Manila, is due later in 2015.

In addition, Ronin Robot Press is putting together an exciting lineup of the best new writers in Westerns, Romance, and Children's Books. Check them out on Amazon's Kindle eBooks and at **www.roninrobotpress.com.** *Undefeated Love,* a story of growing up in 1972 among the strange teenage subcultures of suburban Philadelphia by Bruce Bennett, was released in June 2015. *Gold for San Joaquin* by Cliff Roberts was the first Western released by Ronin Robot Press, followed by *Texas Spitfire,* a Western romance by Chloe Mayer, and *Timmy and Stacey's Adventure at the Carnival* by Dennis Gager and Nathan Beckwith.